SUMMER OF THE APOCALYPSE

"James Van Pelt is a wonderful writer, whose science fiction appeals to both the mind and the heart. His debut novel *Summer of the Apocalypse* is not to be missed."
          —Robert J. Sawyer, author of *Hominids*

"James Van Pelt commands the history of science fiction as the instruments of his narrative. His award-winning prose is informed with a deep empathy for the human condition which highlights the genre in novel ways. After the amazing *Strangers and Beggars* and *The Last of the O-Forms*, *Summer of the Apocalypse* marks his first foray into single-title fiction. . .expect to be amazed again.
          —Jay Lake, author of *Trial of Flowers*

"A writer with unique insight into the human condition and mind-blowing imagination. I'd read a grocery list by James Van Pelt."
          —Julie E. Czerneda, author of *Regeneration*

"James Van Pelt is one of the most humane writers in science fiction today. His writing has a sensitivity and insight that is often lacking in the genre. Whatever technologies, wonders, fears and terrors his stories contain, at heart every one of them is about people—human beings living human lives. Best of all—and this quality is truly hard to come by in our age of cynicism—his stories show a humanity that is worth saving and very much worth reading about."
          —Carrie Vaughn, author of *Kitty and the Midnight Hour*

"Every time James Van Pelt writes a story, the world gets a little richer. This time he's written a novel. You do the math."
          —Jerry Oltion, author of *Anywhere But Here*

More Praise for James Van Pelt

"A supple, inventive, and ambitious writer who handles any genre with expert ease."
—Gardner Dozois, editor of *The Best of the Best*

"James Van Pelt is a Grand Junction schoolteacher quietly building a career as one of the top writers of short science fiction."
—*The Denver Post*

"One of the freshest thinkers and most original voices in modern science fiction."
—Robert J. Sawyer, author of *Hominids*

"A versatile and talented author."
—Connie Willis, author of *Passage*

"Van Pelt's work is consistent, strong, and occasionally crackling. Like many of his protagonists, he's answered a difficult challenge well."
—*Tangent Online*

"James Van Pelt has a gift for opening strange new windows on familiar events, revealing the world from a perspective you never knew existed."
—Jerry Oltion, author of *Abandon in Place*

"James Van Pelt not only enthralls and amazes, but [reminds] us of what it is to be human."
—Julie E. Czerneda, author of *In the Company of Others*

"Equally adept at science fiction, fantasy and horror, Jim Van Pelt is one of those rare writers who swoop effortlessly across the landscape of the fantastic. I read him with admiration and envy."
—James Patrick Kelly, author of *Think Like a Dinosaur*

"Van Pelt's fiction crystallizes the journeys of his characters, examining their lives between one heartbeat and the next before releasing them and you, the reader, to voyage onward, profoundly affected by the experience."
—Jay Lake, author of *Rocket Science*

"James Van Pelt is a serious writer in the very best sense. His stories are literate, gripping, and meaningful."
—Jack Dann, author of *The Memory Cathedral*

SUMMER OF
THE APOCALYPSE

Also by James Van Pelt

Strangers and Beggars
The Last of the O-Forms & Other Stories

SUMMER OF THE APOCALYPSE

JAMES VAN PELT

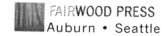
FAIRWOOD PRESS
Auburn • Seattle

SUMMER OF THE APOCALYPSE
A Fairwood Press Book
November 2006
Copyright © 2006 by James Van Pelt

Fairwood Press
5203 Quincy Ave SE
Auburn, WA 98092
www.fairwoodpress.com

Cover image by Paul Swenson
Cover and Book Design by Patrick Swenson

ISBN: 0-9746573-8-7
First Fairwood Press Edition: November 2006
Printed in the United States of America

For Tammy,
who watched this book's long gestation and birth

Chapter One
SAD NEWS

Eric wished he could enjoy the warm August sun that penetrated deep into his old muscles, but he could hear Dodge and Rabbit talking in front of his house, and he knew the two children came to hear about the Gone Times. Almost no one else visited—they didn't care to listen to his stories—but the children liked to talk about the old days, and their company was appreciated. Lately he'd been restive. He enjoyed sunsets less. He took longer and longer walks, always toward the foothills, sometimes getting home after nightfall. People in the village didn't do this. Fear of wild animals kept them indoors after dark, but Eric couldn't shake the habit and the notion that the night was safe for man. He felt the urge to travel again, to see new places one more time before illness, or just plain age, forced him to stay home.

This afternoon, though, stretched out on a hammock, with the late spring sun so pleasant, a breeze blowing cool off the mountains and a glass of pungent herb tea beside him, he'd rather drift into a doze.

"Are you sleeping, Grandfather?" Dodge, a tall, skinny ten-year-old with dark hair neatly cut into bangs above his eyebrows, pushed the creaky gate open. Rabbit, his sullen twelve-year-old friend, whose face bore heavy scars from wild dog bites suffered when he was five, followed.

"Why bother an old man?" said Eric. He pointed at the pitcher and the boys poured themselves tea. "Don't you have productive things to do? Maybe you could pull weeds for me."

Dodge emptied his drink with one gulp. Rabbit retreated to the shade of the grape vines and sat cross-legged on the grass. His broad shoulders and thick chest hinted at the bulk of the man he might become. "You tell him," said Rabbit.

"What?" Eric swung his feet off the hammock and sat up. His back twinged and he grimaced. Beyond the fence that encircled his vegetable garden, the dusty road was empty all the way to the cottonwoods that lined the river. Most people napped during the heat. Later, when the sun moved closer to the mountains, horse drawn carts would pass occasionally, but generally life in Littleton was slow in August. People tended their gardens. Field workers walked past his house at dusk. Some would wave, but most ignored him. He was just a crotchety old man who not only wouldn't let go of the Gone Times, but who also upset the town meetings with his criticisms.

"What news do you have?" Eric asked.

Dodge said, "Dad wants to see you. Don't tell him I come out here all the time, okay? Dad says, 'Family gatherings are bad enough. I don't need you coming home with his garbage.' But I think he's stupid."

Eric sighed. This was a common gambit of Dodge's, to not answer questions. It was a family trait. "Your father isn't stupid. When you're thirty, you'll wish you listened to him more now."

Dodge looked longingly at the pitcher. Eric nodded and the boy filled his glass again. "You don't have a dad to make you do chores or go to school. 'Look for cloth today, Dodge,' he says, or 'Find some tools for trade.' You'd think that he doesn't want me to have any fun. Besides, there isn't anything to find here anymore. All the easy pickings are gone. Not like when you were a kid. We brought something for you, though." Dodge dug into his backpack and removed a thick book. He handed it to Eric. "I know you don't have this one."

Eric turned the volume over. It was an anthology called *Major American Authors*. He opened the cover. The pages were slightly wrinkled, as if the book had been exposed to moist air at one time, but other than that, it seemed in good shape. He read the ending lines of a quote from Nathaniel Ames' Almanac, 1758. *O ye unborn inhabitants of America! Should this page escape its destined conflagration at the year's end, and these alphabetical letters remain legible when your eyes behold the sun after he has rolled the seasons round for two or three centuries more, you will know that in Anno Domini, 1758, we dreamed of your times.*

I doubt it, Eric thought.

He frowned. "You shouldn't be scavenging. That's work for men who know what they're doing."

Dodge said, "We can get places they can't. They're too big. Rabbit found the case of knives last year. The glass wasn't even broken on the front. We don't touch anything we're not supposed to. We're not kids, you know."

The case of knives had been big news the summer before. Eric used it as part of an argument to the city council. "When was the last time someone got good stuff?"

"What do you think, Rabbit?" said Dodge. Rabbit looked into his tea. His hair hung over his eyes. The scars puckered the right side of his face, and he seldom met Eric's gaze even though he'd been coming to his house for years.

Rabbit tilted his head back and stared into the vines. Eric noticed he kept the good side of his face turned toward them. He said, "The knives, I guess. Camaro's Mom found some canned goods last week, but they were all bad. No labels and swelled up. Doc Renke says we shouldn't eat anything from cans anyway, swelled or not."

Eric laughed silently at the mention of "Camaro." Lots of children born in the last twenty years or so had been named after automobiles. There was Dodge, of course, and Rabbit, but he also knew a red-headed girl named "Blazer," a pair of twins, "Plymouth" and "Neon," and the miller's son, "Mercedes." None of these children had ever seen a working automobile. The last one Eric remembered was a Volkswagon Bug that drove by his house twenty-five years ago. That was when the Bowles Avenue bridge repair still stood. The cars were gone, but the names lived on.

"We've been hunting for treasure troves," Dodge said to Eric. "There are basements with guns and knives and tools on the other side of the river, if you know where to look."

Rabbit laughed derisively. "That's a lot of bunk." He pushed the hair off his forehead. "If you believe that, then you must think we'll find good 'lectronics or a car that'll start."

Dodge smiled. "Who knows what's on the other side of the river? Dad told me just yesterday that lots of stuff must still be out there. But hunting around here is a waste. Just a chore."

"You boys been crossing?"

They looked at each other guiltily. Finally Dodge said, "We know a shallow place we can walk through. But we're real careful and we watch out for each other all the time. You won't say anything will you?"

Eric leaned back in his hammock. He guessed that it had been eight or nine years since he had crossed the river. A rumor that an undiscovered sporting goods warehouse existed in the ruins of downtown Denver drew him and four others, but after a week of poking though rubble and climbing down into treacherous mazes of steel, brick, rotten wood and sheetrock, they'd given up. All of the street signs were gone, many of the streets impassable, and the fifty-year-old map they were using had gotten wet early in the trip and was unreadable. A skunk bit Herbie when he reached blindly into its den, and rabies killed him by the end of the summer. All in all, it had been a useless effort. Still, he remembered when Denver *was* a treasure trove, when he could walk onto any car lot, break into the office to find keys, and drive away with anything he wanted.

He looked the boys over carefully. The book rested heavily in his hands. "I'll tell you what. I won't talk about your expeditions, and maybe next time you head out you could show me where you got this."

Both boys shook their heads. "No way, Grandfather," said Dodge. "Dad would whip my butt for sure."

"I don't want you crossing the river again by yourselves."

Dodge bit his lip and looked down into the bottom of his glass. "Okay," he said.

Eric closed the book. "I appreciate the gift, but it's too dangerous for you." He felt awkward and sad. He'd seldom chastised Dodge, and he didn't know what to say now. The silence weighed heavily on him.

Rabbit finally said, "You'd better tell him."

Dodge brightened. "Oh, yeah. Grandma Pao died."

Eric turned his head away from them, his eyes stinging. Emotions ran close to the surface for him lately. Age, he figured. Deaths, births, a change of weather, and he misted up. "I guess I need to go into town then," he said. "You boys want to come?"

*

The breeze that felt cool under the trees, stirred dust and baked Eric's skin as he followed the boys into town. Unlike most people, he lived isolated, with no near neighbors. In the Gone Time, this road was named Bowles Avenue, and it would have been crowded with suburbanites driving to Southwest Plaza, a huge shopping mall west of town. Now, the path was a broad swath of cracked and weeded asphalt and dirt. As they passed mounds of brick, Eric remembered the expensive, tree-encircled homes that once lined the street. Most of the neighborhoods had been burned in the final days of the plague. He could still see the flames leaping from house to house. He'd run for his life that day. No signs of fire now, not even a burned whiff in the air.

What remained of the trees after the fire had long since been chopped down for fuel. Grasses and sage covered the area that had once been the housing developments of Bow Mar South, Columbine, Columbine Hills and Columbine Knolls.

The mile walk to the river would have taken him less than two minutes in a car in the Gone Times. He remembered driving with his parents sixty years ago, and the thought weighed him down even more.

"Come on, Grandpa," yelled Dodge over his shoulder. "If you walk any slower, we'll be going backwards."

When they reached the river's bank, they followed a well-worn trail to the Treasury. Two men sat on the porch and nodded as Eric and the boys went in.

Sunlight streamed through high windows, revealing rows and rows of boxes piled on top one another. Many contained liquor. Old Crow, Seagrams, Kentucky Bourbon, the town's chief trading goods. But there were also cases of nails, screws and irreplaceable hardware; hammers, saws, rasps, clamps and other tools, and then boxes filled with completely useless things like TVs, food processors, computers, flashlights, video games, and stereo components. The town council stored these last items, even though almost none of them had ever seen them in operation.

A man bent over an open box, counting bottles, straightened as they came in. "Father," said Dodge's dad. A deeply tanned, wiry man of forty, he nodded curtly in Eric's direction.

"Good to see you, Troy," said Eric. "Dodge tells me that Susan Pao died."

"You get right to it, don't you."

"So, it's true."

"This morning. Her daughter found her. Never woke up, I guess. She was eighty-two."

"That's the end of the sixties," said Eric. He sat on a large box marked MICROWAVE OVEN—FRAGILE. "The Beatles were still a group and man hadn't been to the moon yet when she was born, and now she's gone."

Troy said, "Uh huh," unencouragingly.

"She used to tell me about television shows she saw. God, that woman had a memory, I'll tell you. Knew 'em all. *Beverly Hillbillies*. Did she ever tell you about the *Beverly Hillbillies*? I don't remember watching that one, but the tune's stuck in my head. Idiotic song. We'd sit in her living room and sing that, and then . . ."

"We've got business to attend to here, Dad."

Eric looked down at his hands resting on his legs. They were liver spotted, and a couple of the knuckles were swollen with arthritis. He thought about Susan Pao telling him about a concert she had been to at Red Rocks Auditorium, a blues concert, and how everybody showed up early in the day with blankets and coolers filled with beer, and how they tossed frisbees and beach balls up and down the stadium seats until the music started. People smoked pot, and if you got there after 6:00, there'd be no place to sit. He'd hiked to Red Rocks thirty years ago. Most of the stage was torn up for the metal, but the auditorium itself, carved out of stone, huge and empty, looked like it was still waiting for rock and roll. He'd left a broken cassette player on the stage, electrical tape holding the head phones together. That was after he had spent three years looking for batteries, and there were none left with any juice in them. He'd never gone back.

Troy said, "Dad, the business?"

"Sorry."

"As the oldest member of the community, and the last person who actually remembers anything of the Gone Times, you got a vote now on the council. A lot of people depend on you making good decisions. They can't be based on wild theories or old fears. You've got to keep your head."

Blood rushed into Eric's face. He felt his cheeks flushing. "School's not a wild theory. Our kids have got to be able to read, or we're going straight into barbarism."

The contempt showed on Troy's expression. "That's just what I mean. You get going on the school thing, or the library idea, and people won't listen. We've got important community projects, and it's hard enough to convince people to pull together on them without you distracting the committee with these pet ideas of yours. The crops have to come in, we've got to widen our search for tradable goods, and you just make everyone angry by hanging on to old ways."

Eric slapped his knee. "Look at this stuff in here. I'm not the one hanging on. America used to be a great place. We built cities. We flew around the world, and now you're scrounging through garbage dumps, hoping to find things we can't make anymore. I tell you, if we don't teach the kids, the next generation will be nothing more than nomads following deer herds, or subsistence farmers barely surviving from summer to summer."

Troy shook his head. "Hogwash, Dad. We do fine. There's no reason to think we won't keep on this way. People are happy until you go telling them they're doomed." He closed the box lid with a snap. "This is the world, now, but you hang on to a past that no one knows. Your people died. Mine are alive. You've got nothing to say to the living."

"What about the sicknesses in the last couple of years? And I don't see anyone dancing for joy about their stillbirths." Eric, breathing hard, turned from his son. "Something's changing. Ignorance doesn't help."

Troy walked back and forth behind him. He started to speak several times—Eric heard his lips part. Finally he said, "I hate this. Every time we talk you make me say bad things." Troy gripped his shoulder. "What are we going to do?"

Through the open door, Eric could see the river. Heat waves shimmered the ground and the water flowed silently through the old bridge's broken pilings. Across the shallow expanse, jumbles of brick marked the remains of downtown Littleton. "I think I should leave for a while," he said.

Troy wiped his sleeve across his mouth. Eric shivered. For a second, he saw in Troy his own father. Troy was now about the same age as when Eric's father had died.

Troy said, "Don't be childish, Dad. You're hiking days are long past." He laughed, suddenly jovial. Eric cringed. He heard the patronizing behind the tone. He's humoring me, Eric thought.

Troy continued, "Besides, we need you here. As the oldest person, people are going to want your opinions on all kinds of things. We'll probably have to move you into town to save everybody the walk."

Eric remembered the steady stream of visitors to Susan Pao's house. Some brought old 'lectronics, radios or TVs, as if by laying on the hands she could heal them. Some came to her when they were ill, carrying with them boxes filled with medicines, most bad with age, hoping that she would identify the Gone Time cure that would save them. Lately there'd been a lot of sickness. She presided at weddings and christenings, funerals and festivals. Every day people dropped off baked goods or fresh-caught fish, like she was some sort of icon, which, of course, she was.

He pictured himself sitting in a house, people lined up to see him, like Susan Pao, his eyes glazed with age.

He shook the image away. Whatever else happened, he couldn't see himself as a symbol for these people, not the ignorant children of the Gone Time. One more time before he died, he needed to wander in the world.

"I'm serious, Dad. You don't know what's out there anymore."

Eric almost laughed out loud. He'd seen superstitions and fears develop in the community over the years. The latest one was that bad spirits, some said "ghosts," protected the countryside. The ruins of the city were safe, or as safe as ruins could be, haunted by nothing more than rusted metal and unstable foundations that collapsed on the unwary, and expeditions as far north as downtown Denver weren't uncommon, but no one went past the fields to the east, south or west. When he'd proposed an exploration to Colorado Springs two years ago, Troy reminded the council of the seventy miles of country to travel and that ended the discussion.

Eric once talked to one man who claimed to have heard something at night when he'd gone after stray cattle. "I'm not saying I was scared," he said. "But after that, I figured cows weren't worth it and I came home." He'd never said exactly what it was he heard.

"Maybe because we don't know what's out there, someone ought to go," said Eric.

"Don't be ridiculous, Dad. You're old."

*

At home, Eric packed. As he'd walked the dusty two miles to his house, the idea of a long trip made more sense. He'd been half joking with the boys about scavenging with them, but only half. Lately his muscles ached all the time. Not the good ache of a hard workday, but a queasy throbbing ache, like they wanted to be put to rest, and that frightened him. So he packed. Maybe a voyage would set my mind to ease, he thought. Maybe if I wandered north I could find other communities, places where they weren't giving up on the spirit of the old America. But mostly he just wanted to walk, to feel the long pull of the road like he did when he was young, to set his eyes on a distant spot and watch it swell as he approached, to choose his direction without regard to where he was going or when the journey would end. Yes, a long walk is in order, he thought.

But the more he arranged items in the pack, the less sensible an *aimless* walk seemed. There *was* sickness in the community. He'd seen it; the Iversons on the river's edge were all down with a wasting disease that robbed them of energy and appetite. The Sanduskys and Washingtons were nearly as bad, though they'd seemed to be making a recovery in the last week. Brent Washington had even worked a morning in the fields he'd heard. But the stillbirths—that bothered him. Too many labors ended in quiet burials.

No, a walk to indulge a whim, that would be senseless. He thought, I need to find an answer—to prove to them the value of the Gone Time learning. Ignorance is no shelter.

An old idea came back to him, the place to go. It was north, farther than anyone had gone in years, but still a reachable hike for an old man if he took care of himself, if he was careful: the library at the University of Colorado, in Boulder. If any learning still existed, if there were one place where science might provide an answer, that would be it. He would go there.

Smiling, he stuffed into the pack a collapsible fishing pole and lures, a good sheath knife, insect repellant (some things never rot, no matter how long they're stored), a worn hard back copy of *My Antonia* that he'd been meaning to read, a rain poncho, a small first aid kit, binoculars, a compass, a Colorado map, and enough food to last for three days.

He walked through the house looking for anything else he felt he might need. Most of the ground floor rooms were filled with books, the largest collection he knew. He taught reading to children and adults who were interested, a group of four on Tuesday night and another group of five on Sunday afternoon. In a community of almost a thousand people, only a hundred or so were literate, and most of them were over forty.

Lit only by the small rectangles of the window wells, in the basement where canned preserves crowded the shelves, he chose a jar of strawberry jam and one of pickled watermelon rind. In the back of the room, he contemplated the boxes of irreplaceable goods he'd stockpiled over the years. He had three good artificial-fiber sleeping bags, two nylon one-man tents with fiberglass poles, and four rifles but only ammo for one of them. Sixty-year-old shells weren't trustworthy. Some might work, but most of them wouldn't, so the rifles were practically useless. Everyone had one they never used. He also had a small store of hardware to keep the house from falling apart. He looked into a box with one of his most valuable assets, a rare supply of hardwood axe handles that people came from miles away to trade for. Eric hadn't worried about food for the winter for some time.

He needed a change of clothes, and he went to his bedroom where he kept the wardrobe he'd paid dearly for. When he was young, and realized new clothes might be hard to come by, most of the stores and houses had already been looted. He'd traded for the supply he had now, but, sadly, even though he protected them with mothballs and kept them dry, the fabric was not as sturdy as it had once been. He pulled apart the legs of a pair of jeans he'd never worn, and a seam ripped. Only a couple of threads popped on the second pair he tested. He put them in the pack. He hoped that before all the clothes from the Gone Times were unwearable that trade with the south would be reestablished, assuming the south was growing cotton again. There had been no news of the world from more than twenty miles away for years. Every once in a while, the younger men left on explorations, but they either came back after a few days, frightened and silent about what they'd seen, or they didn't return at all. No wonder, Eric thought, they believe that ghosts protect the wilderness. He wondered how long it would be before the people would make maps that said in the unknown white space around their little world, "Here there be dragons."

Eric grabbed his walking stick that doubled as a quarterstaff, a large-brimmed leather hat, and his slingshot to complete his outfit. Many of the men in the community carried bow and arrows, but he'd always been most comfortable with the sling. Of course, just like everything else people used from the Gone Times, he couldn't replace the most valuable part, the surgical tubing rubber bands that provided the power. Once those broke, he would have only the weapon's memory. He kept the tubing he had now in an airtight box in a cool spot in the cellar, and it hadn't deteriorated too badly. Even at seventy-five, Eric could nail a wild dog at fifty yards. It was a skill that had saved him more than once.

He locked the front door, closed the shutters on the windows, and walked away. The afternoon sun cut long shadows through the prairie weeds and grasses that grew up through the road. Eric figured he could get a fair amount of hiking done in the cool afternoon, find a safe place to camp in a few hours, and be near enough to the mountains by noon tomorrow to start north.

He pulled the brim over his eyes. The pack straps clung agreeably to his shoulders. I might be old, he thought, but I'm a long way from dead. I've left home before and made out all right.

Just after the sun dropped below the mountains, Eric found a rocky outcrop with a flat top where he could spread his sleeping bag. The land darkened into deep blue shadows, though sunlight still glowed in the clouds. He guessed he had hiked eight miles or so. That would put him west of Chatfield Reservoir, which was now called "The Swamp," but another ten miles away from the real beginnings of the foot hills.

At first, he was afraid that Troy would take his talk of leaving seriously and send someone to the house to watch him, and then, after he'd started hiking, he was convinced someone was following him. He twirled in his tracks several times at sounds he soon dismissed as nothing. Troy never believed me when he was growing up, thought Eric. No reason to think he'd change now. Within a couple of miles he began to enjoy the road. The pack settled comfortably. Water sloshed and gurgled in his canteen. The walking stick planted solidly. He breathed deeply of the afternoon air, sweet with sage and columbine.

When he came to the rock outcrop, it seemed perfect. He had resigned himself to camping in one of the many ruins along the way, always a spooky experience, when he'd spotted it poking up on the horizon like a blunt thumb. Tall enough to keep animals away, but not unclimbable, foot and handholds offered easy access to the top, and when Eric reached it he realized they must have been carved in by some other traveler who recognized the value of a safe campsite. A blackened pit and chunks of charcoaled wood confirmed his guess.

Dangling his feet while gazing east, Eric sat on the cool stone. A line of clouds on the horizon flashed sporadically with lightning, but was too far away for him to hear thunder. A breeze kept the mosquitoes away. He pressed his hands into the small of his back and arched. Muscles cramped, and he awkwardly rubbed them until they relaxed. His legs throbbed.

Seventy-five, he thought, is a lot of years. He gingerly crawled into his sleeping bag, lay on his back and watched the sky. Troy, he thought, you will see what the old learning is worth. You'll learn that lesson you never knew.

By the time the last shades of daylight disappeared, and the stars shone like bright ice, he was asleep.

Chapter Two
THE BEGINNING AND AN INCIDENT

E ric mashed his Cheerios with his spoon until the milk was a uniform tan color. The end of the world, he thought, that's what they're calling it. Everyone is heading to California and I'm stuck in school. He turned his cassette player up another notch. The sun poured through the windows, silhouetting his father, and casting a bright morning glow on his mother's face as she read a magazine. The very image itself, Mr. and Mrs. America in their perfect little home, riled him. So he concentrated on the headphones, where he was at Red Rocks Park listening to U2 playing "Sunday, Bloody Sunday."

He lifted his bowl and turned the pages of *The Denver Post,* looking for school closure listings. Over the top of the paper, Eric noticed Dad's grimace. Dad wrote for the *Rocky Mountain News,* and Eric's subscription to the rival daily irritated him.

Long articles about the disease's progress on the East Coast dominated the front section. The banner headline read "80% FATALITIES!" The only pictures were of an overcrowded hospital in Boston and a panicked crowd at an unidentified airport. He turned past them. Boulder schools closed two days earlier, and today was the last day for the Colorado Spring schools. He didn't find a listing for Denver, though. He pulled the head-phones around his neck. "I'm staying home," he said.

Mom, a heavy woman with three chins and hair streaked with gray—Eric thought of her as a white Aunt Jemimah—reached across the table and felt his forehead. He jerked his head away. "You're not feeling sick, are you?" she said.

Dad folded the classified ads of his own paper and laid them in his lap. He had been reading the classifieds a lot lately. Eric picked them up once after Dad was done and saw that he had circled various gun ads, mostly shotguns. As far as Eric knew, the only gun that Dad owned was a funny looking over/under 20 gauge that he used to hunt pheasant years ago. Eric had a hard time imagining Dad hunting anything. He reminded him of Barney Fife and Walter Mitty rolled together.

Dad looked through his bifocals at Eric for a long time, and then rubbed his own forehead. "Today's as good as any, I suppose," he said. "Let's pack."

"Are you sure?" asked Mom.

"Take all the practical clothes," Dad said. Eric hated it when his dad didn't answer questions. It made him sound stupid, like he didn't know, so Eric had made it a point of honor to never ask Dad anything.

Eric filled his box, the only box Dad would let him take, with personal items. At the bottom he layered thirty comic books, all Conan the Barbarian adventures; then his slingshot and a marble bag filled with steel ball bearings; beside that, his cassette player and tapes (Run DMC, the Rolling Stones, Men Without Hats, The Cure, AC/DC, U2, and a Willie Nelson tape that none of his friends knew about); two paperbacks (*The Hobbit* and *The Stand*); a rabbit's foot; one hundred and forty seven dollars saved from his paper route; a *Playboy* (November, 1992); a Blue Oyster Cult tee shirt; a picture of a Porshe 911 he had lovingly cut out of *Car and Driver* magazine the month before. A NUKE THE GAY WHALES FOR JESUS bumper sticker. A small frisbee (the competition-weight disk was too large for the box); a thick bundle of wallet-sized photographs that his friends in the Eighth Grade had given him in the last two weeks (Mostly girls who signed the backs with "Have a nice summer," or "It's been a blast having you in class this year." None mentioned the disease). He topped the bundle with an old MTV towel of Martha Quinn at the MTV beach party. He looked at the posters on his bedroom walls that the black light made glow like nuclear accidents, the rest of his books and tapes, and everything else he had to leave behind, forlornly. He went into the kitchen to help Mom.

Eight hours later, near sunset, the van, filled not only with boxes and suitcases of clothes but also with all the food from the cupboards, pulled off U.S. 6 next to Clear Creek in a canyon west of Denver. Traffic passed them sporadically, heading west. Eric supposed that most people stuck to the newer, multi-lane I 70 rather than the two lane, winding, older highway.

"What are we doing here?" Eric asked Mom.

"You'll see," she said.

The canyon wall across the highway rose steeply to their right, and the thirty-foot-wide stream tumbled noisily over the rocks to their left. Other than the pullout their van almost filled, nothing seemed distinguishable about this stretch of road. "Do you feel like some climbing?" said Dad.

Eric decided he definitely *didn't* feel like climbing by the time he was far above the highway, as the sun set, one hand bleeding from cactus needles and his back burning under an overloaded pack. He stepped into a space between two rocks where Dad pointed. He handed Eric a flashlight. "Help your mom set up house." He turned away and started down the "trail," which Eric couldn't believe Dad had led them up. Mom leaned against a boulder, breathing heavily.

"How is it in there?" she said.

Eric shrugged off his pack, held his flashlight in front of him, and crawled into the hole at the boulders' base. The light penetrated deeply into a room that quickly grew wider and higher the farther in he went. Far from being empty, boxes lined the walls, each marked with thick felt-pen labels in Dad's handwriting: soup, tuna, ham, beans, corn, chili, spaghetti, sterno, gas, kerosine, charcoal, and dozens of others he couldn't see. Light reflected off something big wrapped in black plastic. Eric pulled a corner of the sheet off the shape revealing three mattresses stacked on each other.

Another light cast sharp shadows around him. He pointed his flashlight at the entrance, and his mother, just getting off her knees, shielded her eyes. "You all right?" she said.

They used the plastic as a ground sheet and put the three mattresses side by side on a relatively flat spot on the floor.

Eric said, "What is this place?"

Mom pulled the lid off a box and looked inside. "A fault cave. Your dad learned about it when he was at the Colorado School of Mines."

"Fault cave?"

"Caves normally form in limestone, but this is granite. Not many people know about it. Your dad has a map of all the passages and entrances. We can explore it later."

She found sheets and blankets in one of the boxes and just finished making the last bed when Dad crawled into the room. "Why didn't you light one of the Coleman lanterns?" he said.

Later, with the lantern extinguished, Eric snuggled deeper under the blankets and sleeping bag Mom had spread over him. He strained his eyes, but saw nothing. He remembered once when the family had toured Cave of the Winds at Manitou Springs. The guide had turned out the light. After the group had stood in the velvet darkness for a minute, he said, "This is what a blind man sees every day of his life."

Dad breathed softly next to him. Eric guessed he was asleep. He couldn't hear Mom. After a long while, when he almost felt the rocks of the mountain creaking beneath him, when he was sure that snakes or scorpions or demons were hovering in the air, he said, "Mom . . ." His voice sounded flat and small in the cave's space. ". . . are you awake?"

Cloth rustled against cloth. "Yes."

"Did Dad carry all this stuff up here by himself?"

She moved again. A blanket scraped across the plastic ground cloth. "When he heard how bad the disease might be, he started buying things and bringing them up on the weekends or after work."

"No, really?"

"It tired him, Eric. He couldn't tell anyone."

"Did you help?"

"This is the first time I've been here." She sighed. "He said he would be fine."

"How did he get the mattresses? I mean, I could see a box of beans or something, but the mattresses? Arnold Shwarzenegger couldn't get up that trail with a load like that!"

"He's persistent when he's got a goal," she said.

Eric stood eight inches taller than Dad, which made Dad as small as the smallest kids in his class. "He's not strong enough!" Eric caught his breath. Dad moved on his mattress, rolling on his back. Eric's bed, which was pushed against Dad's, shifted slightly.

Dad cleared his throat, then said, "A man needs a hobby. Now get some sleep."

But Eric couldn't. Not with the total blackness settled over him, not with the rustle of leaves in the entrance crawlway or the skitter of rodent paws over rock. He smelled mice droppings. Eventually, Eric reached under the blankets for his cassette player and put the headphones over his ears. He listened to Run DMC at low volume, figuring the batteries might last longer that way, and he wondered if Dad had the foresight to bring some double A's among the other supplies. He doubted it.

In the morning they ate breakfast on a large flat rock behind a ridge above the cave entrance: Mom, sitting on a camp stool, Dad standing, back to them, surveying the canyon, and Eric leaning against a branchless juniper trunk that stuck out of the ground like a twisted pole. After they were done, they carefully policed the area of any scraps that might show they had been about. Dad was adamant about this. Then he led Eric to a rocky outcrop that overlooked the trail to the cave and the highway below. While Eric followed him, he silently critiqued Dad's outfit. The flannel shirt seemed okay, although it was warm for it. Already the sun-washed rocks were too hot to lean against comfortably. But the blue corduroy pants were definitely wrong, and so were black socks with Hushpuppy shoes. The outfit was embarrassing, Eric thought. Dad gave him a canteen and told him to keep a watch for "tourists."

Even though he had sworn not to ask Dad any questions, the words blurted out. "What do you mean?" The canteen hung low on Eric's hip and the weight pressed coolly against his thigh. Eric wished he had a cola.

Dad said, "You hear that?"

He's not answering again, thought Eric, and he listened. Below the river mumble covered the passage of cars. Nothing else. Then he heard it, chirping somewhere in the rocks above him. A canyon finch, he thought, but he shook his head.

"It's a canyon finch, son. You know that."

Eric shrugged, as if he still didn't hear it. For years Dad had been identifying bird calls, and lately the exercise wearied Eric to no end. He'd taken to not playing the game.

Dad pushed his glasses up his nose. He turned away from the bird and looked down the steep trail. His hair was matted and skewed to one side. Eric realized he'd never seen Dad before he'd showered and shaved. "We might get sick, Eric. There's nothing we can do about that. But if we don't, then there may be . . ." He paused, as if searching for the right words. ". . . dangerous men. We'll be safe as long as no one thinks to come here." His hand fluttered to his face, took off his glasses. He rubbed the lenses with his shirt tail. "Stay alert, and if you spy anybody coming up don't let them see you. Tell your Mom. She'll know what to do." Dad clambered over a rock and headed for the trail. When he was twenty feet away, he turned and looked at Eric. Eric thought he might say something noble or encouraging like, "You must be the man while I'm away," or "We're depending on you, son," but what he said instead was, "And don't wear those darn headphones either."

When Dad was out of sight, Eric popped the headphones on and listened to the radio. News and talk dominated: warnings from the Denver Police to be wary of looters, information about possible quarantines from the Governor's office, lists of school closings (Denver schools were dismissed. Eric frowned. He'd only missed one day.), and health tips ("Stay away from crowds and keep your immune system healthy by eating right and sleeping well"). Eric roamed through the channels, but couldn't find any music except for a Ft. Collins station playing spirituals that kept fading out.

Cars passed steadily by 150 yards below, household goods pressed against the windows. Families, mostly, as far as Eric could tell. Usually a man and woman in the front seat, two or three kids in the back, a dog maybe or a cat. They moved from left to right, their motor sounds swallowed by the stream's constant rumble. Eric rubbed the rock he sat cross-legged on with his thumb. Tiny glints of mica or quartz caught the sun and reflected them like stone-frozen stars. Most of the rock in the canyon was dark, almost black, granites and schists.

Something moved on the canyon wall across the stream at about Eric's height. It was a small mountain goat picking its way across the steep slope. He observed it until it hopped over a ridge and disappeared.

The rest of the day Eric watched Dad carry box after box up the trail to the cave. Dad would stand at the side of the highway below and wait until there was a break in the cars. Then he would dash across the road and into the young cottonwood trees that screened the trail's base. Eric snorted each time. Dad was such a ninny, practically a coward, he thought. Hiding in a cave! Nobody cares if we're up here. We'd be tons better off if we stayed in Denver, or if we'd gone to California. Surely by the time the disease gets to the west coast they'll have a cure for it. In the meantime we could be soaking up rays.

To kill time that afternoon, Eric practiced with his sling shot, firing irregularly shaped pebbles at targets he set up on the slope. The whiz of the rocks cutting through the air and the sharp crack when they hit entertained him until Mom brought him dinner, a bowl of hot chile and a hunk of bread.

"Enjoy the bread, Eric. We might not have any more fresh food for a while." Her hair was pinned back and looked greasy. If Dad really cared about her, he thought, we wouldn't be stuck on this stupid mountain.

Eric set the bowl on the rock beside him to cool. "So what's the plan?"

"We're living up here until your dad thinks it's safe to go home."

"Dad's a nut."

"Think of it as a camping trip. Dad's afraid that the city will be bad. Exposure to the disease, and there's already been riots."

"He's still crazy."

Mom frowned. Eric thought for a moment that she might yell at him, that he had pushed too far. She said, "He's your father. He's trying to protect us." Her face screwed up, like she was going to cry. "The world, Eric. It's all going away. Don't you care about the world?"

Eric put a pebble in the sling shot's leather pocket, aimed it across the canyon and fired. The rock shattered against a boulder on the other side. "I'm getting pretty good with this."

She shook her head and walked back to the cave. Eric wished he'd said instead, "I love you, Mom." He put on the headphones, cranked up the volume and watched the cars passing below until the sun set and the evening mosquitos drove him inside.

*

When Eric took his slingshot and cassette player to his post the next morning, the air was already hot, and gnats rose from the scrub oak like nasty tempered clouds. Two motorcycles were parked in the pull-out across the road from the trail. He scanned the canyon and what he could see of the path for the riders, but didn't spot them. Several times yesterday cars had parked there, mostly to let faster cars pass, although once a woman had jumped from her truck and run down to the stream to squat behind a bush where she was hidden from the road. Eric looked away until she was gone. He didn't worry about the cycles.

He put a tape in the player, adjusted the headphones and pressed "play." Nothing happened. The battery cover slid off easily and he cupped his hand below the batteries to catch them when he thumped the player against his knee. He shook the batteries like dice in his hand, which he hoped might revive them, and carefully wiped the terminals against his shirt to remove oxidation. But when he put them back, the tape still would not run.

The radio worked, for what little use it was. The stations were either off the air or broadcasting news. He couldn't find rock-n-roll anywhere. Finally he settled on KBPI, where at least he recognized the DJ. The governor had declared a general emergency the night before and called for National Guard support at hospitals and "food distribution centers." Also there was talk about possible vaccines and how the scientists were saying that people shouldn't panic. Meanwhile, reports from the eastern United States sounded bad, but no one would say how bad. Europe, where the disease started, wasn't reporting anything now. What bothered Eric was the DJ's voice. He sounded wheezy and he cleared his throat a lot.

Eric leaned against a rock and watched the clouds. It's hard to believe that anything is wrong, he thought. A jet dragged a contrail high against the blue. Probably a military flight, he thought. Commercial service was suspended. The shady side of the rock cooled his back, and lichens flaked off beneath his fingers as he rubbed them. Far up the slope, scrub oak leaves twisted in a breeze that hadn't reached him yet. The announcements droned. The DJ started coughing and couldn't stop. After twenty seconds or so, they switched to the station's call signal and kept playing it over and over. Eric held his cassette player in his lap, his hands around it, and cried.

After a while, he closed his eyes and fell asleep.

*

The heat woke him. The shade that had protected him earlier had retreated, and three quarters of his body was in the sun. He sat up groggily, his head foggy with sleep. His first thought was to check the trail. After all, he thought, I'm supposed to be on guard duty. The motorcycles were still there. Traffic slid slowly through the canyon, bumper to bumper now. The windshields reflected brightly, and he couldn't see the occupants. Baggage was strapped to the car tops. His second thought was of how lucky he was that Dad hadn't caught him sleeping. He'd have freaked out for sure.

He clipped the player to his belt and walked back to the cave. Maybe Mom knew where some batteries were. If not, he might be able to talk her into running into town with him for some more. If Dad was so set against going into Denver, they could go west to Georgetown or Idaho Springs.

Eric stopped at the cave entrance. Voices came from within, his father's and one he didn't recognize. He scooted into the crawlway and crept closer. The Coleman lantern's harsh light left deep shadows through the room.

"You have more than enough for three people," said the man sitting on a box with his back to Eric. A big soft-looking hulk, over two-hundred pounds, he wore a jean jacket with the sleeves cut off at the shoulder, short, spiked hair, and a dangly earring. Dad stood on the other side of the lantern, his arms across his chest, and another man, tall and scrawny, maybe high school age, sat on Eric's mattress.

Eric pushed himself up slowly and scanned the room. Mom wasn't there. He thought she might be in one of the back corridors he hadn't gotten around to exploring yet. She had said that there was a lot more to the cave.

Dad said, "There's not so much. I'm planning on staying for the winter."

The jean-jacket man leaned forward. "So we go get more when this runs out. Lots of food there if you know where to look."

"Looting you mean."

"A strong man takes what he wants."

Dad stepped back toward a stack of boxes.

The high school kid said from the mattress, "Might be we could team up. You got a good start here. Three guys working together could do all right. We get some women and wait for things to blow over."

"You're not too old for witch wool are you?" said jean-jacket. "All kinds of babes would be happy to come out here and get away from the city. Scared, you know."

"I like it alone." Dad looked relaxed but Eric suddenly felt cold. The leaves beneath him seemed to crackle like firecrackers and the darkness of the crawlway felt like poor cover.

"Maybe he's already getting some," said high school. "You notice he got *three* mattresses here?"

Jean-jacket walked over to the beds. "Three. You said you were on your own. Who you hiding?"

"Used to be three of us. My family. They didn't make it. I buried them out there." He nodded toward the entrance. Eric tried to look like a rock.

Jean-jacket said, "That's too bad. Shit happens, doesn't it?" He seemed to mull over Dad's news. "Maybe you're right, old man. You'd do better on your own. So I'll tell you what. Why don't you leave?" High school laughed.

"This is my place. I found it and I did the work to stock it." Dad stepped back again. Eric slipped his hand down to his waist and loosened the tie on the sling shot's ammo bag.

"Other people know about this cave," said jean-jacket. "Getting here first doesn't make it yours. I figure I got just as much a right to it as anybody."

"Why you talking to this guy?" said high school. "Let's toss him off the mountain." Dad looked back and forth between them.

Jean-jacket paused, as if considering the idea. "Cops. We can't let him go." He sighed. "They're pretty busy, those that ain't falling down sick, but someone might get interested."

Eric loaded a ball bearing into the sling shot. His hands trembled and he could barely hold the leather patch around the shot.

"You going to do it?" said high school. Eric got up on his knees. They were both looking at Dad. Eric took a deep breath and pulled the shot to his ear.

Then Dad moved. He planted both hands on high school's chest and pushed. The young man yelped as he stumbled back and tripped over the mattresses. Dad dove to the back of the cave. Eric let go of the shot. The lantern burst into a hundred shards of glass, and the room went black. "Run, Dad!" Eric yelled.

He turned and sprinted on his hands and knees out of the crawlway. He stood too quickly at the entrance, slamming his back into the rough ceiling, and then he was out and running to a boulder above the cave entrance. He wanted to be higher than them. He loaded another ball bearing into the sling shot and spread a handful more on a flat spot where he could easily reach them. The entranceway was fifty feet away. An easy shot. But he was gasping. Where was Dad? A bearing rolled off. He didn't take his eyes off the entrance. One minute passed. Two. He wiped sweat from his eyes. A flicker of movement a hundred yards away. Maybe a squirrel. It kept moving, and then it grew longer. An arm. A head. Dad squeezed himself out from under a rock. Another entrance, Eric thought. He wanted to yell to him, but he was afraid the men would come out any second and know where he was. They shouted to each other in the cave. Eric couldn't hear their words. He figured they hadn't found flashlights, and they were feeling the way out in the dark.

Dad climbed to a cairn of rocks higher on the slope and dug into them.

"Here it is!" hollered jean-jacket as he stepped into the light. High school joined him, and they both shaded their eyes.

Eric pulled the shot back, not sure what to do. If they moved toward Dad, he would shoot them, but would the shot drive them off or just make them furious?

Dad yanked a long bundle wrapped in canvas from the rocks and started untying the rope that secured it.

The men saw him. Jean-jacket pointed one direction for high school to go, and he went the other.

Eric let go of the shot. The ball bearing hissed and nailed high school.

He went down, holding his arm. "Hell, hell, hell!" He rolled under a scrub oak in plain sight. "I'm shot!"

Jean jacket ducked behind a rock. "I didn't hear anything."

"Must have had a silencer."

"How bad?"

High school took his hand off his arm and looked at it in wonder. "There ain't no blood," he said. "But I think it's broke."

Eric rose and aimed at jean-jacket, who saw him.

"It's just a goddamned kid!"

Eric let go and the shot smacked loudly into the rock by jean-jacket in a small puff of rock dust. The ricochet whined into the distance. Jean-jacket dropped out of sight.

"He's just got a damned sling shot," he yelled. "It's not like he can kill you."

Dad stepped onto an overhang that looked down on all of them. "I can," he said and cocked the shotgun he carried. On the pinnacle of rock, the sun high behind him, he looked ominous and deadly. "Time for you men to go home."

Jean-jacket stood. Dad swung the barrel in his direction. There was a long silence. Then jean-jacket put his hands on his head. High school did the same, and the two marched down the trail. "We're coming back, suck-nuts!" screamed high school when they were almost out of sight. Dad didn't move. The shotgun pointed toward them until they got on their motorcycles and rode away.

Eric sat. Dad jumped from the overhang and sat next to him.

"You did all right, son," he said.

Eric gazed at the dirt between his feet. He didn't want to look at Dad. If he hadn't fallen asleep, this wouldn't have happened. "I thought you were going to die," Eric said finally.

Dad patted him on the shoulder awkwardly. "I thought so too." He broke open the shotgun. The chambers were empty. "I didn't have shells in it."

Eric stared, open-mouthed.

Dad said, "I got in a hurry when you started shooting at them. I forgot to load."

A voice above them said, "Good thing I didn't." Gravel skittered down the slope. Eric looked up. Mom, holding Dad's 20 gauge, picked her way among the cactus and granite. "Someone has to have some sense in this family." She answered Eric's unasked question. "I went out the back door when they came in the front. Watched the whole thing." She smiled. "Sure scared me when the lantern went out. You shot it?"

Eric nodded.

She looked down at the highway, where the line of cars rolled slowly westward. "Will they come back?"

Dad snapped the shotgun closed. "No. I don't believe they will."

Eric said, "They said they would."

"I think they were sick, Eric. Sick people do desperate things, but they don't live long."

Dad stood and brushed dirt off of his pants. He helped Mom stand, and they walked hand in hand to the cave. Eric, walking behind them, began to laugh. He laughed so hard that he had to sit on the trail.

"What is it, Eric?" said Mom.

Eric looked at them both again. Their hair was dirty, clothes smudged. She stood over him, shotgun balanced on her hip. Dad rested his gun on his shoulder.

"You look . . ." He laughed even louder. "You look . . . so different." He rolled onto his back, short of breath.

Dad held his hands out and examined himself. "Well," he said, "it's not Norman Rockwell."

Chapter Three
A DAY WITH WOLVES

A sound woke him, or perhaps a flash of heat lightning from the clouds that still hung in the east. He couldn't tell. His right shoulder throbbed where his stone bed pressed through the sleeping bag, and his backbone felt compressed and warped. He sighed comfortably. These were the sensations he associated with sleeping outdoors. He looked for star patterns for the time. When he'd drifted off, the mountains to the west were just touching Gemini, which would have made it around 9:00, but now Ursa Major, the Big Dipper, was a couple of degrees off the horizon. The world turns, he thought, as it always does. He figured it was 2:00 a.m. or so.

He identified the constellations: Bootes, with brilliant Arcturus anchoring it; Draco snaking around Ursa Minor, the Little Dipper; and right at the cloud line, Hercules facing the next brightest night light, Vega. Clouds hid Andromeda, Cassiopeia, Cygnus, Capricornus, Pegasus and Aquarius. His dad used to sing a song about the "dawning of the age of Aquarius." Eric pondered on it for a moment, trying to come up with the tune, but he couldn't.

He stared into the sky. One good thing about the Apocalypse, he thought, is the stars shine brighter without city lights to wash them out.

The air murmured distantly like a deep, deep growl. He guessed the storm might be fifty miles away and slowly approaching. He remembered how Huck Finn described thunder as a "rumbling, grumbling, tumbling down the sky towards the underside of the world, like rolling empty barrels down stairs, where it's long stairs and they bounce a good deal, you know." That was Troy's favorite part of the book when Eric had read it to him years ago. Troy had sat on his lap and turned the pages night after night by the uneven light from a kerosene lantern. Sometimes Eric could read eight or nine pages before Troy's head sagged, and Eric would carry him to bed.

Lightning flickered again, like a far away flash bulb, and Eric flinched. Something moved at the rock's base. He saw it in the corner of his eye. He rolled to get a better look, but the ground was absolutely black to him. The lightning hadn't been that bright, but for a moment his eyes were blinded to whatever the starlight might reveal. Gradually, though, he made out the outline of the rock he lay on, and then the clumps of grass below it, and then the asphalt road he'd been hiking, a silver path in the dim light. Nothing moved. He strained his eyes watching the dark mounds of grass until the bass whisper of thunder shook the air again. All was dim silver or black. Cold air slid past his face. Spring was still young and he knew that for many mornings more he'd waken to frost on the ground. Other than the swish his own sleeping bag made as he turned, and the far off thunder, the night slept silently.

A black hump moved. Eric had been looking to its left, but he was sure that it changed positions. His eyes ached trying to discern this shadow from any other. Another one moved. This one he tracked as it glided ten feet and then stopped. He kept his eyes on it, sure that if he looked away that it would be indistinguishable from every other black shadow on the starlit, silvered backdrop. The top of the stone suddenly seemed too close to the ground. When he'd climbed it at sunset, his backpack dragging him backwards and each handhold a shade too far of a reach, the eight or so feet had seemed plenty tall enough, but now, with shadows drifting around its base, the stone afforded little protection. He pushed his hand into his pack and grasped the handle of his sling shot. The steel ball bearings clinked softly as he opened the leather bag's neck and grabbed one between his thumb and index finger. Another shadow moved.

Lightning flashed, flickering brightly for an instant. Eyes below reflected the light back, and then Eric was left to contemplate the afterimage floating before him. Long legs, solid bodies, huge feet. For a second Eric thought they were dogs, but the next burst of lightning confirmed what he feared. They were too big, too similar to each other. Feral dog pack's members showed all the remnants of their mixed ancestry. In the same group might be a few that looked like collies, a few like German shepherds, some like Dobermans. Their snouts and heads varied in shape and size. And they barked a lot. Dog packs were almost always noisy, but Eric had heard nothing from these animals. They were wolves. He placed the ball bearing in the sling shot's leather patch.

Here is something worth telling them in town, he thought. He'd read that wolves were hunted to extinction in Colorado by 1930. No wild wolves lived in the contiguous 48 states, except for a small population in Minnesota and an experimental pack in Yellowstone. It's taken 50 years for them to get here from Canada, but they're back. He remembered stories he'd read about wolves, all of them frightening: how wolves would attack lone men hunting in the woods; how they were the animal kingdom's equivalent of mass murderers, killing way more than they could eat; how one wolf might fatally cripple a dozen cows in one night, eating none of them but leaving them to suffer until the poor rancher the next day would be forced to destroy them. He'd read a book once about famous outlaw wolves, the kind that terrorized communities and defied hunters to kill them: Queen Wolf in Unaweep Canyon, Colorado; Split Rock Wolf in Wyoming; Old Whitey in Bear Springs Mesa, Colorado, and perhaps the most notorious, Three Toes of Harding County, South Dakota, who took thirteen years to hunt down, and whom ranchers credited with destroying fifty thousand dollars worth of stock.

Wild dogs the town can handle. A couple of guards on horseback, with their own dogs to help, managed to keep stock loss to a minimum; a sick cow now and then, or sometimes a calf that wandered off. But if wolves are back, he thought, then precautions will have to be doubled.

In the next flash of lightning he counted a dozen of them. Some lay down; four or five were standing, sniffing the wind perhaps. He wondered if they knew he was there. Surely they do, he thought. How could they not? He'd read that a wolf's sense of smell was a hundred times keener than a man's, and that its eyesight was phenomenal at night. He scooted himself to the edge of the rock, taking his sling shot with him, although now all he thought was that if the wolves tried to climb the rock, he might be able to scare them off. The chances of striking a fatal blow in the dark seemed remote. He felt the edge of the stone beneath his hand. Something moved below him, and then the lightning flashed again. A wolf standing with its forefeet on the rock, stretching almost five feet vertically, its head only three feet away, met him eye to eye. Eric froze.

The wolf whined. It seemed such a small sound for an animal this size to make and so ridiculous that Eric almost laughed, but instead he screamed, "Back off!" Claws scrabbled against the rock, and the next flash revealed all the wolves looking up at him, heads cocked to one side or the other, tongues lolling lazily out of their mouths, their eyes like bright lights shining out of their dark faces.

Eric held the slingshot ready, but the next flicker showed none of them had moved, and when it flashed again, the wolves seemed disinterested. For a long time, maybe an hour, Eric sat up watching the wolves by lightning. One was much larger than the rest, the one who'd partially climbed the rock. Eric guessed he might be one-hundred and fifty pounds or so and at least three feet tall at the shoulder. The rest ranged from sixty pounds to maybe a hundred. They seemed well fed. No lean and hungry look in them at all. Of course there were range cattle to eat, he thought, and the deer population had soared once man wasn't around to harvest the surplus each year. He should have guessed that wolves, the natural predator, would eventually return.

Dogs' days were numbered. They'd either interbreed or be driven out of the ecological niche. He thought about the others, mountain lion and bear. They'd probably made a comeback too. Maybe out on the plains of Kansas, buffalo herds were slowly building. If the fences were down, and they undoubtably were, and if the pathetic little populations that lived on the tiny preserves hadn't died the first few winters, then even now the plains might be the home of the buffalo again. He imagined them nosing through the abandoned streets of Kansas City. The thought tickled him, and then frightened him. If the animals come back, where will the men go? Man had to reassert his place in the new world. The thought reminded him of why he started this trip. Tomorrow he would reach C-470 and start north to Boulder. The best library in Colorado was at the university. Boulder might have escaped the general destruction that Denver suffered. If the building stands, the books might be safe.

A sound rose from below, but Eric couldn't pin its source. It seemed to swell out of the air around him, a cool, piercing animal siren, and then another joined it. They all started, a huge, primeval harmony of sound. In the lightning, the wolves strained their snouts up, howling at the sky. Eric shivered. They continued, two barks and a howl; two barks and a howl.

He realized they weren't afraid of him. They weren't threatening him; they weren't hungry. He probably could climb off the rock and walk away and they wouldn't do anything, because a five-foot wolf would have no trouble jumping to the top of an eight-foot rock. Eric tilted his head back to see what the wolves saw. The clouds covered the sky now, hiding the stars, and the lightning flashes within the clouds lit up their fantastic shapes: bottomless valleys and prodigious mountains of mist, fantastic rollings of shapes birthing and swallowing each other, like a slow motion ocean gone mad. Profound rumbles shook the air regularly.

The wolves howled, and after a moment of this, Eric cleared his throat and joined them. The sound rose up from deep in his chest. He joined their harmony. Despite his fears, despite his imagining of a world without men, it felt good to yowl at the sky.

*

The clouds hid the sunrise the next morning, and when Eric awoke late, it took him a minute to place where he was. He sat in his sleeping bag. To the east, almost on the horizon, a dark line of trees marked the course of the South Platte. To the south, the gentle hills rose and fell until they blurred in the distance. North, ruins of houses and dark foundations marked the same hills. On the north side of Bowles Avenue, several large houses behind a long line of crumbling brick wall still stood. Unlike so many others, they looked as if they had escaped the burning during the great panic, but their roofs had long since collapsed, and they sagged like tired old men. He shuddered, thinking about the great fire that had almost killed him when he was young.

The remnants of the western edge of Denver and its suburbs stretched for twenty-five miles in that direction. Eric planned on walking beyond Denver's western edge before heading north to Boulder. The dogs were worse in the city, where they roamed in large packs, and a man traveling alone would be too tempting.

To the west, the hills sloped until they leapt into mountains only a half a dozen miles away. Snow still covered the front range, but the low clouds kept him from seeing them.

Except for tracks as big as his hand, he found no sign of the wolves after he stowed the sleeping bag and climbed off the rock.

Before he started, he finished twenty push-ups, fifty sit-ups and a series of stretching exercises—his morning routine for years. His back felt much better when he'd worked the kinks out, and by the time he hefted his pack to his shoulders, he was whistling. Twenty minutes farther down the road, he realized the tune was "Aquarius."

By the time the sun popped from behind the clouds an hour later, when he guessed he was still two or three miles from the C-470 interchange where he would turn north, he realized he was being followed. Nerves, he thought at first. A man spends an evening perched above wolves, and he gets jumpy. He twirled at a clatter, like gravel being kicked, but the road stretched as empty behind him as it stretched in front. Plenty of brush for something to hide in, he observed. An army could sneak along ten feet from the road, and he'd never know a thing. He walked on, ears finely tuned.

He calmed himself by contemplating the changes in the road since the last time he went west fifteen years ago. First, weeds commanded more of the path than asphalt now. Fifteen years ago, at least in most spots, the road was still a road. Double yellow lines, faded to near invisibility, still marked the middle. But this hadn't surprised him. The first spring of the Now Time he'd been amazed at how bad the roads were. Cracks had formed. Weeds had pushed through in some spots already. Winter swelling had buckled the as-phalt in some places and pulled it apart in others. Without constant traffic and road crews, the elements and nature went to work. Each year after that, erosion undercut some parts. Wind-blown dirt or mud overflows from rain covered other sections, and plants rooted in every crack and every deposit of soil, so that even if he had a car now, he wouldn't be able to drive a quarter of a mile without falling into a gully or stopping at an obstruction. In Europe, he'd read, the Romans built a road called the Appian Way, and some sections of it were still passable 2,000 years later, but they built with stones. As-phalt was too biodegradable.

He pushed through a line of weeds a yard wide that cut all the way across the road. Weeds and grasses skirted the next thirty feet of relatively clean asphalt, then a grass peninsula covered the path, and if he didn't know better, he could have sworn that there had never been a road. Glass crunched behind him. He twirled again. Grasses, weeds, scrub oak, but nothing else. He sniffed: a hint of Pinyon and ozone in the air, a remnant of last night's storm. He wet his finger and held it up. The sound was downwind. If it were ani-mal, it'd be smelling him, not the other way around.

He'd left the outskirts of Littleton and although ruins no longer dotted the landscape, he'd reached the line of gutted and rusted cars that ended at the C-470 intersection. All were rust red or brown and resting on their rims. Not a speck of paint left on them. Eric knew of at least four big grass fires in the last fifty years that must have burned any paint that weathering alone wouldn't have removed. Through open doors and broken windows he saw black seat springs and bare metal. All the vinyl, rubber, leather and plastic were long gone. Tumbleweed filled some cars and poked out so that they looked like weird planters in need of watering. Eric guessed that in the panic to flee Denver, a monstrous traffic jam gridlocked this road west. People must have abandoned their cars and walked. Later, the civil authorities, or the army, had cleared the road with bull dozers or tanks. Pieces of safety glass glittered wherever he looked. He kept to the middle, as far from the wrecks as he could. The empty headlight sockets, broken grills and dangling wires kept a somber witness. A breeze whistled hollowly.

Eric picked up his pace and glanced quickly side to side. It couldn't be the wolves, he thought. Too noisy. And not dogs. Not noisy enough. Then ahead he saw what he'd been hoping for: a bus. When he reached it, he glanced over his shoulder, then bent low and ran behind the crumpled metal mass. He gasped; his heart throbbed solidly in his ears. Ruefully, he admitted to himself that although he was in fine shape for seventy-five, he was seventy-five. Dots circled through his vision.

He braced himself against the bus's cool bulk, and rust powdered his hands. Then he crept to the back of the bus so that he could see the road without being seen. Why do I want to know? he thought. It'd be best to keep going and let them play their hand. He wasn't worried about death by violence, he realized. It was more like idle curiosity, or the challenge of turning the tables on whoever was following him. Not feeling fear was wonderful, liberating. He realized that staying at home he had become afraid. Fighting with Troy over how to direct the town, he'd become a shut-in. The only reason to leave the house was to go to town meetings, and all he'd thought about for the last few years was how afraid he was for the future of humanity, or at least that segment of humanity he knew. Cut off from other groups, salvaging manufactured goods, making nothing for themselves, he feared their death by ignorance. As he lay in the shade of the bus, half buried by a tumbleweed, miles from home, followed by who knew what for who knew why, he felt glad. He smiled.

A half hour passed. Eric pinched the back of his hand to stay awake. A mouse ran across the road. A bird sang the same six notes over and over. A meadow lark, he thought. He smiled. He'd never forgotten his dad's bird calls. The breeze stopped and heat waves shimmered off the asphalt and broken glass.

Eric thought about a hunting trip he taken when Troy was twelve. Carrying compound bows, they'd left before dawn for a blind set near a salt lick by McLellan Reservoir. Rains had come down hard for several weeks before, softening the ground, and a visit to the lick the day before showed deer used it. With luck, there'd be fresh venison on their table. But nothing went well. At the blind, Troy refused to stay still, jumping up at every sound, notching and un-notching an arrow, rummaging through his day pack, and when a deer did come, he scared it off with a hasty, ill-aimed shot.

Eric thought, I was too rough with him. I shouldn't have yelled. But the missed meal was too real in his head, and Troy was crushed. He didn't speak to Eric for the rest of the day, and the next day, when Eric called him in for his reading lesson, Troy said, "I don't need to read, I need to hunt." A week later Troy brought in a deer he'd shot on his own. Exhausted, he dropped it at Eric's feet. Dirt covered his face. A long scratch ran down the side of his cheek, but he didn't look proud; he looked angry, and Eric didn't know what to say. Confronted with this new version of his son, this defiant hunter, he felt at a loss. Finally, Eric put out his hand. He wanted to hug him, to pull him close to his chest and say, "Ah, son." But he didn't. He knew now, at the time when he most needed to show he loved him he'd made a mistake: he only offered to shake his son's hand. Troy kept his own hands at his side for a long time before he reached out and shook with Eric. He never read with his father again.

Eric's chin rested on his forearm, and he knew he'd been sleeping. Whatever had been following him had either been a figment of his imagination, or it had spotted him leaving the road and was now holed up on its own waiting for him to move. He rolled onto his side and dug into his backpack for a jar of preserves and some bread. He decided he had no need to rush. Traveling in the heat drained him. If he reached the intersection by evening, he could find a good campsite on the hill beyond. There used to be a stone hut above a gully a few hundred yards up the hill, and if it still stood, he would sleep there.

When he spotted a coyote trotting up the road, he paused in mid-bite. He thought, this is my day for the dog family. No wind now to carry my scent, he's probably tracking me. As if to confirm this thought, the coyote paused to smell the asphalt before continuing towards Eric. Then it stopped a hundred and fifty yards away, perked its ears, and stepped toward a car on its side. A rock sailed from behind the car; the coyote ducked and sprinted away.

Got you, thought Eric. He moved his backpack to the corner of the bus where it'd be visible, put his hat on top of it, as if he'd decided to lay down, then crawled into the underbrush, carefully keeping out of sight of whoever hid behind the car down the road. Out of the shade, the sun beat hard on his back. He partially stood, and, using bushes for cover, maneuvered himself closer to the car. I'm on a stalk, and we'll see just who you are. He felt strong, springy, like a twenty-year-old. He slipped a rock the size of an egg into his pocket, and when he found another about the same size, he kept it in his hand.

Slowly now, he crept closer. Twenty yards away, he squatted behind a Volkswagon Bug with Colorado plates. The embossed mountains still showed in the metal. The rock he tossed over the other car clattered loudly in the silence of the afternoon. Somebody said something and somebody else hissed a loud "Shhhh!" Eric weighed the second rock in his hand. After considering what to do with it for a moment, he threw it directly at the other car. The "clang" still echoed when a head popped up, looked around, then dropped out of sight.

Eric yelled, "Dodge! You can come out now." He heard frantic whispering. "You too, Rabbit."

Sheepishly, the two boys stood. "How'd you find us, Grandfather?" asked Dodge. Rabbit said, "I told you he was too smart for us."

Eric smiled at them. "You boys eat yet?"

When they finished lunch, Dodge showed Eric their inventory. Dodge had packed five one-pound packages of beef jerky, a roll of dried crab apple leather and a package of rock candy. Rabbit's pack, which Eric decided must weigh sixty pounds, had twice as much food, two knives, a first-aid kit box filled with various herbs, a tool kit complete with hammer and saw, a hundred-foot length of rope, a tent, a shovel, and a complete change of clothes for both of them. "I like to be prepared," he said.

"You can't come with me, boys," said Eric.

"I knew he'd say that," said Rabbit. He scowled and turned his scarred face away.

Dodge wasn't bothered. "Where you going to anyway?" He sucked on a piece of candy. "Dad don't even know your gone. He's going to bust a bow string for sure."

Dodge told him that they'd discovered him missing the day before, probably only minutes after he'd left, and they decided to go after him. They'd run home, packed, and been on the road for an hour when nightfall came. They'd slept in a Chevy van that was partially protected by a collapsed garage. "Old man will kill himself if we don't catch him," is what Dodge said that Rabbit had said. "Said no such thing," said Rabbit.

"Did to," said Dodge. "We figured you know some great scavenging, like a treasure trove we talked about. Caught up to you this morning. Still don't know how you guessed us out."

Rabbit turned back to them. "All the good stuff's gone."

Eric chewed on a tough piece of jerky thoughtfully. "You hear anything last night?"

Dodge blanched. "Nothing." Eric recognized Dodge's lie. At ten, Dodge didn't have a poker face.

Rabbit said without flinching, "Some thunder."

"You didn't hear anything like this?" Eric howled.

Dodge's jaw dropped. "That was you?" He looked at Rabbit and then back at Eric. "You?"

Rabbit slapped his thigh. "Told you it wasn't ghosts."

Dodge snapped back, "I didn't say they were ghosts. I said it sounded *like* ghosts."

"You were scared."

"So were you." Dodge looked back at Eric again. "How'd you do all that?"

"It wasn't all me, son. It wasn't all me." He wouldn't say any more about it. They finished lunch.

"So what about the treasure trove?" asked Dodge.

Eric thought about the library at Boulder. Thousands of books: books on farming, metallurgy, medicine, astronomy. "I guess maybe you're right about that," he said. "I've got a treasure in mind if I can get to it. If it's still there."

Dodge said, "You're gonna need help carrying it back, then, right?" Rabbit nodded in agreement.

Eric picked at a piece of meat jammed between his front teeth. "Your dad . . ."

"Dad's scared your gonna teach me something he don't want me to know," said Dodge. "You ought to hear him go on. He's asking me all the time, 'What's he saying to you now? What's the old man saying?' And he keeps telling me to stay away from you." Dodge bit his lip. Eric thought it a sad expression. It was a habit Troy had when he was young. He'd bite his lip so often that sometimes it'd turn blue from the bruises underneath. "I don't want to stay away from you, Grandfather."

Eric explained why they couldn't go, how the trip might be dangerous, how an old man who knew the ways of the world would be safe but if he had to look after two kids that they all might get hurt, how their parents would worry about them. He used all his best arguments, so it was with more than a little amazement, when he reached the intersection of Bowles Avenue and C-470 and moved up the hill towards the stone hut, that he realized the boys were still with him, and that he had agreed to take them.

As they cleared trash off the hut's floor so there would be room for their sleeping bags, Rabbit said, "You know, somebody's been watching us."

Eric said, "Excuse me?"

Holding the corners, Rabbit snapped his ground cloth out and it settled gently to the stone floor. "They been spying on us since lunch. Surprised you didn't notice." It was the longest speech he made all day.

Chapter Four
HOLDING HANDS

Four days after the motorcycle thugs shouted their parting curses, hopped on their motorcycles and roared away,
traffic on the highway stopped. The night before, the bumper
to bumper parade had crept west, headlights glinting from the chrome
and windshields of the cars in front of them, taillights winking bright
red as they tapped their brakes. Sometimes someone would beep,
and the horn echoed from the granite wall across the stream. Two
or three hours after sunset, Eric's mother relieved him. They'd been
keeping twenty-four hour watch of the path to the cave. But in the
morning, when Eric took the lookout again, the empty, silent road
greeted him. He put on his headphones and thumbed on his radio
for news, hoping that the batteries had somehow recharged in the
night, but they were dead.

Three days later, when he took the morning watch, he still wondered what no traffic meant. Had they cured it? Did the doctors fix
everything and no one was scared? He sighed. There was no way
to know without a radio. He couldn't believe that Dad would have
had the foresight to store all the food and other supplies in the cave,
but forget to include a radio. He looked around at the familiar ter-
rain. A thin coating of frost covered the shaded part of the rocks. A
quarter-inch band of moisture marked the boundary between the
shade and sun. He pressed his hand against a rock and left a five
fingered shape in the frost.

He pulled the useless headphones around his neck. The cold
metal raised goose bumps on his legs and arms. He tried not to
touch his hair, which felt heavy and flat. Oil coated his skin like
paint. Dad had said they'd wash at the river, but he hadn't said it
was safe yet. He said he didn't want to risk being seen on the road.
Eric believed himself lucky that Dad let him brush his teeth.

He thought about Amanda Grieves, a girl he liked at school. What would she think of him now, dirty and hiding in a cave? She sat next to him in the band, the flute section, an instrument he'd picked two years earlier because Ian Anderson, the lead singer for the group Jethro Tull, played it. She was second chair; he was third. Each day he'd think about how close they were. Their legs sometimes touched. He felt her warmth through his jeans. He had dreamed about holding her hand for weeks, but he didn't tell anyone, not even his friend, Mike, who talked about "scoring" constantly. "I really bagged one last night," he'd say. "We back-seat bopped till we dropped." But Eric just wanted to hold Amanda's hand. He imagined them walking down the hall, fingers intertwined.

Rocks clattered behind him and he jumped. His dad was coming toward him, methodically kicking pebbles on his way, keeping his head down as if he were purposefully clearing the path.

"Quiet?" Dad asked.

Annoyance flared in Eric. The canyon was empty from end to end. Obviously it was quiet. He considered something clever like, "You just missed the floats and bands," but said nothing.

Dad rested his hands on the boulder Eric used for a watch post. As big as a refrigerator on its side, it offered a perfect view of the only approach to the cave and was easy to hide behind. Dad bent his elbows until his chest met the rock, doing a kind of leaning push-up. Eric doubted his dad was strong enough to do a real push-up, then he thought about the boxes in the cave: cases of canned fruits and vegetables and the other supplies. He still marveled over the mattresses. No matter how he tried, he couldn't imagine his scrawny, unathletic, bookish father muscling the mattresses up the scrub oak choked trail from the road. A black holster hung from Dad's belt. Eric couldn't imagine his dad carrying a gun either, but there it was, dark wooden handle sticking out of the dark leather.

Dad said, "I have to go to the van."

"I thought you'd got it all."

Dad grimaced and pushed himself upright. "Is your radio working?"

Eric shook his head.

"I'm going to find out about this." He waved his hand at the road. "Then I'll drive into Idaho Springs. I want you to go with me."

Normally, before this horrible, weird week, Eric hated driving with his father, partly because Dad braked a half block earlier than he needed to, as far as Eric was concerned, and he always took the shortest route, even if a slightly longer one had ten fewer stop lights. He also hated driving with his father because of the silence. Long, dry, uncomfortable minutes would pass, and neither of them said anything, then Dad would say something stupid like, "How's school?"

In Idaho Springs, though, Eric could buy batteries. "Sounds great. Let's go!" He slid his arms into his pack straps and followed Dad down the path.

A half mile east of the cave, US Highway 6 went through a short tunnel. Dad had hidden the van down a weed-choked access road that cut away from the highway right before this tunnel. He'd parked it behind a thick stand of Cottonwoods. Eric walked ahead, though Dad kept urging him to stay back. The air smelled wet and cold next to the river. By the cave, a hundred feet above the canyon floor, it smelled dusty, like pinyon.

Eric was thinking of Amanda again. She had baby-fine blonde hair that brushed her shoulders. When she played the flute, her head tilted to the side and he could see the pulse in her neck, the way her lips pursed over each note. He had wanted more than anything to hold her hand in the hallway, so he made a plan, a stupid plan, now that he remembered it, but the only one that he thought might work. The door out of the band room was wide enough for two people to walk together. If he left the room the same time she did, if he let his hand swing as he walked, he could time the swinging of his hand with her hand, then naturally, oh so naturally, let them meet. Then, they would be holding hands.

"Eric, stay back," repeated Dad. The darkness of the tunnel loomed before them. It amplified the river, making the splash of water on rocks sound like clapping. They turned onto the access road. A patch of brambles caught Eric's sock. He bent and carefully brushed them away. Dad walked past him.

When Eric caught up, Dad stood to the side of the road, his arms crossed on his chest. The van, Eric saw, rested on four flats. The windows were broken in and the hood was up. Eric didn't need to look at the engine to know that it too was vandalized. "Sheesh. Now we're in for it." Eric peered into the van, careful to keep his hands off the jagged edges around the windows. The seat covers were slashed and white stuffing pushed out of the slits. Dad climbed the slope above the car and rolled some rocks off a pile.

"Hah! They missed our stuff though." A corner of a box showed between two of the stones. "We'll get this later." He looked at the van for a moment. Eric tossed a handful of pebbles into the creek where the foam swallowed them without a splash. He thought they might hitchhike to town, then he remembered there was no traffic. "Sheesh!" he said again.

Dad covered the box, then slid down the slope. "We walk," he said and moved resolutely up the path to the highway.

When they passed the hidden trail to the cave, Eric was thinking again of Amanda. She smiled often. Sometimes, when they played a section of music particularly well, she smiled at him, but they didn't ever talk. He didn't know what to say once he got past "Hello," and "How are you?" He thought, why did I think she'd hold hands with me? He blushed remembering how his plan hadn't worked out, and he was glad his father was ahead of him.

School this year was so weird anyway, he thought. Everybody talking about the disease. The newspapers called it "Mega-cold" or "The Austrian Cold," or "Beggar's Fever," because doctors first identified it among the homeless in Vienna. We were still cheering at football games when the T.V. started reporting the disease. It was a curiosity, something happening to people far away. First they'd act as if they had a cold, sniffing and coughing, then, after a week or so, the fever would start, and within twenty-four hours they'd be dead. The fever wouldn't break, even after they died, the newspapers said. For hours afterward the virus ate at the body, creating its own heat. The disease's progress was simple: two weeks contagious, one week of the cold, one day of fever, then death. He'd heard that airborne droplets from coughs transmitted the virus a mile downwind. So did sweat. Brian Knudson told him, in a horrified whisper, just touching a doorknob an infected person had handled a week before gave one the disease.

Adults acted funny too. The band director, even, told everyone in the woodwind section not to swap reeds. All the fuss, though, didn't touch Eric. Teachers talked about the disease. Students staged benefit concerts, and the school nurse gave talks in class about health issues. But Eric could only think about Amanda's hand, Amanda's beautiful, remote and lonely hand.

He shook his head ruefully. Four days in a row he'd tried for it as they left the band room. The first time, Theresa Ortiz got in the way. The next three times his nerve failed him, but the fifth time,

Friday, the last week in May, he lined himself perfectly. They reached the door, shoulder to shoulder. He smelled her perfume, he was so close, and underneath that, he imagined, something else, lilacs, like her bath soap perhaps. The thought made his head swim: her *bath* soap! He could in a moment be walking in the hall, hand in hand with Amanda Grieves, the prettiest girl in the flute section. Heck, the entire band. She wasn't like those women in the Metallica posters, the Prince posters, with black mesh stocking and metal studded leather bikinis. She was real. His forearm brushed hers. He wiped his hand on his leg, then timed his reach. There! He caught her hand in his. For a second, all was perfect. He had her hand. Then she stopped, jerked it away and said, "What do you think you're doing?" She looked at him, puzzled. "Were you trying to hold my hand?" she asked. He couldn't speak. Someone bumped her from behind, and she joined the crowd in the hall. Other band members pushed past him where he stood, blocking the doorway.

Later, Eric sat in the lunch room poking at his Salisbury Steak. At the table next to his, a couple sat facing each other, foreheads almost touching, holding hands. He wondered, how do they do it? How do people ever get to hold hands?

A few weeks after that, he got a girlfriend, but he couldn't shake the sight of Amanda's sculpted and impossible fingers, lightly curled, brushing her thigh as she walked.

*

The high tech, straight-as-a-mountain-road-could-be multi-lane I-70 replaced the old, curvy, two-lane US Highway 6 in the mid-1960s. Until 1991 when Colorado made small stakes gambling legal in Black Hawk and Central City, only slow-paced tourists and fishermen used the old road that followed the course of Cripple Creek, crossing occasionally. When the road builders could figure no other way, the road dove through short tunnels where children in station wagons urged parents to beep their horns. The scenic route ended where the old highway merged with the new via a long, steep entrance ramp.

Just before noon, Eric trudged up this ramp behind his dad, who had not rested since they began hiking three hours before. The creek gurgled over rocks to Eric's left. Other than their feet scuffing the asphalt, the lively chatter of the water was the only sound he had heard since they left the van. Neither Eric nor his Dad had spoken. The wet sounds reminded Eric that his throat ached from thirst. His shoulders throbbed where the pack weighed them down. His feet hurt; he could feel blisters forming where his perspiration-soaked socks rubbed on each step. He glanced at his dad. A broad swath of sweat stained the back of his shirt to his belt.

Eric broke their sustained silence with, "When are we going to get there?"

Dad stopped, put his hands on his hips, the right hand cupping the holstered gun, and sighed loudly. He didn't turn to face Eric, but looked up the ramp until Eric reached him.

"We better talk," Dad said.

Eric closed his eyes for a second. Dad's "talks" were always a bore, or bad, or both. He opened them and tried to look interested. "Okay."

"Your mom is sick. I've been trying to figure a way to tell you while we've been walking, and I don't know any way but this."

It hadn't occurred to Eric to wonder what Dad was thinking. Hours of silence from him weren't unusual. Eric assumed he wasn't thinking. The idea that Dad was churning something in his brain at the same time he was struck him peculiarly, like finding out that escargot was snail. Then the words themselves sunk in. Mom is sick.

Dad continued, "She's sick; maybe you and I are too, so we've got to get to Idaho Springs for medicine. They may have a doctor and a clinic. We can bring her into town if there's room. Perhaps it's not the . . . the . . ." He paused, searching for a word. ". . . disease, but it might be. We can't be too careful."

"We should be with her." Eric wanted to run down the ramp and back toward the cave. He could almost see her, alone, frightened, a big, heavy woman who needed someone to care for her.

"She'll be fine. It's just a cough now, an itchy throat. She has aspirin. She wanted you to go with me."

"But she would have expected us hours ago. She'll think we're dead."

Dad wiped his face with a bandanna he pulled from his back pocket. Then he tied it around his neck. "She's a tough bird, Eric. Besides, she saw us go by this morning."

"I didn't see her."

"You weren't paying attention. She waved from the lookout. Anyway, we may not be walking much longer."

"What do you mean?"

"Listen."

Eric turned his head side to side, like a hound dog catching a scent, then he heard a rumble over the cascade of water. It rose in volume, then fell, and Eric realized he'd heard the sound several times while they were standing on the ramp.

"It's trucks on I-70. We can catch a ride. We're only a couple of miles away, now, but I'm getting tired," said Dad. Eric started toward the highway. Dad caught his arm like a clamp. Eric tried to shake him off, an automatic response. He hated his dad to touch him. It made him feel like a baby.

Dad said, "We're not done talking." Eric relaxed in his grip. Dad let go. "If we get sick, son—I mean your mom and I—we've made some preparations, some things at the house you need to know about." Dad fished in his pocket. Eric heard the clink of coins, then Dad handed him a key. "This opens a drawer in the back of my desk in the office. It's not likely anyone would find the drawer, even if they broke into the house. In it are instructions for you." Eric looked at him uncomfortably. Dad continued, "You know, if we do get sick."

Eric put the key in his pocket. "You'll be okay." He looked away. He didn't know how to deal with this. He thought maybe he should hug his dad. Dad coughed into his hand.

"If things don't work, you'll have to make decisions on your own. We've got plenty of supplies in the cave to get you to winter, but I think you'll need to go back to Littleton before the snows hit. I'm thinking the worst will be past by then. The disease will have burnt itself out. Do you understand what I'm saying, about us getting sick, about what you should do?" Dad put his hand on Eric's arm again, but he didn't squeeze it this time.

"Sure, Dad. I got it." Dad's hand pressed a shade harder on Eric's arm, and Eric looked directly into Dad's eyes behind his glasses. They were dark brown with little flecks of brightness like gold in them. He couldn't remember ever looking into his dad's eyes like this before. "Sure, Dad." Dad pulled his hand away.

*

Most of the trucks were military, flat green diesels hiding their cargo behind green canvas that snapped in their own wind as they passed Eric and his dad. They walked west toward Idaho Springs, keeping their thumbs out. Dad had put the gun and holster in Eric's pack. The weight felt scary. He could feel its presence like a black heart.

An eighteen-wheeler blasted by, driving wind past his ears. Eric waved his fist at it. Mom needs us to hurry. She could be huddled under a blanket now, unable to reach water, wondering if her son deserted her.

After ten minutes, a silver and red U-Haul truck slowed as it passed and stopped a hundred yards up the road, its emergency lights flashing. They ran to it.

The passenger door opened before they reached the cab. Dad stepped onto the running board. "Thanks. We just need to get to Idaho Springs." Eric couldn't see the driver. Dad sat, then stuck down his hand to pull Eric up.

"You folks aren't sick, are ya?" The driver, a young man in army fatigues, lay across both of their laps and yanked the door shut. He checked the rear view mirrors and drove onto the highway. "We got lots of sick'uns in Denver that are trying to get out. You wouldn't be one of those, would ya?"

Dad said, "No, we . . ."

"Crazy in Denver, you know. People just up and driving and they don't have half a mind to Tuesday where they're goin'. Government's right to shut the roads. If it were up to people, ever'body would be contaminated afore they can get this thing licked." He moved through the gears smoothly. "I heard there was shooting at some of the blockades. Can't take a man's car away in America." He laughed. "My name's Beau. How do you do? Haven't seen many hitchhikers. Fact, you're the first." He spoke with a Southern accent, but rushed from word to word so fast that Eric wondered when he took a breath.

Eric's dad smiled. "I'm Sam and this is my son Eric." Eric couldn't believe he could be so friendly, so unhurried. The road unwound before him like a slow-motion film. He half thought he could get out and run faster than the truck was moving. The speedometer needle inched past forty miles an hour. The soldier shifted again.

"Like I said, name's Beau. Got to make this haul to Salt Lake City, but they didn't say I got to do it alone. You only going to the Springs? Well, it's a short trip to heaven, too, they say."

Dad said, "What's this about blockades? We haven't heard the news for a week."

"Cut off, are ya? Marshall law. Civilians can't drive, and they can't leave the city. Utah shut its borders, and so I heard have the rest of the states, but that kind of news is hard to come by. I ain't telling you no secrets neither. Army isn't saying anything to us. We just drive the trucks. Got to keep supplies moving. Commandeered anything that can roll and the Army and Reserves are doing the delivering. Some second assistant to the Surgeon General, guy named Washburn, handles all the medical releases now. Says they got a cure in the works and to 'Be brave in the face of adversity.' I like that kind of talk."

"So, is there a lot of sickness?"

"I ain't sayin' there is and I ain't sayin' there isn't. I got half a mind to believe I got medical supplies in the back of this rig, though. It's a sinful world. That's all I got to say. My minister says you reap what you sow. You watch the T.V. guys on the religious channel. They'll set you straight. A hard wind's a gonna blow. Bible says that."

"Do you think we can buy medicine in Idaho Springs?" They passed a sign warning they were one mile from the Idaho Springs exit.

"You got cash money, sure. Don't expect they'll be takin' checks, and your plastic won't be worth anythin' either if they're behavin' like they are in Denver. Seller's market. Depends what you want to buy, too." He downshifted as they approached the exit. "Can't take you into town. Got a schedule to make." The heavy truck slid to a stop. Dust billowed past the window and, when Eric opened the door, into the cab. He jumped onto the gravel shoulder. Dad climbed down more carefully. The young soldier grinned at them, a little sadly Eric thought. "I got a son just two years old in Texas. Haven't talked to my wife for three days. Can't get through. Hope they're all right. A man ought to be with his children. Good luck, guys." He slammed the door.

Eric had never been to Idaho Springs, and the town looked tacky to him, from the mining scarred mountains above, to the weathered, cracked-mortar Victorian houses with high-pitched roofs, dirty garages behind them, their doors hanging crookedly. Sand piled against the curbs, remnants from an icy winter. Dad told him there wasn't a mall. No mall! They passed an ugly ski and tee-shirt shop where a "Closed for the Season" sign hung in the window. A woman walking toward them on the sidewalk crossed the street to avoid a meeting.

Dad bought Cokes from a machine in front of a closed Conoco. Eric rubbed the cold can against his forehead before opening it. They stood in the shade of the gas pump island and finished the pops. Eric hopped from foot to foot, ready to go minutes before Dad, who leisurely, it seemed, shook the last drops into his mouth.

The Safeway in the middle of town was open—a checkout clerk wearing a surgical mask eyed them as they came through the doors—but most of the merchandise looked picked over. A few lone cans dotted the shelves in the soup section. Much of the toilet paper was gone. The produce bins were empty. Dad headed for the pharmacy in back. Eric picked up a red plastic shopping basket with wire handles, wandered through the cereal section and looked longingly at the Cocoa Puffs. He'd already noticed the empty refrigerators. No milk. A man, shivering under the bulk of three or four sweaters, rolled a cart filled to the top with dried pasta: spaghetti, macaroni, fettuccini, lasagne and green spinach noodles. "Buy stuff that stores well," he said. Eric nodded at him.

He found batteries by the film display and took all the triple-A's, eight packs of four, enough to replenish his cassette player sixteen times. Then, thinking about how he wanted the player just for cassettes, he picked up a transistor radio shaped like a Teenage Mutant Ninja Turtle in the toy section, one of the few items the store had in abundance. The turtle in his hand left a gap in the ranks of identical turtles like a missing tooth. He went back to the film display for the right size batteries.

Eric's stomach hurt. What was keeping Dad? No one stood at the Pharmacy desk and the light in the Pharmacist's station was off. The man with the sweaters, he thought, has the disease. He's in a supermarket buying noodles and he's maybe dying. Mom's maybe dying. Where's Dad?

He remembered a Metallica lyric. Nobody ever listened to Metallica lyrics except some of his head-banger friends, and they didn't care what the band said. They just liked the image and the sound. They liked skulls on tee-shirts. The lyric was, "I'm inside. I'm you. Sad but true."

A door beside the pharmacy clicked open and Dad stepped out. He shut it quietly, then stuck a white sack, the kind that held medicine, in Eric's backpack "Come on."

"What'd you get?"

"Shhh." He took two bottle of rubbing alcohol from a shelf and put them in Eric's basket with the batteries. "I found out there isn't a clinic, and the doctor commutes from Denver."

At the checkout counter, the surgical-masked clerk leaned back from them. Eric could almost see him holding his breath, and Eric wondered what the man would do if he or Dad sneezed or coughed. Eric emptied the basket. To the alcohol, batteries and the Ninja Turtle radio, Dad added a handful of M&M packages.

The clerk didn't reach for the products. His eyes glittered blackly above the mask. He said, "You people from out of town?" Dad nodded. "That'll be two-hundred dollars."

Dad said, "That's ridiculous. If you think..."

A sawed off baseball bat, a foot and a half long, appeared in the clerk's hand. He tapped it on the counter. "It's our going out of business price."

Dad stiffened, his knuckles going white as they gripped the edge of the check stand. Then he said, "Fine," and opened Eric's backpack. The gun in its holster still pressed Eric's back. He wanted to yell, "Don't, Dad! Don't do it!" Dad pulled his wallet out of the pack instead, took two bills from it and laid them by the cash register.

Outside the store, Eric said, "Hundred dollar bills?"

Dad shrugged his shoulders. "I thought things might be pricey."

*

Dad walked briskly, almost trotted, farther into town, looking at store signs as he passed them. He stopped at a bike shop and rattled the door, which was locked. He cupped his hands around his eyes and peered through the window into the darkened building, then shook the door again. A second story window slapped open. Eric stepped into the street and looked up. An elderly woman, gray hair wrapped in a yellow scarf, looked back.

"We're closed. Can't you see, dear?" Her voice squeaked pleasantly. "The radio just said we're in quarantine now. You boys should be home."

To Eric's relief, she agreed to open for them and sold them a pair of mountain bikes and helmets. Dad paid cash. She gave them a circular about a recreational bike rally from Idaho Springs to Georgetown in July. "This little fuss should be over by then, don't you think?" Dad smiled and agreed. "Glad I could be of help," she said. "Biking's very healthful, you know. Don't know why we ever bothered with cars."

A few minutes later, after she adjusted the seats and handles for them, they pedaled away. Eric turned and she waved. He waved back.

The trip to the cave went quickly once they left I-70 and its roaring trucks that kept them on the shoulder. The route was mostly downhill. Eric pedaled as fast as he could, then glided for minutes, the new knobby tires buzzing on the asphalt, before pedaling again. Dad kept close. Their shadows raced ahead as the sun dropped behind them.

When Eric reached the path to the cave, he hopped off the bike. Mother was not at the lookout, as far as he could tell. Dad skidded to a stop beside him. "Wait," he said. "I need to show you something first. Turn around."

Eric fidgeted as Dad dug in the pack. He heard the crackle of paper. "Here," Dad said. Eric took the pharmacy bag from him, opened the top and shook out a bottle of pills. There was no label on the bottle.

Cyanide, Eric thought. Dad's flipped like that Jim Jones fellow in Jonestown. He shook the bottle. "What are they?"

"Pain killers. Tylenol four. Tylenol with codeine in them. I want you to know about them in case you have to be on your own." Dad took the bottle from him. "I made a deal with the pharmacist. I paid fifteen bucks a pill, and he didn't ask to see my prescription. People were lined up out the back."

Mom was sleeping behind the lookout rock. She'd made a bed with their blankets and set up a beach umbrella they'd taken to Florida the summer before to shade herself. Eric yelled when he saw her. She jerked awake and grabbed for the shotgun before she realized who he was. He hugged her for a long time, letting go only when he heard Dad struggling on the steep path with the two bikes.

*

Mom and Dad sat up late, talking by the light of the Coleman lantern. Their voices rose and fell in a gentle mumble. Twenty feet away, Eric lay on his sleeping bag, looking at the shadows deep in the cracks of the cave's ceiling high above. He'd washed in the river as the sun set, the water so cold that the shampoo wouldn't lather, and when he finished, his jaws ached from shivering. Now he was warm and clean. The cassette player rested on his chest. He'd put the batteries in an hour ago, but he wanted to delay listening until his parents went to bed. Their talk, probably stupid stuff about mortgages or car payments he figured, sounded comforting.

I wonder where Amanda Grieves is right now, he thought. I wonder if she ever thinks about that day in the doorway. I wonder what she thought as she walked down the hall with her friends.

Mom coughed once, and the conversation stopped. She coughed quietly again. Eric rolled to his side and propped himself on his elbow. The Coleman lantern glowed brightly on a rock shelf behind his parents who faced each other. They were very close, their foreheads almost touching, not saying anything. Eric watched them for a long time before he realized, there in the darkness of the cave, surrounded by boxes of canned goods, shotguns close by, miles from home, Dad held Mom's hands.

Chapter Five
PHIL'S PLACE

Eric woke slowly and saw a slim shaft of dust-filled light slanting across the stone room. He thought for a moment he was back in the cave high above the river and that the soft bubble of breathing by his cheek was his father. "Dad?" he whispered in the dark room. How could light come into the cave? A crack in a wall we've never seen before? A place from where bats come and go, the seam invisible every day of the year except this one when the long hole in the wall lined up exactly with the sun? He puzzled over this question until slowly he remembered he was in a hut a few hundred yards from the intersection of Bowles Avenue and C-470. He closed his eyes and savored the feeling of being fifteen, of sleeping beside his father and mother. But the image slipped away until he barely felt it, until all that remained was the breathing, the gurgle that reminded him of Dad, but wasn't. It was Dodge, head covered in his sleeping bag. Today they'd start north.

Eric rolled and the stiffness in his back woke him further. Rabbit slept beside Dodge, the scar side of his face down. In the shadows of the room, Rabbit looked angelic, like a baby and unlike the silent, brooding boy he was.

Outside the hut Eric grunted through his morning exercises, his breath fogging the cold morning air. Seven miles east, the Platte River glimmered like a golden ribbon in the rising sun. From this vantage point he saw all south-west Littleton. Most of the buildings along Bowles Avenue were burned down, and even huge structures like South-West Plaza Mall sprawled, a pile of broken bricks and rusted girders on its own weed-covered parking lot, but many buildings miles away seemed untouched by the years. Glass still glinted in their windows. They stood solid and geometric, and Eric could envision them as they had been. People would be going to work about now; cars would stream purposefully along the road. Eric guessed by the sun it was past six o'clock. Helicopters would be buzzing above the main roads, reporting on the traffic. People would be buying donuts to take to the office. Eric had a sudden, solid memory of Winchell's donuts. Cinnamon Crumb. He used to stop on the way to school for two Cinnamon Crumb donuts, still warm. Even late in the morning after sitting through three or four classes, he might find a grain of brown sugar clinging to his shirt, and his fingers smelled of Cinnamon.

*

"What's that?" Dodge asked. He pointed down the long stretch of four-lane highway. Ahead of them the top of a sign peeked over a hill. As they walked closer, more and more of it showed until Eric recognized the familiar logo.

"It's a gas station. A Phillip's 66."

"What was their slogan, Grandpa?" The slogan game was one they played often. Dodge skipped ahead. Eric guessed that Dodge didn't feel the weight of his backpack the way he did.

"You can trust your car to the man who wears the star." Eric tightened his waist belt to take some stress off his shoulders.

Dodge laughed. "No way. That's Texaco. Was it the 'Hottest brand going'?"

Eric said, "Conoco." He thought as they walked closer. "I don't know. Maybe they didn't have a slogan."

"We can find out in the books at Boulder, can't we?" asked Dodge.

They climbed into a gully that had washed away fifty feet of the road. Eric said, "I suppose, but there's much more important information in books."

Dodge nodded agreeably as he scrambled up the loose bank and back onto the blacktop. "Books will tell us everything."

Eric watched where he put his feet, making sure there were no wobbly stones, planting his step firmly before putting his weight on it. More old folks die of broken bones, he thought, than anything else. They're doing fine right up to the time they break a hip; then they're doomed. "Well, maybe not everything. Books don't know everything."

Dodge grabbed his arm and pulled him the last step. His strength surprised Eric. Good grip for a ten-year-old. Dodge said, "You told us books got stuff about the Gone Times, like cars and computers. What else we need?"

Rabbit had found another spot to get out of the gulch and squatted on the road waiting for them. He had stripped his shirt and tied it around his waist. Sweat glistened on his chest. Eric thought, they're like horses. He realized that the pace he set must seem terribly slow to them. They were only twenty-two or twenty-three miles from Boulder now. If the boys were on their own, they'd make it by sunset. He figured he might make it by tomorrow evening, but that would be pushing it. A ten-mile day was a lot of walking.

He took a long drink from his canteen. "I've been reading books for sixty-five years, and I've read amazing passages. Poetry, mostly, and fiction. Beautiful stories about wonderful people living adventures. And there were books on science, and picture books."

Dodge grinned, "Tell us about how you see pictures in your head."

"Not really pictures. I mean, reading is like being there sometimes. I'll be reading along, and I'll forget that I'm holding a book. Suddenly I'll be Joan of Arc, or Moses rolling back the Red Sea." He hadn't had much luck teaching Dodge to read. Unlike most children his age, Dodge could work his way through a page of a book, but it was painful and slow as he sounded out each word. Troy had been partly successful at limiting Eric's influence on the boy. Eric could only teach Dodge and Rabbit two or three times a week. He suspected that Rabbit had picked up on the lessons better, but he seldom read out loud.

Dodge said, "I never see pictures."

"It takes practice. You've got to keep doing it. Then one day you'll be reading along, and the words will vanish off the page and you'll be in the story."

"Like that television stuff, right? And all the magic from the Gone Times are in the books, right? Like 'lectricity?"

Rabbit cleared his throat. "You said books can't tell us everything. What's wrong with books?"

He wondered where to start. He'd spent days and days reading books after his parents had died. There was no place to go, and in the books he could get lost. Later, he'd read for information, for medicine, for mid-wifing. He'd delivered Troy on his own. He remembered the sun streaming through the rips in the rotted curtains in the living room where Troy was born, how the sun heated his back as he supported Troy's tiny, slippery head, but the books hadn't told him enough and Leda died an hour later. She was small hipped and thirty-nine years old, and they'd assumed that one or both of them were sterile. The pregnancy surprised them. They'd been together for fourteen years. He marked her grave with a stone he took from a mortuary storehouse and an epitaph that had taken him a week to carve:

LEDA

"We don't need last names no more."

Eric said, "Reading about life isn't the same as living life."

*

The Phillip's 66 sign, maybe a quarter mile away he guessed, looked odd. He studied it. At first he thought part of the sign was broken out, but as they got closer, he saw that a piece of plywood covered some letters, so now it read *Phil's*. No signs of the gas station remained other than the low concrete benches where the pumps would have been.

Dodge said, "Do you hear that?"

Eric stopped and turned his head from one side to the other. "What?"

"That." Dodge pointed up the slope to their left. A huge brick building, its windows boarded, sat at the end of a footpath that started at the *Phil's* sign. Eric heard it now, a soft, quick thumping. He listened intently.

"An engine," he said. "I'll be darned! A diesel engine." He started up the path. Dodge dashed ahead.

Rabbit ran to Eric and grabbed his arm, then looked at the building and shook his head. The boy said, "Check it out first." He frowned at the building at the end of the path. "What is this place?"

The three-story brick building stood at one end of a long stretch of grandstand. Weeds covered the remains of a chain link fence that started at the building and reached for a half mile north. Eric said, "Bandimere Raceway, I think. There use to be drag races here."

Rabbit raised his eyebrows.

Eric explained, "Two specially built cars—very fast—raced from one end of the track to the other. Lots of people came to watch. Probably five-thousand or so depending on who was racing."

"It smells."

Eric sniffed deeply, "Diesel exhaust. Probably a generator. You boys are in for a real treat."

A broad, cracked but neatly swept sidewalk bordered the building and led Eric and Rabbit to a pair of glass double doors. A hand painted sign hung above the doors proclaimed, *Phil's Place*. Eric looked around for Dodge. A long series of stairs tumbled down the hill to what must have been the pit area for the racers. A huge, heavily rusted though mostly intact, girder and sheet metal canopy protected the stands on the west side of the track that stretched for three-quarters of a mile and ended at the base of another hill. Eric thought the knife edged abruptness of the road's end was odd-looking and somehow disturbing, like a door that opened into a wall or a book with blank pages.

He imagined Friday nights, the parking lot full, high-octane dragsters roaring fire from their exhausts, the spectators murmuring expectantly, and he smelled beer slopped out of plastic cups, rubber burnt from smooth-treaded funny cars, and the close, humid warmth of the crowd pressed shoulder to shoulder. "We loved our cars," he said.

"'Scuse me?" Rabbit stood by the doors.

"Sorry. Just reminiscing. Where's Dodge off to do you think?"

Rabbit shrugged, opened the door, then disappeared inside. Eric followed.

The artificial lighting caught Eric's eye first. Ceiling-mounted panels of translucent plastic glowed brightly. He hadn't seen electric light for two decades. It took a few seconds for him to look away at the rest of the room. He stepped to a green metal railing and saw on the floor below a dozen highly polished, factory-fresh show cars. Dodge was peering into the side window of a lemon-yellow Ferrari. Rabbit jumped down the stairs and joined him.

"'Lectricity!" yelled Dodge.

The showroom floor glistened under the lights. The darkly tinted windows opposite Eric reflected the scene. Somebody must be watching us, he thought. We're in a museum. He dropped his backpack to the floor. "Don't touch anything, boys."

A door in the middle of the tinted window wall swung open. "Why not?" a voice boomed. A tall man in stained mechanic's overalls shut the door behind him. "Touch 'em. Bang on 'em. Hell, you can even make love to 'em if you can get 'em on their backs." His bald head gleamed as he walked toward the boys. He ran his hand over the polished metal of each car he passed. Eric guessed he was in his mid-thirties. "Heaven knows you aren't going to drive 'em."

"Why not?" Dodge asked. Rabbit backed away, putting the Ferrari between him and the stranger.

The man patted Dodge on the back. "The gods are dead, son. This is a hollow church. Gas is no good, and their batteries are shot. I've got a couple of diesel cars in the garage that'll run if I start 'em from the generator, but I don't use 'em much. Roads are awful, you know." He smiled at Eric, a big smile that bared his upper gums and folded his eyes into a confusion of wrinkles.

Eric said, "You must be Phil."

"Mom named me after a service station. Hard to believe. Why don't you come down, old-timer? There's enough stew in the pot for the three of you, and I can use the company." He tousled Dodge's hair.

"Sure," said Eric. "Nice of you to offer." But as he was saying it, Rabbit caught his eyes and shook his head, almost imperceptibly, no. Eric hesitated, then continued down the stairs. First chance he got, he'd take Rabbit aside and find out what bothered him.

Electrical appliances packed the room behind the car museum. Pinball machines lined one wall. Above them, shelves held blenders, food processors, mixers, espresso machines, electric carving knives and hot air popcorn poppers. An expanse of televisions, their screens dust free and blank, covered another wall, a VCR tucked beneath each. Video tapes filled cabinets from floor to ceiling. Dodge stopped, obviously awed. The screens tossed back fish-eyed reflections of him.

Phil said, "You ever see one of these working, boy?"

Dodge's face lit up. "Oh, no." He spun around. "Grandpa, can we? You can see pictures?" He clapped his hands to his mouth. "Gosh."

Phil punched a button on the VCR in the middle. The numbers, 12:00, blinked on and off in the clock display. The machine buzzed and ejected a tape. "Don't think you want to watch this one," he said. The way he slid it behind the other tapes in the cabinet made Eric wonder what was on it. "How about this?" he said as he selected a title. "*Star Wars*. Third copy I've used. Wore the others right out. Of course I've got a whole case of 'em. Long as I keep the generators running and the juice hooked up the force will be with me." He laughed at his joke.

The screen flickered. Then Phil fast forwarded through the FBI warning. "Long ago . . ." read Rabbit, "in a galaxy far, far away . . . ."

"We'll bring you boys some stew," said Phil. He motioned to Eric, and they left the room. "Figure that'll keep 'em for an hour or two. Got some things I want to ask you."

They walked through a long hallway, doors on both sides. "My mom's cathedral," said Phil. He opened the first door and turned on a light. "Have to watch how many lights I have on. Generator poops out with too much of a load." Eric glimpsed cases of light bulbs piled to the ceiling. Mirrors packed the next room. Long ones, the kind people used to put on the backs of bathroom doors or at the ends of hallways leaned against the wall. Hand mirrors, their handles pointing in all directions, filled boxes on shelves. "You know how hard it is to manufacture a mirror?" asked Phil. "Mom says you have to store the goods people can't make."

"What do you mean when you say this is your mom's cathedral?"

Phil closed the mirror room door. He wiped the handle clean with a rag he pulled from a back pocket. "Cathedral, man, a church. She says, 'Keep the flame of technology burning.'" He cleared his throat, then spit into the rag.

Boxes of electric tools filled the next room: drills, saws, screwdrivers, air-hammers, power painters, sanders and others Eric didn't recognize. "'America was great,' she used to say. 'We ruled the Earth.'" They walked past two doors that Phil didn't open. "'Gods,' she said. 'We were gods.' We used to go into Denver. U.S. 6 out of Golden is still passable. She knew where stuff was stored, or she had a nose for it. We collected goods. Mom called it 'harvesting the fields.' When I could drive a truck, I helped. Of course, even then we had to push start everything."

"Batteries," said Eric. "We can't make a battery."

"Don't you know it. It's a problem of shelf life. Things just don't last. If Mom had any sense, she'd have frozen a hundred car batteries while they were still good. We had a huge fight about it. She whacked me, she always whacks me, and said, 'Hindsight is twenty-

twenty. I'd like to see you do better.' Well, I know now. You keep
something perishable like that cold, then take it out later and it'll be
good as new. That's where most of my electricity goes now, keeping the freezers and refrigerators going."

The hallway's end door opened into a cavernous garage. The
building was much larger than Eric had suspected. He guessed there
might be over a hundred vehicles parked there: cars (all on blocks),
trucks, tractors, boats, motorcycles and earth moving machines.
Back in the shadows, far from the string of lights that ran through
the middle of the garage, Eric saw the unmistakable outline of a
tank, its gun pointing phallically up. The air smelled vaguely of oil
and tires.

"For years," said Phil, "Mom worked on converting gas engines to propane or natural gas, but she couldn't get them to run
reliably, and other people hoarded the fuel too."

Phil led him down a long flight of stairs. The air cooled percep-
tibly as they went deeper underground. Every twenty feet, a wire-
encased light provided illumination.

"Your mother sounds like an extraordinary woman."

Phil laughed derisively. "She's a fool." He looked over his shoulder, suddenly fearful. "I didn't mean that. I mean, it's a joke. I love
her, really." Phil's eyes rolled, and he clenched his jaw so tight Eric
heard his teeth grind. Eric let Phil get farther ahead of him, and he
decided the narrow stairwell felt too small and confining.

The stairs ended at a heavy metal door, like a bank door. Phil
pulled on the wheel in its center. "Welcome to the inner sanctum.
The highest of the holies. I control the whole building from this
room: light, heat, water and security. It's Mom's, really, but she lets
me use it."

An old couch dominated the center of the room. Behind it, a
long chest freezer buzzed loudly. A pile of clothes filled a hamper by the door, and a couple of dirty plates and empty glasses
crowded a small TV table. Eric decided Phil spent a lot of time
here. Like the television room where they had left Rabbit and
Dodge, screens lined one wall. These screens were lit. One
showed the path that connected the highway to Phil's Place.
Another showed the gully that cut across the highway. On two
other screens were outdoor views Eric didn't recognize. The
rest seemed to be rooms or hallways in the building. On one,
Rabbit and Dodge sat on the floor watching *Star Wars*. Phil

touched a knob on a control panel and the image of Dodge swelled until his head in profile nearly filled the screen. Phil said, "Beautiful boy. A real heartbreaker."

Eric warily said, "Thanks. He's my grandson."

Some video cameras were mounted on motorized swivels; the view on their screens scrolled from side to side. "I've got the entire building covered. Nothing goes on inside or out that I don't know about." He flicked a switch and all the screens changed to new views, most of them exteriors now. "I saw you folks coming an hour before you got here."

Phil took a video tape out of a drawer and held it self-consciously. He said, "You mind me asking where you come from?"

Eric sat on an overstuffed couch with badly sprung springs. An unpleasant sweat odor puffed from the cushions. Phil must sleep here, he thought. "Not at all. Littleton."

"Ah, I didn't think of Littleton. You live by yourselves or in a community?"

Eric thought Phil looked uncomfortable, like the questions meant more to him than they ought to, as if he was asking something personal or distasteful, but he didn't seem as intense, as manic, as he did on the stairs. "About a thousand live there now. We farm the land west of the river."

Phil's eyes glanced around the room. Eric felt that he was consciously avoiding looking at him. Eric said, "Is there something special about Littleton?"

"No, no. It's just . . . well . . . I didn't think about trying south."

"What do you mean?"

"Mom always says go north or east. I've been trading in Commerce City and Northglenn my whole life. I'd drive a jeep into town and swap tools for food and stuff. I didn't know about a community to the south." Phil wrapped his hands tightly around the video tape.

Eric could see Phil was disturbed. "You don't trade there anymore? What's the problem?"

Phil stared into the video screens. His eyes glistened damply. "You and your boys are the first people I've seen in three years. Must have been four or five-hundred folks between the two towns. Last time I went, they were all gone." He looked intently at Eric. "I haven't seen a soul on that road for three years before I saw you today. I said to Mom, 'Company's coming,' and I turned on the lights." He paused to clear his throat. For a second, Eric thought

Phil might be on the verge of tears. "I've been afraid to go anywhere. I haven't been fifty feet from home since the summer before last. People don't just disappear, and, of course, there's this." He held out the video tape.

Phil pushed it into a VCR. "I run a continuous record on the outside cameras. Mom told me it's better to be safe than sorry." All the screens flickered, then showed the same scene, a patch of aspen and scrubby pine in the background, a stretch of dirt reaching to them. "This is the field behind the place here. It's the back approach to the generator. Filmed this two days ago, but I've seen it before."

A breeze swayed the aspen branches. White letters at the bottom right corner of the screen read, "6-04-56 4:14 p.m."

"Watch close," said Phil. He moved his face a foot from one of the TVs, giving his skin a spooky pallor. "There . . ." He pointed. "See it?"

Back in the shadows, a white form drifted from left to right behind the aspen. Eric guessed it might be five or six feet tall, but darkness and the fuzzy picture prevented him from discovering anything more. The white form itself wasn't particularly disturbing, but the situation felt so creepy: the tall, bald man frozen in front of the television like a gargoyle; the cool, close room deep underground. Eric said, "Is it a man?"

Phil stroked the screen as if trying to feel the image. He said quietly, to himself, "No tracks. I ran out when I saw it. Mom said to stay inside, but I ran after it. Three years, you know, is a long time. I ran out but it was gone."

A figure dashed into the middle of the picture. The time read, "4:16 p.m." It was Phil. He wasn't wearing a shirt. The camera showed a roll of fat and a soft mid-section. He glanced quickly left and right, as if hunting for a scent, then ran into the trees. The white form had moved off screen.

Phil turned off the VCR. Now all the screens showed the closeup of Dodge watching the movie. Phil stared at him. "A man needs companionship. We weren't meant to be alone. But I don't think what I've recorded is human anymore."

"What do you think it is?"

"I saw 'em first the summer Northglenn and Commerce City were deserted. I thought they left because of me—you know—like I did something to upset them. There *was* some trouble." Looking down, he sat on the edge of the freezer. "They thought I'd kidnapped a kid, but I didn't. The boy wanted to be here." Phil stretched and leaned back until his head rested on the wall. Eric had to turn to see him. Phil said, "I lost him too. He left the same summer."

Confused, Eric said, "I don't get it. What's the shape in the video? Why does it frighten you?"

Phil slid off the freezer, put his hands on the back of the couch and whispered, "Millions of people died. Mom told me about it. I remember we went into a storehouse once—she thought it might have car parts in it. I didn't want to go. Old building, windows boarded, filled with crates. But she whacked me and told me to go in, so I did. Took a crowbar to this crate, must have been eight feet tall, and I popped the side off." Phil breathed deeply, shakily. "Filled to the top with clothes and bones. For a second they stayed packed in the crate; then they slid out around me. Bones up to my knees. I tried to run, but . . ." He wiped his lips. ". . .something grabbed my ankle. Something in that pile of corpses wasn't dead."

Eric thought about all the bones he'd seen in the last fifty-five years, bones in cars, in broken down and rotted beds, in dumpsters, under overpasses. In the end, no one was around to pick them up. "People died. Their bones don't mean anything. You must have panicked."

"That's what Mom said. She laughed, called me a scaredy-cat, but, I tell you, something is out there now. It's ghosts. They've been searching and searching and now they've found me. This place, my mother's temple, is all stolen stuff, stolen from those people."

"Why don't you leave?"

Phil shook his head and laughed. He took a couple of deep breaths, composing himself. "It's Mom. I can't leave Mom." He patted the freezer.

"She's in the freezer? She's dead?" Eric stood and backed away.

"Oh, you can't tell. I roll her every couple of weeks so she won't freezer burn, but you can see why I have to stay. Sometimes I think that it's her they're after, not me; then I remember that pile of bones. I can feel that grip on my ankle. They know about me."

*

Phil toured Eric through the rest of the building. The generator, he explained, was originally a part of Bandimere Raceway. So far from Denver, Bandimere had decided to rely on its own electrical generating capabilities rather than tie into the city's system. His mom, after just about everyone died, had the foresight to scavenge Denver's five main hospitals, each with its own generator. He used the parts to keep Bandimere's generator operational. She also found enough diesel to fuel the system. "I figure I can keep the lights on until I die," Phil said when he slapped the side of a tanker truck parked in the garage.

Littleton didn't have a working diesel generator. Eric remembered the tedious, fractious town meetings years ago when the last one provided enough power to light a handful of houses. The town decided then to give up on generating power. He'd argued for expanded scavenging. "There are other ways to keep the electricity," he'd said, but he was outvoted. Troy, in his first long speech to the council countered, "What do we need electricity for anyway? What would serve us best is using the daylight more productively. Farm, hunt and fish during the day. Rest at night. These are values we should embrace." Eric could see the natural politician his son was becoming, but he couldn't help arguing. "We are entering a new Dark Ages, and you are leading the way!" That meeting marked the beginning of Eric and Troy's political split. Eric called Troy's followers the "New Barbarians," and Troy called Eric's camp the "Gone Timers." Most of the "Gone Timers" lived before the plague and remembered what technology could do, but the passage of time dwindled their numbers. The New Barbarians, led by Troy, opposed almost all Eric's suggestions. Eric often believed Troy took positions solely to spite him and not because he believed them.

Every door Phil opened revealed some remnant of technology. In the radio room, Phil turned on the short wave receiver and roamed through the bands. "Mom said she last heard someone on this the year I was born. I've never heard anything other than static or this." Through the crackles and hiss of static came a steady beeping.

Eric listened intently. "I'd bet that's a weather satellite." Phil agreed then turned the system off.

After an hour of other rooms, they came to the kitchen. On the stove simmered a large pot. "Beef stew," said Phil. Eric peeked into the pot suspiciously.

"How old's that meat?" he asked.

"I told you, I traded. This is three years old. Vacuum packed for freshness. I threw out the meat Mom stored ages ago. It was like shoe leather." He ladled big spoonfuls into bowls. "We'd better get a meal up to the boys. Movie will be about over by now."

Dodge dug into the stew eagerly, but had a hard time eating and talking at the same time. "The Gone Times were wonderful!" he said through a mouthful. "Floating cars, light sabres, star cruisers. Do you think Luke lived through the plague? I'll bet he did. He hopped in the Millennium Falcon and got away when people started getting sick. I'll bet he's coming back for us."

Rabbit sniffed his stew before tasting it. "None of it's real, Dodge."

Dodge glanced angrily at him. "I know that. I'm not a baby. It's make believe."

Eric wondered how much Dodge meant when he said, "It's make believe." Did he include airplanes? Doctors? Everything he'd been telling him about the Gone Times? If it weren't for Phil's interest in Dodge, Eric would encourage him to stay, to see what technology could do.

Phil sat next to Dodge on the floor. "You're right, though. Make believe is wonderful. I've probably got the best collection of tapes in Colorado. Hell, best in the world, and I've got the electricity and equipment to show them." He put his hand on Dodge's shoulder. Eric stiffened. "Would you like to see more?"

Dodge said, "Sure!" Then he looked at Eric. "Maybe when we finish our trip, I can come back?"

"Maybe," said Eric. He breathed easier.

"Well, at least you boys can get a decent shower and spend the night. When was the last time you had a hot shower?"

"We have running water," said Rabbit. Eric guessed what had upset him earlier. He must have sensed that Phil wasn't "safe."

"Sounds great to me," said Dodge. "Maybe we can see another video?"

After they watched *Indiana Jones and the Temple of Doom,* Phil took them to a locker room with gang showers. The drag racers, he explained, used the lockers to change before their contests. He found towels for them, then said, "Have to shine up the cars. Mom insists."

He closed the door behind him. Rabbit said, "Let's leave." Eric turned on a spigot. In a few seconds, clouds of warm steam billowed off the tile floor. He wondered where Phil stored the water and how he heated it. Two days of grime decided the debate for him.

"I think we'll be okay. I don't think he's dangerous."

Dodge looked from Rabbit to Eric, puzzled. "What do you mean? I like him."

Rabbit started to strip. "Wait a minute," said Eric. He searched the locker room, carefully covering the four video cameras he found.

When he was sure he'd got them all, he said, "I don't think he's dangerous, but I don't want you alone with him either."

Dodge said, "I don't get it."

Rabbit smirked. "He wants to bugger you, dolt."

*

Something woke Eric. He hadn't been sleeping easily anyway. The strange bed, the excitement of the electric lights and the other Gone Time triumphs that Phil had shown him, conspired to ruin his night's rest. Finally, though, he'd drifted into a doze. Now, a night light (a green glow-worm from a baby's nursery) provided the only light. Dodge slept on a bed near a boarded window; Rabbit slept on the floor. He'd smelled the mattress and insisted.

He heard a noise again, a slight rattle, the door. It creaked as if someone were pushing against it. He propped himself on his elbow and said, "Go away, Phil. We're sleeping." Quick footsteps padded away down the hall. Eric got out of bed and checked the chair he'd jammed under the doorknob. It still held firmly. Eric smiled and went back to bed.

*

After a breakfast of pancakes and syrup, Phil walked them to the front doors. He seemed worried. "Get into the city," he said privately to Eric. "Maybe they aren't ghosts, but I don't believe they're human, and those people in Northglenn and Commerce City couldn't have just gone without a good reason. I figure they got scared or carried off." He put his hand on the small of Eric's back, conspiratorially. "You ought to leave the youngster with me, for safe keeping. When you go home, you can pick him up. If it's dangerous, you wouldn't want him with you anyway."

Eric stepped away from him and didn't say anything, as if he were considering the idea. Then he said, "What would your mom think?"

Phil's face clouded. "You're right," he said. "She wouldn't like it at all." He wiped his face with his rag. "What's a son to do?"

Dodge and Rabbit waited for him at the end of the path.

"Let's not come back this way," said Rabbit.

Dodge nodded in agreement. After he walked for a while, head down, kicking pebbles in front of him, he said, "But he did have nice toys."

Eric thought about the cars in the showroom, mirror bright. Phil wandering among them, dusting each grudgingly for his dead but omnipresent mother. He thought about him sitting alone on his couch watching sixteen televisions at once. He thought about all the rooms filled from floor to ceiling with electronic gadgetry. He thought about Phil's dwindling supply of non-renewable, non-repairable resources and what else Phil had told him when he showed him the tanker truck filled with diesel. "There's enough to last me until I'm gone, and what do I care after that?"

"Yes, they were nice toys," said Eric.

He guessed they would be in Golden before noon, and he realized they would be within a couple of miles of the cave where his mother was buried. "We're going to take a little detour today," he said. "Want to show you something."

A breeze from the hills to the west cooled them. The clear sky was blue, high and vibrant. Eric felt good. He felt as if he could hike forever.

Chapter Six
KING KONG

Eric heard his father talking, and that was all he heard. His soft voice filled the cave. "I read a book once that discussed the filming of the 1933 *King Kong*, a wonderful movie. Great special effects. When that sad ape climbed the Empire State Building, and all those biplanes buzzed around like mosquitoes, I cheered. Smash those planes, I said. Crush them out of the sky."

It had been a week since their trip to Idaho Springs. Dad held Mom's hand. Eric supposed he'd held it all night as her coughing worsened and the fever built. With a wet washcloth he'd wiped her forehead, but he never let go. When Eric awoke, Dad was holding on. Mom's face glowed with fever. She'd lapsed into a coma. An hour later, she died. Now the lantern's light dimmed and brightened. It was low on fuel. Eric sat cross-legged on the rock floor of the cave near his mother's feet. He reached out to touch her leg, brushed the rough blanket, then pulled his hand back. He imagined her leg would feel hard, wooden. He didn't want to know. Dad talked. Eric had never heard him like this, non-stop, a droning monotone.

"The funny thing was, about this film, the Hays Office censored it. Nowadays they'll show any god-awful thing, but *King Kong* they censored."

Dad leaned forward as if his stomach hurt. "There's a scene on Skull Island, before Kong goes to New York, where he chases Fay Wray to the giant barricades that are supposed to protect the village from him and the prehistoric monsters on the other side. He reaches over the wall—they used a sixteen inch model for all the shots; I didn't know that—grabs a villager and bites his head off. That's what the Hays Office censored. Too graphic, I guess. But the next scene Kong pushes down the barricade, crushing twenty or thirty villagers."

He'd been talking steadily for two hours. Eric supposed he should feel grief, but he didn't, really. His eyes felt pressured like someone was pushing thumbs into them, and his face seemed heavy; the corners of his mouth dragged down and no effort could move them, but he didn't want to cry. The woman lying under the blanket wasn't his mother, not the one who toted a shotgun so jauntily the last weeks, not the one who woke him for school or bought him milkshakes when they went shopping. She was just a body, and Eric had never seen a dead person before. He didn't know how to behave around one. He sat, and his dad talked.

"I didn't understand why they censored that scene. Stupid thing to do. Hundreds of people died in this movie. Why'd they take out one death? The expedition chased Kong, trying to save the girl. Kong crossed a log over a chasm, and, when the men followed, he picked up one end and shook them off, down and down into the ravine. Why not that scene? So I read in this book a theory that the death of one is more horrible than the death of many. It's psychological. Kong nips off a head like you'd bite the end of a hot dog and the censors cut it out, but he can smash a faceless crowd."

He rocked back and forth. "One death," he said, "hurts too much."

The Coleman lantern sputtered, then lapsed into the rapid fire fut-fut-fut that meant it would go out any second. The light turned Dad's face into a dancing moonscape of black shadows. He started coughing, a long series of dry, painful sounding explosions that made Eric flinch.

When he finished, he moaned quietly and leaned forward again so that he trapped Mom's hand between his chest and his thigh.

Behind Dad a pile of canned goods caught the flickering light but the cave wall beyond reflected nothing. Its gray and black surface sucked in light, returning darkness. Eric stared at it for a long time until he saw high on the dull stone that someone, some earlier explorer, had carved a heart and scratched within it in barely visible, shaky letters:

Martha W. loves George

"Dad," Eric said finally, "we should take her home."

The lantern flared for an instant, then winked out. An afterimage of the inscription on the wall drifted in front of Eric, the letters and heart now dark on a lighter background. His dad inhaled shakily, held the breath, then let it out in a long hiss. He said, "I'll go into town and bring back an ambulance." Clothes rustled and Eric heard his dad's back crack as he stood. "You stay here with your mother."

After lighting a battery lantern, then covering Mom's face, Dad took a filled canteen and dragged his bike out of the entrance to the cave. His parting words were, "I'll be back before sunset."

As Eric sat on the cold stone floor an hour later, he suddenly wished very deeply that before Dad had left that he would have held him close, then kissed him goodbye as he had when Eric was a child.

*

Three hours after sunset, Dad still had not returned. Eric took a flashlight to the watch post and listened to the creek rumbling beside the highway below. Clouds obscured the stars, but the night was not dark. To the east, toward Denver, the clouds glowed redly. In the nights before when it was overcast, the lights of Denver lit the sky a pleasant, even electric white, but tonight the clouds boiled like bloody sheets.

He retrieved the Mutant Ninja Turtle radio from under a rock where he stored it, but it gave him almost no news. Over the last weeks, fewer and fewer radio stations stayed on the air. Tonight he found several channels squealing out the emergency broadcast signal, interrupting themselves every few minutes with a message to tune to KTLK for information about the "current situation." KTLK, however, played elevator music, and the only announcement Eric heard was one warning people to obey the curfew and to report looters to the proper authorities.

He flashed his light down the trail, hoping to see his father, though he knew Dad wouldn't attempt to climb up without using a light of his own. Eric wrapped his sleeping bag around him. His muscles ached as if he'd lifted weights for hours. He'd never been so tired in his entire life, so old and drained. A breeze rattled branches. He flicked the flashlight on again, and its dim light penetrated the thin cloth of his sleeping bag. He thought he might go to sleep, but the idea that he could miss his father frightened him, so he pinched his leg hard. The pain almost felt good. It was real and immediate and normal, not like the body lying in the cave or the horrible red clouds that rolled languidly above him. He thought he should be mourning, and it worried him that he wasn't. Don't I love my mother? he thought. Am I a beast, some sort of sociopath? (He'd heard the term on television one night applied to a serial killer.) He thought about going to school. If everything straightened itself out, or if this is just a nightmare, I'll never hate school again. I'll go to class and smile at teachers and do homework and I won't call anything stupid ever.

The cliff walls across the canyon lit brilliantly. Eric blinked back tears, the light was so bright. Then all was dark. What? he thought. The air swelled like a crack of thunder, a great slam of sound that pushed on Eric's chest. He screamed, but he couldn't hear himself. Then echoes sounded for several seconds. He thought, this is nuclear. The end of the world for sure. In the distance toward Golden he thought he heard rocks falling, though the ringing in his ears prevented him from being positive.

Movement down canyon caught his eye. A wall of darkness slid toward him, swallowing the highway, blanking the glimmer of the river. He stood on the rock, trying to see better as the darkness rolled by below. Whatever exploded between him and Golden had kicked up a cloud of dust; he decided it must be the tunnel. Someone blew up the tunnel.

After a few minutes, the air cleared, and the canyon was quiet again. The river noise sounded unchanged.

An hour before dawn, he fell asleep. Dad hadn't come back yet.

*

A black, muscled, immense shape heaved itself over the South Glenn Mall, scattering cars in the parking lot like children's blocks. Its knuckles scraped the pavement. Sirens howled on University Boulevard behind Eric. He flattened his back on a brick wall and tried not to move, to not breathe. (He knew it was the Littleton Saving and Loan building that stood on the corner of the mall's parking lot on the corner of University and Bellview.)

The ape tore a light pole from its fixture, studied it briefly, then flicked it a hundred feet. There were no people in the scene, just empty cars and the giant black figure. Eric smelled him, a vast animal odor like a hundred zoos on a hot summer afternoon.

In the background, a harmony of engines hummed, then grew louder. (The biplanes are coming! The biplanes are coming!) Eric tried to shout, "Run away! Run away!" but his best effort sounded no louder than a squeak. He wanted to wave to him and warn him but he was too frightened. What if the ape spotted him? Eric's inarticulate love bubbled within, but he was afraid of the size, the strength, the unbridled power. A creature so big shouldn't die, he thought. They'll drive him up some tower so they can knock him down. They'll shoot him and he'll never understand why they won't let him live.

In the dream—Eric knew he was dreaming—a blue van, its windows knocked out and its tires flat, limped into the parking lot. His mother was driving. "Stop, Mom!" he tried to yell. "Don't let him get you." But she drove to the monster's feet. The ape looked at the van with his vast, glistening eyes, then bent down to peer in the window. Mom stopped and got out. She put her hands on her hips and stared up at him unafraid.

Eric struggled, but it was as if the wall held him. His voice called out in slow motion notes that were deep and incomprehensible. Don't you know the story? The ape picks up the single person, plucks her from the ground and bites her in two. It's his nature. It's not his fault, but you can't get close to him. He is death.

It is Mom, isn't it? The woman standing at the ape's feet became slender and blond. She was Fay Wray. Eric knew she was his mom, but she was also Fay Wray. The ape cupped her into his hand and lifted her from the parking lot.

Eric shouted.

He brought her close to his face, his teeth visible.

He rubbed his cheek against her.

The engine noise rose to a deafening level.

King Kong clutched Mom/Fay Wray to his breast, straightened and shook his fist into the sky.

The first biplane circled high above, then winged over and began its attack. The next one followed. The next one followed. The next one followed.

*

The sun woke Eric, and he lay in his sleeping bag by the boulder for a long time before he remembered yesterday's events. He slid out of the bag and brushed the goose bumps off his arms. On the rock, the radio still played, but now it repeated one message continuously, "The Denver Public Health Department asks you to please stay in your homes." Then it listed the hospitals that were no longer accepting patients. From the size of the list, Eric wondered vaguely if they wouldn't save time by announcing the hospitals that were open instead.

He folded the sleeping bag mechanically, trying to think about what he should do next. His brain seemed full of fog, though, and thinking was like walking in knee-deep mud. Maybe Dad passed him while he slept, and was in the cave right now. Eric crawled through the cave's entrance, pushing the flashlight ahead of him, but Dad was not there. He avoided looking at the mattress where his mother's blanketed body lay. The idea of waiting for Dad held no appeal, but he didn't want to leave her either.

Last night's explosion finally decided the issue for him; he needed to search for Dad. He needed to do something, though, about Mom before he left. The blankets didn't seem enough protection, some- how. He envisioned mice nibbling on the corpse, shuddered, and quickly spread the sheet of black plastic that Dad had used to pro- tect the mattresses originally over the body. He tucked the edges under and checked carefully for any spaces a mouse might try. When he finished, his hands felt soiled, as if the plastic were slimy. He rubbed them hard against his jeans, but that didn't help, so he washed them with drinking water.

Squatting next to the body, he watched the play of light reflect off the plastic. Finally, he placed his palm where his mother's shoul- der would be. The plastic crackled and gave off no warmth; it was the exact temperature of the rocks around him. He spoke into the silence, "Goodbye, Mom," and the quiet that followed felt like the closing of a book.

He threw packages of beef jerky, several cans of fruit and an extra canteen into his backpack, made sure the desk key Dad had given him was secure in a side pocket, wrote his dad a note, and left the cave, dragging his bike after him.

As soon as he rounded the corner on the highway he saw the result of last night's explosion. A jumble of rock choked the tunnel opening, and a bare spot on the mountain above the entrance showed where rock had sheared off to drop on the road. A refrigerator- sized boulder sat in a crater in the asphalt seventy-five yards from the rock pile.

A fisherman's trail, the only way out of the canyon, followed the river, where it vanished into a light morning mist that drifted off the water, giving the scene an otherworldly look. Eric hoisted the bike on his shoulder and walked past the remnants of their van, which reminded him of his dream ("The biplanes are coming!") and generated within him a strong feeling of deja vu; not a bad feeling, but very creepy, like the top of his head was floating away, as if he'd stepped out of time. The farther he walked, the stranger he felt. The trail didn't seem connected to the real world. Water tinkled musically over the rocks, and the air smelled moist and clean. All the colors vibrated, even through the mist.

An animal crossed the path fifty yards in front of him. Eric thought it was a German shepherd at first, the biggest shepherd he'd ever seen, but it moved so smoothly that he couldn't believe it was a dog. It trotted up the hill on its big paws (What big teeth you have grandma, Eric thought), and just before it disappeared behind a ridge it looked back at Eric with clear, light blue eyes. Eric almost waved at it.

Eric turned around. The van was out of sight; he couldn't see the road. For a second, he wasn't sure which direction he'd come from; both were unfamiliar. He noticed hip high, broad-leafed plants a shade of green he'd never seen before growing next to the water. He dropped his bike and scrambled down the slope. Their leaves were thick and waxy. He broke one in half. A thick, milky fluid oozed out of the wound, and he caught a strong citrus odor like a tangerine. Triangular, dull orange beetles scurried up and down the plant's stalks. He couldn't shake the feeling that he'd stepped away from reality, that these weren't Colorado plants, that this wasn't the Colorado he knew. He climbed back to the trail, picked up his bike and continued on.

Suddenly he realized he wasn't alone. Sitting on the slope above the trail fifty feet away, their backpacks beside them, three hikers, an old man and two boys were eating a meal. A complicated series of wrinkles criss-crossed the old one's leather-colored face. He smiled and spoke to one of the boys, but Eric didn't hear what he said. When he walked just below them, the old one glanced up and met Eric's eyes. Eric's throat constricted. The creepy feeling of being displaced in time swept through him so intensely, he thought he would fall over. He didn't want the old man to say anything to him. Don't talk to me, old man, he thought. I don't know what to say to you. Something in the man's eyes, something compassionate, made Eric think he understood.

Eric looked away, and as he did he observed a heavy scar marked the side of the boy's face on the old man's right. Eric walked a few more steps, then glanced at the group again, but they were gone. A breeze swirled tendrils of mist past the empty spot where the hikers had sat. The sense of deja vu vanished as if someone had thrown a switch, and Eric shook his head. His bike drug at his shoulder and he staggered a couple of steps. He realized he was near fainting; he hadn't eaten for thirty-six hours. That's it, he thought, I'm delirious.

He rested on a stump by the river and ate two beef jerky strips and a can of peaches. This is a beautiful spot, he thought, and he reflected on all the people who had driven through the tunnel for years and years and never seen this section of the river that the highway cut off by diving through the mountain instead of following the canyon. For the moment, he forgot where he was going and why. The jerky tasted salty and good, and the peaches were sweet and cold.

*

A junkyard lined the highway on the other side of the tunnel. Starting at the rock-choked tunnel entrance, and stretching for several hundred yards, a mess of cars crowded the road. At first Eric thought someone had painted black dots on the cars, then he realized that holes peppered them. Standing on the trail below, he saw that the closest car, a green Chevy Nova, sat unevenly. Three of its four tires were flat. A tight web of cracks frosted the windows. He clambered up the slope, pulling the bike behind him. A shift in the breeze wafted gasoline fumes over him and another smell, deep, bad and nasty. He snorted to clear his nose and mouth-breathed. When he stepped onto the road, he noticed that many cars had burned, their paint blackened and blistered from the heat.

Thousands of brass shell casings glittered on the highway by the tunnel entrance. He picked one up; it was much larger than the ones Dad used for the deer rifle. He imagined what must have happened. Weeks ago, when the traffic stopped, the police or the National Guard established a road block. Panic in the last couple of days forced people to flee. They were stopped here. He marveled that his family hadn't heard any of the shooting. Last night's explosion, the final act to seal the road, provided the only clue of the battle.

Fearfully, he approached the Nova's open passenger door and peeked inside where a black stain discolored the driver's seat. The stain shifted and Eric jerked back. Dozens of flies boiled off the stain; some flew out the window, but the rest settled on the seat again. He swallowed hard to keep his stomach down. Dad might have been caught here. Maybe he was coming back with help and whatever happened stopped him. Eric checked the next car. It too was empty.

The third one wasn't.

He thought at first that someone had left a pile of clothes on the seat until he saw the bare foot sticking out. Two lines of dried blood like the outline of a carrot traced their way from the heel to the curled toes. A swarm of flies lifted itself angrily from the corpse, then settled back when Eric stepped away. He sat hard on the pavement and rested his forehead against the cool metal door. By wrapping his arms tightly around his midsection, he forced himself not to throw up.

One afternoon in the sixth grade he'd sneaked into an adult Driver's Ed class that the elementary school sponsored in an unused classroom. He'd heard they were watching a "cool, gross film," and he and two of his friends dared each other into ditching class to see it. The movies, *Signal 30 for Danger* and *Highways of Death,* featured real life footage of automobile accidents, and even from the back of the room, the images sickened Eric. One scene stuck with him particularly. A man lost control of his car and it careened into a field of tree stumps. He probably would have been all right, but he wasn't wearing a seat belt; his door popped open and he was tossed from the car. When he was half way out, the door crashed into a stump, slamming it on the man's chest. The camera lingered on his bloated torso for a long time. Later the friends invited Eric to a sleepover where they promised they were renting *Faces of Death I* and *II,* Eric declined. For months afterward he had dreams about bodies pulled out of twisted wreckage.

Dad might be in one of these wrecks. Eric had to check them all, and he couldn't afford to be sick to do it. Besides, he reminded himself, he didn't know any of these people.

Very few of the cars contained bodies. He found guns in some. Suitcases and boxes of clothes filled many. He read a poorly printed leaflet that fluttered on the front seat of a wood-paneled station wagon. It was a call to arms and said that the Coors management had immunized themselves from the plague and that they were withholding the cure from their employees. Eric didn't make the connection at first, then he remembered that Coors had its main plant in Golden. Much of the populace worked there, and almost all the rest of the town's economy depended on the plant. He was starting to get a picture of the panic and desperation in the cities that the radio hadn't provided.

After he inspected the last car, he mounted his bike and pedaled toward Golden. Smoke discolored the horizon ahead, and the smell of burning grew stronger. Eric kept his bike close to the shoulder, listening for the sound of an approaching car or anything else threatening. He watched for places to hide if he had to. The best plan, he thought, would be to stay out of sight. Whatever happened at the tunnel, people were shooting at each other and a boy on a bike could be fair game.

The closer he got to town, the slower he pedaled. The road, he remembered, ran above the north side of town. From it, he should be able to look down to see what's happening, but he felt too exposed. On his left, the canyon rose steeply, in many places unclimbable, and there wasn't a bush any bigger than a fruit basket to hide behind. On his right, the shoulder sloped to the river. His forearms ached from gripping the bike handles so tightly, and his heart raced. Blood pounded in his ears.

This isn't fair, he thought. In the movies, the hero isn't scared every second. Rambo sneaks right into the enemy's camp. He looked at his hands. His knuckles were white. Stopping the bike, he unclenched and forced himself to breathe slowly. He recited a mantra he'd learned when he was little, a tongue twister that made him feel better though it didn't mean anything. "Sixteen stainless steel twin screw cruisers," he said. He repeated it twice more, then moved on.

He knew when he rounded the next bend that the canyon would open up and he would be able to see Golden. Smoke filled the sky. The air in the canyon was hazy. He stood on the pedals—the bike glided downhill—to get a first glimpse.

When he stopped the bike finally, he should have been able to see all the way into Denver, but Golden was burning. Much of the center of town, made up of turn-of-the-century Victorian homes, was blackened, and nothing remained of the quaint brick homes except a few, low, broken walls or a handful of chimneys poking out of the rubble. Some fires still burned there, though mostly the excitement appeared to be over. On the north side of town, however, thick, black smoke poured out of the Coors plant.

Eric watched for several minutes. He didn't hear sirens and he didn't see anyone moving below. The streets were empty, no traffic at all.

Initially he thought of the burning of Atlanta from *Gone With the Wind*, but then the more obvious connection came to him. It looked like King Kong had visited Golden, maybe in one of his later incarnations where he met Godzilla. Eric could imagine nothing else that could cause so much destruction. King Kong lives, he thought.

How will I find Dad in all this? The world had never seemed so big.

Smoke billowed from the Coors plant. Wind swirled the impenetrable darkness, and for a second, the black clouds formed the shape of the great ape. Just for a brief instant, Eric could see King Kong straddling the wreckage of Golden. Just for an instant he could hear him shrieking his challenge at the powers of the earth, and at this instant, there was no one to answer.

Chapter Seven
CROSSROADS, COMING AND GOING

A re we still being watched?" asked Eric.
    Rabbit shrugged his shoulders. "Maybe." He stopped,
    scanned the edges of the canyon, then tilted his head to
the side as if listening. "Yes."

"How do you know that kind of stuff? I can't do that," said
Dodge crossly. "You give me the heebie-jeebies."

Rabbit shrugged again. "Sometimes I get a feeling."

Eric laughed. Sometimes he'd felt they were being watched
too. It wasn't anything big, a shiver when he wasn't cold, a sense of
being on stage, of things moving behind him or just below the horizon. It made him want to run around bushes and yell, "Boo!"

Rain clouds swelled to the east. Thunderhead piled on thunderhead like mushroom clouds, and flickers of lightning flashed at their
base. The plains are getting a washing, Eric thought. During the
Gone Times, he didn't pay attention to the weather. Buildings were
air conditioned, artificially lighted and always dry. Car heaters held
out cold or rain or snow. Now, he checked the weather automatically. Red sky at morning, sailors take warning. Red sky at night,
sailors delight.

They hiked quietly for several minutes. Eric decided the storm
would stay out on the plains. They needn't worry about finding shelter from wind or rain tonight. He snapped a glance over his shoulder, trying to catch whatever might be following them, but he saw
nothing. Rabbit walked in front of him nonchalantly. If Rabbit wasn't
frightened, then there was probably no need for him to fret. Rabbit
"intuited" better than anyone he had ever met.

"What kind of car did you have, Grandpa?" asked Dodge.

Eric surveyed the path before them. Following U.S. 6, they had
turned into Clear Creek Canyon a half hour earlier, but a rock slide

covered the highway now and they would have to pick their course carefully over the broken and loose rock. Heat waves shimmered off the rock-strewn slope. He could see almost no evidence of the line of gun-shot riddled cars he remembered from years ago. The slide had buried them.

"I drove several, but I didn't really *have* one." He decided to head down to the river. The rocks looked less steep and jumbled there. "I was too young to get a driver's license before the plague, and there didn't seem much point in owning one particular car afterward. For a year or so, everybody who was left could own a hundred cars if they wanted to."

Dodge jumped from rock to rock like a mountain sheep. Eric shook his head ruefully. He couldn't recall the last time he felt that limber and careless of his well being. He continued, "Of course, that was only for a year as I said."

"How come we don't have cars now? Phil said he still had some that worked. I sure would have liked to drive in one. It'd save us from a lot of walking."

Rabbit sat next to the river, waiting for them to catch up. "Car won't do you any good where we're going," he said. He gestured up stream where the river tumbled through the clutter of boulders.

"We'll be on a path soon enough," said Eric. He remembered the fishing trail that went away from the highway at the old, blocked tunnel. "But Rabbit's right. Most places I expect a car won't go too far. A car needs a very special environment, a road, and the roads are falling apart." He lowered himself onto a rock that overlooked a deep pool in Clear Creek. Five trout a foot or so long each lazily swam to the other side when his shadow fell on the water. Heat broadcast from each sun-baked rock. Eric jerked his hand off the black granite. The stream looked refreshing and cold. "I suppose in some parts of the country, the roads will stay good for centuries. After all, when I was a child there were places in the prairie where one could still see one-hundred year old ruts left by covered wagons. If ruts can last that long, highways ought to also. Mountains and winter, though, are tough on roads, and a car needs good ones to get anywhere."

"Why don't we fix them?" asked Dodge.

Rabbit said, "Cars don't work."

"Phil said something interesting I hadn't thought about." Eric led them upstream. A rusted mass of metal jammed between two rocks showed that they were at least to the point where the cars had been parked, which would put them within a few hundred yards of the tunnel, but looking ahead, Eric couldn't tell. Time had reshaped the canyon. "He said it's all a problem of shelf life. Some things last and others don't. A car will last a long time if you keep it out of the weather, but two of its elements won't, the battery and gasoline. You can run a car without a battery, but gasoline has additives that evaporate over time no matter where it's stored. A couple years after the plague, it became very hard to find gasoline that was usable. Without fresh gasoline, most cars can't run, and no one has made gasoline for sixty years. So, gasoline's shelf life stopped the car a lot sooner than bad roads."

"Why is diesel still good and gasoline isn't?"

"Diesel has no octane." Dodge looked at Eric blankly. "Octane is what gives gasoline its power. Diesel is mostly oil. It doesn't evaporate or change chemically as quickly as the octane in gasoline. We can find out more about gasoline and chemistry if the library in Boulder still stands."

Dodge grinned, "Books will tell us everything!"

Eric sighed. Dodge's enthusiasm for reading as a cure all depressed him. "Reading, study, and careful thought may teach us how to make gasoline again, but cars are just a small part of this shelf life problem."

Climbing around a particularly treacherous stretch of sharp-edged rock silenced them for a minute. Eric spotted where the slide ended and the fishing trail, as fresh and vivid as when he last saw it, began.

After they stepped off the slide, they splashed water in their faces and cooled their necks on a grassy shore by the creek. Dodge refilled their canteens.

They picked up their backpacks, but didn't put them on as they looked for a comfortable place to eat lunch. Above the trail, Rabbit found a spot of soft grass shaded by a juniper, and they sprawled comfortably.

"What else about shelf life?" asked Dodge.

Eric wished he had a cigarette. He had only smoked tobacco for two or three years after the plague, but the urge still hit him strongly sometimes. "This is kind of a lecture," he said.

"We don't mind, do we, Rabbit?" Rabbit shook his head. Dodge said, "We like your stories."

"Well, this isn't a story." He dug into his pack for a jar of crabapple jelly. "A loaf of bread stays fresh for a week if you keep it wrapped up, right?"

Dodge held out a hard biscuit for Eric to put jelly on. "Right."

"Well, then we can say its shelf life is one week. Shelf life is how long something stays good. Bread has a short life unless you freeze it; then it lasts longer."

Dodge said, "But we can't freeze things because we don't have 'lectricity."

"Right. But this isn't a problem because flour, salt, sugar, eggs and yeast either have long shelf lives or are always available. Shelf life, though, doesn't just apply to food. Lots of technology from the Gone Time had limited shelf life. Batteries, for example, are fairly obvious. A battery stays good for up to five years, or so, then it's dead. Even a rechargeable one. Ammunition, gasoline, florescent light bulbs and many medicines chemically degenerate. The problem is that we don't have access to the raw materials, or we don't have the technology in place, to replace the items with limited shelf lives. Imagine if we didn't have flour, salt, sugar, eggs and yeast how long it would take to run out of bread."

Dodge said, "Well, we could store up a bunch and it would last a long time."

Rabbit said, "Shelf life. One week. Doesn't matter how much you have."

"So, is this what you were arguing with Dad about?" Dodge rested on his back, looking into the sky.

"Exactly," Eric exclaimed. "Your dad wants to have his cake and eat it too. On one hand he says that we don't need to read, and on the other he wants to keep finding Gone Time technology to maintain the community. He wants to scavenge, but he doesn't want to learn how to make these things ourselves. What's important is not finding a warehouse filled with leftovers from the Gone Time, but teaching ourselves how to make them again. The answers are in the books, and that's where we don't see eye to eye."

Thinking about Troy normally depressed Eric, but today, sitting with his grandson, eating crabapple jelly by Clear Creek, he felt fine. Something about this spot was restful: the way the light reflected from the water, or maybe its musical clattering as it swept around the canyon's bend. Now he could see their disagreement as philosophic, not solely personal. If he could figure a way to bridge the argument about relearning Gone Time knowledge rather than relying on or abandoning Gone Time technology (Troy seemed to want to do both), then they could work on their real personal differences. The philosophic chasm just complicated matters.

"I don't understand," said Dodge. "Why did people forget?"

Eric thought, this is the essential problem: why people forgot. "The plague scared people. For a long time after, they kept expecting to die. The ones that didn't go insane, and there were many, grieved over their dead and worried about living. And during this time, so much technology was lying around that no one thought how to make more of it. The water plants shut down and the electrical generators quit working, and nobody knew how to run them. They were too big and required too many knowledgeable technicians to throw the switches. People just survived, sort of like we are now. Some of us forgot because we didn't want to remember."

Rabbit munched on a handful of sunflower seeds. "Cars sound like fun, but I'm happy here, right now. A car or a book won't make lunch better. Don't you like this?" He waved his hand at the creek, the trail that ran below them and the spray of wild flowers along the bank.

Surprised, Eric looked at him. Rabbit never talked about himself, how he was feeling.

"This is a nice spot," agreed Dodge. "I like the way the mist floats on the river. Kind of like ghosts."

Eric noticed the heat from a half hour earlier had dissipated. A mist was rising from the water, and a cooling breeze bent the grass around them. "Yes, it is," said Eric. Goose bumps rose on his arms and neck. He was trying to remember. He had been here before. He inhaled deeply. The air smelled, oddly, of tangerine.

Dodge spoke, but Eric missed it. "Excuse me?" he said. He looked at Dodge.

"I didn't say anything," said Dodge.

In the corner of his vision Eric sensed movement, and a flash of delicious inevitability flooded his head. He didn't have to look to know what was coming. He *had* been here before, not just this place but this time.

Trudging toward them on the trail, a teenage boy, a bike slung over his shoulder, looked up at Eric. What struck Eric first was the boy's unwashed hair plastered to his forehead. Smaller details, the cassette player hanging from his belt, the wire leading to the speakers around his neck and the Air Jordan sneakers he noted, but what Eric concentrated on most were the boy's sunken and exhausted eyes. No one had ever looked so alone to him; so abandoned, lost and alone.

The boy glanced down. Eric almost called out to him, but he realized there was nothing he could say. Eric wasn't even sure if the boy could hear him. He doubted it. Then his eyes watered, and he blinked the tears away.

The boy was gone.

*

From the old watch post, U.S. 6's appearance had changed considerably. Despite the height, Eric could see weeds pushing through the asphalt and rocks cluttering the road. Eric found it hard to imagine the same road crowded with traffic. He remembered the scene, but he couldn't feel it anymore.

"Come on, Grandpa," yelled Dodge. "I want to see the cave." He and Rabbit stood at the cavern's entrance holding hastily constructed torches. Eric guessed they might give them five minutes of light if they were lucky.

Dodge said, "I've never been in a cave before."

Rabbit lit one torch, handed the unlit ones to Dodge and Eric, then led them into the crawl way. On his hands and knees, Eric followed Dodge. The acrid smoke from the torch stung his eyes, and he couldn't see anything anyway, so he squeezed them shut and continued to crawl.

He butted into something soft. "What . . . ." Suddenly, Dodge's rump pushed into him. "What . . . ." Eric said again.

Dodge screeched, "Back! Back! Back!" Deeper in the cave, Rabbit swore. Eric tried to turn around, whapped his head against the rock wall, then backed up as fast as he could. The stone roof snagged his shirt and pulled it snug against his armpits before ripping. Dodge smashed Eric's fingers twice and kicked him in the chin as they retreated.

Panting loudly, they stood outside the cave. Rabbit had lost his torch and his left elbow oozed blood. Dodge's nose bled freely from a kick Rabbit had delivered, and Eric rubbed his chin gingerly.

"Rattlesnakes," said Rabbit. "I got into the room, saw the boxes you told us about, then I heard buzzing. Cave's full of them. Must have been two-hundred." He sat heavily. "I don't mind a snake or two, but sheesh!"

Dodge held his nose to control the bleeding and said nasally, "I thought your face was on fire or something."

Cautiously they inspected the other entrances. All were homes for rattlesnakes. The system of cracks and crevices provided an ideal environment for a large rodent population, and the snakes were evidently well fed. They could find no way in.

"So what's special about this cave anyway?" asked Dodge. The sun touched the canyon rim to the west. Although it was only mid-afternoon, they could expect no more direct sunlight.

Eric thought about the last time he'd been here, the summer after the plague. He and Leda had parked their four-wheel drive at the blocked tunnel, then carried a shovel and pick to the cave. He'd dug in the rocky soil most of the day to excavate a hole deep enough to hold his mother. Leda inventoried the items in the cave and packed the most useful ones to the highway.

They'd wrapped the black plastic tightly around Mother, carried her out and buried her. He'd thought of her as a big woman, incapable of being budged once she set her feet, but her body seemed so light. She was no trouble at all to carry to the grave.

He had a hard time relating the two versions of himself in his memory: the one who listened to rock and roll under his headphones and worried whether school would be canceled or not, and the one a year later who with his wife drove a car he'd taken from a Chevy dealer's car lot to bury his mother. It seemed as if he'd lived two lives.

"This is where I started to grow up," Eric said. "I wanted to see it again."

He led them to the grave, a flat patch of ground between matched boulders near the top of the ridge. He'd chosen the site because the rocks sheltered it from the wind, and it was a good high place to rest.

He barely recognized the spot. No sign remained of the wooden cross he'd made, and the ground was no longer bare. A knee-high bed of Columbine covered the entire area like a blue fog. Their delicate stems and petals trembled in a breeze too slight for Eric to feel. He paused at the edge of the bed.

"Where's the grave?" asked Dodge.

Eric knelt and passed his hand over the flowers, letting the fragile blossoms brush his palm. He remembered Mom in the backyard of their Littleton house, knees firmly planted in earth she'd just turned over, carefully pushing bulbs into the garden in expectation of the spring. Mother had always believed in the spring, in regeneration. She'd said once, "A flower proves nature is an artist."

"She's buried by that boulder," Eric said. "Underneath this . . ." The Columbines shimmered in the canyon dusk. ". . . this . . . blue quilt."

Dodge said, "Doesn't look much like a grave, Grandpa."

Eric sighed deeply. His breath shook a little when he exhaled. On his knees, the flowers spread out before him like an affirmation of beauty and life, and he recalled when he first went to school how he'd kneel on a footstool in front of his Mother so she could comb his hair. He felt her hand on the back of his neck and her breath in his face.

"That's the way it should be," he said. "Nothing ought to look like a grave."

*

"Shush!" said Eric. He put his arm across Dodge's chest to stop him. They were almost to the old watch post. "I saw something." Rabbit stepped past Eric and surveyed the road.

Sun shone on the canyon wall east of them, but deep blue shadows filled the valley Eric had stood watch over years ago. He looked west, toward Idaho Springs. Whatever caught his attention wasn't moving now.

Rabbit said, "I see them."

"Who?" asked Eric.

"Don't know, but they're sitting by the creek."

Eric strained his eyes. All he could see was foam on the rocks and a scattering of low plants lining the river. He squinted. Nothing.

"Where? Are they ghosts?" said Dodge.

"By the bank, there," said Rabbit. He pointed. "Two by that rock and another on the shoulder."

Frustrated, Eric gritted his teeth, then turned his head—an old hunter's trick—and let his peripheral vision go to work.

Dodge said, "Ah, I see."

Eric dug into his backpack for binoculars. When he found them, Rabbit was halfway to the road. "What's he doing?" Eric hissed.

Dodge sighed. "He's always going off on his own. Lots of times when we scavenge he'll leave me, and I won't see him for the rest of the day."

Eric focused the binoculars where Rabbit had said he saw the figures by the creek. "He's not going to find anything. Nobody's there."

Dodge said, "'Course not. Soon as Rabbit moved, they took off."

"Where?"

"Up the slope." Dodge shivered. "They *might* be ghosts. I watched them until they reached those bushes. . ." He pointed to a half dozen scraggly clumps of rabbit brush that couldn't hide a good sized marmot, ". . . then they kind of melted into the ground."

Eric raised his eyebrows.

"Honest. Like coyotes. You see them for a few feet, then they're gone."

"Were they people?"

"No." He gulped. "They were b . . . ." He colored and looked away.

"Dodge?"

"You won't believe me." He crossed his arms across his chest. "You'll laugh. It's just a story they tell little kids to scare them after dark."

"What's the story?"

"You won't make fun?" Dodge asked. Eric shook his head.

Rabbit reached the road, crouched low and ran on the shoulder next to the canyon wall, keeping out of sight of the creek. Eric swept the length of the canyon with the binoculars. Nothing.

"It's about the Gone Time. Dad told me the story when we went hunting. He said that in the Gone Time people were very proud. That they flew higher than birds and clouds, that they drove faster than arrows in their cars on the roads, that they lived in the buildings we scavenge, but that the buildings were beautiful and rose thousands of feet in the air. He said there were so many people that I could never count all of them because babies would be born faster than I could tally."

Dodge paused and looked at Eric. "Is all that true, Grandpa. Are all the stories you told us true?"

Surprised, Eric said, "Of course. Why would I lie to you?"

"Grown-ups make up stuff. I know about Santa Claus, and he's a lie."

Rabbit reached the spot where he'd said he'd seen the three figures. He stood on the edge of the road, looking left and right.

Eric stroked his grandson's hair. Dodge reminded him of Troy, who had been hard-headed and skeptical. Troy had never believed man had walked on the moon, or that Denver used to glow at night like a sea of stars.

"Santa Claus is different. The Gone Time is history, and history is real."

"Like *Star Wars?*"

Eric sighed. How could he teach Dodge the difference between reality and fiction when both sounded so fantastic? "I'll have to explain that later. What was the story your dad told you?"

Dodge looked disappointed, but he continued. "He said the Gone Time people got so proud that they spread all over the Earth building towns and driving their cars and watching their TVs. He said no one had to work because machines did everything and all they did was write poetry and go to parties."

Eric smiled at Dodge's fractured version of history.

"The stories you tell about the Gone Time don't sound like that, but I'm just saying what Dad told me. Anyway, he said the Gone Time people kept knocking down forests and filling up the world till there wasn't any place for the Bugbears."

"The Bugbears?"

"Yes. Dad said they lived on the Earth before people did, and they didn't mind sharing, but when there was no place for them to be private anymore, they came out of their holes in the ground and their secret places in the trees that were left. They touched people on their foreheads when they were sleeping, and when they woke up they got sick and died. The Bugbears went to everybody's houses and decided who was bad, and they touched them." Dodge pressed his finger in the middle of his forehead. "Good people they kissed and let live."

"You think those were Bugbears by the river?"

Dodge nodded. "Dad said that sometimes you can see one if you're real quiet for a long time. I figure it's Bugbears that have been following us."

Rabbit trotted on the road toward them.

Eric said, "That's as good an explanation as any, I suppose." He shouldered Rabbit's backpack and his own. "Let's get off the mountain. Unless you want to spend the night with rattlesnakes?"

Rabbit waited for them at the bottom.

"Did you see them?" asked Dodge when they finally reached Rabbit.

He shook his head. "Nothing there but a footprint on a rock. One of them must have stepped in the water."

"But where did they go?" said Dodge.

Rabbit took his backpack from Eric and slipped the straps over his shoulders. "Don't know. They'd have to be mountain goats to climb that hill."

Dodge started hiking toward the blocked tunnel. "Bugbears," he said.

Eric expected Rabbit to laugh or say something derisive about Dodge's theory. Instead, Rabbit looked at Dodge and raised his eyebrows as if to say, "Could be."

*

After they pitched camp and doused the campfire with creek water, Eric lay on his back staring into the canopy of stars, each as bright and sharp as a new needle. He felt that tonight, if he stared hard enough, he could separate the individual stars in the Milky Way. If he just concentrated, he could pick out the planets circling each, count their moons, follow the paths of wandering comets alone and cold with no sun to burn them.

The grave had him thinking about his parents. I'm seventy-five, he thought, and I miss my mom. I miss them both. Of all the people he'd ever known, of all the reactions he had seen to the plague and the change in the world, they had seemed the most flexible and resilient.

He pushed his hands under the small of his back. The extra support always felt good when he wasn't sleeping on a mattress.

"Are you awake?" asked Rabbit. Eric rolled his head to the side and saw that Rabbit was sitting up in his sleeping bag, leaning against his backpack. The night was too dark to show his features, but his eyes glistened, reflecting the little light there was.

"Yes," said Eric. He looked back into the stars. Willow tree leaves rustled at the edge of the glade near the junction of U.S. 6 and Colorado 93 where they had eaten dinner in the dark before bedding down.

"Do you believe in ghosts?" asked Rabbit.

"Yes," said Eric without hesitation. The answer hung in the air between them for a long moment. For some reason, with the stars piercing the blackness above, with the little bit of breeze fluttering through the willows, he felt Rabbit had asked the most important question a human being could ask. We're on the brink of understanding our world, thought Eric. It's about ghosts, almost six-billion of them, and everything they left for us. Real ghosts, mythical ghosts and metaphorical ghosts. They're everywhere. I can't ignore them.

From the first day he'd left the cave, sixty years ago, he'd felt their presence in the empty streets of Denver, the broken windows, the parked cars. Ghosts and ghosts and ghosts. He remembered a sheet of newspaper blowing in front of him as he walked up Littleton Boulevard toward his home. It touched the pavement, then shot twenty feet up, then spiraled down again. It was if some invisible being were playing. And ever since, he'd felt ghosts like the pressure in the air before a storm. Did he believe? There was no way he could be who he was, he thought, if he didn't.

Rabbit said, "I've talked to one."

Eric shook his head. "Who? I mean, what do you mean?"

"Last month I talked to one. I was in the basement of a Big-O Tire store, scavenging, and when I came out, a girl was going through my backpack. She looked like she might be seven or eight years old. At least I think she was a girl. She looked like a girl, red hair tied back in a ponytail, leather skirt, no shirt. Anyway, she saw me and said one word, then ran. I yelled at her not to be afraid. Then I chased her, but she was fast. Squeezed through a crack in a brick wall and was gone."

She must have been fast, Eric thought, to get away from Rabbit, who was the quickest boy Eric had ever known. "What did she say? What makes you think she was a ghost?"

"I was south of town, east of the river."

Eric thought about the map of Denver in the Town Hall. Every community Littleton traded with was marked with red pins. All of them were north along I-25, what most people called the Valley Highway now. As far as they knew, no one lived to the south. If people lived in Colorado Springs, seventy miles away, the people of Littleton didn't know about them. For all they knew, and all the fear they had of travel, the area south could be marked with "Here there be Dragons."

Rabbit continued, "I didn't recognize her either, but that's not what makes me think she was a ghost. I ran around the wall she jumped through, and she wasn't there. There was no place to hide or anything. She just vanished."

"What did she say to you?"

Rabbit lay back. In the darkness, Eric couldn't read his expression.

"She called me a name." Rabbit put his hands under his head. He stared into the sky like Eric had earlier. "Maybe 'called' isn't the right word. It's more like she identified me, like if I looked into a box and there was a squirrel in it and I said, 'squirrel.'"

"I understand," said Eric.

"I startled her, I think. She looked at me and said 'Jackal.' Then she disappeared through the crack."

Far away, a long, lonely howl rose in the night. Another joined it. It's the wolves, Eric thought. Rabbit shuddered at the sound.

"What's a jackal, Grandpa?"

Eric listened to the wolves for a few seconds. Their voices mingled in eerie harmonics. "A jackal . . . it's an animal that lives in Africa . . . a kind of dog." He thought about it. The air suddenly cooled, like the breeze had pushed a patch of arctic atmosphere over them. He wrapped the sleeping bag tighter around his shoulders, then he chuckled. "Of course," he said. "It makes sense. A jackal . . ." He pulled the bag around his ears. ". . . is a scavenger."

Chapter Eight
BODY BAGS

The smoke on the streets in town didn't look that bad. When Eric looked up, the swirls of ash turned the sky gray, and the stench of burning rubber and insulation seared his throat. He covered his nose and mouth with a bandanna. None of the houses or stores he passed on this side street were damaged, but boards covered many windows, and locks secured the gates. The buildings had a closed, protected look to them, as if they cowered in the face of the destruction. He couldn't hear any birds. Since he'd entered town, he hadn't heard a bird, a dog, a car horn or a siren. Nothing. He heard only his own sounds.

Eric pushed his bike, approached an intersection slowly, peered both ways, then hurried across. He had no idea where the hospital or police station might be, the logical places to look for Dad.

The light "ping" of a loose spoke every revolution of the wheel made him nervous. What if somebody heard him? What could he say? If people were shooting at each other on the highway the night before, maybe he would be mistaken for a thief or arrested for violating a "stay inside" order. His eyes watered, and half in frustration and half in fear he angrily wiped them with the heel of his hand.

A glass-partitioned public phone kiosk on the next corner was vandalized, the glass shattered, and all that remained of the receiver was a nub of protruding wires. In the phone book he found an address for both the hospital and the police station, but there was no map, and the street names didn't mean anything to him.

A white van roared down the street. Eric pushed himself against the remains of the phone, trying to disappear. A man in the passenger's seat looked right at him. His eyes were small and cold, like a beetle's. His mouth was straight and hard. Eric was glad they didn't stop. He wouldn't want to meet a man who looked like that.

Pieces of paper swirled in the wake of the van; its taillights flashed when it turned the corner a couple of blocks away. Eric rested his cheek against the phone booth's cool metal. A minute later, a police cruiser with darkly tinted windows turned onto the street. He started to step out, to wave, then fear welled up, making him weak. Across the sidewalk, he saw a deep doorway to duck into, but there was no way to get there without being seen. He stayed in the kiosk and tried to act like he was busy, which felt ridiculous since the phone was broken. He opened the directory to the yellow pages and studied them. The car stopped at the curb, and the window rolled down.

A tired voice from inside said, "Sir, would you mind stepping next to the car?"

Eric looked behind him. Nobody had ever called him "Sir" before.

"Me?" he said.

The voice deepened, became threatening. "Don't make me get out."

Eric moved by the cruiser and bent so he could see in the window. What he noticed first was in the back seat, a stack of what he took to be heavy, black plastic tarps. Eric didn't understand why tarps would have zippers on them though. Then he saw the officer's revolver. His stomach gripped into a tight ball. The revolver rested on the seat, and the officer's hand was on it. His mirrored sunglasses reflected a distorted picture. "Give me the stereo," he said.

For a second Eric didn't move. He didn't know what the officer meant, then he unclipped the cassette player from his belt, disconnected the headphones and offered the player to the policeman. When he didn't stir, Eric dropped it on the seat. It bounced once. Without moving his head, the officer's hand floated from the gun and picked up the cassette player. He held it in front of his glasses, then floated it back to the seat. His movements were smooth and careful. Eric didn't want to make him angry. The man made Eric think of a snake, a meticulous, cautious predator, ready to burst into motion any second.

"Now, the backpack," he said.

Eric shucked the strap off his shoulder and placed it next to the cassette. The hand drifted from the gun, undid the straps and explored the contents. He lifted each item out and placed it carefully on the seat until the empty bag sagged beside him.

During the process, Eric thought about fidgeting, but he held himself still. He knew he should be frightened, but now he felt detached, almost meditative about what was happening, as if he were hovering above the sidewalk watching the scene unroll. Maybe the event was too surreal, like one of those weird paintings he'd seen in art books where mountains levitated in living rooms and watches melted over tree branches.

He couldn't see the man's eyes, but it suddenly occurred to him that they wouldn't be malicious eyes, not the eyes of a killer; they would be crazed eyes. Below the officer's sunglasses, even in the tinted window shadows in the car, Eric saw deep, purple circles like twin bruises. The man's face sagged from his cheekbones. His hair, brown streaked with gray, stuck out in uncombed angles from under his hat. Crumpled fast food sacks and crushed Styrofoam cups covered the floor of the cruiser. The car smelled strongly of old coffee and sweaty clothes. Eric knew—he didn't know how—that the rigidity of the man's posture, the unnaturally precise hand movements, masked exhaustion and madness. For the first time in his life, Eric felt like he understood something about someone else. He felt a connection to him, an empathy, as if for this instant they were sharing the same thoughts. The policeman must have been patrolling for days, maybe never getting out of the car, just driving and looking and upholding the law because he didn't know what else to do. Eric felt very sorry for the policeman, though Eric knew he was a hair's width away from being shot.

He wanted to say some kind thing to him, but he didn't know how to start.

The officer said, his voice gravelly and no less threatening than before, "Looters don't last in this town."

"Yes, sir. I'm just looking for my dad," said Eric.

The man started to replace Eric's goods to his backpack. His hand shook slightly as he lifted a can of peaches.

"Let me help," said Eric as he leaned into the car and reached for the can.

The peaches dropped from the policeman's hand, and in it he held the gun. He was very fast. Eric tried to swallow, couldn't. The end of the barrel, only a foot from his face, looked a mile wide and infinitely deep.

Trapped, his head in the car and off balance, Eric heard the policeman's hard and heavy breath. The man said, "Do you know Gloria?" The gun didn't waver.

Eric tried to answer, but he couldn't force a word through his throat. He shook his head no.

The gun sank to the backpack, and the officer gazed out the front window, turning away from Eric. His voice became distant and soft. "She's about your age. At the hospital with her mom now. They got a touch of something," the policeman said. He focused suddenly on Eric, and his voice became business-like. "I thought maybe you went to school with her."

Cupped loosely around the pistol grip, the man's hand fascinated Eric. He tried to speak again and squeaked out, "I go to Littleton High."

"A Littleton Lion." The policeman slid the gun onto his lap and stuck it between his legs so the barrel pointed down and the grip was still visible. "I was a Golden High Knight. Played football." He licked his lips.

Eric let out a long breath silently and realized he hadn't been breathing. "Uh huh," he said.

"Thousand people buried in that football field now." The policeman gripped the steering wheel. He was wearing a black glove on his left hand. "Don't think the Knights will have a good season this year," he said.

He plucked the radio microphone from the dash and held it to his lips. "Tanner, this is Buck. I'm on 12th and Jackson talking to a Littleton Lion. What you got?"

The radio crackled feebly.

He rested the microphone on his lap and continued to stare out the front window. "Gloria thinks she might be a cheerleader. She's a little bony, but she can do the gymnastics. Eight years of lessons." His chest expanded as he took a deep breath, and when he finally let it out, it shook. "Her mother's real proud. Bought us shirts that say *Gloria's Mom* and *Gloria's Dad*."

He tried the radio again. In the quiet of the car, the steady hiss sounded baleful and lonely. "Nobody home," said the policeman. "Burnt to the ground . . ." He paused and took another deep breath. ". . . just like the hospital. Forgot for a second."

His chin dropped to his chest as if he were too tired to hold it up any longer. "I'm a ghost cop," he said. "Except I'm alive and the city died." Then he waved his hand vaguely in Eric's direction. "You can go."

Quickly, Eric filled his backpack and grabbed his headphones and cassette player. The policeman didn't move. When Eric backed his head out of the window, he started to thank the man—he felt like he should—but then Eric realized the policeman had fallen asleep. His face looked peaceful, and Eric made a sudden connection, an understanding of the policeman in a different role. Eric shook with it, the empathy was so strong. The policeman looked like a man at halftime at a football game, tired from his day's work, but at the game because his daughter was going to cheer. Eric wished that he could tell him the day was okay, that his bony daughter dazzled the crowd, jumping high, clapping her hands, throwing back flips for the team as it entered the field.

Instead, Eric stepped back quietly. Brightness of the sun through the smoke, after the darkness of the car, made him blink back tears.

*

Smoldering ruins dominated the north end of Golden, and the closer he pedaled to the Coors plant, the fewer intact buildings he found. Two jewelry stores side by side, A Touch of Gold and a Zales, had been cleaned out. A spray of velvet display pads littered the sidewalk. After a few blocks, he turned and headed south, but he had no idea where to go now. Should he return to the cave and wait for Dad? How long should he wait before searching again? The image of his mother's body lying still under the plastic chilled him. Thinking about crawling into the cave again to face that lump under the black visqueen made him shake his head. He would ride the bike to Littleton. Dad might have gone there, though he couldn't think of a reason that he would. What really decided him, was the idea of being home. He imagined his bedroom, the posters on the walls, the books lined neatly on the shelves, and his bed, a place of safety and normality. If he could just get home, things would be all right. All of this would go away. He wouldn't have to think about policemen who lost their daughters or cars filled with frightened, angry people being shot at a road block.

At the bottom of Jackson Street, he reached the high school. "Have a good summer!" read the marquee in front of the school. A pair of unattended backhoes squatted on the torn up remains of the football field. One goal post lay on its side. The other stood, a solitary sentinel. He turned onto 24th Street, hoping that it would take him back to U.S. 6 and out of town.

24th ended at Illinois Ave and he could see the highway at the crest of the hill to his right. In the distance, a long way up the hill with several smaller hills between, the two roads intersected. Breaths came hard in the smoky air as he struggled to pedal up the slope. Because he kept his eyes closed part of the time, or stared at the goose neck of the bike so he wouldn't have to look at the hill in front of him, he missed the first black shapes lying on the road's shoulder to his left. When his legs were too tired to push the pedals any farther, he leaned the bike and rested. Then he saw the body bags, hundreds of them like black seed pods lined side by side along the road, stretching to the top of the hill.

At first, he thought they were trash bags, as if the Highway Department had been running grass cutting crews along the roads and were storing the clippings. But when he put the bike down and stood over the closest bag, he knew the truth.

He blinked slowly. His eyes ached from the smoke, and he took a long time to realize what he was looking at. Sun glinted dully off the slick plastic, and the bag was unzipped. Inside, he saw a glimpse of pink flannel. The woman—though the bag covered her face, he guessed it must be a woman—had died in her pajamas. Her hands lay on top each other on her stomach. The top hand was disfigured; it was missing the ring finger.

Eric looked down the long row of bags to his left, toward town. All the bags were unzipped. Hands dangled over the sides of many, and even from here he could see others without ring fingers. He stepped to the next bag. A man's well-tanned arm sprawled across the plastic as if he had tried to extricate himself and then died in mid-effort. A pale band of skin circled his wrist where he must have worn a watch.

Eric knew he should feel something about all these bodies, some sadness or revulsion, but he couldn't. He walked up the hill, pushing his bike. In some bags he saw faces, eyes open or closed, mouths gaping or neatly shut. Some bodies were naked; one man wore a three piece suit. A few bags had more than one body in them, mostly children. All the bags were open, and all Eric felt was a mild curiosity about why.

Near the crest of the hill he heard an engine idling and then a voice. He put the bike down and, bending low, scurried to the top.

In the little valley below, thirty yards away, the white van was parked in the middle of the road. A man, the beetle-eyed one he'd seen earlier, unzipped a bag, reached in, pulled out the body's hands, inspected them, then moved to the next one. A gun in a shoulder holster swung from his chest when he bent over. He held a three foot long pair of bolt cutters. He unzipped again—the harsh rasp reached Eric—and grabbed a hand.

"Got one," he said to the hidden driver in the van. Beetle-Eyes pinned the hand to the body with his foot, maneuvered the bolt cutters into position, then, without pause, snipped off a finger. Eric heard the click of the bolt cutters closing.

The man stripped the ring from the finger, then tossed the finger beyond the body bags into the long weeds beside the road. He put the ring into a heavy sack that hung from his belt and moved to the next bag.

Eric pressed the side of his face to the pavement and closed his eyes. Sun-warmed asphalt burned him, but he didn't move. The enormity of what he was seeing boggled his imagination and sickened him. Surely nothing can top this, he thought. Nothing could be as gross.

He wondered how he was going to get past the van. He couldn't see just riding by, and he thought about going back and finding another way to the highway, but he also wanted to stop them, to turn them in maybe—whatever it would take to get them to leave the bodies alone.

He heard another loud snip. The van rolled a few feet forward to keep up with Beetle-Eyes, who moved from bag to bag with ghoulish efficiency. He unzipped another one and looked the body over speculatively. "Nice tits," he said, then threw the ringless hands back in the bag in disgust. "Why don't I drive for a while?" he said. A voice from the van murmured back. Beetle-Eyes shrugged his shoulders.

As the van move farther away and higher on the hill, Eric crept backwards to stay out of sight. He could no longer hear them, but he saw the pantomime as Beetle-Eyes crouched, opened, inspected, stood and cut, taking rings and watches as he found them, bag after bag.

Finally the van topped the next hill. Eric mounted his bike and rode past the abused bodies, still unsure of what to do, but determined to do something. Once again he was within earshot. Zippers whisked open. Bolt cutters clicked together. Beetle-Eyes cursed the driver's squeamishness. "You'll like what this stuff will buy later," he said. Another finger flew into the weeds. "You got to cut bait to fish." Eric felt his gorge rise.

From the bottom of his backpack, Eric grabbed his slingshot and a handful of ball bearings. Without thinking, he folded the leather patch around the first bearing, stood, drew back, and fired at Beetle-Eyes. The bearing missed but whanged off the van leaving a very satisfying dent.

The man yelled something and hit the asphalt. Flying end over end, the bolt cutters vanished into the weeds. Eric loaded and fired. The shot zinged off the pavement a foot from Beetle-Eye's head, who was trying to crawl backwards under the van. He hadn't seen Eric yet.

Eric placed a third bearing in the slingshot, then Beetle-Eyes spotted him. He unsnapped his gun from its holster and started to aim it, but the van moved forward a foot and Beetle-Eyes panicked, dropped the gun, rolled to his back and pounded on the side of the van. "Stop, you stupid shit. Stop!" he yelled. "I'm under here!" Brake lights flared red.

He glared malevolently at Eric and slid himself from under the van. Without breaking his stare, he reached for the gun.

Eric drew the bearing to his ear; his arm was straight and steady. "Don't do it," he said. Forty yards separated them.

Beetle-Eyes froze, his hand a foot from the pistol. "I don't have to kill you, kid," he said. "You can put that squirrel shooter away and walk right now, but if you try to hurt me again, I'm going to pick up this gun here and blow your head off." His hand inched downward.

Sweat trickled down Eric's face. One good shot, one perfect shot, and Beetle-Eyes would be done, but if he missed, he wouldn't have time to reload. Far away, a bird sang. Eric thought, meadow lark, and released the shot.

He missed.

Beetle-Eyes came up with the gun and straightened from his crouch. Holding it in front of him, he walked toward Eric. "You stupid little kid," he said, then clicked the hammer back.

The meadow lark trilled through his song again. Eric's dad had taught him many bird calls. He couldn't believe that the last thought he would ever have would be the name of a bird song.

Beetle-Eyes stopped. "Oh, shit."

A rumble behind Eric startled him and he stepped aside. Like a black and white boat, the police cruiser flowed past Eric. Through the tinted windows, Eric saw the glint of mirrored sunglasses. The car's brakes screeched loudly when it stopped. Beetle-Eyes stepped backwards, gun at his side, until he bumped into the van.

The police car's door clicked open and Gloria's Dad, the ghost cop, unfolded himself from the driver's seat, his gun gripped in his right hand, the black glove on his left.

Without looking at Beetle-Eyes, he walked to a body bag. Caked mud clung to his boots. Eric wondered if it were from the football field.

The ghost cop bent, inspected the bag, pulled a mangled hand out, then, holding the hand gently in his, bent farther, briefly pressed his forehead to the dead person's hand, then tucked it back into the bag. He zipped it shut and stood.

"We just got here," shouted Beetle-Eyes. "The kid will tell you!" He pointed his gun at Eric, as if he'd forgotten that he held it.

The ghost cop brought his revolver up and fired. Echoes bounced back. Eric had seen many movies. He'd seen a million shootings, but this wasn't like anything he'd seen. The shot was sharper, more crisp, but less loud than he'd imagined. A very distinct puff of smoke drifted away from the gun. He followed it until it dissipated.

Beetle-Eyes sat, his legs spread in a V, his head resting against the bumper. Tears slicked his cheeks.

"You didn't have to do that," he said. Eric couldn't see any blood on Beetle-Eyes, but a single rivulet of red streaked the white van where he had stood. He sniffed, "I wasn't doing anything." His sack had ruptured at the bottom and rings and watches reflected sunlight in a pile beside him.

The ghost cop dug into his back pocket and brought out a pair of hand cuffs. Keeping his gun trained on Beetle-Eyes, he clipped one wrist and reached for the other.

Out of sight from the cop, but where Eric could see, the passenger door swung quietly open. Slowly, a sneakered foot, then a bare leg slid into view. The ghost cop struggled to cuff the other hand, but the mechanism seemed jammed. Beetle-Eyes blubbered, "I'm sorry. I'm sorry. Don't hurt me." Stunned by the nearness of his own death, by the violence of the shooting, Eric watched slack jawed, as if the event were television. Whatever anger had motivated him to confront Beetle-Eyes was gone.

A short-skirted woman hefting a baseball bat emerged from the door. She raised the bat above her head and ran around the corner of the van where the ghost cop knelt over Beetle-Eyes.

Eric snapped out of his lethargy. "Watch out!"

Arching her back like a woodsman, the woman paused before swinging the bat.

The ghost cop rolled, fired; the woman fell.

Beetle-Eyes stretched for his gun, got it, swung it around.

The ghost cop fired.

Two puffs of smoke floated away like carnival balloons.

Dusting his pants off, the ghost cop trudged back to the cruiser, gun hanging from his hand as if it weighed a hundred pounds. From the back of the car he took two of the black plastic tarps Eric had seen earlier and unfolded them. They were body bags.

As Eric watched, the cop uncuffed Beetle-Eyes, fitted a bag over him and rolled him over so he could close it; then he bagged the woman. He tossed her bat in the bag with her and drug both of them to the side of the road along with the other bodies. Everything he did, he did tiredly, seeming to barely have the strength to move himself from place to place.

Stooping over the last bag Beetle-Eyes had robbed, the ghost cop placed the hands inside and zipped it up. He moved to the next one and did the same.

Eric turned and looked behind him at the hundreds of open bags and beyond them where oily black smoke poured into the sky from the Coors plant. A meadow lark lilted through its notes again and the sun shimmered in waves off the road. Eric went to the nearest bag. Trying not to look in, he gripped the large, square zipper tab and pulled it shut. Soon the cop caught up with him and, not speaking, they worked together moving from body bag to body bag, softly putting hands back inside and closing them.

An hour or so later, when they finished, Eric straightened painfully and rubbed his back. The cop's face was an agony of exhaustion lines, the skin sallow and muscleless.

Eric said, "Maybe you should go home." The mirrored sunglasses reflected blankly back at him. "Nobody will know."

Wind flicked hair across Eric's eyes. He brushed it back. The cop said, "I haven't been relieved." And that seemed to settle it for him.

They walked back to the cruiser. Eric collected his bike and
backpack from the road. When he left, the cop was sitting in the
car, door open, his hands wrapped around the steering wheel.

At the top of the hill, where Illinois Ave. met U.S. 6, Eric looked
back. The line of body bags stretched almost to town, a black border on the road. Distinctly, Eric heard a car door slam and an engine start. Then the cruiser rose out of a valley in the road and
headed for Golden's smoke and fire and emptiness. Eric watched
until it vanished from sight.

Chapter Nine

THE FLATS

O ur fourth morning, Eric thought, and we're still in good spirits. Dodge led, dashing from side to side to pick flowers, Indian Paint Brush and Rocky Mountain Bee Plants. Rabbit hung back and whistled tunelessly. Eric strode up the highway, pleased by the hardness in his leg muscles that a few days of activity had given him. He did a skip step. Highway 93 roller-coasted generally uphill north out of Golden in front of him along the foothills to Boulder. Eric compared the landscape to what they had passed through before; this was the first that had not been a part of the suburbs. Ruins of shopping malls, subdivisions and shopettes dominated the ten miles west from the Platte River, and the fifteen miles north to Golden. But here, he hiked through real country. Clean of brick walls, concrete foundations, or houses in varied states of decay, the grasses dropped away from the road through a gentle valley to lap against a scrub pine shoreline at the foothills a mile away.

He rubbed his sun-warmed right cheek. Four days of stubble scratched his palm. He felt poetic. Perfect weather, he thought.

> Sun rises . . . like a great red whale.
> Mid-afternoon: cloudless, arching blue
> storm builds on mountain
> cool breeze wipes the day.

He shook his head at that last part. Weather poems, he thought, are never as good as the weather. That bit about a red whale, though, that's nice.

He remembered last night's sunset. The clouds broke and bands of color flowed from the west, first yellow, then orange and red, then indigo and violet. What a spectacle! As he hiked, he found himself thinking about dust in the atmosphere. The dawn and evening displays this year reminded him of the first few years after the plague, when the sun rose and set in sullen glory, which he attributed to ashes from fires in cities filled with the dead.

By midmorning, Eric's legs that he'd been so proud of burned with fatigue. He bit his lip and struggled not to limp. He envied the boys' energy to run back and forth across the road in front of him, showing each other things they had found: a length of PVC pipe, a glass telephone line insulator, a rusted hammer head without a handle. They're as fresh as the first day, he thought.

Pain rose for another half hour, each step driving spears into his hips and calves. Small fires embered behind his knee caps. Head down, he watched his foot placement. A flat step hurt less, but any roll to either side flared new pains. I'm just plain old, he thought. Old and out of gas. The phrase made him smile. Dodge used it occasionally, so did Troy. Neither knew what it meant. Several expressions came to him: "Run it up the flag pole and see who salutes." "Give me a ring." "Drop me a line." "That does not compute." He said aloud, "Put the pedal to the metal boys." Dodge looked back at him. Eric shook his head. "Nothing, son. Just a thought."

He concentrated on walking. Heat radiated off the buckled and fractured asphalt, and the weeds that grew with such enthusiasm a few miles earlier, looked dispirited. Everything about the landscape now seemed beaten down and tired. By the road, large parcels of caked and cracked ground were free of grasses altogether. He imagined how the dust must kick up here on windy days. Only bushes, laurels and what his dad used to call greasewood, thrived. He struggled with why the look of the land would change so drastically in just a couple of hours of walking, but his legs' pains messed up his concentration.

Step, step, step, he thought; even the sky has lost its color. It pressed down like a slab of gray slate, and the sun pulsed in its midst, its edges fuzzy. He kept his eyes down, watching his feet. Dust covered the road. Little puffs marked each footfall. Dodge's small sneakers left perfect imprints and made Eric think of black and white photographs from the moon, where he supposed the astronauts' footprints still existed around the pile of unrusting equipment they'd left behind.

He bumped into Dodge, who had stopped. I'll never get momentum again, he thought, and almost snapped at the boy until he looked up and saw what was in their way. Three wooden poles jutted from the asphalt, and impaled on their tops at eye height, animal skulls. Suddenly grateful for the rest, Eric fingered one, a cow skull, bleached and toothless. A fringe of bone pieces dangled on short strings threaded through holes bored in the back of the skull. He stuck a finger through an eye socket and wiggled it for Dodge and Rabbit to see. The bone fragments clattered against each other.

"Don't," said Rabbit. "It belongs to somebody."

Eric wiped his hand on his shirt. Totems, he thought. Every hundred yards in both directions, other poles held their bones to the sky. An uninterrupted line stretched east across the plain into the city, and to the west the line vanished into the pines. "We have to go this way," he said, and shivered when he stepped across the boundary the totems drew across the road.

Somber now, Dodge stayed close to Eric, whose leg pains had been replaced by a loose, empty feeling. Eric feared he might fall any moment. Rabbit quit whistling and walked next to the side of the road like a coyote ready to bolt. The grasses, what few patches there were, hissed in a hot breeze that didn't dry the sweat on Eric's forehead, and he caught himself weaving as he walked.

The bones, he thought, mean something to someone. Something primitive. He imagined how wind must moan through the bone holes in the bone heads, how lonely it would be to walk upon them if he'd been by himself. He looked back. Heat waves shimmered off the road, and the skulls in the distance wavered and danced. Eric stumbled.

A hand grasped Eric's wrist, steadying him. Dodge's eyes met his, and Eric could see the worry. "I'm okay," said Eric, but Dodge held firmly, and Eric let him support some of his weight. Dodge's fine-boned fingers reminded Eric of Troy at two, walking along the river. Troy loved to throw rocks in the water, and they'd spent hours making splashes. Dodge's clasp on his wrist brought the memory back like it was all new again, and Eric's eyes' watered.

"Maybe we should camp early today, Grandfather," said Dodge. Rabbit looked back at them and nodded.

Eric didn't argue, and let himself be led to a shaded spot part way up a hill above the road. Cottonwoods will keep the sun off my head, he thought, and after a lunch that seemed bland and a little nauseating, he laid back, enduring his legs' throbbing. Dodge gathered leaves to spread under their sleeping bags. Eric pressed the heels of his hands into the tops of his thighs, rolling the muscle down to his knees. He bit back a cry. How can so little muscle hurt so much?

Closing his eyes and pushing hard, he started the massage again. Then he felt hands on his. Rabbit bent over him, his long hair obscuring his scars, and rubbed Eric's legs. His strong hands kneaded the calf muscles, pressing them against the bones hard enough to hurt. He winced, and Rabbit let up a bit. Such a strange boy, Eric thought. So quiet, so distant, and he does this for me. Eric rested his hand on Rabbit's shoulder. The boy didn't look up, but he didn't shrug the hand away either. After a few minutes Eric relaxed; the pain subsided to waves of comfort, and not soon after, he fell asleep.

*

Something punched him, and Eric roused himself from a dream of a cop car appearing at the crests of hills, then disappearing until it was just a dot that blended into the burning town at the end of the road.

"We're not alone," whispered Dodge.

Blue-gray predawn shadows colored the bushes and cottonwoods. Dodge huddled against him. "I'm scared," he said.

"What is it?" Eric said as he groped in his backpack for the slingshot. He sat up and looked around. Only the faintest blush of light of the horizon told him it was other than night. The trees stood starkly in their shadows. The grasses were a wash of gray.

Dodge pointed. "Can't you see them?"

A gust rustled the cottonwoods. Eric shivered. At the edge of where a cooking fire would cast light if it were lit, sitting or crouching in the grasses, a dozen still figures surrounded their camp site.

"Are they men?" asked Dodge.

Eric squinted, tried to use the dim light to discern more of the watchers' features. "Yes," he said. "Who are you?" Eric called. Leaves brushed together, muttering in the wind. The figures didn't answer. After a moment Eric said, "Go away. You're frightening the boy."

One figure stood. He carried a staff or a long, unstrung bow. Darkness hid his face and the kind of clothes he wore, but Eric saw a flicker of light in his eyes when he turned and walked into the shadows. The other watchers faded into the landscape. Eric blinked. The visitors had made no sounds.

"Where's Rabbit?" Eric asked. A flat sleeping bag marked where the boy had slept. Eric scrambled from his bag, ignoring the stiffness in his legs, over to Rabbit's spot. Where is he? He dashed a few steps away from camp. As far as he could see, black, blue and gray shapes formed the landscape. To the west, the foothills and mountains behind them loomed like tidal waves on the horizon. Below their camp, the two-lane highway cut through hip-high weeds. "Where'd he go?"

Dodge said, "A noise woke me." Now that the dark figures were gone, he seemed more self assured. "Maybe what I heard was Rabbit. I didn't see anything. Then the men came."

Eric placed his hands into the small of his back and pushed. He worried that the men had taken Rabbit, but he said, keeping his voice calm, "We won't find him until it's lighter. Let's eat, then we can look."

As they finished their breakfast of dried fruits and beef jerky, the sky lightened and the wind died down. A couple of hundred yards away, on the crest of the hill overlooking their camp, Eric saw the group that had surrounded them, sitting. They too appeared to be eating. Watching them closely for hostile movement, Eric put on his backpack and prepared to track Rabbit. From the dew-cleared path of grass leading from his sleeping bag, it was clear that he had headed north, parallel to the highway, but as soon as Eric and Dodge broke camp, the group on the hill stood and walked down toward them.

"Stay close," said Eric. He kept himself between Dodge and the strangers.

The men drifted toward them like a mist. In the dawn light, they moved . . . deliberately. He could think of no better word. Each watched where he was stepping, missing twigs or patches of dry leaves, like deer crossing a meadow. They wore leather skirts—their bare legs were sun browned—and what looked like home-spun-wool shirts. Moccasins. No socks. Each carried a bow, a spear or a staff. Several were weighted with heavy, leather water bags. He guessed they were in their twenties except for the one leading, who might be forty or fifty. A broad-chested man with a weathered face and light blue eyes above a gray-flecked beard, he planted himself in front of Eric. The others spread out in a semi-circle.

He raised an empty hand to Eric and Dodge. "I'm sorry, old one, but you can't go farther on this road." The voice rumbled.

"Where's the boy?" demanded Eric. His own firm voice surprised him. The smallest and weakest of the men out-weighed him by at least thirty pounds. They seemed like cave men, hard and rangy and animal like.

Gray Beard looked puzzled. He gestured at his men. "We have no boys here." The deepness of his voice impressed Eric. The man spoke from the bottom of a well.

"Our boy," said Eric. "Where is he?"

Gray Beard glanced around, then signaled one of his party. "Skylar, you had the watch. Where is the other one?"

A man carrying a heavy water bag looked embarrassed and shrugged his shoulders.

"Find him," ordered Gray Beard. Skylar dropped the bag and circled the camp. He found the trail Eric had noticed earlier and pointed north.

"He's gone into the Flats," said Skylar.

Gray Beard threw his staff on the ground and stamped his foot. "After him, all of you!" The men melted into the underbrush, and Gray Beard, Eric and Dodge were left to contemplate the rising sun.

The rush of men hurrying off, the strangely dressed man standing next to him, and the mystery of Rabbit's whereabouts confused Eric. He took a step to follow Rabbit's trail, but Dodge tugged on his arm. "We're supposed to stay here, I think," he whispered.

Gray Beard picked up his staff, inspecting it for cracks. "The Flats," he said. "One job to do, and I ruin it." He turned to Eric. "The boy won't go far, do you think? He'll come back on his own?" Concern creased his features. Eric thought his posture was odd—forced and uncomfortable—as if he expected Eric to scold him.

Gray Beard twisted both hands slowly on the staff. "Damn."

Eric said, "What is this about the Flats? Do you mean Rocky Flats?" Rocky Flats were a few miles to the north and east, he remembered. They used to make triggers for nuclear weapons there.

"The Flats," he said. "We just call them the Flats." Gray Beard bent and rubbed his hand over the fabric of Eric's sleeping bag. "You're jackals," he said, "but that won't keep you safe."

Eric remembered Rabbit's story about the little girl who called him a jackal. "What do you mean, safe?"

The man smiled at him, a strained smile but an honest-seeming one that softened his face and crinkled long laugh lines from the corners of his eyes. Eric felt less threatened by him, although still frightened for Rabbit. Whatever was happening, this man was scared.

Gray Beard said, "I don't believe the stories, but some of the others do, that Jackals are protected from the spirits in the Flats."

"Spirits?"

The man leaned on his staff and looked past Eric to where the others had headed in their pursuit of Rabbit. "Spirits. Gods perhaps. But my parents told me the Flats were *always* evil, that even in the Gone Times people feared it. Not because of spirits though. Plutonium contamination." He pronounced "plutonium contamination" a syllable at a time, as if they were foreign words. Eric wondered if he had any idea what they meant. The man continued, "Animals don't go into the Flats. People who are stupid enough to go in get sick. Some die."

What a strange superstition, Eric thought. "So you patrol the border, to keep people out?"

Gray Beard shrugged his shoulders. "Foolish people come and go as they please until an animal eats them or they fall off cliffs. Nobody patrols the boundary. If they ignore a clear warning, who can help them? We have been following you since you sang with the wolves." He paused, embarrassed-looking, as if he were waiting for Eric to laugh at him. "Some of the men think you are a spirit, a manitou. Wolves carry power. To sing with them is a rare gift."

Dodge stiffened beside when Gray Beard mentioned following them. "Bugbears, Grandpa. They're the Bugbears."

Eric put a hand on Dodge's shoulder and pulled him close. "I know." After being trailed the entire trip (and why?), after listening to Phil's fears, actually meeting them seemed anticlimactic. They're just men in badly made clothes, and what do they want with us?

Too many mysteries here, he thought, but he didn't let his confusion show on his face. He remembered the first night he left Littleton—it seemed long ago, now—and howling with the wolves in the middle of the night. Their long, sturdy shadows milled around the base of the rock he slept on, and they made harmonies to the sky.

Gray Beard said, "It's a small thing, really, I told them, but the young men see the world differently. Lots of ways you could've acted around the wolves, and maybe we'd have stopped you from going into the Flats anyway. No one has come so far from the Jackals in years, and you're old—we don't see many old ones away from their homes—but of all the things you could've done, you sang, so we've been watching. We wouldn't want you to come this far, then have plutonium get you." He glanced north into the brush.

Eric looked too. Surely the man's fear of Rocky Flats was un-justified, but he realized he knew nothing about how plutonium was stored. All he remembered was the incredible toxicity of the ele-ment. A millionth of a grain, less than a dust mote, on your skin would kill. When the plague hit, was the facility safely shut down? Were they even still working with plutonium? He shivered.

Dodge handed Eric a coat. "You should wrap up, Grandpa," he said. Clouds glowed on the horizon. Sunrise was a few minutes away. "How far north would be unsafe?" asked Eric as he pushed his hand into a sleeve.

Gray Beard shrugged. "A mile or two maybe. Who knows what plutonium will do? We don't trespass." He turned, concerned again. "It will kill him if he gets too far. I've seen men who've tried to cross. They . . ." He paused. "Their deaths are . . . ugly." He stopped as if contemplating a bad memory. "He won't get too far. A town boy. My men will find him soon."

Eric thought about the way Rabbit could move in the under-brush, his preternatural speed and sense of self preservation. "Not if he doesn't want them to," Eric said.

*

A half hour after the sun rose, one of the men dashed into the campsite. Gray Beard still stood, leaning on his staff. Eric and Dodge had rewrapped themselves in the sleeping bags. Eric had been guess-ing at what Rabbit had done. When he heard (or sensed?) the ap-proach of the strangers, he must have awakened, realized there were too many to stand up to, and fled. He must have figured that he could do more good if he were free than if the men captured him. But why did he go north? He wouldn't leave us, would he, and try to reach Boulder on his own?

The man said, "He lost us, Teach. Got off the soft ground. Skylar split the group, though. He can't stay gone long." Gray Beard nodded an acknowledgment, and the man ran back into the brush.

Gray Beard shook his head. "Boy must be as fast as blue blazes."

Eric pulled the sleeping bag off his shoulders. It was a climbing expedition bag, and too warm for the summer. "He called you Teach. Is that your name?"

Gray Beard squatted and faced him, the sun flush on his face. "It's what I do. Teacher. Teach. It's a good name. You're Eric. Littleton's oldest resident. The last of the Gone Time survivors."

Eric started at his own name. Teach said, "We've heard you talking. That one," he pointed to Dodge, "is your grandson, Dodge. The other is Rabbit."

"But who are you? Where are your people? Why were you following me in the first place?"

A different man ran into the camp. Teach looked up at him. "Skylar picked up the boy's trail and we followed it for a while, but he doubled back. Then we figured out he lead us in a big figure eight. The little demon has us going in circles."

Teach thought for a second, then said, "Ignore the trail. Tell Skylar to spread the men out and come back toward this camp. Better poke a stick into every hole or pile of leaves. The boy knows what he's doing."

He turned back to Eric and Dodge. "I've told you who I am." He scratched a figure in the dirt at his feet, a circle, then smoothed the image away. "We live upstream." He nodded toward the mountains, now drenched with light, the high peaks of the continental divide still white and glistening with snow.

Eric didn't know what to ask next, but there was something alien about Teach, not just his clothes, but his demeanor, something wildly awake about him. When he wasn't speaking, he listened, not just to Eric, but to the air. He rested his head on the breeze. His nostrils flared, like a blink, a couple of times a minute. He didn't behave like someone who spent time indoors a lot. It would be hard to sneak past this man at night.

Teach tilted his head to the side, then stood. The man he'd called Skylar stepped through the bushes and approached Teach. "We cornered him," said Skylar, "but he got away. The boy's a devil, Teach. I say we let him go and the Flats can have him." A large purple knot swelled below the young man's left eye. He touched it gingerly with his fingertips. "He's good with rocks too. Jackson caught one in the knee, and I think we'll have to carry him home."

Teach said, "He's not going north, then?"

Skylar spit. "Bah! He's gaming with us. He stuck his tongue at me before he threw the rock."

Teach laughed. "How'd you let that happen? You were a sharp little rock thrower yourself once."

Skylar scowled at him, then stalked out of camp.

"They won't catch him, I think," said Eric, "unless he thinks Dodge and I are safe."

"Good," Teach said, "if that means he's not heading into the Flats."

They waited for an hour. Three times men came to report no progress. Eric and Dodge packed their sleeping bags. Dodge didn't seem to be afraid for Rabbit or of Teach, and Eric found himself more relaxed around the man, even though he wasn't sure if he was a friend, an odd stranger or their captor. Finally Eric said, "You followed us for days secretly. Now that you've come out in the open, what's your plan?"

Teach said, "Today, the wind is my plan." He added, "Getting off the flats." He scuffed the dirt at his feet. "And maybe asking you to talk to my students about the Gone Time around a campfire. They love ghost stories. Or you could tell them about singing with wolves."

Teach cocked his head to the side, listening. In the distance, a bird chirped. A bit closer, another answered. That's like no bird I've heard, thought Eric. Sounded like nut-hatches, sort of. From the hill above them, a third chirp drifted down. Ah, he thought, not birds at all. Men. He listened intently. After a few minutes he knew approximately where all of Teach's men were, and Rabbit probably knew too. If they kept chirping, they'd never catch him.

Eric touched Dodge's shoulder. Leaning against his backpack, the boy was almost asleep. "Dodge, can you do a meadowlark for me?" He nodded, pursed his lips and blew. The first try came out airy. The top note of a meadowlark's call is high and hard to hit. He tried again, and the call trilled down perfectly.

"That's good, boy," said Teach. "Meadowlark's a tough one."

From the middle of a bush fifteen feet away, a meadowlark answered. The bush shook, and Rabbit rose from the center of it like a wood sprite, twigs and leaves caught in his hair, a goose egg-sized rock clasped in each hand.

Teach didn't even look particularly surprised. He sighed, put two fingers in his mouth and whistled. Within a couple of minutes all of the men returned. The last one limped in, supported by two others, his knee darkly swollen. "I was looking the wrong direction," he said cheerfully. "I figure I can walk on it. Might have to go slow, though. Heck of a throw from thirty yards." He gave Rabbit a thumbs up.

*

"My parents destroyed the old Coal Creek Canyon Road from the highway to the canyon itself," said Teach. Eric walked behind him; Dodge and Rabbit followed. Spread to either side, the rest of the men hiked, sometimes in sight, other times hidden behind thick stands of scrub oak. We can't be leaving much of a trail, observed Eric.

Teach continued, "They told me they blocked all the ways into the mountains. Some they blew up, like the Boulder Creek Road. Knocked down half a canyon. The Peak to Peak Highway to Black Hawk and Central City they cut the bridges. But this one, they obliterated. Earth movers, my dad told me. He and a handful of others dug it up, spread the asphalt and replanted. He called it a 'deconstruction project' or 'highway beautification.'" Teach's thick, bare calves flexed as he stepped onto a deadfall branch and pushed himself over. Unscarred foothills rose before them, and the land looked clean and untouched. If there had been a highway here fifty years ago, they did a darned good job hiding it, Eric thought.

Eric puffed. Legs, achy and weak, protested at the pace, and they'd generally been climbing since they'd walked into what looked like an open field to the west of Colorado 93. "Must have been afraid of people coming," he said, finally. "Somebody got the tunnel on U.S. 6 west out of Denver the summer I was there."

Teach looked back over his shoulder. "U.S. 6?"

Eric rested, pressing his hand deep into his side, thought a second, then said, "Clear Creek Canyon Road."

"Oh, yes." Teach stopped. "Here, let me handle that." He took Eric's pack. A broad sweat patch on Eric's back cooled quickly, and as soon as they started again he felt like Teach had subtracted years, not pounds. Teach said, "Couldn't do anything about the maps, Dad told me, but a line on paper doesn't mean much if you can't find the road it belongs to."

Eric tried to reconstruct a map of Colorado. He had a good head for geography. The Coal Creek Canyon Road led to . . . to . . . Golden

Gate Canyon State Park, he thought. And above that, a couple of little towns. He couldn't remember their names, but he didn't think the road cut north soon. Every step took them farther from Boulder. If we could just go straight, we're probably not ten miles away. He looked north, past the hills, to Boulder and its library, if it still existed. "How far do we have to go?" he asked.

"We might make Pinecliffe today." Teach looked back again, obviously gauging Eric's fitness. "Maybe not. Then it's another day and a half to Highwater."

Eric couldn't place the name. "Highwater?"

It was Teach's turn to think a second. "Nederland in the Gone Times. That's where we live. It isn't safe to cut any closer to the Flats than that, and there isn't a good trail anyway."

Nederland, Eric recalled, was an old mining town twenty or thirty miles into the mountains and not too far from the Continental Divide. A big difference between twenty and thirty when you're walking, he thought.

A granite boulder blocked their path. Eric drug his hand across its rough face as they walked around, but another one the same size stood next to the first. A wall of boulders choked the mouth of the narrow canyon they were about to enter. "Your dad did all this?" Eric asked. He thought, what an immense project!

"Persistent man," said Teach as he ducked into a narrow passage. The rest of the men had vanished. There must be many entrances, thought Eric. Dodge and Rabbit pushed into the corridor behind him. Rock framed a narrow band of sky. Dust kicked up in the passage scratched Eric's eyes, and he rubbed his wrist across his nose to keep from sneezing. Then they broke into the open on the other side and Eric could see the extent of Teach's father's work. From side to side boulders choked the skinny opening of the steep valley. A man on foot would have no trouble getting through, but Eric doubted that one could lead a pack animal through the jumble, and a car, of course, would be stopped.

Coal Creek, a three-foot wide ripple, tumbled down beside the two-lane asphalt road and dove under a pair of the boulders. Dodge walked to the creek's edge and knelt to take a drink.

In a move frighteningly fast for a man his size, Teach reached him and grabbed his wrist. For an instant the tabula was frozen, the hulking, leather-clad savage bent over the slight child. Eric's breath seized in his chest.

"Don't, son," Teach said. "Not till we're at Highwater." He released Dodge and turned to Eric and Rabbit. "Let me see your canteens." After sniffing them disdainfully, he dumped the water on the ground. "You'll drink from our supplies till I tell you different."

Friend or foe? thought Eric. The ribbon of asphalt wound up the valley. The group walked single file now, Teach in the lead, then Eric, the boys, and the rest of Teach's men, his students as Teach had called them. Students of what? What does Teach, teach? Not too far ahead, maybe a mile, the bush-covered hills gave way to more rugged mountains, and Eric could see that granite, canyon walls swallowed the road and Coal Creek.

Dodge pressed close behind Eric and whispered, "They're Bugbears, Grandpa. I was just thirsty. He's mean." Dodge sounded more angry than frightened. Eric reached back and patted him on the arm.

They rounded another corner. Here the old road builders had calved away a portion of a landscape to make way for the road. The bed cut deep through a hill, leaving almost vertical walls on either side. The clean cut revealed layers of different colored rocks. A million years an inch, thought Eric, and when mankind is done, we'll be no thicker than a coat of paint on top of all of it.

He walked close to one wall and saw that the road builders had cut into a seep. A line of dampness oozed at about head height and stretched the length of the cut. He reached to touch it, then drew his hand back. The seep looked unhealthy. Instead of clear water, it was red, and it thickly stained the rocks below. He stopped walking. For fifty feet in front of him, the red moisture coated the rocks, and he smelled something from it, coppery and foul. Coal Creek, only a couple of feet wide here, and fast, rushed by the base of the cut. Red leeched into the stream. Tendrils of it eddied in little pools, then vanished in the water that snatched it downstream.

In the length of creek from the boulders to here, not a thread of algae waved in the current, and, he realized, he'd seen no minnows, water striders or tadpoles, and not a single bird near the stream. He thought of the poem he'd made up that morning, where he'd compared the sun to a red whale surfacing on the horizon, but now he thought of the Earth as the whale, and somehow it was cut, and here it was wounded. Layers of rock scraped away like skin.

As if reading his mind, Teach stepped beside Eric and gazed at the red slime that slid down the crusty rocks into the tiny stream. "The land bleeds," said Teach.

Chapter Ten

MORE PRECIOUS THAN WATER, AND NOT SO THIN

After five miles of riding his bike down U.S. 6, throwing himself to the gravel shoulder once when a truck rocketed by on the other side of the median heading west, cringing at the sound of a distant shot, too drained and frightened to consider crying, Eric decided to jump the waist-high concrete divider and head south to Littleton on the smaller streets. He crossed the two-lane frontage road into Union Ridge Park, where the grass was uncut but well watered. Sprinklers at the far edge of the park popped up and sprayed long streams. Sun rainbowed in the mist, and the air smelled wet and green. He paused at the swing sets. Their metal seats hung motionless above well-worn grooves in the grass. I used to swing, he thought. Feet in the air, head down. Whoosh. He imagined sitting quietly, hands wrapped around the chains, his feet dragging in the dust, waiting for Dad to give him a push. When his hip began to go numb from the bike leaning against it, he realized he hadn't moved for minutes.

A sound behind him made him start to turn. Then it seemed his head swelled, the ground slipped away—he was falling—and as he fell, he twisted and saw the sky. Slowly, so slowly it seemed, it turned to black.

*

Waves marched out of the horizon, green and glassy, building as they got closer. A hundred feet from shore, Eric saw a dark form in the water. A seal? he thought. Dad said there might be seals, but it was a patch of seaweed riding up the solid-looking slope. A frond waved forlornly at the crest, then disappeared as the wave slid in. Seconds later the smooth, cascade leaned too far forward, toppled from the top into foam and noise to rush up the beach, spent at his toes. Sizzling like bacon, the water slid back into the ocean to be swallowed by the next wave.

He scooted a foot closer to the sea, playing a game with the waves.

Far away from the beach, in another world, Eric strained against consciousness. His head hurt, and something pulled against his chest, holding him under the arms.

I'm dreaming I'm three. It's the San Francisco trip when I was three, and we spent an afternoon on the coast.

He didn't want to wake up—the world was bad; awful things waited for him there—he forced himself back to the dream.

Wind pushed spray into his face. He wiped the salt from his eyes. The next wave spilled itself on the sand, but stopped a yard short. He scrunched closer, and the next wash of water sent him scurrying backwards like a crab. He giggled. We're playing tag, he thought. The film of water, no thicker than his hand, rushed away from him. Eric jumped up. Sand fell off his calves, and he brushed the back of his overalls. He loved the brass buttons that snapped the shoulder straps on because he could do them himself. Not like his shoelaces; they still gave him trouble. He rushed down the firm sand after the retreating wave. Water wants to play, he thought. I'll chase it. But the wave retreated too quickly. I'll catch you. He ran, hands outstretched, reaching, laughing, toward the ocean.

Then, the next wave towered above him, and he stopped, his feet rooted to the sand.

The dreamer Eric whimpered—he heard himself make the noise out of his dream—it was one he had often. The wave, that huge, unstoppable wave looming up, and panic, like frozen oil filling his head. Oh, Dad, he thought, and in the dream he looked back up the beach and saw his dad, a tiny figure, miles away it seemed.

"Daddy," he yelled, and the ocean roared above him. "Daddy!"

Nothing could save him; time stopped. He squirmed, and whatever pinched him under the arms squeezed even tighter, and then, in the dream, his dad was there, swooping Eric up and out of harm's way, the water reaching no higher than Dad's waist.

Dad held him high, hands locked under Eric's armpits, and he laughed with Eric as the wave bubbled and foamed on the sand. Eric reached down and hugged his dad's head.

The dreamer Eric thought, I'm alive. I'm alive and safe with my dad.

I can wake now. The dream is over. Everything is okay.

*

He awoke.

Nothing was okay.

Eyes closed, he struggled to breathe, but a tight band of pressure constricted his chest.

Also, in dull, thudding rhythms, the back of his head throbbed. He tried to touch it, sure he'd find a baseball-sized lump, but his hands were trapped behind his back, and, oddly, he still felt his dad's strong grip supporting his armpits. He was swaying, as if Dad were carrying him, but he knew he was awake. Finally, Eric forced his eyes open.

Slowly, the room rotated to his left. Eric felt nauseated, and clamped his eyes shut again. I'm in a basement, he thought. He'd seen a small window high on the wall. No other lights. Open rafters. Cement floor. A dusty water heater and furnace in a corner next to a beat up, wooden door; the edge of a toilet beyond in a darkened room. His inner ear told him he was still moving, so he sneaked another peek. I'm hanging! Below his feet, a tall, backless bar stool lay on its side. He kicked once and started swinging side to side. The rope creaked above him.

"Stay still," said a voice behind him. Eric kicked himself around. As he rotated, he saw two other people on stools next to the wall. The closest one, a woman in her mid-twenties, dark hair, said, "I told you to not move. You'll just get sick."

The man sitting beside her *did* look sick. Eyes shut, face drawn, he sagged against his rope. On the next circuit, Eric saw that their ropes were tied to their necks, not their chests, and their hands were tied behind their backs too. He wondered if the sick man were dead, but the man shifted in his stool without opening his eyes. Two empty nooses hung from the rafters beyond them. An unlit stairwell led upstairs. Beside it, on the wall, hung a Budweiser mirror, and on the other side, a dart board, one of the fancy kinds with levered doors. Light blue or gray paint covered the walls except in the large patches where it had peeled away to the cement. He spun slowly, and when he stopped he faced the wall behind his stool.

Duct tape held a Grateful Dead poster to the wall, the poster of a violin-playing skeleton with a long stemmed rose in his teeth.

"Are you all right?" asked the woman.

"It's hard to breathe," said Eric. Dots swam through his vision. On the other stool, the man coughed weakly.

The woman said, "Listen close. I'm going to call for help, but we're in a fix here and probably going to die." She had a narrow face, fine boned, and her dark hair fell in ringlets to the collar of her blouse. "But we're not dead yet, so don't do anything stupid."

Her voice was low and hoarse, like she'd bruised her throat, and Eric strained to hear her.

She continued, "There are two of them. I know what they want, so they won't kill us right away, but don't tick them off. The man, Jared, is the worst, but Meg is dangerous too." She paused. Eric tried to take a full breath; the pressure was too much.

"You got that?" she said.

"Yes," he gasped.

She faced the stairwell and yelled, "Hey! We need some help down here!" Except for the wheezy breathing from the man who still hadn't opened his eyes, Eric heard nothing. The woman shouted again, then the ceiling squeaked, and he heard heavy footsteps. A door opened and light filled the stairwell.

Jared was a fifty-year-old slob. Eric guessed he might be five and a half feet tall, but he probably weighed over two-hundred and fifty pounds, most of it in his gut that hung out of the dirty t-shirt and nearly covered his yellowed underwear. Brown hair with streaks of white stuck straight up on the left side of his head, as if he'd slept on it. His breath reeked of alcohol, his pocked complexion was flushed, and his eyes watery. He stretched up and put his hand on Eric's forehead.

"Not hot. No fever at all," Jared said to Meg. He coughed hard, doubling over, then hawked phlegm onto the floor. "I told you so." He smirked and gave Eric a push that swung him hard enough that his feet hit the wall behind him. Eric clenched his teeth so he wouldn't scream. The rope bit under his arms and pulled underarm hairs out.

Meg snorted, stepped forward and put the flat of her hand on Eric's chest, stopping his motion. She was big too, huge, maybe the same weight but a couple of inches taller than Jared, and younger by fifteen or twenty years. Eric's momentum didn't jolt her at all. He just stopped. She bent down, picked up the fallen stool and, supporting Eric's weight with an arm wrapped around his waist, slid it under his butt.

The pressure off his chest, Eric almost fell over. She steadied him. He could feel the fever baking out of her. "You gonna stay there?" she said. Her bloodshot eyes looked right in to his from six inches away, and her breath smelled sick, like old cough drops. Underneath that smell came something else, something sad and slippery and rotting. Eric didn't flinch away, but tried not to inhale too deeply. He looked at her lips, which were incredibly chapped. Cracked scabs covered the corners of her mouth.

He nodded, and she stepped back. She was wearing jeans and a red flannel shirt. Eric had never seen such an expanse of flannel before. Neatly combed blonde hair fell to her shoulders from a dead-centered part.

"I'm gonna change your rope, youngster. Now that you're awake, I don't want you thinking about going anywhere." She stepped behind him. "Jared," she snapped. He snatched his hand off the dark-haired woman's thigh and got a club from beside the water heater. It looked like a cut-in-half baseball bat. Duct tape, the same type holding the Grateful Dead poster, wrapped around the end of it. Jared rubbed his hand up and down its length, glaring at Eric as Meg undid the rope, then retied it around his neck. "If you get too rambunctious here, you'll choke to death. You got that?" She put her hand on Eric's chest again, tipping his stool backwards. He kicked his feet out to maintain balance. The rope snugged tight, and Meg held him there, feet out, stool tipped, rope cutting off his air for a handful of seconds. He couldn't swallow. "Yes," he tried to say, but it came out a gurgle.

"Good," she said, and tipped him forward.

Eric squeezed his eyes shut against the pain in this throat, then opened them. A tear spilled out of each eye, and he brushed his cheeks against his shoulders to wipe them off.

Jared said, "I'll check the girl," and put his hand on her forehead. She grimaced but didn't pull back. "Not bad." He caressed her cheek, his hand cupping the side of it. "I don't think she's fevered," he said and moved his hand down her neck and onto her chest. "No sweat." He chuckled and pushed his fingers inside the top of her blouse. A button popped off and clattered to the floor. Eric stared as Jared worked his way farther down the woman's chest. Her face was grim, lips bloodless, but her eyes were open and defiant.

Meg stepped around Eric and slapped the side of Jared's head with a loud pop. The blow staggered him, and he retreated. "Hey, I didn't . . ." he said, and she slapped him again. He seemed to have forgotten the baseball bat he was holding as he tried to protect himself. Meg didn't say anything. "Wait!" She brought her hand around again, connecting smartly across his mouth. He fell back, saying, "Lay off . . . lay off," and knelt in the corner of the room, arms wrapped around his head. She stood over him, palm raised, and held the poise for several seconds.

Finally, she put her hand down. "Get up," she said. He looked at her from between his arms, like a clam peeking out. "Get up!" Spittle flew from her mouth.

Jared pushed away from the wall, stood up, looked at the bat as if he'd just discovered it, and pointed it at Meg's face. "Bitch." The vivid imprint of her hand glowed on his left cheek and his ear was bright red.

The man on the third stool started sneezing: wheezy, wet expulsions of air that sounded silly and empty in the basement. Eric saw the scene as so unreal that he wanted to scream. Turning to the sick man, the dark-haired woman hissed out a quick, "Shush."

"Shoot," said Jared, tucked the bat under his arm, and felt the man's forehead. "The guy's burning up." He snapped his hand away and shook it, as if the germs might fly off.

The dark-haired woman said, "It's just a cold." She sounded as if she were begging. "He's fine, really."

Meg sniffed. "I told you he was no good from the start." She started up the stairs. "We'll bring the needles down later." She didn't close the door when she reached the top.

Eric looked up. The floor above creaked so loudly that he could spot her position without trouble. Needles, he thought. What needles?

Breathing heavily, Jared stood in the center of the room eyeing the woman speculatively. A swollen, fat, sick old man in his underwear, badly in need of a bath, Jared scratched his bare leg. "We're alone, missy, at least for a second," he said to the woman and moved toward her. Breath bubbled deep in his lungs, and he smiled through a couple of strangled coughs. She strained backward on the stool, risking her balance. The rope pulled taut.

From the floor above, Meg's voice thundered, freezing Jared in mid-reach, "And stay away from the goddamned woman!"

The other man sneezed again and groaned low in his throat. He seemed to be barely conscious, slumped to the side and letting his noose support part of his weight. Jared leaned toward the dark-haired woman, caught himself, then shook his fist at the ceiling.

"Fish," he said. Eric wasn't sure he'd heard him right. The word seemed . . . inappropriate. "Fish guts," Jared said.

Then, looking at the dark-haired woman's chest the whole time, as if he could undo the buttons with his eyes, he carefully placed his bare foot on the sick man's stool and pushed it out from under him.

*

Twenty minutes later, long after the sick man had died, his sneakered feet only a couple of inches off the floor, a strange sound came from upstairs. Eric didn't pay attention to it at first. He couldn't take his eyes off the dead man. Thankfully, the man's face was hidden, but the noose pushed his head to the side, and his shoulders tilted slightly, so one hand dangled free, fingers slightly bent and relaxed-looking. Eric stared at the hand, not thinking about it really, but thinking about the difference between dead and alive. A moment. A little push was all it took. No more strength than to knock over a stool.

So he didn't pay attention to the sound at first, but, eventually, he looked up. From upstairs came a rhythmic pounding and a distinctive squeak. After a few seconds, he placed it—bedsprings—and not long after that, he heard moaning. A soft voice cried over and over again, "Oh, oh, oh." It was Meg.

*

"They're dying, you know," said the dark-haired woman.

Late afternoon light cast a pale square on the wall opposite the window. Eric had been watching it crawl up the wall so he wouldn't keep staring at the dead man. An hour or so had passed since he'd last heard noise from upstairs, and he'd almost forgotten someone else was in the room with him.

"It's the sickness, isn't it," he said. "My mom . . . my mother . . ." He swallowed hard. "She died."

The woman nodded.

"You're not sick at all?" she said. "No cough? No pain swallowing?" Her voice was still hoarse, throaty, but not unpleasant. It sounded weighty, the voice of someone competent.

"Uh uh."

She stood on the stool legs' crossbars and stretched her back. The rope fell across her chest and pushed her blouse part way open where the top button had popped off. Her bra's thin white strap was twisted, and Eric wanted to straighten it for her, like when his mom would fix his collar in back if it was sticking up.

She sat. "I hope one of them comes down soon. I have to pee, and I'm thirsty." She smiled and looked at Eric. He liked her smile; it seemed unforced, as if she didn't care that she was tied by her throat to a wooden beam in some profoundly frightening people's basement. Her eyes were deep and dark. "Doesn't seem right to want both, does it?"

Eric almost laughed, then he remembered the corpse. "I've got to go too," he said soberly.

A few more inches, and the square of light would be at the ceiling. It must be near sunset, Eric decided.

"It's getting dark. When will they turn on the lights?" he asked.

"Hasn't been any electricity for a week. Either that knock on the head rattled something loose, or you've been living in a cave."

A door shut upstairs. Somebody walked a few steps, then there was silence. They both looked at the ceiling.

Finally, Eric said, "The second one."

"Excuse me?"

"The second one. I've been living in a cave. Do you want to yell for them, or shall I?" Now that she mentioned it, he really had to go.

"I'll do it," she said, "but listen. They're sick, like I said, and scared to death about dying, like everybody else, but most handle it with more dignity. I mean, they accept it. They watched the news, listened to the President, and followed the emergency procedures. And when that didn't work, and they got sick anyway. They died in their homes."

Eric remembered his mom lying on the mattress in the cave, holding Dad's hand.

The woman continued, "Some, of course, panicked. Riots, looting. But most people gave up the ghost sort of peacefully." She leaned forward, as far as the rope would permit. "These two, though, these two plan on beating it."

"How?"

"They think it's in the blood. Everybody who catches the disease dies. Zero recovery. Not everyone catches it though. Doctors said some people may never get it, so you're either dead, dying or safe. Not too many people left either. Lots of quiet houses with dead people in their beds. I drove from Aurora to Northglenn yesterday and went for blocks and blocks without seeing anyone, just houses with their drapes drawn. Then, there are a few homes like this, with the last of the living, but they're sick. And there's some, like you and me, not sick yet."

"So what do they want to do with us? We might get it eventually." *I* might get sick, Eric thought. He hadn't considered that before. Maybe the whole world will die. He tried to picture his own illness, but he couldn't do it. He thought, the idea is too ridiculous, and, like she said, we're not dead yet. She seemed so unafraid that he began to feel better too.

"Transfusions. Meg was a nurse a long time ago, and she's got this plan to round up the healthy and take blood from them to keep her and Jared alive. At any rate, they don't want us dead as long as they believe we're not sick and their plan might work, so if we cooperate, we might get out of here."

Eric looked at where the rope ran through the pulley in the beam above and continued to a ring bolted in the wall. He couldn't see anyway, with his hands behind his back, that he had a chance to get loose. If they die or decide to leave us here, he thought, it will be impossible for us to set ourselves free, and if everyone is dead or dying, then we won't be rescued. The feeling of confidence faded. "What good will that do? If it works, they won't let us go, and if it doesn't, we're stuck."

She smiled again, her teeth bright in the now almost dark room, then said, "And the horse might talk."

Before he could ask what that meant, the door at the top of the stairs opened, and Jared and Meg started down.

*

"I need to go to the bathroom too," said Eric. Meg had placed on a TV table in front of him a small pile of clear, plastic tubing, several plastic connectors, a syringe and a couple of I.V. bags.

Meg recinched the woman's rope to the ring bolt. She had untied it from the bolt and walked the woman into the bathroom while

Jared gave her slack. He jerked the rope when the woman was almost in the bathroom, and she squawked. "Makin' sure you know I'm here, dearie," he said, but he didn't do it again after Meg gave him a venomous look.

"You take him," she said, and moved over to loosen Eric. She talked quietly, without opening her lips much. The chapping at the corners of her mouth looked worse. Big cracks deep with pus.

"Undo his hands," said Jared.

"Wimp," said Meg.

"I'm not holding another man steady so he can take a piss."

The mechanics of how he was to go to the bathroom hadn't occurred to Eric. He envisioned overpowering Jared, maybe beating him with his own bat and becoming the hero. Old, slow and drunk, thought Eric. I can take him. But the thought of trying the same with Meg made him reconsider. She'd moved like a prize fighter when she'd beat Jared earlier. Her upper arms were meaty. She probably couldn't run a hundred yard dash, but underneath the weight lurked a perilous and strong woman. He'd better not.

As if reading his mind, Meg said, "I can haul you off the floor in a second, fellow. You're not too big for that."

When Eric stood, he realized what Meg meant. He was clearly taller than Jared, and had an inch or two on her. Jared referring to him as a man earlier, and Meg's careful hold on the rope made him think about how they might see him. I'm not a kid to them, he thought, but I feel like a kid. Maybe if I keep my mouth shut, they won't figure it out.

Any hope of finding a razor blade, or a shard of glass in the bathroom to use on his rope later vanished when he walked in. Jared pushed the door shut on the rope, and the thread of dim light through the door's crack revealed nothing. Eric felt for the toilet. Then, as he went to the bathroom, he wondered if the dark-haired woman thought of him as a child or an adult. Maybe we're just equal, he thought.

Eric caught the dark-haired woman's eye as he walked back to his stool, and smiled a little to let her know his spirits were up, that he wasn't going to surrender. She lifted her chin slightly in acknowledgment.

As Meg tied his hands again, she said, "I'm going to take a bit of blood from you." She yanked on the rope. Eric flinched. He'd been tightening his wrists, figuring that when he relaxed, the knots would be loose, but Meg must have noticed. It felt as if his bones were being pushed together. She continued, "This'll go better if you don't fight me. If you move around, I might have to stick you a few times. I'm a bit rusty at this." She slapped her thigh, as if she'd told a joke, but she didn't smile, and her movements were sure and swift.

"Quit your jabbering and get on with it," said Jared. He stood by the T.V. table, looking worse than he had earlier in the day. Could be the light, thought Eric, but he couldn't tell. Black circles underlined Jared's eyes, and his breathing seemed faster and more watery.

Meg fastened a needle to one end of the plastic tubing, and the other to a three-way stopcock. The syringe went into the middle plug on the stopcock, and the I.V. bag fastened to the third.

Jared said, "Is this gonna work?"

Meg turned Eric toward the water heater—he couldn't see Jared or the dark-haired woman now—and swabbed his inner arm with a wet cotton ball. "Don't know," she said. "Better than the alternative."

Eric bit his upper lip, afraid he would yelp when she poked the needle in. Then he said, "Don't you need to know what my blood type is?" He knew from biology classes that blood types had to match for transfusions.

She gripped his upper arm hard and pushed the needle through the skin. He barely flinched. "I'm AB positive. Anything will work for me. Universal recipient," she said. "Don't know about Jared." She drew back on the syringe. The plastic tubing turned red. "Got to do this is a hurry. Little bit of heparin in the bag'll keep it from coagulating, but not long."

"What do you mean, you don't know about me?" Jared asked angrily.

"Don't. Ain't that clear? If the types don't match, might make you sick. Might kill you. I've got no way to type blood, and I don't know how. I figure the way your cough's going, and the way that fever keeps spiking, that you ain't good for three or four more days tops as it is." She turned the stopcock and pushed blood into the I.V. bag. Eric couldn't connect the blood to him. The process was more interesting than frightening.

Eric said, "How much are you going to take?"

"Filled with questions, ain't we?" Meg turned the stopcock again and pulled out another syringe full. "Hospitals only take a pint, but I figure they're extra cautious." Blood squirted into the bag. "Couple pints. Might take more." She filled the syringe again. "Worried about it?"

He didn't answer. Where the needle was taped to his arm began to burn a little, and he felt dizzy, so he shut his eyes. He heard the blood squirt into the bag several more times, then she jerked the tape off and put a band-aid over the tiny wound.

When she finished with the dark-haired woman, she piled the two blood-filled bags and the rest of the equipment onto the TV table, picked it up, and started out of the room.

Swaying on her seat, the dark-haired woman said, "You can't leave us like this all night. We've got to sleep."

Meg stopped. The room was nearly dark now, so her face was lost in the shadows. "You stay there till morning, child, and if the blood works, we'll see about chaining you to a wall or something, but until then, a night without sleep won't kill you."

And Jared said, "If the blood works, we might see about getting you some more lively company too." He spun the dead man on his rope. Then—Eric couldn't be sure in the half-light—he winked at the woman and licked his lips.

*

Long after the last light faded, Eric asked, "You all right?" His stomach ached and he still felt dizzy.

In the darkness, the silence scared him. He peered hard in the dark-haired woman's direction, eyes wide, trying for any sense of where she was.

"Yeah," she answered, finally.

"Do you think they're still in the house?" He hadn't heard a noise from upstairs for sometime.

"Probably." Her throaty voice floated in the air. "The blood idea, it won't work."

"How do you know?"

He heard her move on her stool, maybe to face him. "Scientists aren't stupid. If the plague could be treated this easily, no one would have it. They'd figure out what it was in the blood that keeps some people well, then they'd duplicate it. Nope, they're doomed."

He thought about that for a while. He could hear her breathing, the room was so quiet. "What did you mean earlier," he said, "about a horse learning to talk?"

The dark-haired woman chuckled. It was a tired sounding chuckle, but Eric liked it. "Oh, it's an old story. Goes like this. In an ancient kingdom there lived a cruel king who executed anyone who upset him. Well, one day a man is hauled into the king's court for some minor crime, and the king's just about ready to pronounce sentence, which will be death, when the man says to the king, 'If you give me a year, your Majesty, I can teach your horse to talk.' Well, this intrigues the king, so he tells the man to do it, but if the horse isn't talking at the end of the year, the man will be executed. As the man is being hauled down to the stables, the guard says to him, 'What a stupid thing to do. You'll never make that horse talk. Why'd you agree to try it?' The man looks him over, then says, 'This is the way I figure it. A lot can happen in a year. I might die. The king might die. Or hell, the horse might talk.'"

Eric smiled in the darkness. His arms hurt. His stomach ached. He was dizzy, but he said, "Good point."

*

Eric thought the story would have been a good place to end the night, but it didn't. They talked for a while longer. He learned she'd lived in Aurora in east Denver, and that Jared picked her up on the highway when her car broke down. Eric told her a little about the cave, since she asked about it, but he didn't feel comfortable talking about his dad, so the conversation trailed off, and after a bit he found himself drifting. I might dream about the ocean, he thought, if I don't fall off the stool. With that thought, he rested his chin on his chest and relaxed.

Sometime later, a noise snapped him into attentiveness. He couldn't place it. A squeak and a rattle. It was rope playing out of a pulley. He twitched his head side to side, trying to catch another sound, or a glimpse of anything. Something wheezed, like a dragon, he thought. Something's in the room.

The dark-haired woman whispered hoarsely, "Don't, goddamn it."

Cloth ripped.

"I told you I'd be back, missy."

Eric stood on the crossbars. What's happening? he thought, what's going on? A scraping noise. Must be the stool.

"Don't!" Then a muffled yell, like a hand was over her mouth. A metal clink. Belt buckle? A swishing sound. Cloth on skin? Another muffled yell, a pained moan this time.

Eric leaned forward, the rope snagging him short. His pulse beat in his ears like surf. Darkness pressed around. He recognized the feeling. It's like the dream! I can't stop the wave. I can't do anything. The water's coming in. I'm stuck. I'm stuck.

The noises came from below him. They were on the floor.

Fear, or something, anger, rose in him. He wanted to jump down, but he could feel the rope on his neck. The wave towered within him, dark, solid and unstoppable. There's nothing I can do! He'll kill us both.

The noises struggled on the floor. Eric whimpered. His daddy wasn't up the beach. What could he do? The nightmare never ends, he thought. In the dream he was frozen; in the dream he could do nothing to save himself. And in the dark, it was himself. *He* was being attacked. *He* felt hot breath on his chest, hands pushing down his jeans. He was in the dark-haired woman's head.

Jared's voice filled the dark. "Lay still, you bitch."

Then he couldn't stand it any longer. I'm not in a dream. I don't have to do nothing. I'm not a child. He opened he mouth and yelled, "Meg! Meg! Come down here quick!"

He felt the rush of air at his face before the blow reached him that knocked him off the stool.

Chapter Eleven
EARTH DANCING

D on't get up," said Teach.
        Campfire light flashed rhythmically against the bluff's tan wall of stone where a swath of black marked the smoke trails of previous fires. Eric rested his back on his still rolled sleeping bag. The rest of the party sat equidistant from the fire, their faces yellow in the light; the back of their heads lost in the shadows.

"'Scuse me?" said Eric. His stomach bulged pleasantly from dinner, a savory squirrel stew, and he felt tired and lazy. The night was so warm he thought he might just go to sleep as he was, without unrolling the bag, like Dodge and Rabbit.

Teach put his hand out to Eric, motioning him to stay still. "A rare privilege. Earth dancers." He pointed beyond the fire behind Eric. The other men looked past him, holding their dinner plates still, as if frozen. "Move slowly," said Teach.

Eric dropped a shoulder and turned. At first, blinded by the firelight, he saw nothing, then white shapes resolved themselves from the blackness. Men. They were clearly men, naked and painted white, dancing at the edge of the clearing.

Teach said, "Have you seen them before?"

The dancers, perhaps fifteen or so of them, bent low, brushing their hands against the ground, then jumped for the stars, throwing their hands wide open. Other than the crackle of flame, Eric heard nothing, but the dancers bounced in rhythm, all of them low, then they burst up, as if on cue, hanging in their outstretched poses, a mountain ballet.

"No," he whispered. He remembered the white figures in Phil's videos, the ones driving him crazy with fear. "Maybe," he added. "Who are they?"

One of them broke toward the fire, running, hands low and open. Forty feet away, he put his arms out like wings and veered away, rising from his crouch as if he could fly. One after another, others followed his lead, some coming as close as a dozen feet before curving back to the dark.

"First men," said Teach.

When they ran particularly close, Eric could see that the white was a powder, like chalk, some places smeared thickly enough to crack at the elbows and knees, and almost worn off in other places. Their hair was thick with it.

"My boys think they're spirits, or ghosts. Their momma's scared them with stories of Earth Dancers, and now they believe them to be supernatural."

Someone hissed, "We're not babies anymore, Teach." But the voice sounded awestruck.

Teach continued, "Feral men. I think they're the children of the children of the children. No, don't speak to them. They'll run. When the plague moved on, some of the survivors were little kids, four, five, six years old. They must have been horribly afraid, their parents dead, the dogs going wild, so they hid in the city."

Eric hadn't thought of that before. The plague killed ninety-nine percent. In the weeks after, when only the survivors were left, one out of a hundred of everyone still lived. One out of a hundred of his school mates. That would mean twelve of them. One out of a hundred criminals. In prisons, behind the bars with the rest of the dead, waiting for guards who would never come to let them out. Were there a hundred people in iron lungs in Denver? Maybe. How long did the person in the iron lung survive, unable to move, maybe only able to see part of the room in the mirror mounted over his or her face, seeing a nurse slumped over her desk? And, of course, the children wandering in the empty shopping centers. He didn't know why he pictured them in shopping centers. Where would a five-year-old go? One out of a hundred of them went somewhere. One out of a hundred two-year-olds couldn't reach the doorknob, or couldn't turn it.

The image made Eric ill. He rubbed his eyes. The ground was real. It pressed hard against his knees. The slick fabric of the sleeping bag was real. The dancers, leaping unbelievably in the mountain air, beneath a million needle stars, were real. Bad memories shouldn't be real.

One of the dancers charged the fire, stopped at the invisible boundary, and instead of running away, began to wave his hands in the air in front of him, as if to capture the flames. Eric started, almost falling off his sleeping bag. This dancer was a woman, a young one, maybe fourteen or fifteen, naked like the others. The chalk was almost gone from her lower legs, brushed off by grass Eric guessed, and her strong, dark skin rippled with the intensity of her movement as she swayed. She stared directly at Eric. She knows me, he thought.

Teach said, "They must have grown up like animals, isolated, maybe even forgetting their language, until, eventually, they met up. None of them trusting anyone who was not like themselves, avoiding the adults who might have taken them in. Angry, perhaps, at the adults who were their parents who had died and left them alone."

Another dancer joined the first, close enough to the fire that Eric could see the lines in their faces where the chalk had crinkled and fallen away from the corners of their mouths and eyes.

"And after a few years, these kids had kids, and then their kids had kids, each generation farther and farther from the Gone Time until what they are is what you see, true natives of the land."

Five of the dancers gyrated in a line in front of Eric now, another one a woman. Eric thought they were scrawny, all muscle, limbs as lithe as coyotes. The first woman continued to lock her eyes on Eric, as if trying by force of will to get inside his head. The rest continued running and jumping, weaving patterns, sometimes touching each other in passing, a hand on a shoulder or the top of a head.

The eyes were unnerving, the feeling that the woman knew him. Eric said, "How do they live? They must freeze at night this high in the mountains."

A log popped in the fire sending an ember onto Eric's arm. He flinched, and it sizzled for a second, but he didn't want to knock it off, sure the sudden movement would end the boisterous ritual.

"Mostly they stick to the mine shafts. Mountains here are full of them, or natural caves. Pure hunters, too. Don't believe they raise a thing. If they can run it down, they eat it."

Teach's voice stayed low and even, almost as if he were chanting. The dancers either didn't hear it or ignored the sound. "My guess is their homes are deep where the cold can't get them. They store food for the winter and don't come out. Sometimes the boys'll kill an elk or deer, dress it and leave it hanging in the woods. It disappears. Bear might have got it or the Earth Dancers. Don't matter much to them. I've never seen smoke from fires they might make, so I guess they don't use it, which might explain what we're watching now."

Another voice from the fire said, "I dream about them Teach Women Earth Dancers, like that one."

The two women, both tightly muscled, small-breasted, narrow-hipped, moved sinuously in the firelight. The voice continued, "They're, you know, those kinds of dreams."

Someone else chuckled.

The voice snapped, "You never had a wild Earth Woman dream?" Whoever laughed didn't reply. "I have a dream like that and I figure whatever I do the next day is sort of . . . I don't know . . . blessed."

The wind shifted. The tops of pines creaked as they leaned slightly in the new direction. The dancers stopped, looked about as if aware of some danger. None of them said anything; he saw no gesture, but all except one woman turned and fled across the road and into the forest. Eric thought of fish in an aquarium, changing directions at the same time with no visible way of communicating.

The woman watched the others leave, then she crouched, her knees wide apart, arms between her legs, hair covering her face. She smoothed the dirt at her feet, concentrating, unaware, it seemed, of the crowd of men staring at her from the fire. Eric could see them from the corners of his eyes, all intent on the young woman powdered in white.

She traced a figure in the dirt with her finger, shrugged her shoulders, looked at Eric like a portrait artist, smoothed the figure out again and retraced it. Eric shifted position—his back was cramping—and the woman glanced up, like a bird, half rising from her crouch. Her eyes, reflecting fire light, met Eric's and he shook his head, no. Please, he thought, please don't go. There was something inspiring and beautiful in her, some primal element that made her seem more tree and stone than human. He couldn't place it. Scratches covered her legs; her hair was matted and tangled, but the line of her arms and legs, the strength in her thighs. In this position, her muscles bulged, and Eric decided "scrawny" was a wrong word to apply to her. Hard was better. He remembered women who worked out in the Gone Time—he'd had a poster of some on the wall of his room when he was fifteen—aerobic instructors with smooth, rounded muscles, tanned skin, beautiful hair. They were . . . buffed. The Earth Dancer's musculature looked

efficient, not showy, pure animal. He imagined her grandparents
or great-grandparents in the Gone Time, driving to work, probably
in a Volvo, stopping for breakfast at—what was that place?—
McDonalds, having an Egg McMuffin and drinking coffee out of
a styrofoam cup. Eric remembered a friend of his in school talking about a schoolmate of theirs, a pathetic, fat girl who waddled
down the hall, the butt of jokes. He cringed at the memory. Un-
doubtedly both of them were dead now, gone in the plague. Old
friends and bad jokes all lost. His friend had said, "She's built for
comfort, not for speed." The Earth Dancer looked built for speed,
like she could take on a mountain lion.

Teach whispered, "We find signs of them in the woods: cairns
of stones arranged in circles, and animal bones carefully stacked."

"How many of them are there?"

The woman sidled around, looking at whatever she was drawing on the ground from a different angle.

Teach said, "The land can only support so many carnivores. A
hundred and twelve people live in Highwater. I'd guess their tribe
might be half that size."

She stood, hands resting on her thighs, and waved her hand at
Eric, a beckoning. He looked behind himself at the fire and the men
around it, then back at the woman. She waved again. He pointed
his hand to his chest. "Me," he mouthed. She waved a third time,
more emphatically.

"She wants you to follow her," said Teach. "I wouldn't."

"God," someone said. "It's a summoning. It's like a deer asking
you to dinner."

"More like a dream."

"I wish she'd ask me," said someone else wistfully.

She walked a few steps away and motioned to Eric again.

Eric faced Teach. He felt a swelling in his chest. The woman,
he thought, for a moment there was like Leda, intent and focused.
"I'm going," he said. He thought, What am I doing? But she stood,
her hand outstretched to him, and everything felt right. Her dancing, the ceremony to moon light and night, the nakedness and vul-
nerability of it all, felt right, mystical. He would go with her and he
would be safe.

"They must know you," said Teach. "Maybe they watched us
following you, or maybe they've always known you. They've never
tried to communicate with us." He sounded a little jealous.

Eric brushed dirt from his pants and walked into the darkness. A few strides into the clearing he looked back. Teach and his boys stared after him. A couple waved. He turned and followed the woman.

For the first few hundred yards, walking was easy. The Earth Dancer stayed ten feet in front of him on a faint trail that started on the other side of the old highway. A bright moon provided enough light to see his step although he couldn't tell if shadows on the ground were holes or safe places to set his feet. Then the trail grew steep, and the woman, her skin the color of moon, used her hands to brace herself as she climbed.

Sandy soil and rip rap skittered beneath Eric's shoes, and he grabbed tree roots, weeds, and rocky outcrops to keep from slipping. "Where are we going, young lady?"

She shook her head impatiently and kept moving up. The trail was steep, and several times Eric got close enough to smell her. He wrinkled his noise. She was rank, but it wasn't really an unclean smell, he decided. She smelled like . . . deep caves, moist and warm and close, and like crushed leaves. Aggressively female too.

The trail quit climbing. They'd reached a high ridge that sloped away to either side. In the valley to Eric's right, the fire flickered through the intervening trees, and the highway shone like a pale ribbon. Now that his eyes had fully adjusted, he walked as confidently as he would in full daylight.

Ahead, the rest of the Earth Dancers waited, squatting by the sides of the trail. They gazed at Eric as he passed, faces white and neutral, eyes aglitter with the moon. None looked over thirty. He wondered if their life-spans were short, like medieval man. Did they have any kind of doctoring, or had that disappeared too? "Do any of you . . ." The sound of his voice breaking the silence startled him. ". . . speak?" Far away, a coyote yipped and a host of others joined in. No Earth Dancer replied.

Eric said, "I'm feeling over-dressed for this party." One of the men walked beside him, casting quick glances from the corner of his eye. Eric felt like he was being measured in some way. He sighed. "Lots of nights I've kicked my clothes off too." And he had. Since his house was a couple of miles from his nearest neighbor, on hot summer nights he would sit on his porch and watch the stars slip behind the mountains one by one. A wink and they were gone, and after he'd sat long enough, he'd feel a part of the revolution of the

Earth, a speck on a plate, tilting, tilting ever up. After hours on the porch, he had no illusion that the stars moved, and he wondered how anyone could have ever believed that they revolved around us.

Ahead, a mountain swallowed the ridge, and the trail turned right, becoming a narrow shelf road. He kicked a rock over the edge and it bounced and clattered for seconds, starting a half a dozen other rocks on their way before reaching the tree line. The woman led the way, then Eric, then the rest of the party. He started whistling the theme music to *The Bridge Over the River Kwai* to hear the sound. The woman peeked over her shoulder. He launched into a second chorus, and another whistler joined him. Eric grinned. In a moment, they were all whistling, and he laughed at the image of it: a hard, wild naked woman powdered in white, followed by an old man from another time, followed by the rest of the tribe, all whistling a tune from a one-hundred-year-old movie about a war that only he knew anything about.

After a third time through, he stopped, and they walked in silence again. A hand patted him on the back. The man behind Eric ducked his head when Eric looked at him, but he thought he saw a smile.

At the next turn in the trail, the woman stopped and Eric nearly ran into her. She stepped to a rock wall that blocked the trail and slapped her hand sharply on it three times. A rope ladder tumbled from above. When she reached the top, she waved him up and he followed clumsily, having a hard time finding the loose rungs with his feet as the ladder twisted. Swinging from one side to the other, he banged his hip twice. The rope felt ragged and homemade. He wondered what they used to make it.

Another Earth Dancer, this one an unpowdered blonde woman, seven or eight months pregnant, held a torch that instantly ruined his night vision. Eric thought, Ah, they do use fire. She handed the leader a torch, lit it for her, and they waited for the rest of the Dancers to join them.

The flickering light showed the entrance to a mine. Huge, rough beams framed the entrance, and beyond them, bright sparkles reflected the light back to him.

The pregnant woman led.

What is this? Eric thought. The mine's walls and ceiling were pure gold. He inspected closer, but the torch moved several paces farther away, and the bright color faded to gray. Down the shaft, golden light bathed the two torch bearers, while the rest of the Dancers waited for Eric to continue. He touched the wall, and something small and flat fell into his hand. He hurried to catch up.

A turn brought them into a large room that smelled moist and human. Other torches sputtered from niches in the walls, revealing the home of the Earth Dancers. Piles of skins dotted the floor, and Eric thought at first that this was a storage room until he spotted eyes looking at him from each pile. Here the walls were golden too. Eric took down a torch and held the flame next to the piece he'd taken from the shaft. One side was white with a dark stripe along its length. He flipped it over. It was a Visa Gold card. He walked around the room. Thousands of Gold cards covered the rock, each held with a tiny bit of something gummy. It might even be gum, he thought, but where would they get so many cards? He checked the back of the Visa he held. The signature read, *Mason Withers*, which matched the embossing on the front. He checked others; they were all embossed and signed. "God," he said, "what a horrible job collecting them must have been." The Earth Dancers watched him. "Someone was very persistent," he added, holding up the card.

The woman, who he now thought of as *his* Earth Dancer, pulled on his shirt sleeve and tugged him toward a shaft at the back of the room where the rest of the Earth Dancers had gathered. "Okay, I'm coming." He pulled away to stick the cards he held back in place.

Light green covered the walls in the new shaft. He checked. "American Express," he said to her. "Don't leave home without it."

Pure white reflected the light in the small room the shaft led to. Eric chuckled. Sears cards, of course. In the middle of the room stood a large grandfather clock. Earth Dancers formed a semi-circle around it and sat on the stone floor. The woman lit two torches on the wall, then placed her torch in an empty niche. She knelt in front of the clock and pressed her forehead to the floor. How out of place the clock looks, Eric thought. A beautiful piece of work, though. Its mirrored oak finish and polished brass fittings called to his mind paneled drawing rooms. No, smoking rooms, where massive, overstuffed leather chairs held proper gentleman who smoked pipes and read from gilt-edged books. "Your drink, sir," the butler would say, and in the background, the grandfather clock ticked majestically, calling out the hour with measured chimes.

All of the naked Earth Dancers leaned toward the clock until their foreheads pressed against the floor. This is a cathedral! I'm in a place of worship. Why have they brought me here?

After a minute where no one moved, the woman, barely raising her head, crawled to the base of the clock and opened the glass front that covered the weights and pendulum. Blindly she groped in the cavity until she touched the pendulum, then she pushed it so it began moving back and forth. Each swing grew shorter, and the clock didn't tick. She pushed it again, looking at Eric this time.

"It's just a clock," he said. His face flushed, and he felt embarrassed for their posture. He pictured their wild leaps at the moon, their wonderful patterns of dance. They belonged. They were scary and primitive and feral, but they seemed proud. He was the one that was out of place, in his clothes, in his remembrances. "It's just an old, dead clock from a world that never existed." He spat the words. Anger filled him too. They hadn't chosen him from the camp because there was a special connection. They didn't know him from anyone else. He was just the oldest, the most likely to know how to fix the clock. The closest human to their parents' age.

She kept her head on the floor. The pendulum stopped. Eric's head sagged. He felt tired. It's late, he thought, and I should be asleep. Voice thick with irony, he asked, "Does anyone know the time?"

Her eyes pleaded with him to help, and again she reminded him of Leda whose eyes were so expressive, and he said, "I'm sorry." He didn't know exactly why he was apologizing, but he knew he should. "You're not responsible for your gods. I mean, they're not your fault. You've been sold a bill of goods by moms and dads who didn't even know what they were doing."

He thought, at least this god, if that is what it is, when it works is visible. At least this god is dependable and regular. This god keeps good time, and a god could do a lot worse than that.

He stepped into the circle, and, not knowing what to do, bowed a little before peering into the clock. The woman crawled out of his way.

"Have you tried pulling on the weights?" Bottoms of three acorn patterned, brass weights barely showed at the top of the case. "Of course you have." But he pulled one to the bottom anyway. When he let go, it rattled back to the top.

"I had a pendulum clock once," he said. "Here, give me a torch."

No one moved. He got one himself and held it so it cast light inside. This is tricky work, he thought. When the flame approached the clock close enough to see the works, it also scorched his cheek. He didn't want to singe the wood, so he put the torch back, reached inside and worked by touch.

As he hoped, just like his clock at home, the main weight pulley screw was loose so that the gear on the back of it wasn't engaging anymore. Awkwardly reaching both hands inside, he pushed the pulley wheel against the gears, then tightened the screw by hand. This time when he pulled the weight down, it stayed. "Here goes," he said and pushed the pendulum. The ticking echoed loudly in the small chamber.

*

Dawn light doused the last and brightest stars as Eric and the Earth Dancer climbed down the steep path into Coal Creek Canyon. "It's been a pleasure," he said, "being able to help you."

She reached the bottom and waited for him. During the hike back, she stayed much closer than she had on the way to their home. In the morning light, she seemed much smaller than she had in her moon-lit costume, and though she seemed no less animal-like, she was less threatening. Her smell at close quarters was almost over-powering, pure mountain creature.

Eric found himself staring at her as she walked in front of him across the highway, the muscles in her back and butt contracting pleasantly at each stride, and even though she was narrow-hipped, she still had a slight side to side sway.

"Stop it, Eric," he said. "She's young enough to be your great-granddaughter." Then to her, he said, "You know, some of the young men I'm traveling with have dreams about you. Maybe you ought to not be such a stranger." She didn't even look back. He'd been talk-ing to her the whole walk.

No one in camp appeared to be awake yet. Fifty yards from the sleeping men, she stopped, facing Eric. He thought he might have a few dreams about her himself. "I'd invite you for breakfast, but I think you need a coat."

Impassive, she looked at him, and he could tell now, peering through the white power that covered her face, that her eyes were brown. He wanted to shake her hand, or hug her, but he was sure she would run away, and now he didn't want this odd meeting to end. "You'll have to fix the clock yourself the next time," he said.

The woman reached out and held his wrist. Shocked, Eric flinched but didn't pull away. She pressed his hand against his chest, then pulled it to her breast, holding it palm flat to her. She said, slowly and distinctly in a low, throaty voice, another reminder of Leda, "Don't tell them where we live."

Then she let go and ran across the road. Eric stood for a long time watching the last place he'd seen the Earth Dancer. Finally he walked into the camp, trying to decide what he could tell them of the night. Before he bent over to shake Teach awake, he realized he could still feel the shape of her breast in his hand.

*

After a breakfast of strong herb tea and hard bread, where Eric told the party almost nothing of his evening, Teach pulled him aside.

"You got some secrets last night, that's obvious, but maybe you can tell me something about this." He took Eric to a spot outside the camp where a blanket lay on the ground. "We covered it up so the wind wouldn't get at it."

He pulled the blanket away. "It's what the Earth Dancer woman was drawing in the dirt before you went with her. Does it mean anything to you?"

Eric rubbed his throat, and an almost religious ecstacy filled him. The world is a magical stage, he thought; she did choose me. She knew who I was. The drawing, sketched in the dirt she had smoothed so carefully, was a noose.

Chapter Twelve
IN HIS FOOTSTEPS

No breath! **Eric opened his mouth wide**—his jaw pressed against the rope buried in his neck, but no air came in. Pressure pulsed in his forehead and droned in his ears.

He thought, I don't have to die. He pointed his toes and felt beneath him for the stool. Darkness hid it. He was blind. If I catch it with my foot, I can tip it up or maybe stand on it.

His foot bumped something and he stretched, but he couldn't find it again. I'm spinning or swinging, he thought. Reach! Take the weight off the rope. Breathe! His tongue filled his mouth.

Time slowed. His hands clenched in fists behind his back, firmly tied. He opened them—felt his fingertips press together. Consciousness divided. A part concentrated on the sensations: rope, choking, dangling; a part separated and saw him twisting above the floor, and a part went back to his fingers touching behind his back so much like prayer. Dad used to take him to church every Sunday when he was little.

He kicked his feet, weaker now.

The pews were hard and after a few minutes Eric wanted to squirm to find a comfortable position. Once, he remembered believing that the Devil made him feel this way—it was temptation.

The rope dug deeper. I'll last longer if I don't move, he thought.

If he could just stay perfectly still, then God would recognize his virtue, but the longer Eric remained motionless, the harder the pew became. After a few more minutes, he began to itch. First behind his knees, then the middle of his back.

Odd, I don't hurt, he thought.

Finally, even his eyeballs. In agony, he prayed for strength to resist the itching, his fingers pressed together. "Oh, God, come to me now and stand between me and the Devil." He concentrated, strained to hear the voice of God, waited for some sign to show that God appreciated his efforts. A sweat bead dribbled down his forehead and into his right eye. He resisted the urge to wipe the stinging away. He imagined himself like a nun, down on his knees in some bare cell, a plank and a plain blanket for a bed, a severe Christ bleeding from deep wounds hanging from the wall, the only decoration. The Devil comes for the righteous. The Devil wrestles in the privacy of the mind, in the hollow spaces between faith and fear. Speak to me, God, he thought.

Dad leaned over and whispered in Eric's ear, "It's not the prayer part of the service, son," and then Eric knew his Dad and the Devil worked together.

Eric felt his spin slowing, or maybe it was a trick of the inner ear. He remembered a short story title, "An Occurrence at Owl Creek Bridge."

He thought, I should pray. Now I lay me down to sleep . . . Yea, though I walk through the valley . . . I pledge allegiance to the flag . . .

Eric thought, it's the prayer part now, Dad. He could feel himself losing consciousness. His legs numbed. Even if he could touch the stool, he wouldn't be able to control his limbs. He couldn't save himself. But I don't hurt. The rope gripped his neck like a strong hand, and he realized, strangely, that he was happy. I hope the dark-haired woman is okay. Maybe she isn't, but I tried. I'm not a kid. I did something.

He began to rise, pressure dropped from the rope, and he thought, I'm ascending! and he wished he'd prayed more in the last few years. His pastor used to preach about being "ill prepared to meet your maker." Since he was ten, he had thought of himself as an atheist, or at least an agnostic.

"Breathe, damn it," said the dark-haired woman, her voice coming from the black below. Her hands gripped his thighs, and he felt her head between his legs pushing him toward the ceiling piggyback.

He sucked in air down his burning throat, then began coughing.

"That's it," she said. "Open that airway."

His head knocked against a rafter, and spider web covered his face, but he was breathing. He filled his lungs and coughed again, then inhaled deeply.

"Thank you," he tried to say, but it came out a croak. He swallowed and said it again, a bit more clearly, though still rough.

"I haven't got you down yet," she said. "I can't hold you forever."

Eric felt her quiver.

In another part of the house, voices shouted. Inarticulate. All rage. Loud thuds. A gunshot. Silence.

Eric strained to hear more.

The woman spoke urgent and low, "I'm going to move to the wall and untie your rope."

Eric ducked his head out of the rafters. She turned and stepped to the wall. His head bumped the concrete.

"Sorry," she said. "Now stay balanced." She let go of his legs. He gripped her ribs with his feet, and he felt her respiration, quick and even. As she fumbled with the rope, she said, "We got to ambush them when they come down. It's our best chance. You stand on one side of the stairwell, and I'll stand on the other."

His pulley rattled and he knew the rope was free.

"There," she said. She bent and Eric slid down the wall until his feet touched the floor. Her hands steadied him for a second, then untied his neck. "You're lucky the knot didn't slip. The noose should have tightened, and I might not have been able to get it off." She bent to his wrists. "When your hands are loose, grab a stool. We'll nail the first one down."

"What was the shot?" Eric whispered.

He sensed her shrug. The darkness in the basement was complete. "Lover's quarrel, maybe. But it was only one and whoever is left won't be pleasant, assuming either one of them *is* shot."

Eric said, "That would be a blessing." His hands wouldn't work. They were wood. And it was all he could do not to fall over. He felt blindly for the stool, and when he found it, he had to hook his wrists under the seat to lift it. Fiery tingles rushed into his fingertips. He grimaced but said nothing, then slid along the wall until he reached the stairwell.

He said, "How'd you get free?"

She whispered huskily across the space between them, "Small wrists and hands. I almost hoped he'd try something like that. All I needed was to be let down." Her stool scraped the cement, loud in the dark room. "Of course, it was a stupid plan."

Eric set his stool down and rubbed his palms together. "Why?"

"Jared's big. Girls my size who think they can do anything physical to stop a determined guy his size are just fooling themselves. You need a gun."

He remembered the almost out of body feeling he had when she was being attacked, like he had been in her mind. Jared pressed down, an inexorable force, hot gusts of breath in her ear, on her neck.

He offered weakly, "Maybe if you threw your knee, you know."

She snickered, not unkindly. "Yeah, sure."

Black silence stretched between them. He set the stool down, rubbed his hands together. They almost felt normal. "They might both be dead."

"Doubt it." Cloth scraped against cement. Eric guessed she was sidling along the wall. "I'm going to get that bat," she said. "We'll see how he likes his toy when somebody else is playing with it."

"Are we going upstairs?"

She whispered back, "Only thing we got is surprise. They don't know we're free. Jared let me down, but he's got to figure my wrists are tied and that I'm leashed to the wall. I couldn't have undone the rope with my teeth, so he won't necessarily be in a hurry to come back. If Meg shot him, then she probably has no idea at all. Ha! Got it."

Now that they had the bat, Eric relaxed. Not that it means much, he thought. They've got at least one gun, and they could come in blazing. I'll look pretty dumb holding this stool above me when I get shot.

"Don't try for the head," she said, returning to the stairwell. "Hit low. A sharp thwack on a knee or shin will hurt enough so we can get a second swing in. You miss the head and you're dead."

Eric snickered.

"'Scuse me?" she said.

"You rhymed." He thought, I'm not going to die on that rope. I'm still alive. A breath that seemed long and pent up whooshed out of him and he giggled again. "Dead head."

She said nothing for a second, then giggled too. "I saw them once, the Grateful Dead. Used to be my favorite t-shirt."

"I'm more into AC/DC," said Eric.

"So you go both ways?" They laughed. Eric covered his mouth to muffle it.

"Led Zepplin too. When the levee breaks. . ."

"You got no place to go." She said, "My name's Leda."

"Eric," he said.

"Nice meeting you, Eric."

They whispered secrets about rock-n-roll for a long time until, despite his best efforts, he drifted off.

*

Eric shook himself awake. Soft, gray light filled the basement. Leda sat with her back to the wall, her legs flat in a "V" on the floor, the bat resting on her thigh. She snored softly. He rolled onto his side, moving the stool.

"What. . .what?" she said, frantically grabbing the bat and rising to her knees.

"Shhh. . . sorry. I made a noise."

Dropping onto her hands, her hair covered her face. "God, I thought I was dreaming." She looked around. "We'll have to go up after all."

Tension gripped him, tightening his stomach. *They* were upstairs: bloated Jared and hard-hitting Meg. And a gun. Eric sucked air between his teeth. "I'll lead."

Mercifully, the stairs didn't creak. Eric, holding the bat now, slowly tested each step before putting his weight on it. They climbed higher. Looking back, he saw her smile grimly, and beyond her, just visible, the feet of the still dangling dead man.

On the kitchen counter, foul dishes were piled precariously. Eric crept past them, quietly opened a door next to the counter to reveal a washer and drier, and a back door.

"We can get away," he hissed.

She shook her head. "No, I have to know what happened. I won't ever feel safe."

Her eyes were round and deep and intense. "Okay."

He peeked around the corner into the small living room where maroon curtains cut most of the morning light. Dust motes swirled lazily in a narrow shaft that slipped through a gap between them. A shadow of a couch crouched under the window, and a pair of recliners faced a television. He couldn't imagine Jared and Meg sitting in them, watching a show. But the room seemed so suburban. The light beam ended on a pleasant landscape on the opposite wall.

"The bedroom," she said. "Could be they're sleeping." Her voice quavered. She's scared too, he thought, but she's going on. It made him feel braver.

"Smells bad," he said. Holding the bat in front of him like a probe, he moved into a hallway, past a bathroom, then past a bedroom with boxes of canned goods piled to the ceiling. Blotches spotted the carpet. He bent down, touched one. It was wet. The door to the last room was partly closed. He pushed it with the end of the bat and it creaked as it opened. Bad air wafted around him, menthol, alcohol and the distinctive smell of vomit. Eric wrinkled his nose.

Micro-inch by micro-inch, he edged his eyes by the doorway. A dresser covered with empty blood bags spilled from a carton, then, the end of a bed, someone under the covers, someone with bare feet on top. Then, jeans. A red flannel shirt. Meg lay motionless on her side on top the covers, back to the door, her arm across Jared's chest who faced the ceiling, the blanket pulled up neatly under his chin. An almost black stain soaked the blanket above Jared's midsection. Clearly, he was dead, his face rigid and held in a grimace that wasn't quite human. Eric couldn't see a gun.

Leda crowded behind him, pushing him into the room. She held his arm against her. A sheer curtain covered the window, but through it Eric saw a tree, and a car parked on the street. Everything felt surreal. How could he be here? How could he be in danger? The sun is rising. Wind is blowing in the leaves.

Taking the bat from him, Leda eased herself to the edge of the bed and reached out to touch Meg.

Without moving, Meg said, "He was a bad man."

Leda gasped and jumped back, banging into the closet door. Eric almost ran out of the room. He gripped the doorsill, panting like he'd run a race.

Meg pulled Jared close and pressed her forehead to his cheek. "He was a bad, bad man." Gently, she kissed him. "And he died too soon." The bed shook and Eric thought, she's crying, but the shaking went on and Meg convulsed into a fetal position, never releasing Jared, and Eric realized she was silently coughing. He watched for a minute, then the coughing stopped and she relaxed, painfully straightening her legs until once again she lay full length beside him.

Leda mouthed, "Let's go," and they started to back out of the room.

Meg hugged Jared tight, partially pulling herself onto him and said into his ear, "You'll never get to be a father."

*

They walked south through disturbingly quiet neighborhoods. Four houses in a row were burned to the ground, only pipes and chimneys poking from the smoking beams and rubble. An old couple sat on a porch in rockers, faces shrouded in flies, their hands hanging between them like the last thing they did was to let go of each other. Toys littered the yard of a house with a *Wee Care Day Center* sign over the door, the windows closed tight and draped inside.

"Where are we going?" she asked.

Ahead rose a house-covered hill. Eric leaned into the climb. Sun bleached the street. Flattened grass on unmowed lawns lay brown and beat. Last night's storm had done little to revive it.

We, Eric thought. We are a we? Most of the buttons were gone from her blouse, and one sleeve was almost torn off. Her slim shoulder glistened with sweat. "Following my dad," he said. "I think he's gone home."

She opened her mouth as if to say something, then shut it. She shook hair out of her eyes and looked up at the sun. "Hot, isn't it?"

"Yeah." The road flattened and they were at the hill's top. Before them, the city fell away, houses on houses, streets pleasingly parallel and neat. Here and there, plumes of smoke leaned with the breeze. To their left miles away, the Denver downtown pushed its buildings high into the skyline.

"Are you religious?" she said. "I'm not. Seems to me that the end of the world would be more dramatic if there were a god. There'd be some sign."

He thought about it. More of the city was visible now. He stopped. "What is that?"

"What?"

He pointed. Directly in front of them at the bottom of the hill, a narrow streak of houses two blocks long and a block wide was completely flattened.

"Jesus," she said.

Eric thought, it looks like somebody stepped on that spot, and he remembered the dream about King Kong, about how Dad talked for hours about King Kong while Mom died in the cave.

She said, "There's another one." A half-mile farther on, another block of houses were down. "And another." She pointed. He saw three other spots of flattened houses leading away from him to the south. A trail! he thought. We're following his footsteps. And for a second he thought he *had* a sign. God does exist, and he walked right here.

"What could have done that?" he asked, and he half expected her to answer, "It must be supernatural," but she shook her head in puzzlement.

When they reached the first spot, Eric as if he crossed a boundary. Untouched, the last house he passed looked like all the houses on the street, but the next one was gone. the foundation stood out of the lawn, and lumber littered the yard. Wood shards stuck out of a tree trunk broken off like a match stick at hip height.

"This wasn't a fire," he said, levering up one end of a ceiling joist. "No charring."

She stepped carefully over a nail-studded section of roof, the shingles covering one side. "The destruction is so complete." Bending over, she picked up a round object and held it to him. "Dinner plate," she said. "It's not cracked."

Next door, the story was the same, but the next lot, one wall remained, family photos hanging from it. The roof and all the other walls were gone. Just the roof was missing from the next house, but all its windows were broken out, the glass fanned across the lawn from each.

"Explosion came from the inside," Eric said. "Somebody planted a bomb in these houses?"

"No sign of fire, remember?" She put the plate down she had been carrying and winced when she stood up.

"Are you hurt?" Eric asked.

"Just a bruise," she said and gingerly massaged her shoulder, the one under the untorn sleeve.

"Let me see." He walked around a pile of brick between them.

"It's nothing," she said, but she stopped and faced him. Suddenly, he felt awkward. The only way to check the bruise would be to move the blouse off her shoulder, and he wasn't sure how to do it. Taking a deep breath he pinched the lapel of her blouse and pulled the cloth aside. She pressed her hand against her chest so her bra wouldn't be uncovered, and turned her head away from him. She was shaking.

She said, "Don't touch it."

"Oh, god." Beginning at her collar bone, a deep purple mark ran to the top of her shoulder, part way down her back and all the way to where her hand rested on her chest. "Are you sure nothing's broken?"

"Just stiff," she said, rearranging her blouse.

"Was it Jared?"

"Yeah."

"It looks awful."

She smiled. "You say the sweetest things, but you shouldn't be talking."

"What do you mean?"

"If you could see your neck, you'd think I was fine."

Eric touched where the rope had dug in. Pain flared and he snatched his hand away. "Pretty ugly?"

"The worst."

They'd reached the end of the destroyed houses and walked through another undisturbed neighborhood. Most of the homes now were old, brick duplexes with twin sidewalks leading to twin doors.

"My father died last year," she said. "Liver cancer. I didn't know him too well. He and Mom separated when I was little and I mostly got to see him in the summers. He lived in St. Louis."

They crossed a street. On this block, three or four yellowed, folded and rubber-banded newspapers were piled before the doors. Eric shivered at the thought of the dedication of some newspaper boy delivering papers to homes where the subscribers had died. Leda followed his gaze.

"They kept the paper going until ten days ago or so. Guess they thought a newspaper would keep people believing things would get better."

Eric asked, "Did you love your dad?"

"I didn't know him, I said."

"That isn't what I asked. Did you love him?"

"Well, sure. I had to."

He thought that over. A new area of destroyed houses began, much the same as the last one. "This is weird. What do you make of it?" He stood beside a telephone pole. The cross arms at the top were snapped off and the wires were wrapped tightly around the shaft, like giant children had used it as a maypole.

"Don't know. Maybe there is a god. While the people are away, the gods will play."

"Sounds good to me."

Dad might have come down just this street, he thought, and he glanced at the lawn, thinking he might see a mark, a sign that Dad had passed this way. How would Dad have seen this?

"When my father died," she said, "I didn't accept it at first. I told my best friend that he was sick, but not that he died. It took me a while to believe it myself."

Eric thought, why does she keep talking about this? "My dad's not dead."

"Of course not," she said quickly.

"He didn't come back to the cave, so he must have gone home. He wouldn't have just left me there." Eric clenched his hands into stone. *We could be standing in his footsteps!* "He would write a message and tell me where he went." His face screwed up. He could feel the muscles by his eyes pulling in, his jaw tightening. He breathed in hitches.

"Of course. That's what happened."

"That's why I'm going home. I've got to find Dad. We've got to go together and bury Mom."

"Yes, that's what we'll do."

Eric sat on the ground in the midst of the flattened houses, in the middle of God's footstep, or King Kong's. "My dad . . ." He gasped. "My dad is a survivor. He's too strong."

Everything was letting go inside of him. He could feel the unraveling, and inside he tried to stop it, to hold back the wind. He put his face in his hands and he could feel his skin on his skin. Why do I feel this way? Why am I acting this way? She'll think I'm a fool. Dad's fine. I'll find Dad and everything will be like it was. We'll live in the house. We'll play catch. He'll teach me new bird calls. Dad's okay.

"No, it's all right," she said. "I believe you." Her arms were around him and they were both sitting on the ground. She rocked him quietly while he shook in her arms.

After a long while, after he had quit sobbing and the muscles in his back relaxed, she still held him. He felt her chin resting on the top of his head.

"Look at that," she said.

He lifted his head and blinked away tears. "What?"

They were sitting near another broken tree trunk. The trunk

itself leaned and roots hung in the air on one side, clods of dirt still clinging to them.

"Sticking in the wood."

He followed her finger. Protruding from the tree trunk, four inches or so of silver glittered in the sun. He pushed himself off the ground, then pulled on the metal.

"Jammed in there pretty tight." He worked it back and forth several times before it pulled out. He held it to her. "A spoon. What would do that to a spoon? You couldn't do that without bending it."

Taking it from him, Leda turned it over in her hand. "A tornado," she said. "That's what it was."

He gazed at the scene of destruction, and it seemed familiar, like news footage he'd seen before. "You're right. Only thing it could be."

"They skip," she said. "They touch down, destroy everything, lift, then touch down again."

"Darned regular. I've never heard of one leaving a trail."

"Strange storms. Leave some stuff, ruin others. If anything's unusual, it's how much it destroyed. Colorado tornados are generally narrower than this." She gestured to the block-wide path.

"A year ago," Eric said, "this would be the top story. Denver would be cleaning itself up. It'd be in mourning."

She dropped the spoon. "Small potatoes, now, a tornado."

He smiled. It was incredibly hard to make that movement with his face. The muscles felt weighed down from frowning. "Does a house falling in a city make a noise if there is no one to hear it?"

"Come on," she said, "let's find some food. I'm starving."

"I'm sure we'll catch up with Dad soon," said Eric. "He'll be glad to meet you."

She didn't say anything, and Eric glanced at her. "Sure," she said, "I'll bet he will be."

Chapter Thirteen
GONE BUT NOT FORGOTTEN

Teach said, **"Keep your hands underneath you**. Don't look up. Don't separate your feet. Be a rock, and that's what they'll see."

Eric scrunched his face into the gravel on the hillside above the road. The rest of Teach's boys had scattered, and when he'd last looked, he could only pick out a couple of them in the same posture he was taking now, folded on themselves, faces down, practically invisible. Their leather skirts and wool shirts blended perfectly into the background.

"Where's Rabbit and Dodge?" Eric whispered.

"They're okay. Don't move and you'll be fine. Unless they're expecting to see something, they won't." Teach broke a branch off a nearby juniper and jammed it into the ground by Eric's head. He braced the bottom with a couple of rocks. "There, that'll give them something to focus on if they do look this way."

Teach climbed a few feet up the slope and lay down, hands underneath him, feet drawn up, the back of his gray-haired head to Eric.

Eric pulled his limbs in even tighter; his back crawled under the heat of the sun. A bit of sand he'd sucked up when he put his face in the dirt gritted uncomfortably between his teeth, and chunks of gravel dug into his cheek, but he didn't move. They'll be able to see me, he thought. I might as well stand and shout.

*

Before the point-man had whistled the warning that sent them scrambling for cover above the road, they had been walking up-canyon, crossing a slide that hid the asphalt for hundreds of yards,

Eric was hiking gamely, trying not to slow the pace. Teach said, "You've got two problems."

Eric panted, put a foot on a stone, placed his hand on his knee and pressed to help himself up. One of Teach's boys carried Eric's pack, but even without the extra weight, the soreness in his legs and the incessant buzz of pain in his hips reminded him of his age. "What's that?" he said. The mountain air smelled of pine and creek water, of sun on hot rocks, but it didn't fill the lungs.

"First one's easy, but important. Our last Gone Timer died seven years ago, and most of the young ones haven't heard about Gone Time from someone who's seen it. So you're the featured speaker at the town talk-around tonight."

"Okay." Eric almost did a skip step but didn't. The dirt and sand footing was slippery. "You *want* to hear old Gone Time stories?" Nobody in Littleton listened to him. The kids would gather at the hunters' feet and wait for each word about finding elk or killing a bear, but when Eric said anything about Gone Time, they ran off, except for Dodge and Rabbit.

Eric looked for them. He spotted the dark-haired Dodge on the black-top beyond the slide. Rabbit walked in the tall grass on the road's shoulder, as always looking as if he were ready to bolt. "I can do that."

"Talking might not be that easy. We've got a girl up there— name's Ripple, a kind of, I don't know, child prodigy—she's got some strong ideas about Gone Time. You can bet she'll ask some tough ones. Might have some things to say of her own. She was my best pupil, but she left me behind years ago."

"I'll watch myself. What's the other problem?"

"Getting you into Boulder. The roads aren't safe." Teach offered Eric a firm, hard hand and helped him over a slippery patch of gravel.

"You said the Flats weren't safe either. More radiation?" He stepped thankfully off the uneven surface of the slide onto the flat road. Here and there, portions of the double-yellow line were still visible on the pavement. Been a while since a car had to worry about oncoming traffic here, he thought. The long stretch of highway curved in between pine-covered hills a half-mile away.

"Nope. Federal's gunmen." Teach fell into pace beside him. Eric sighed a little to himself; the bigger man visibly shortened his stride to accommodate him. "Your library may or may not be standing, but there's a guy who calls himself 'Federal' or 'The Federal' who thinks something's valuable in Boulder, and he's got the roads."

"Really? Guns? I haven't seen a working one for years."

Teach grinned at him, his gray-flecked beard fanning out beneath the smile. "Neither had I. My dad kept a rifle, but he was down to just four boxes of ammo. Took it off the wall on his birthday and would fire one shot. Never did tell me why he did that. But the last year, it took six tries to get a shell that'd work, and it sounded pathetic; hardly an explosion at all. Mostly smoke. Dad said the shells had gone gunny-bag, said there wasn't much ammo anyway, so I'd better learn how to make arrows."

Eric stretched his gait a bit; the extra effort felt good. He thought, at least I'm not hobbling. "What kind of guns?"

"Don't know, but one of my men has one." He chuckled. "Federal's boys aren't all that bright. One of them shot up a couple of deer and didn't notice Skylar sitting in a tree. Walked right under him, and Skylar dropped a water skin on his head. He got the gun and a good knife off him, and the guy probably woke up an hour later with a sore neck and a lot of explaining to do. But bright or not, they've set up camps on the roads into Boulder. Sometimes we hear shooting."

Teach spat into his hands, rubbed the palms together and wiped them on the front of his shirt. "Lousy hunters, the lot of them. No respect. Take just parts of the meat and leave the carcass in the open. Worst kind of jackals."

A whistle from farther in the canyon trilled down the scale. A lark, Eric thought. Haven't heard one like that before.

"Whoops, speak of the devil, as my dad told me," said Teach. He scanned the slopes on the sides of the road. Eric looked up too. Here, the road snaked smoothly through rounded hills with few trees or boulders. Immediately the rest of the men started climbing. Teach tugged Eric's arm. "Best place to not be seen is in plain sight."

Then he taught Eric how to be a rock.

*

Eric's back itched. He pressed his face down even harder. A particularly sharp piece of gravel dug into his cheek. A spot of dampness slid toward his ear. I'm bleeding, he thought. Feet tramped steadily on the road below, measured, military. Metal clicked against metal. Gun swivels? he wondered. They were less than a hundred feet off.

Someone said, "Don't like this duty. Stupid way to spend a day."

"Shut your hole, private," rumbled another voice.

"Just talking. No harm in that."

They passed. Slowly, Eric raised his head for a peek, marveling that he hadn't been spotted. Marching toward the slide they had just crossed, a line of eight camouflage-dressed soldiers moved down canyon. They wore dark green boots that reached to mid-shin, and on their backs rode small packs, and each carried the same gun with distinctive open-metal stocks, sharply curved banana clips and cone-wrapped snub barrels.

Eric sucked air between his teeth.

"What?" whispered Teach.

"I know those guns." The men single-filed it to the other side of the slide and out of sight. "They're army M-16s."

*

Firelight illuminated the blackened stone face of the natural amphitheater and cast flickering light on the pines that surrounded the site. Split-log benches, two deep, formed a half circle around the fire. Eric, Teach, Rabbit and Dodge had one bench to themselves, although it might easily have held a half-dozen more. The people of Highwater drifted out of the trees and started taking their places at the fire.

Eric hadn't thought much of the remains of old Nederland, what used to be a mining town and then became a tourist trap in the Gone Times. Most of the buildings were gone, part of the "Naturalization Project" as Teach called it.

"Where's the town?" Eric had said. A few foundations poked up, and a bank and small office building still stood. After a long afternoon of nervous hiking, convinced that at any second they would run into more of Federal's patrols, he'd been looking forward to sleeping with a roof over his head on a comfortable mattress.

Teach chuckled. "We've been walking through it for the last half mile." He pointed to a small hill they'd just passed. "Got several families there."

Eric saw nothing man-made at first, then he picked out the shape of a wall. Unmortared, rounded stones slumped to one side. Partially hidden by a boulder, the house was practically invisible.

"Looks small," he'd said.

"Much of it's excavated. Warmer in the winter. Some of the homes have tunnels running back seventy, eighty feet. If they have another kid, they dig out another room." Teach pointed to a pile of rock chips. Eric had assumed it was mine tailings. "Takes a long time, too. Soil's thin. Mostly they're carving into solid mountain."

More people sat at the fire. They moved silently, soft on their feet. Even the children were quiet, muted. He saw one poke another and a woman put a hand between them. They looked up and she shook her head gently at them.

Teach said, "What's different about an M-16? You sounded frightened."

"Not really," said Eric. He shifted so he sat closer to the fire. After the sun set, the temperature dropped quickly, not at all like the late-June conditions they were probably enjoying in Littleton. "It's a powerful gun, though. I saw a few in the year of the plague. Some National Guard units had them, and the people who lived got to be real good at hoarding items like that. I read up on them." Eric noticed that the people around him were listening. He spoke a little louder for their benefit.

"An M-16 is a small calibre weapon, only a 22, but it has a high muzzle velocity. . . uh, the bullets come out very fast. And the way it's designed, the bullets don't fly smoothly like an arrow. They tumble. When the bullet hits, it tears or smashes. I read that one could be shot in, say, the leg, and it still might kill. The shock of the impact would be so great that it could stop the heart."

A man behind Eric said, "Tears the flesh you say?"

"Oh, yes, very ugly wounds."

"Wouldn't want to hunt with one then."

"No. They're designed to kill people. Weapons of destruction."

Another voice, a woman, said, "They're part of Gone Time sickness."

Teach leaned toward Eric, "That's Ripple. She's a deep one."

The woman looked at Eric intensely, a full eye lock, as if she were challenging him, and it took a second for him to break the stare and to see that she was young, maybe fifteen, like the Earth Dancer. Her face was skinny, and even by firelight Eric could see dark circles under her eyes.

"Yes, I suppose, but the world was dangerous, and America needed an army to keep itself safe."

She scooted forward on her bench, bent down and put her hands on the dirt. "No," she said to her feet. "Gone Time sickness had many symptoms. An army was one of them. M-16s were a symptom."

"But you never lived there. Much was good then, too. A lot." Eric felt tense, defensive. "It was a magic time. We could fly, don't you see. We had great learning. Man knew things."

"He'd forgotten all that was important."

Eric thought, she's so young. She knows nothing of me or my time.

As if she'd read his mind, she said, "I know myself. I know my time, and I've heard the stories. I've walked through the cities." She drew a design in the dirt at her feet. Eric found it odd that she spoke to the Earth, and then he thought, she's like the Earth Dancer, drawing designs, and he wanted to leap up and look at what she was making, to see if it were a noose.

"None of you were native," she continued. "The sickness came from not belonging. All the symptoms. None of you belonged."

"Go on," he said, suddenly eager to hear what she might say.

"None of you were native. You had no place you knew of as your own, and because of that you lived in all places as if you didn't belong. You made an army because you feared being thrown out. You were always temporary."

"You mean we weren't Indians? My family had lived in America for several generations."

"No," she said, shaking her head, sitting up and looking at him again. The rest of the people, surely the whole population, listened intently. All the benches were filled. Eric guessed maybe sixty people sat around him. A log popped sharply in the fire sending a shower of sparks up with the smoke. "Birth doesn't make you native. It's a matter of life and mind."

People nodded around her.

"Gone Timers, most of them, lived on land they didn't know. It's true, isn't it, that most Gone Timers didn't build the houses they lived in?"

"That's true, but our technology freed us from . . . from . . . some tasks. We could devote our lives to learning."

"You could, but did you? What you did is what counts, not what you could have done. You didn't build your own houses, but you lived in them. You didn't make your own clothes, but you wore them.

What's important though, what's important is that you didn't know where anything came from. Your house, your clothes, your food, your light, your medicine, your entertainment, even your water. You turned on a tap, and water magically poured out. You flushed a toilet and wastes disappeared. You put your garbage on the street, and others took it away."

"Well, yes, you could look at it that way, but what does that mean? What does that have to do with being native? How does that make the Gone Time sick? We were advanced; we could go to the moon. We could cure sicknesses."

She said, "Not the last one."

Pushed by a breeze, smoke watered Eric's eyes. He turned away from the fire.

She said again, "Not the last one. But it doesn't matter. The real sickness was in life and mind. Gone Timers lived in the world like the world didn't matter. They took upstream and disposed downstream like upstream was forever and no one lived below. The sickness was in metal and coal, in gasoline, in things that could not grow back. The end was inevitable, one way or another."

Eric wondered if Troy and Rabbit were bored. Ripple was preaching, he realized, and a sermon is often a bore, but they were listening too.

Ripple said, "There isn't a rock here that I don't know. Every tree, as far as I can walk, I have seen and touched. I place my hands in the stream and I feel the connection to all the water everywhere, to the liquid in my veins. Everything I eat, I know. I am careful with my wastes. I read in a book the saying, 'Don't shit where you eat,' but Gone Timers always shit where someone else ate, and ultimately, because it's all connected, in their own plates."

A child giggled. Someone hushed it quietly.

"I share . . ." she said, ". . . space with all the living things. If I take a deer, I pray for a deer somewhere to be born to replace it. If I harvest a plant, I see that I leave the ground ready for another. When I die, I will leave a place that another can live. I am native. I belong."

"That's a nice idea," he said. "But people couldn't live like that, not in Gone Time numbers. Mankind was successful. We learned how to make the work of a few feed and clothe many. We spread out, like grass; we covered the ground, and what we made was beautiful. You said you walked through the cities. Did you look? Did you really look? And what did you see?"

A vision of Denver at night rose in Eric's head. He said, "Lights everywhere: street lights, lights in homes, advertisements blinking on and on into the darkness. Cars hissing the pavement dry on rainy nights. Laughter. People laughing, coming out of theaters. And concerts, 70,000 people in Mile-High Stadium on their feet feeling music pounding in their chests. Heart-stopping rock-and-roll so loud your skin hurt. That was beauty, human beauty, and there was nothing sick about it. A good time, my father's time.

"Knowledge too, pure knowledge. We were close, so close to knowing everything. I've seen the books. I know. Scientists could study particles so small that an atom was their universe." He knew most of the people around the fire would have no idea what he was talking about, but he continued. "We studied the galaxies. We looked out with telescopes and electronic measuring devices and saw the face of god. Mankind reached up and in. Backwards and forwards. Our science traveled everywhere, and that's what we're losing now. Our children, my own son, are forgetting the heights we reached. My dad . . ." he said, ". . . my dad's world, my world, was about making people live. We lived longer and healthier. We took care of our teeth. We helped the nearsighted. We reached out, the Americans, we reached out and helped people thousands of miles away in other parts of the world. Technology and science made us more compassionate, more human."

Ripple looked at him sadly. "The beauty you're talking about is denial. It was terminal, the false color of fever before death."

Taken aback, Eric said, "Where do you get words like that? Those are Gone Time terms. How old are you?"

She blushed. "Books. I've read and talked. I've thought. I'm sixteen."

Teach said, "She has, too. Ferocious memory." He turned to Ripple. "A little overpowering at times, too."

Ripple said, "He's been there, Teach. He knows that it's true."

A voice from behind Eric said, "What do you think about the Jackals with M-16s?" He pronounced the name of the gun carefully, making it three words. "They seem more Gone Time than now."

Eric said, "Teach, you said the roads were closed. Your parents dynamited them."

"They did, but foot traffic has no problem going over the blockade. This is the first they've come this far in force, though."

Eric thought for a minute. "The only reason I can think of that they are coming this way must be the same one why we are going their way. They want to get around the Flats."

"What about the guns, the uniforms?"

"A military base somewhere north, perhaps. I can't imagine they're manufacturing the ammo. There must have been a well protected cache of it. Maybe if it stays cool, it lasts longer." He considered some more. The fire crackled softly. "If M-16s still work, I wonder if they have other munitions, grenades, napalm."

Teach sighed. "I guess we'll have to find out. If they're going to tramp through Highwater."

Silently, Eric stared into the fire. Twists of flame danced along the edge of a log, the heat baking his face and shins. The trip to Boulder seemed almost impossible now. First, the wolves, then Phil and his odd museum, then the Flats, now an army between him and the library. He thought about turning around. Troy would be glad to see Dodge again, of course, and Eric could imagine explaining why he'd left. Maybe the illnesses will pass, thought Eric. There are seasons of bad times. The crops grow rich one year and they grow thin another. People might be that way too. What could make facing men with M-16s worthwhile?

A small voice asked, "Could you tell us about the Gone Time monsters?"

Eric looked for the questioner. A girl, maybe ten years old, lifted her hand shyly. She said, "My grandma used to scare me—I remember—about the Sudden Death Playoff and the Twilight Double Header. Were they terrible? Did they really come for little kids?"

Eric laughed. For two hours he answered questions, and the people listened. They hung on his words, and all the time Ripple sat quietly, her head cocked to one side, intent. Eric was convinced she'd not forget a word that he said. And while he was speaking, while the fire burned low until it was just embers and the cool breeze swept gently past his face, he thought over and over again, maybe she is right. *These* are the natives. I am an alien in my own land.

*

"What are they doing, Grandpa?" Eric slid over on the stone ridge so that Dodge would have a better view into the canyon at the camp below. Eric looked for Rabbit again, but the boy had taken a different path once they started climbing, and Eric knew that saying anything to him would do no good.

"Keep your heads still," said Teach. "They might notice us poked up like this, but only if you move. Motion's the key." He lay on Eric's other side. Beside him, Ripple slowly moved into a position where she could see too. Now that it was light, Eric got a better look at her. Her short, cut red hair framed a serious, pale expression. Freckles sprinkled across her cheeks only made her seem more frail. Her eyes were green, and intense. Her movements, deliberate. She might be sixteen, he thought, but I wouldn't have put her at twelve. He looked back at the camp.

Sixty yards away and fifty feet down, a handful of drab, green tents stood in a small clearing beside the highway. Thin, gray streamers of smoke stretched straight up from a pair of campfires. Beyond the tents, farther down the valley, the rocky sides of the canyon covered the road and choked access. A shallow lake at the rock wall's base reflected clouds and sky.

Three soldiers were unpacking bulky metal pieces from green chests and assembling them on the other side of the road from the tents.

"Looks like a gun emplacement," said Eric. "That's some kind of heavy machine gun they're putting together."

"It's the Gone Time sickness coming back," said Ripple. "The head has died, but the body still twitches."

"What do you mean?" asked Eric.

"The guns and technology are irreplaceable. They can't be remanufactured. Their ammo fires now, but even stored in perfect conditions, it will become inert."

"Why can't they make new shells? All the equipment exists." Annoyed, Eric rolled to his side so he could face her. "The Gone Time is not gone, just forgotten. If the children will learn, then the machines will run again. Our great-grandchildren could live in cities under the lights. We aren't starting from scratch you know."

Below, the men had nearly finished their work. A black, swiss-cheese-looking sleeve covered the barrel, and twin, heavy kegs rested at the butt end. One of the soldiers reached into a keg and pulled out a bullet-lined strap. The leading end he clamped into the gun.

Ripple said, "The delivery system is gone. No more mining. It's high tech and there are too many missing pieces. We'll never be able to do what the Gone Timers did. Their ancestors had it easy. Metal ore was easy to find. It was on the surface. As they made better tools from the easy metals they mined, they could dig deeper, work less productive ore, extract using more complicated processes . . ."

Eric could hardly believe that a person as young as Ripple could talk the way she did. She's not just a prodigy, he thought, she's a genius.

". . . but now the knowledge and tools are gone. We can't start from scratch again."

"What about the metals that are already out, cars, buildings, all the stuff that won't work but are already processed? Wouldn't it be easy to use them as our raw material, even easier than the easiest mines for primitive man?"

Ripple glanced at him. "They're not raw. Even if you could melt them, they're blends. I'll bet we couldn't find pure iron anywhere, and the more time passes, the more difficult it will be. But even if we could do it, we shouldn't. We'd start the sickness all over again. What would be the point?"

The soldiers at the gun flurried into motion. One picked up an M-16 and strode across the road into a tent. The others swung the gun around so it pointed at a large boulder thirty feet from them. Then, from the tent, the soldier backed out. A older man followed him, not in uniform, his light hair catching the sunlight. Then a second man came out, a younger one with the exact shade of hair. They could have been father and son. The soldier gestured with his gun and the two men walked across the road. As they approached the machine gun, Eric realized their hands were tied.

"They're prisoners!" said Eric. "Do you know them?"

Teach said, "No, but Federal has all the roads into Boulder blocked. They could be from the city."

The soldier said something to the men. From this distance, Eric couldn't tell what it was, but the tone was angry, commanding. The older man held his head high and said something back. The young one looked frightened and defiant.

"Does he take a lot of prisoners?"

"I don't know," said Teach. "This is the first I've seen them on this side of the blockade. They're moving up canyon, that's for sure. Maybe they're trying to get into south Denver."

"I could go down and talk to them," Eric said, "and find out what they want." But even as he said it, he knew he wouldn't. Something felt bad about the men. His urge was to run.

The soldier pointed to the boulder. The older man sagged. His head dropped, as if all the life had been taken from him. He turned and walked toward the rock. The younger man hung back until the soldier prodded him with his M-16.

"What are they doing?" repeated Dodge.

A swell of sickness rose in Eric. He could feel it pushing against his ribs. "Oh, god," he said.

Teach said, "They wouldn't."

Keeping his M-16 trained on the two men, the soldier directed them to stand with their faces to the boulder, their backs to the machine gun. One of the soldiers manning the gun put his shoulders into a yoke on the gun and aimed the barrel at the men.

Eric's jaw dropped. Even as he watched, horror filling him up like ice water, he thought, I'm not going to see this. I can't, and he reached out to cover Dodge's eyes. In the distance, crows cawed loudly.

Someone yelled, "No!" The soldier beside the gun buckled to the ground, his limbs loose. "No!" yelled the voice again. In the bushes at the base of the cliff, Rabbit stepped forward and threw a baseball-sized rock. It zinged off the barrel of the gun. The other soldier swung around his gun and let fly an angry rip of sound. A line of dirt jumped up in front of Rabbit, and he ducked into the bushes. Firing stopped. The soldier pounded on the clip of his gun, cursing. Rabbit burst from the bushes, running low away from the men. Eric could see the cleft he must have climbed down to get into the valley.

Ponderously, the muzzle of the big gun swung around toward Rabbit.

"Run!" shouted Eric. He was standing. He didn't remember getting up. A hand grabbed him and yanked him back.

"Don't be a fool," said Teach.

The big gun opened up, slamming explosions. Eric scrambled to the ridge and looked over. Dust hid the base of the cliff. He couldn't see Rabbit.

The gun quit firing. Smoke obscured it for an instant, then cleared. The soldier Rabbit had hit still lay on the ground. Gesturing angrily, the soldier with the M-16 directed the two civilians back to the boulder.

A minute later, the big gun fired again, briefly, a short burst. Eric watched the execution, dry-eyed. Then Rabbit joined him, a long scratch across the non-scarred side of his face, but otherwise unharmed.

Ripple lay next to him. Long after the smoke had cleared and the blood had quit running off the deeply pocked boulder she said, "The Gone Time is gone, but it's not forgiven."

Chapter Fourteen
LOOTING

The four lanes of Hampden Avenue stretched before them, empty and still. To their left, a tall chain link fence separated them from a deserted cross-street lined by long rows of brick tract houses. A waft of smoke burned Eric's eyes as he strained to see through the haze. He had this vision that at any moment a lone figure would resolve itself out of the distance. His father. Eric almost whistled with the relief of it. He wiped wetness from his cheeks with the back of his wrist. Like a pall of wispy ghosts, smoke drifted between the houses. On all sides, up and down Hampden, at each side road, gray swirls floated over the lawns, among the houses and above them.

We're finding Dad, he thought. Leda's wrong about him. I can feel it. He's out there, just ahead, looking for me. I know I'll find my dad.

Leda said, "Whoops. We're in trouble."

Before Eric could answer, he glimpsed a shadow rushing through the air above the street, then it slammed over them and was gone. He was sprawled on the pavement. "What was that!"

"Maybe he didn't see us," she said, voice steely calm, her face a foot from him. "It's a gunship."

Eric could see it now, maybe a half-mile down the road and a hundred feet up, a beige and brown camouflage-painted helicopter. It turned nimbly and headed back.

"What does he want?" Roaring past, the copter's prop wash kicked up dust. Eric tried to melt into the asphalt.

"I'd heard that some of the pilots went crazy in the last days—this was a couple of weeks ago—and that they were strafing people on the streets." The copter turned again. Eric watched, amazed. It was so fast!

Leda continued, "A rumor said a copter pilot shot up St. Joseph hospital. Went back and forth pumping bullets into the building. Lots of people dead."

This time the craft came slower, its blade a blur, a cloud of dust beneath it.

Eric said, "He knows we're here."

They stood. The copter hovered just off the road, twenty yards away. Bits of sand stung Eric's cheeks. The mirrored cockpit glass revealed nothing. He didn't feel scared, really, but he stepped in front of Leda, putting himself between her and the ship. She moved beside him.

"What's he going to do?" asked Eric.

"He's doing it." She pointed to a multi-barreled device that hung on a mechanized swivel arrangement below the cockpit. The barrels were whirling around and around. She said, "He's shooting us."

After a minute, the copter howling on the road, the ineffectual guns spinning, Eric said, "Let's keep going," and he walked toward the copter. Leda stayed beside him. As they approached, the craft moved aside, and the guns swiveled so they were pointing at them the whole way. When they'd walked for a couple of minutes without looking back, the tenor of the engine changed and the copter rose and flew away.

"That was odd," Eric said. He felt like he imagined an athlete would who had just done some amazing feat—a half-court shot that touched only net, or a grand slam homer that wins the game at the bottom of the ninth—then walks away like nothing had happened, the epitome of cool and calm. Just another day. It was too bizarre to comprehend.

She said, "Glad he didn't have ammo."

He said, "Yep."

Later, as they passed a station wagon parked on the shoulder, Leda bent at the driver's window, cupped her hand on the glass and peered in. It was the third car she'd checked.

His heart still racing from the close call, he noticed her torn shirt drop away from her side, flashing a long stretch of white skin from her belt to just below her bra. This time Eric didn't glance away. She's pretty fit, he thought. Good looking for a twenty-five-year-old. He remembered his ex-girl friend at the high school, a sallow-faced blonde plagued with a band of pimples at her hairline that she could never clear up despite her most dedicated efforts. Last winter she'd decided to attack them with heat and cold and Eric had watched her wash her face with snow, then rush into the house to steaming hot hand cloths that she'd drape across her forehead like an Indian head dress. Twice they'd made out on her living room couch. The second time, Eric had experimentally tried to French kiss, and she'd said, "Don't. That's gross." They'd broken up a couple of weeks later. "I can't get into this pimple thing," Eric had said. It all seemed so childish now.

"What are you looking for?" he asked.

"Keys." She straightened and smiled, her face smudged and tired (but clear-skinned, he noticed). "We don't need to walk to Littleton."

Eric hooked his thumbs into his backpack straps and pulled them together in front of his chest. Despite the mid-day heat, he shivered. "I saw a cop shoot two looters yesterday. They were robbing bodies."

"Really?" She banged the door shut; the echo came back off a distant surface. "The National Guard took over police duties a couple of weeks ago, and my guess is most of the Guard are dead or home with their families. You sure he was legit?"

Eric thought of the ghost cop methodically pulling zippers closed on body bags, the liquid speed he'd demonstrated gunning down Beetle-Eyes and his girlfriend. "I don't know." He imagined the cop sitting on the edge of the Golden High School Knight's football field that was now a mass grave, his wife and daughter somewhere under the torn-up sod. "He believed he was. I haven't seen a car yet today. We'd attract attention."

"All right, we walk." She started down the road again, sniffed, then waved her hand in the direction they were headed. "Kind of creepy, don't you think? Like dry fog."

A reddish nimbus circled the sun above. He felt adrenalized by the brush with the copter, as if it had awakened him from a deep sleep. "Maybe. It's more somber than anything." He caught up to her and matched her pace. Her hands swung easily to her stride.

She turned and walked down an off-ramp to Wadsworth Boulevard. "Look, a Wal-Mart. We can get some stuff."

Resting on four cinder blocks, a rusty Pinto sat on the street side of the otherwise empty parking lot. Didn't she hear what I said about looting? he thought as they passed the abandoned vehicle. The broad reach of blacktop made him feel like a bug on a slide, like God was looking down on him so in the open. He walked backwards for a few steps, scanning the street for traffic, but there was nothing. No trucks. No cars. No copter. He cocked his head and listened. Not even a bird. His left shoe squeaked. Her footsteps padded on the asphalt; her jeans swished lightly.

As if catching his thoughts, she said, "I'll leave money. We can find food. Clothes." She plucked at her shirttail. "Not much left of this one," she said, then rubbed the side of her index finger across her teeth. "I have to brush too."

Crunching over broken glass, Eric stepped through the shattered front door. Produce littered the floor, as if there had been a riot. He kicked aside an Oreo box, skittering black cookies across the tile. A whiff of old popcorn, the scent of butter soft as plush, lingered. Leda called into the dark store, smiled back, the flash of white startling in the gloom, and said, "Come on. They're having a sale."

Last summer, he'd gone with Dad to a Wal-Mart to buy a lawn-mower. For hours, it seemed, Dad agonized over the merits of Briggs and Stratton versus Jacobson. Finally, Eric said, "They cut grass just the same," and Dad met his eyes in answer, leaving Eric speechless as always. After a frightening second, where something mute and dark bubbled between them, Eric dropped his gaze to the mower. "Grass is grass," he mumbled. Then he wandered over to the music department, and spent the rest of their time in the store deciding between a classical music collection or the latest group he liked.

Leda stepped through a mess of Saltines boxes and other crushed cookies and chips packages, heading to the back of the store. He grabbed a plastic bag of Zingers and tore it open as he followed her. It had that flavorless, pure sugar taste he liked. The farther they moved from the windows, the darker it became, and the cavernous echoes of their footsteps made him jump. "Flashlights?" he said, and she cut down an aisle toward hardware.

"Good thinking."

Another turn later, he could barely make out her silhouette. She tripped. "Can't see a thing."

"Here, let me," he said and helped her up. Her arm felt warm and firm, and she came up so easily he realized he must outweigh her by thirty or forty pounds. "I've been living in a cave. This is almost home." But it isn't, he thought. He slid his feet cautiously, holding her hand, waving his other hand in front of him. The cave was never home, not like Littleton. He thought of his own room, the posters thumb-tacked to the wall, speakers perched on their pedestals. How he used to lay in bed with his hands locked behind his head, staring at the ceiling, letting the steady thrum of rock-and-roll wash over him hour after hour. Some days he'd pretend to be sick so he'd miss school, and while his parents were at work, he'd crank the sound up, shut his eyes and feel the vibration of the bass in his lungs.

As his eyes adjusted, he realized that the dark was far from complete. A gray wash of light illuminated the high, suspended florescents, and the corners of the displays were just visible. Many of the shelves were empty, or their goods were knocked about. Something frantic had happened here.

"Where are we?" she whispered, her raspy voice loud in the silence.

"Households." He let go of her hand and picked a box off the floor. He shook it. "You want a blender?" he asked.

She snickered.

"I'll bet I can get you a good one. Ten speeds."

"Will it slice and dice?"

He put the box down. "Sure," he said, and reached back for her. She took his hand again, and her fingers felt good against his, not like holding his mom's hand, where he wanted to hold her. More like he wanted her to hold him.

"I'm seeing a little better now," she said, and Eric let go reluctantly, suddenly embarrassed. "Thanks," she added.

He still moved carefully. Goods lying on the floor were indistinguishable from shadows, and both looked more like holes he was about to step into rather than things to step over.

"Think we can go back to sporting equipment?" he asked. Hammers hung to his right next to saws. On the next aisle, camping gear blocked his path. He rummaged through the pile, searching by feel for a small pack for Leda. Finally he found one that might work, though he couldn't tell if he'd grabbed a day-pack or a duffle bag. Padded straps gave him hope it was what he wanted.

"No guns in any of the stores, if that's what you're thinking. The guard and police cleared 'em out weeks ago. First thing people went for when they got scared."

Eric shook his head, then realized she couldn't see him. "Shot for the slingshot," he said. "If they've got it, and a slingshot too for you. I don't like guns."

"Here's what we want," she said triumphantly. He heard a click. "I'm glad they sell these with batteries in them now."

Squeezing his eyes shut, Eric turned away. "Great, I'm blind."

"Sorry. Here's another." She handed him a flashlight. "I'm going over to clothes. Do you need anything?"

"No. Take this," he said and handed her the pack. He shone his light on her, and she blinked at the brightness. Curls of her dark hair fell across her face, and her eyes glittered behind them.

"Um," she said, and she shifted her weight from foot to foot. "Maybe it'd be a good idea if you looked for something new to wear too."

"What? Why?"

"Well, I mean, something fresh." She blushed. Eric stared at her. He'd never seen anyone blush so brightly. Even beneath the grime of a half-day's walk and everything that happened before, in the sharp cone of flashlight her skin glowed all the way to her hairline.

He sniffed. "Oh, jeeze. Do you think they have a shower? An employees locker room?"

Shielding her eyes, she said, "Not that I ought to be talking. If the water's still running . . ." She hooked her thumb toward the back of the store. ". . . It'd be there."

Through a pair of swinging doors, Eric entered the employee area. By flashlight he read notices on the bulletin board. One in bright orange said, "STAY FREE FROM DISEASE: WASH YOUR HANDS." And another read, "BE A PART OF THE WAL-MART CULTURE: WE'RE FAMILY."

Styrofoam cups, dried coffee in their bottoms, littered a round table in the center of the room. He ran his hand across a plastic-backed chair's top. Another swinging door led to a small locker area and a shower. Since the door didn't have a latch, and feeling slightly absurd, Eric propped his pack against it. He showered in the cold water by the light of his flash he'd placed on the floor.

While the water pounded down, and he lifted his face in the cold stream, he marveled at himself: how mundane everything seemed. Even now, the world as dead as dead could be, his father gone (maybe needing rescue!), he could still take a shower, raise his hands above his head and stretch. Palms on the wall, head down now, the water ran off his back. He could almost feel layers of dirt peeling away, and it was normal. He remembered a friend of his telling him once, after going to his grandmother's funeral, how everything seemed so weird. He'd said something like, "They're putting her in the ground, and my mom's crying and stuff, and all I could think about was how nice it was they covered the grave dirt with artificial grass. My grandma's dead, and I don't feel a thing. I just looked at that astroturf like nothing special is going on. You know what I mean?" Eric hadn't then, but now it made more sense.

When he finished, he turned the water off. Shivering so hard his teeth ached, he rubbed vigorously with a towel he'd plucked off a pile in a canvas hamper. "Shoot," he said explosively. "Nothing to wear." His kicked his dirty clothes aside and rummaged through the lockers. In one he found a clean pair of overalls. A draft caught him, and he shivered hard again, but this time it wasn't cold. The room suddenly felt spooky. He rubbed his hands down his legs, and he wondered about who the clothes belonged to. Who'd worn these before? Would he mind? He picked up the light and shined it around the room: lockers, shower, changing bench, towels, and door. Something wasn't right. Something was different. Backing to the wall he looked again. What had changed? Then he saw it: his pack. It had fallen over and was a foot from the door. Slowly he approached it. Shadows bent and moved with the light. Falling over, I believe, he thought, but then it slid a foot? No way.

Then he thought, did I actually leave it against the door? I might have thought about putting it there, then didn't. That's more likely.

But why was he so sure there wasn't someone else in the store? It was a big place. A natural safe haven. Plenty of food, albeit mostly candies and cookies, and there was that normality he'd thought about in the shower. The world might be falling apart, and all of your friends could be dead, but at the Wal-Mart you could still find queen-sized comforters and camcorders and bicycle tires and Sam's Cola. Sure, a person might come here to save his sanity, he thought. He could sleep on a brand new mattress every night.

He picked up the pack, then cautiously pushed the door open, the flashlight gripped like a club. Grit scrunched under his bare feet; the floor needed sweeping. Nothing. The employee lounge looked the same. Past the double doors, he saw Leda's light. Moving quietly, light peering around every corner, he found her in the clothes section. She'd draped a blouse over her arm, and was stuffing a pair of jeans into the backpack.

"Doesn't hurt to have a spare," she said, then pointed her light at him. "Nice overalls, but do you think something that long will be good to hike in?"

"There might be somebody else in the store," he said. "Did you hear anything?"

She shrugged. "Was there a noise?"

He didn't want to tell her about the pack now. It seemed childish. The feeling he'd done it himself came back even stronger. *I'll bet I moved it without thinking.* "No. I guess not."

"Then don't worry. It's a big place. Bound to make someone nervous. I didn't want to say anything, but there's no way anyone is in here. They'd be crazy to go into a store."

Eric's jaw dropped. "What?"

She smiled, "They shoot looters. Didn't you know that? Now, be a pal and find me some toothpaste and a toothbrush. I'll go shower."

While he wandered through each department, his light showed the odd interests of the last "shoppers." All the electronics were gone, even the display models that had been anchored to their shelves by stout plastic-coated wire. The neatly snipped pieces showed someone with foresight enough to bring wire clippers had been there. In sporting goods, as Leda had predicted, there were no guns. He doubted anyone had waited five days for a government check-up on their fitness to be gun owners before walking out of the store with these weapons. Anything else that might shoot was gone also. No bows, or slingshots. No shot either. A pair of glass cases, their lids shattered, were all that remained of the knife displays. He sighed. A heavy duty knife might have been good to carry.

He pirouetted. Was someone behind him? In the aisle he'd just come down, fishing poles criss-crossed the path like long toothpicks. No one could walk through them without making noise unless he had a light to direct his steps. Broken display case glass on the tile all around made it seem unlikely that he could be approached soundlessly. He thought, *I'm just getting the creeps.*

Toothpaste looked like an item no one had been interested in. He grabbed a couple of different brands and a pair of toothbrushes.

As far as he could tell, not one roll of toilet paper remained, and almost all the drugs were gone. In a corner, behind a bag of cotton swabs, he found a box of aspirin. It was the only pain killer left. All the cold remedies were missing. He grinned sadly. How pathetic that people would try to treat the symptoms of the virus that killed the world with Nyquil or Sudafed. Antiseptics were gone; so were bandages and tape. He wrinkled his nose; a strong smell of bad meat told him what to expect behind the prescription drug counter where he found the long dead pharmacist, still in her blue smock, on her back, a messy wound on her neck. Not a single bottle graced the shelves.

Eric took another route back to the employee area. The garden area seemed untouched. Droopy-leafed plants hung forlornly above bags of fertilizer. Neat displays of garden hoses cast odd shadows. Some boxes blocked the path in the toy section, but generally most of the goods still crowded the shelves. He looked at a red fire truck whose ad said "REAL EMERGENCY SOUNDS. TRY ME," and an arrow pointed to a row of buttons below the cab. He pressed one. The red lights on top flashed and a tiny voice announced, "We have a hot one boys! Start her up."

Back in the employee area, he heard the shower water. He sat in one of the chairs and turned off his light. Leda hummed a song. He couldn't identify the melody. Water sounds came to him unevenly, the sounds made when someone is moving under a shower. She's nice, he thought. Not half bad for an adult. Dad probably would like her. She's independent. He imagined her in the shower, water cascading, cleaning her arms, bending over to get behind her knees, hair hanging nearly to the floor, and he found himself standing at the door into the locker room, listening. He didn't consciously remember making a decision to stand up. Pressing his ear gently to the door frame, he heard water hitting skin. She still hummed. It's cold, he thought. She won't stay in there long. He thought of the way she walked, how her shirt dropped away from her belly when she bent to look in the car window earlier, and he imagined himself pushing the door open. Her flashlight must be on the floor, he thought, pointing in on her like his had been when he showered. She would never know the door had opened. She'd never know I was standing there.

He remembered necking with his pimpled girlfriend in high school. Lips together, she'd breathed on his cheek, evenly. It wasn't like he'd thought it would be. No real passion, but he'd been so aware of where his hands were: one around her shoulder, the other on her waist, and he thought of what other guys had told him, what he'd seen in movies, what he'd imagined. It would have been so easy to slip his hand up, across the shirt.

He stood, listening. Leda hummed. Water splashed on the floor. His stomach ached with tightness. His hand rested on the door. But is it right? he thought. Is it right to look at her, and he found his mind tumbling. What did he think of her? Who was she? A friend? A woman? A sister? A mom? What would it say about him if he did look? His other hand hurt, and he realized it was clenched. Painfully, he straightened his fingers and made them relax against his thigh.

When he'd kissed his girlfriend, he'd put his hand on the back of her neck and caressed the fine little hairs there. Just when he thought he might slide that other hand up, she'd put her hand on it, stopping any chance for motion. It was then he'd opened his lips, reached out with the tip of his tongue. Pulling back, she'd said, "Don't, that's gross." But he hadn't really heard it that way. No, not that way at all. For weeks after, and even now, he heard it as, "Don't, you're gross." What did Leda think of him? He had saved her life, and she had saved his. They'd talked for hours in that basement, not sure if they would live or die. But he had cried in her arms earlier today. She'd let go of his hand in the darkened store. Don't, he thought, you're gross.

The water still fell. He could almost hear soap sliding on skin, around curves, up and down. He wiped sweat off his forehead. Why is she staying in there so long? She must be goddamned frozen by now! Through the crack in the door, he could see the light on the floor. It was pointed toward the shower. The tile glistened where some water had splashed out, or maybe it had fallen off him when he'd dried. She must know I'm out here, he thought. Why else would she stay in so long. She must want me to look! He breathed hard. Oh God. He pressed his hand against the door, trying to remember if it squeaked, then deciding it wouldn't matter since she couldn't possibly hear it. He swallowed and pushed harder. It moved a half inch, then stopped. Something was against the door. Dropping to his knees, he looked under the door. A shadow a foot or so wide blocked the light. He reached under with his fingers and felt slick nylon.

Sitting back in the employee chair, his flashlight still off, Eric looked at the light under the door, at the shadow. The shower turned off. Silence replaced the throb of falling water. He heard her walk. He heard a towel rubbing briskly. It's her backpack, he thought. She leaned her backpack against the door, and a thought came to him very clearly, like a wave crashing on a beach: sometime while I was showering, or maybe even when I was toweling off, Leda pushed open that door and looked at me. That's why my pack was moved. She looked at me, then went back to the clothes section so I would never know. I stood naked in the water, and she watched me.

He didn't know what to think of the thought.

But it made him happy.

Chapter Fifteen

BACK ROADS

Eric was unhappy. Dodge and Rabbit stood in front of him in a gully removed from the road. Farther down, just out of earshot, Teach argued with Ripple, his gestures wide and sweeping. She stood defiantly, arms across her chest, chin thrust out. High and bright, the sun glared off tiny mica specks in the surrounding rocks, while a fresh breeze swept the bitter smell of cordite away. Federal's blockade was out of sight, but only the curve of the canyon hid them from it.

Eric shaded his eyes and said, "This has to be my last word, boys. As long as we were just hiking, you could come along, but men with guns are too dangerous. Go back to Highwater with Ripple. Teach says she knows a safe way. He and I will go on alone."

"Grandpa, you'll need our help," said Dodge. He jammed his fists on his hips and glared. Eric could see Troy in him, clear as if his son were there. He wanted to hold him, and for a moment, tears quivered beneath the surface. Dodge was younger than Troy was before the disastrous deer hunt that changed everything between them. Troy had never read with him again, had never said again, "I love you, Dad."

He cupped the side of Dodge's face; the skin felt smooth and warm. His eyes glistened. The brown orbs reflected back the sun. "You will be helping," said Eric. "I'll travel better knowing you are safe."

Dodge's lips set grimly, and his ten-year-old expression looked tragic and adult. He nodded, then turned away. Eric almost ran after him. The thought that Dodge might grow to hate him the same way Troy did made him queasy. Rabbit picked up their backpacks and followed. When Ripple finished her argument with Teach, she joined the boys, and the three of them climbed over a ridge above the road and disappeared.

Teach's voice rumbled quietly behind him. "They'll be off the road." He clasped Eric's shoulder. "Of course, she's like a shadow, that one. I don't expect Federal's men could catch her in these mountains if she didn't want to be caught, and from what I've seen of Rabbit, he could hold his own too. About the only mortal there is your grandson, and he's got a touch of quickness himself."

Eric grunted uncomfortably. "They're just kids. I'm responsible to the boy's father."

"Hah," Teach chuckled. "All you had to do was lie like a rock and Federal's gunners walked right by." He pointed after the children. "Keep your eyes to your hind side. My guess is they'll double back and trail us anyway. We're gonna have to catch them, then send them on their way."

Eric thought for a second. The breeze rustled in the pines on the other side of the road, carrying the smell of water rolling past sun-hot rocks. "You're right. They probably will." His spirits lightened. He thought, you can't crush a ten-year-old's spirit. Dodge wouldn't hate him. Only a teenager can truly hate his parent. "Don't know what I was thinking. Of course they'll do that. So, let's take off. How far do we have to go to get there?"

Teach scratched his chin. "Only a dozen miles if you were a crow. Crow wouldn't fly as much up and down as we'll have to walk though."

Teach took him up the road away from the blockade, then pushed through a screen of creek-willow. Wet ground sucked at Eric's boots for a few steps until the path climbed steeply up and turned into a series of rock handholds. Within a few yards, it was all Eric could do to keep moving. "Not much . . ." he gasped, "of this, is there?"

Teach grunted and heaved himself out of sight. He helped Eric to the top, where a long grassy trail paralleled a stretch of man-high rusted iron conduit that reached in both directions around the curve on the mountain.

"Part of old Boulder's water supply," said Teach. "The intake is in Barker Reservoir upstream."

A shower of red flakes fell from the pipe when Eric rubbed it. He wiped the red stain onto his pants. "Does it still work?"

"You're looking at the longest unbroken section, I think," said Teach. "Machinery's all rusted or busted at the high end, and it's got dozens of ruptures. Whole piece a few hundred yards long is gone a couple of turns from here."

They began walking. The service path, a pair of ruts at first, grown over with thin mountain grass, deteriorated, and soon they were pushing through thick, pungent brambles. Eric swore and pulled a long thorn from the fleshy pad at the base of his thumb.

Making a path in front of him, Teach continued, "We can follow this to Kassler Lake, about six miles from here. Then we'll take the maintenance road under the Bear Canyon power line to The National Center for Atmospheric Research. That'll put us on Boulder's southwest corner. Unless Federal's drummed up a whole hell of a lot of men, we shouldn't have any trouble getting into town. If he's got all the roads covered, I'd be surprised. Must be fifty of them."

"How far total did you say?" asked Eric. A mile of this and he'd be done for the day. He was leg-weary. But it was more than that, he knew. It was age. Plain old age. The first few days were fine, but lately, any path uphill strained in his chest and sent creepy tingles into his arms. He'd caught himself walking a couple of times today, lost. Not just where he was, but who he was and why he was there. For a few seconds, the effect had dizzied him. Boulder was gone. His son was gone. It was like he'd been dropped into the world, a blank slate, and it took a shaking of the head, a look at his own wrinkled and liver-spotted hands to bring himself back. It occurred to him, while he watched Teach pushing aside a bush to make his way easier, that he might not finish this trip. He could drop any moment. No one would blame him. His seventy-five years felt like a long, dry desert road. Behind him it reached, fine and distinct, but the wind was blowing fierce and he couldn't see much before him. Just dunes.

Leda had said something to him once about dunes. They'd been walking away from the Wal-Mart where they had found fresh clothes. The street was hot, and his new shirt collar rubbed a sunburn he hadn't realized he'd had (following a few feet behind her, watching her walk, he was thinking about the sound of water, hearing the water fall in the shower, soft then loud, a sudden splash as she must have moved beneath it). She said, "Have you ever been to the Great Sand Dunes National Monument?" A moment of shame stopped him from answering. It didn't feel right to be thinking of her in the shower. It seemed like a tiny betrayal. "Yes," he said, finally, and she didn't comment on his pause. "The park ranger there said the dunes marched. I thought it a funny word, 'marched,' since they looked so solid, but he said they did and he said they swallowed everything in their way. Then he read us a poem." She looked back, shyly Eric thought, the color high in her cheeks. "It's the only poem I've ever memorized. Do you want to hear it?" He said, "Sure," and she recited the poem. Later he had looked it up and memorized it himself.

Steeply, the hillside sloped away from them, and to keep from falling, Eric braced his hand in the dirt, careful to avoid the spiny milk-weeds that sprang up everywhere. In places, the aqueduct's footings hung suspended above the ground that had once held them sturdy. He breathed unevenly, and the poem came back to him, all of it. He hadn't really thought about it in years. Her hair had dried in shiny dark ringlets that fell to her shoulders, and as he half slid, half walked behind Teach, he remembered her low-throated voice:

> *I met a traveller from an antique land*
> *Who said: Two vast and trunkless legs of stone*
> *Stand in the desert . . . Near them, on the sand,*
> *Half sunk, a shattered visage lies, whose frown,*
> *And wrinkled lip, and sneer of cold command,*
> *Tell that its sculptor well those passions read*
> *Which yet survive, stamped on these lifeless things,*
> *The hand that mocked them, and the heart that fed:*
> *And on the pedestal these words appear:*
> *"My name is Ozymandias, king of kings:*
> *Look on my works, ye Mighty, and despair!"*
> *Nothing beside remains. Round the decay*
> *Of that colossal wreck, boundless and bare*
> *The lone and level sands stretch far away.*

"Shelley," she'd said, and waved her hand at the city where smoke rose in the distance, and the silence sounded like the end of an epitaph.

"Eric," said Teach, and Eric gasped. His next step would take him over a ledge and a sixty foot drop. Pine tops fell smoothly away to the bottom of the valley, where a glitter revealed an otherwise hidden stream.

"Sorry," he said, disoriented. Leda's voice echoed in his head.

"I wandered." He backed away and leaned against a hip-high, gray boulder sticking from the hillside, gnarled as an old knuckle.

"This might be a place to catch the kids," said Teach. "They're clever, but the only way through is right here. No cover. We hide ourselves up in those trees and wait awhile, then we can send them home."

He's taking this rest for me, thought Eric, and the knowledge didn't make him angry. He sighed thankfully. If I could get off my feet for a few minutes, I'll feel better. A half hour maybe, and I'll be strong until sunset.

Teach cleared an area under a crooked pine for them, then dragged a heavily limbed dead-fall in front for cover. His back against the tree, Eric had a perfect view of the way they had come. The conduit curved around the side of the mountain, more clinging to it than resting on it. Below, the mountain steepened into a short cliff, and a face of unbroken rock set at a steep angle rose above. If Troy, Rabbit and Ripple were following them, there would be no place here to hide. Sunlight stretched shadows up the valley. Eric guessed they had only a couple of hours left before they'd need to bed down.

"How far from Kassler Lake now?" said Eric.

Sitting cross-legged on the ground beside him, tightening his boot's leather lace, Teach answered without looking up. "Another four miles or so. We've got a little dirt road to cross in about a mile." The lace snapped. He dug into his pack, found another length of leather, and began restringing the boot. "Don't believe we'll make the lake today at this rate," he said without rancor. "Not many miles, but it's all slow going."

"I'm sorry," Eric said, and he was about to say something more about brittle bones, but Teach interrupted.

"I like the pace." Pushing the stiff string through worn holes, Teach kept his head down, then said, "You're almost a legend, you know. My boys are half convinced you're part god or ghost. You're of cities, television, cars . . . that stuff."

Not knowing what to say, Eric rested his head against the pine's trunk.

After many minutes of silence, a clatter of rocks in the valley startled Eric out of a near doze. I *am* tired, he thought. He crawled to the edge a few feet away. A line of deer ran up the stream, their hooves striking rocks as they went.

Teach said, "I heard that during the Gone Time you couldn't

see animals unless you went to a zoo."

Eric grinned. He liked the big, friendly man. "I'll bet you believe a lot of half-truths. Where I come from, I'm constantly straightening people out about it."

"Now's a good time. Educate me. Like, start by telling me about being there, things I haven't heard before." Teach ruffled his beard, knocking dust into the air.

"I don't know what you've heard."

"Start with yourself. Gone Time's a long time gone now. Doesn't it seem almost like a fairy tale to you?" Teach asked.

Eric thought about Leda's poem. For a moment, it was if he could have lifted up his hand and touched her, her freshly washed face, her half-smile as she recited the words. "No, not like that," he said. "In some ways I feel more there now then I did then. Does that make sense?"

"Some," said Teach. The clatter of deer hooves had faded. Eric strained to hear, but all that was there was the water music of the stream.

"I miss odd parts of the Gone Time," said Eric. "Contrails, for example."

Teach looked up, interested.

"Jets, 30,000 feet up or even higher left cloud tracks called contrails. On a clear, blue day, the jets wrote their path across the sky. You'd hear them, humming away, and when I was a kid I'd look for where the sound was. Jets were so fast their sound couldn't keep up, but they'd leave those contrails so you could find them, a tiny pin of silver reflection pulling that long cloud. I miss that."

"Yeah," Teach said. "That would be something."

"Chocolate bars." Eric shifted, felt beneath him and found a pine cone under his thigh. Its rough surface was tacky with sap on one side. He flicked it away. "I remember walking into a store and standing in the candy aisle, the smell of chocolate heavy as a quilt. You'd peel away the aluminum, and there it was, dull, dark and delicious. Umm, the thought's enough."

"My dad complained he missed cigarettes."

Eric hardly heard him. He half closed his eyes. "On Christmas, they used to string all the trees on Littleton Boulevard with tiny, white lights. When it snowed and those lights were on, it was like a postcard." He remembered walking down the street one bitter night when he was five or six, holding the little finger on his dad's glove.

Snow squeaked underfoot, and lights filled the trees. Breath froze in his nose.

"That doesn't sound bad," said Teach. "Ripple's hard on the Gone Time. I hope her version of it isn't the one that survives."

"Maybe it will be like memories," said Eric. "We'll remember the good stuff and forget the bad. I'm not an apologist for the evils Ripple talked about. She's right in some ways, but I think we're losing more by throwing technology and science and knowledge away than we gain by becoming . . . becoming . . . barbarians."

Teach stood up and tested the newly strung boot. "I don't feel like a barbarian."

With his rough leather vest, short skirt and homemade pack, with his full beard and long hair, Teach looked barbarian to Eric.

"But you know what I'm talking about," said Eric. "You've read about the Gone Time and the things we did. The cities . . . well, that's a part, but a small one. The books hold what the Gone Time really has to offer: the science, the mathematics, the poetry. When we get to Boulder, that's what we'll find, the knowledge to beat whatever makes my people sick. That's what I've tried to instill in Rabbit and Dodge; it's what my son never learned, that knowledge and knowing where to go to get it is the difference between man and animal. No matter how far back we slide, as long as there are books, we have a chance."

He thought Teach looked embarrassed. Eric sat up a little straighter. His legs really did feel a bit better now. "I'm sorry," said Eric. "I know I'm preaching to the choir. You've read books too."

Teach didn't speak. He walked around the screen of dead pine and peered up the valley. He slapped his hand against his leg. "Dang, I've an idea we've been had," he said.

"What?"

"I'm gonna check something. Stay here and I'll be back in a half hour or so." He grabbed a piece of jerky from his pack. "One for the road, as my dad would say." He stepped around the screen again, then paused. He said, "Oh, Eric."

"Yes."

After Teach spoke, Eric sat dumbfounded while the big man sprinted to the steep part of the mountain beneath the aqueduct, then vanished around the corner in less than a minute, covering the same ground that had taken Eric fifteen minutes to traverse.

What Teach had said was, "I can't read. I never learned."

Eric sputtered, then said, "But I thought . . . I mean . . . Who taught Ripple?"

"Taught herself," said Teach. "She couldn't have been more'n six or seven years old either. Amazing, huh?"

*

While the afternoon wore on, and the sun dropped closer to the horizon, Eric thought about teaching six-year-old Troy to read. For hours they sat at the kitchen table, drapes drawn wide, a pile of primers and paper at one end.

"Can I say the alphabet again, Dad?" Troy had asked, and he smiled when Eric nodded. Troy's forehead knitted into a series of wrinkles as he struggled with the letters after "P."

"What's this word, son?" Eric said and pointed at C-A-T under a cartoon picture with goofy eyes.

"Cat, Dad. Everybody knows that."

"Did you read the word, or do you know the picture?"

"Read it."

Eric found the D-O-G flash-card, covered the picture and asked, "And what's this word?"

"Cat," said Troy.

Eric sighed and slumped in his chair.

"Fish?" said Troy hopefully.

Eric shook his head no.

"Why don't we go scavenging, Dad? I'm tired of reading."

Out the window, Eric saw the long, prairie grass waving in the breeze. The day before they'd dug through the rubble of a Radio Shack, looking for parts. The only useful item was an intercom kit. All afternoon they'd worked together assembling it. Troy bubbled over each transistor slipping into place, and the intricacy of the wire patterns. Just before they'd finished, Eric had realized that it ran on batteries, which they didn't have, but Troy didn't seem to care. He thought it was an art project.

"Yeah," Eric said. "Maybe we can find a *Hooked on Phonics* book."

*

Footsteps woke Eric. When he rolled to see who was coming,

deepening purple above, orange streaks on the horizon, and the creaks in his back and neck told him that he'd slept against the tree for some time.

"Ouch," he said, rubbing his neck.

Teach squatted next to his pack. "Good thing I wasn't a bear. You looked a lot like dead meat to me."

"What'd you find out? Are they following us?" asked Eric.

Teach pulled gently on his beard. "We're gonna have to leave at first light. From the looks of their trail, I was right about them not heading to Highwater."

Eric smiled. He could imagine Dodge and Rabbit putting their heads together to do what they'd done days ago, follow their grandfather.

"Did you send them back?" He thought, they are good boys. Once caught, they'd do what they were told. Willful kids though; you have to catch them first.

Teach shut his eyes and sighed deeply. "I trailed them until I ran out of light. They're not behind us. They doubled back, skirted the blockade and are headed to Boulder on their own."

Eric's hands felt suddenly clammy.

Teach said, "They're moving into more danger than they can possibly know."

Chapter Sixteen

A HARD WIND

L eda said, "Fifteen? You're fifteen?"
He realized she had thought him older, and he wished he could take the words back. "Nearly sixteen. Next month." His voice sounded lame to him, so he clapped his teeth tight over whatever else he was about to say.

They walked almost directly east, down Bowles Avenue, their shadows stretched before them. They passed one mini-mall after another: Ace Hardware, Target, Big-O Tires, Cost Cutters, Walden's, Bennigan's, Wendy's, McDonald's, Arby's. All empty. Where windows were not boarded, glass shards reflected dully the smoky sunlight.

At South-West Plaza, the largest shopping mall in the Denver area, gun-shot cars, some of them little more than burnt-out hulks, littered the lot and reminded Eric of the line of cars on U.S. 6 he'd passed after leaving the cave. Eric guessed they only had three or four miles left. They'd arrive at his house by sunset. He figured Dad would be waiting for him, or there would be a note of instructions. Dad might be sick or hurt. Why else hadn't he come back to the cave?

They reached an expensive housing development. For a few blocks, high privacy-fence lined both sides of the street, and they glimpsed huge houses through cracks. Beautifully finished, six-foot high brick walls replaced the wooden fence and separated them from the wide, dry yards. Wilted flowers and neatly manicured bushes grew from the median strip beside them.

A gust of wind pushed his back, skittering scraps of paper along the pavement. On both sides of the street, dry leaves rustled loudly in cottonwoods and willows, and it sounded almost like fall. Spring and summer had been dry, and Eric realized it'd probably been a month or more since most people had watered. At the cross street he saw long, uncut grass rippling in parched, brown lawns.

"It's not a big deal," said Leda. "You're as old as you act."

Eric's feet felt lighter. "Right," he said. He remembered something his mom used to say that never made any sense to him before. "Age is as age does, huh?"

"Sure," she said, but she seemed distracted. Another rush of wind smacked his back, and this one was distinctly cooler, like an open refrigerator door, and he wished he had a soda, something sweet and bubbly in a glass with ice-cubes clinking. He felt like he'd been breathing soot for weeks.

"It's smokier," she said.

"Might be cooling off," said Eric. "Maybe another storm."

Leda dropped her backpack and sleeping bag to the pavement and flinched when the breeze hit the broad patch of sweat where the pack had rested. She pulled the shirt away from her back, ran to the brick wall and climbed to the top.

"What're you doing?" asked Eric. She faced back the way they had come, shading her eyes from the sun. She looked . . . jaunty up there, her hair stretched back, white cotton shirttails fluttering behind. He turned and gazed down the road, squinting as the wind picked up, carrying dust and smoke and a strong, harsh, burning odor. A dark barrier rose from the mountains: thunderclouds, ebony and deeply gray. Shapes boiled up within them, like a sea of fists and black babies' heads. As he watched, the storm's top edge touched the sun and swallowed it. The temperature dropped another five degrees, reminding him of something, as if he'd done this before. He shook his head to clear his thoughts.

"I need to get higher," Leda said. "Come on." She jumped to the other side of the wall and out of sight.

Eric caught up to her as she pounded on the front door of a brick tri-level. She waited a second and pounded again, three quick whaps that rattled the window.

"Nobody home," she said. "Or dead. We've got to get into the garage."

Confused, Eric said, "It's going to rain. Maybe we should find some place to wait it out." But she'd already disappeared around the corner. He shrugged his shoulders and followed.

The sky grew darker.

The deja vu returned and he suddenly placed the memory: it was the eclipse, and with the darkening, the dropping temperature, he felt an overwhelming sense of doom.

When he was six or seven, Dad had started talking about a "total eclipse of the sun," and he talked about it for weeks. One day, he seat-belted Eric into the car and the two of them left. Mom stayed home. He didn't know why. They drove south until late that night, Eric reading comic books. Air blasted through the open window, ruffling Dad's hair. Eric snuck shy looks at him. Once their eyes met, and Dad winked. He seemed so confident and strong, so focused on the road. Palm on top of the steering wheel, he made tiny corrections to keep them on course. Eric tried to rest his elbow on the door's edge too, but he was too short. When it became too dark to read, Eric watched the lights out the window: farm houses mostly. Occasionally they'd flash by a gas station alone on the highway, its neon sign a pool of radiance in the night. "You'll appreciate this when you're older," said Dad. "You'll only get to see this once."

They'd slept in the car at a truck stop. Dad crammed in the back seat, his head against the armrest, his knees bent, and Eric took the front. For hours, it seemed, Eric lay on his back, sleepless, watching the stars through the windshield. He had no idea what a "total eclipse of the sun" was, but he was excited. It's Christmas, he thought. It's better than Christmas, because we have to drive a long way to get there. A tiny flutter tickled in his stomach, and he almost squealed for joy. Eric scrunched his eyes closed and tried to will himself to sleep.

The next day, after another nine hours of driving, and after crossing the Mexican border, they pulled to the side of the road. Dad kept checking his watch. Puzzled, Eric climbed out of the car and sat next to his dad on the hood. Up and down the two-lane highway, Eric could see other cars parked like theirs. Some people had telescopes, and others held up sheets of paper or cardboard and let the sun's tiny image fall through a pinhole onto another sheet of paper. Dad had a similar contraption and showed Eric the circle of light no bigger than a pea.

"It's starting," Dad said, almost in a whisper. Eric looked at the paper, but nothing seemed different. He glanced up.

"Don't," said Dad, startling Eric. "You can't look at some things straight on." He pulled Eric around and held onto his shoulder. "Here," he said.

Eric looked at the pea-sized light again, but now he saw a tiny notch taken out of one side. Under his dad's heavy hand, Eric squirmed uncomfortably. Why have we stopped out here? he thought. What's the big deal? He wanted to climb back into the car and read a comic. Then a horrible realization came to him: this is it. This is why we've come so far. This is a total eclipse of the sun. Choked with disappointment, he looked at the image, and slowly, ever so slowly, the notch grew bigger.

"I don't want . . ." began Eric.

"Shush!" said Dad and tightened his grip. Over half the sun's image had vanished, like a dark coin sliding across a bright one.

Eric looked up, and he blinked. Everything seemed shadowy, and the after-image of the partially eclipsed sun kept crossing his vision. He tried to blink it away. A happy buzz of talk from a group of people standing by a car fifty yards up the road caught Eric's ear. They too stared at the sun's image. One of them, wearing sunglasses, stood apart looking directly into the sky.

Then, gradually, the air dimmed more and chilled. In the mutated light, the land looked alien. Even with other people in sight, Eric felt isolated, like he and his dad were lone explorers in a new world. Birds he hadn't really noticed before quit chirping. Without knowing why, Eric began crying.

Now, in Littleton, clouds covering the sun, the houses and lawns almost purple in the odd light, Eric felt like he was once again at the eclipse. Dad hadn't explained to him what had happened until they were driving home. He'd assumed Eric knew what an eclipse was. For the weeks before, he'd thought Eric was excited as he was about the chance to see one. "It was a once-in-a-lifetime opportunity," he said repeatedly.

Leda twisted the garage door handle, but the door wouldn't budge. "Dang," she shouted. Her vehemence startled him. The wind pushed her hair in front of her face, and the bitter smoke caught in Eric's throat. He coughed hard, once, and squinted his eyes against it, then rubbed goose-bumps off his arms. This is weird, he thought. Wind's cold, like winter cold, but the smoke smells hot.

Leda said, "You going to help, or what?"

"How about that window?" he said. A clean, pink and blue geometric patterned drape hid whatever was in the garage. He pried a decorative border-brick out of the garden and heaved it through the glass without a qualm. Careful of the glass, he looked in. It was hard to imagine that they were actually breaking into someone's house. Not only did he feel that in some way no one owned this house anymore, but that the whole city was unowned. Even though two tricycles were entangled by the back door, that a tennis racket, three baseball bats and a fishing pole stuck out of a cardboard barrel by a work bench, and that a sign above the cluttered bench read, "BLESS THIS MESS," he couldn't imagine the people they belonged to. He felt like an explorer as he had with his dad, like a Conquistador. Absurdly, for an instant, he thought about "claiming" the house, but he couldn't come up with a sovereign to claim it for, and he decided Leda might think it stupid. She was clearly agitated.

"Help me up," said Leda.

Eric stepped between her and the window. "You'll cut yourself." He tugged sharp-edged glass teeth out of the frame. Leda stared to the west, where the sky grew increasingly dark.

"Hurry," she said. "We need to find a ladder."

Eric shook his head without understanding and removed the last piece of glass. "Okay."

Once inside, Leda yanked the manual release on the garage door opener and slid the door up its tracks, but the outside wasn't that much lighter than the leaden interior. Eric spotted a ten-foot extension ladder hanging from a pair of hooks. He took one end while Leda carried the other, and they set it against the side of the house. Leda swarmed up before Eric was even sure the ladder was firmly planted. He rattled the ladder, then followed her.

Leda, bracing her tennis shoes against the siding, leaving a pair of smudges, chinned herself from the low garage roof to the higher roof above the second story. Running lightly, Eric jumped and caught the edge of the roof on his chest, easily levering himself up beside her.

"It's an advantage to be tall," he said, but she was peering west and didn't seem to hear him, or the clamor of wind might have swallowed his words.

"That's what I thought," she shouted.

"What?"

Eric looked back the way they'd come. Through the smoke at first he noticed the clouds, now directly overhead, blackening the sky and hiding the mountains. They'd lost their shapes, and become a single, sullen, flat gray plate seeming to rest only a hundred feet above and stretching north, south and west. To the east, a thin line of blue vanished as he watched.

"Not there," Leda said. "There." She pointed to where the road crested over a hill they'd come over a mile or so away. Smoke obscured his vision, then the distance cleared and he could see the intervening ground: closest to them, hundreds of house roofs poked through a broad expanse of trees bending in the wind. Beyond that, closely packed stores and warehouses crowded Bowles Avenue. Open field, golden with waist-high, dry prairie grass stretched both north and south behind the business areas. He saw nothing odd.

"Check the horizon," Leda said. Her hand traced the shape of the hill, and she waved to show the clouds above.

More smoke blew in their faces, and Eric turned away until it lessened. He wiped his eyes and studied the empty reach of road. A flicker of movement caught his attention. It was a black dog, maybe a Labrador Retriever, racing down the street. A few blocks farther, he spotted another pair of indeterminate breed, running their direction like greyhounds. He thought, what are they running from? and he looked at the clouds again. On the horizon, outlining the hill and the line of building and fields on either side, the cloud's color was different. Not the flat gray like that above them, but a seething, dark, dark red.

He started to ask, "What is that?" but he knew. A bright line of flame crested one side of the hill. Pushed by the wind, it flowed through the grass like water and washed against the backside of one of the mini-malls. A flash of light and flame enveloped the building, and a few seconds later, the dull whump of the explosion reached them. Flame broke over the top and the other side of the hill simultaneously. As far as he could see, in both directions, fire flew along the ground toward them.

"We've got to find a safe place!" yelled Leda. She hopped onto the garage roof, lost her footing on the pitch and almost slid off the edge before catching herself.

Eric leaned into the gale, which was really brutal now, and watched the flames for another instant. Wind flattened it out. It didn't look like a campfire, but like a blow-torch, nearly horizontal. A building in the path caught fire *before* the flame reached it. He realized the air in front must be super-heated. Nothing could stand up to it for long. He hopped down, careful not to fall, and followed Leda down the ladder to the ground.

"No place will be safe, Leda. We've got to outrun it." They hopped the brick wall. Leda recovered her pack and sleeping bag, shoving her arms into the straps.

She breathed hard, but not panicked. "The wind's forty or fifty miles an hour. It'll catch us." A piece of plywood large enough to cover a picture window blew across the lawn behind her and splintered in two against a light post.

"Listen," Eric said. He grabbed her arm. She tensed as if to pull away, then relaxed. The sound of a few more explosions reached them. Probably gas tanks, he guessed. Leda's dark hair streamed in front of her face. She cleared it away impatiently. Eric continued, "We don't have to run far." He pulled her along with him. "The Platte River is a half-mile, maybe less. If we can get to that, we'll be safe."

She looked over her shoulder, nodded and started running down the street. Eric followed.

For a block he kept up with her, his long legs matching her efficient jogger's rhythm, then he stumbled and almost fell. She didn't see him, and he regained stride. His legs were like rubber, and he remembered he hadn't eaten anything decent for . . . he couldn't come up with the last full meal he'd had, but it must have been at the cave. Since then he'd had a few handfuls of beef-jerky, a couple of cans of peaches, some Oreos and Twinkies from the Wal-Mart, and that was it.

The street dropped down a hill and through an intersection. Eric looked both directions as he crossed under the dead traffic signal. Then Bowles Avenue angled left. Leda turned with the street, and Eric stopped himself from yelling at her to go straight. He figured the river must be just beyond those houses, but he wasn't sure. Maybe the river curved, or, more likely, the fences and hedges would slow them down more than the distance to the water they'd cut off. He kept running.

Two blocks later sparks flew overhead, and he glanced back. He almost fell again, watching the treetops. Flame and smoke hid the center of the four-lane street a few hundred yards behind them, and he guessed that the house they'd stood on was already burning, but what was happening to the trees caught his attention now. Like long-fingered hands unclenching from fists, the wind stretched balls of flame from one tree to the next. For a second, the flames caressed the next victim, then the green tree burst into yellow, sickly light. Eric gasped at the sight and took in a lung full of caustic air. All the ornamental oaks, the willows and aspen, the birch and pine planted on the expensive front yards in little stands of three or four, lined along the property lines like sentinels, unwatered and dry as tinder, provided jump points for the fire.

Wind creaked the trees' branches as he ran, and he realized that the closer they got to the river, the thicker the trees were.

A house behind a low brick wall and across a long stretch of lawn directly to his left exploded. A billow of white and orange pushed the windows out, throwing a piece of the roof into the sky. "What?" Eric yelled in surprise. There wasn't fire within four blocks of them yet. Then he tripped.

Pavement rose toward him. He saw it coming, and he rolled his shoulder. As he fell, he thought, I've got to bounce right up. Dad's waiting. A second explosion ripped the house. Something whistled just above his head and whanged into the matching brick wall on the other side of the road. He hit partly on his shoulder, partly on his back pack. He heard a crunch, and his shoulder-blade went numb. Against the wall, bent in half, rested a snow shovel. A light pink gash in the darker brick showed where it had hit. Dully, he realized he'd smacked his head too.

A heavy thud in front of him shook the ground, and he looked up. At first what he saw was Leda, still running from the fire. Good for her, he thought. Go, Leda. Then, a few feet to the side, almost to the sidewalk, a metal semi-circle stuck out of the pavement. It took him a second to recognize it: a manhole cover. Gas in the sewers, he thought. The house must have filled with it. The whole street could go. He imagined the network of pipes under him loaded with natural gas. Why don't they all blow up?

Eric didn't hurt, but when he tried to push himself up, his right arm wouldn't hold his weight. He fell back to the road. He couldn't feel his hand. He lay there for a second, focusing on the pavement, looking at his fingers stupidly, as if they belonged to somebody else, and suddenly, the idea of rising and continuing the race to the river seemed too hard to him. His head throbbed. It'd be so much easier to stay here and rest a bit. And even as he thought this, another part of him knew he should be running. But the pavement feels so good. I'm tired, he thought. I've done more than anyone can ask. More than Dad could ask.

He shifted his weight so he could look back at the flames, and he heard the crunch that he'd heard when he fell. Shaking his shoulders, he heard it again. It must be the flashlight, he thought, not a bone. A tingle in his hand and arm confirmed it as feeling flowed back into them.

Blast-furnace hot, the wind pushed against his face. He screened his eyes and peered between his fingers. There was something beautiful about it. Up the street, a two-story cedar-sided house stood silhouetted against the fire. Then, a corona formed on the sides and roof, bright, so bright the house became a black form in the middle of the burning border. His mouth opened wide in surprise. The image was close and familiar; he'd seen it before, on a sheet of paper standing with his dad on a Mexican highway: the dark dot in the middle surrounded by light. An eclipse. A two-story, suburban, cedar eclipse.

"Come on, Eric. Get up!" Leda yanked on an arm, almost throwing him to his feet. "How far now?" she yelled. A steady roar like a freight train filled the air.

Shuffling his feet, Eric started after her. She pulled him into a run. He felt muddled. "Did you see the eclipse?" he asked, and he knew she would have no idea what he meant, if she even heard it.

She ran backwards, dragging him by his hand. "Come on. Come on. Come on," she chanted. Eric thought, She's holding my hand again. Just like Wal-Mart. Orange light reflected in her eyes. Eric caught the urgency and lengthened his pace. She shouted, "That's it. That's my boy."

In front of the aching, scorching wind, Eric ran. On the backs of his legs, he could feel it. Running full stride now, Leda beside him, he felt heat on the back of his head, like a hot compress, singeing his ears. Bowles Avenue curved right, and he saw the river. Beside it, River Front Mall, a huge, all-glass shopping center, glowed with the light of the fire behind them.

"The bridge," Eric tried to say, but the air was too hot and caught in the back of his throat so he nearly gagged. To both sides, houses burned. Leaves curled up, darkened and caught fire as the storm raced ahead of them. Eric pointed at the bridge, and he could feel the skin on his arm prickling like a sunburn; the bridge was down. A fifty-foot slice was missing from the middle.

It's okay, he thought, and no part of him was afraid. He felt calm. Like he had before at the cave when Jean Jacket and High School held guns on his father; and when Beetle-Eyes nearly killed him, and again when Meg started drawing blood, he remained unemotional. The situation was clear. We don't need to cross. We need to get in. Sparks whirled around him, in front of his face, in his hair, on the back of his neck. And he tried again to speak, but breathing the toxic air hurt too badly. His voice was gone. Without hesitation, as if she heard him anyway, Leda pulled him off the road, down the river embankment. A canopy of fire whooshed just overhead, barely missing them, nearly reaching across the river. Only the sudden slope of the bank saved them.

Water rose to their knees, and Eric lifted his knees high, forcing himself deeper. The inferno howled above. Mid-thigh now. Wind snapped their splashes straight away from them, then Eric stepped into a hole, pulling Leda down with him.

For a moment, silence: cold, clean and clear. Nothing. No explosions. No snapping, crackling, shattering roar. Mossy rocks slid beneath his hands as he let the current move him downriver. Water wrapped around him and held him: cool and calm and wet. The river bathed him, and it was only with real regret, seemingly minutes later, that he pushed himself up to gasp for breath.

Leda, panting, hunched over beside him, her face close to the waist-high water. Water streamed out of the bottom of her backpack, and her sleeping bag hung below it, a sodden, heavy weight, still partly in the river. Back to the wind, all the west bank a mural of fire behind them, they sucked in the moist air on the water's surface together. Eric stepped next to her, careful of the slick-rock bottom, and put his arm around her shoulders. He could feel each of her breaths. She steadied herself with a hand at his waist.

"I thought you said . . ." She breathed in four or five more deep gulps of air. ". . . that the river was less than a half mile run." She looked up at him, her face only inches away and smiled.

Embarrassed, and not sure whether to laugh or not, he said, "Sorry." He searched for words, but all he could finish with was, "Thanks. You know. For helping me get up."

"You're a lousy judge of distance, Eric." She looked back down at the water an inch from her nose and leaned her head against his. "It's a mile if it's a foot."

A hundred feet up-river, something exploded, sending a shower of glass into the water, turning the surface temporarily into foam. Eric said, "We ought to move to the middle."

"Yeah," she said without pulling her hand away, and they shuffled side by side, Eric's arm still around her shoulder, farther from the bank.

The water didn't get any deeper, and the current wasn't swift. He had no trouble keeping his balance. When he judged they were far enough away, he stopped, bracing one foot against a moss-strewn rock on the bottom that he thought might be a cinder block. Fighting the wind was a harder task than the current, so he stayed bent down and let the water hold him in place. Explosions thumped deep in the flames. A foot from his hand, something small splashed into the river. Then, a yard on the other side, two more quick splashes.

Leda slapped her hand over her ear. "Ouch!" She glanced up at him. "Shrapnel?" She pulled the hand away and studied it. Eric saw a spot of blood. He was about to look at her ear, when a piercing pain in his back jerked him to an upright position. All around them, the water turned to foam. Something bounced off his shoulder. Leda scrambled to take off her backpack.

"Help me," she said. "It's hail."

Trying to protect his head, Eric jerked at the sleeping bag's water-knotted strings. Dozens of more marble-sized hail stones hit him before they opened the bag up. Leda flinched when they struck, but didn't say anything, working quickly to unzip the bag and spreading it out over the water so they could hide under its thick protection.

They crouched in the cold water of the Platte River while hail hammered down, stinging Eric's hands even through the heavy bag. Floating ice pellets piled up against his back. Eric shivered, shifting frequently to let them by. After a while, Leda closed her eyes, and Eric guessed from the line of her jaw she was struggling not to let her teeth chatter.

Drips fell steadily from the soaked bag. It ran down their arms. Eric could feel her leg quivering against his under the water. "Are you all right?" he asked.

"I'm cold," she said. Hail stones crashed the water's surface into spray, and the chorus of tiny splashes sounded like bacon frying.

"You'll be fine," he said. "You're tough."

Her face close to his, the weight of the bag resting on their heads, she smiled a thanks at him, and he understood that he had said exactly the right thing at the right moment. He had given her a present.

As suddenly as it had come, the wind slowed, and the hail fell nearly straight down. Without the wind to back it, the fires on shore seemed to lose their spirit, and instead of being an avalanche of unbroken flame, they became individual fires. From eye level, the river looked like liquid popcorn, still popping as the hail continued, flowing smoothly past. At his feet, the water seemed almost warm, but under his chin and down his chest and back, the coolness that had at first been such a miracle twenty minutes ago, had turned rock cold, and he found himself quivering in spasms so tight his face ached.

Hail turned to rain, pressing down the fires. It didn't look like the flame had crossed the river anywhere, and Eric realized that if the conflagration had begun on the other side of the river, his house might have burned down. Dad would have had nowhere to hide. The close call made him shake even harder, and Leda said, "Are *you* all right?"

Eric unclenched his jaw, and found he could barely move his arms to put the sleeping bag down. He stuttered, "Ye. . .yes."

She pushed their cover away and turned him toward her, holding his face in her hands. The sleeping bag rolled slowly down stream, and the rain became slushy, not hurting, but mushing against him sloppily. "Your lips are blue," she said. "Come on."

"We've lost the packs," he said. He searched the river surface for any sign of them.

"Doesn't matter," she replied as she guided him across the water. Eric tried to help, but his legs seemed far away and unresponsive. Every rock reached out and tripped him. He fell several times, once banging his elbow on the bottom, but that didn't rouse him. He tried to make a joke of it as they staggered out of the river, but his words slurred and sounded unfamiliar in his own ears.

Although the wind had died somewhat, a breeze still fluttered a torn American flag hanging in front of the bank, and Eric found himself staring at it because it looked strange. At first he decided it was the sunset light through the storm clouds—he was dimly aware that Leda was still tugging on his arm, dragging him up Littleton Boulevard, and it annoyed him; the flag was interesting—but then he saw the snow. The flag looked peculiar because the sleet had turned to giant white flakes, spinning lightly down. He thought, In June. Who'd have thought it'd snow in June? It stuck in Leda's dark hair. He reached up to pluck a flake out, but his fingers wouldn't pinch together, and he bumped the back of her head.

She said, "You're frozen." He thought her lips looked pretty blue too, and he didn't want to say this, but he liked the way her blouse stuck to her. "We've got to get you warm," she added.

He tried to say, "I just need to rest," but it came out, "I yusht nee to resht."

After what seemed like hours of Leda pulling, and Eric pausing to lean against light poles or mail boxes, he found himself in a front yard alone. Where's she? he thought. Snow still fell thickly. He couldn't see the grass at all. Rotating slowly, he looked for her. Their footsteps marking the snow showed where they'd come from. Soberly, he followed their path with his eyes until he reached his own feet. I'm here, he thought. I'm not lost. It's her fault. He turned and tracked her steps to the house, a white bungalow with blue trim. On the door, someone had painted a blue goose with a "Welcome" sign on it. Her steps led to the front window, and it took him a moment to notice that it was broken in. Nearly all the glass was gone.

The front door opened, and Leda hurried out. "It's empty," she said. "Furnace is off, but I found blankets." Her teeth did chatter now, loudly. She led him up the step, through the living room, and into a bedroom. It was so dark inside he could barely see her. He started shaking again.

She moved around the room, but he couldn't tell what she was doing. She said, "We've got to get warm." He could see the outline of the bed, and the urge to lay down moved him toward it. I'll be better after some sleep, he thought. We're in Littleton now, and Dad's not far away.

"No," Leda said. "You're sopping wet."

He felt her hands against his chest, holding him upright. Then she fumbled with the buttons. He could barely stand, the shivering was so hard, and he couldn't tell what she was doing anymore.

He was cold though. He knew that. Damn cold.

The room tilted. He tried to keep balance, but it was inevitable and irresistible, the bed rising up from the floor. I am, he thought, delirious, and that felt good, to let go, to let his guard drop. He could feel himself losing it.

And in his mind's eye, fire haloed a two-story cedar house, a ring of light around a circle of dark. He could feel his dad's hand on his shoulder. "Some things can't be looked at straight on," he said. Leda spoke from the darkness, her voice kind and low and subtle, full of breath. "Fifteen? You're fifteen?" Then, from out of the eclipse, rose her face, and she smiled.

Chapter Seventeen

FIRST TIME

T here are so many of them," Eric said as another pair of soldiers marched by their hiding place, a pile of wood and brick rubble, the sunken remains of a house next to an intersection. A bent street sign leaning over the cracked sidewalk said "College Ave." The other sign said "Broadway." He had an awful premonition of hundreds of men like the ones who had executed the prisoners in the canyon the day before, a whole army overrunning Highwater and Littleton. There'd be no way to hold them back.

"No," whispered Teach. "I think this is *all* of them, but they're surrounding the campus, so it seems like a lot." The patrol turned onto a path cut through head-high sage that grew between the distinctive red-stoned architecture of the University of Colorado. The building to the right of the path looked like a shell, its doors gone, the glassless windows gaping darkly. The smaller building on the left looked better cared for. Its windows were boarded, and the doors were barred tight. A thinning of the bushes showed where the sidewalk led to the door. In town, the streets were relatively clear of vegetation, the normal grasses pushing through cracks, but sage and greasewood crowded what used to be suburban lawns. On the campus, the growth seemed even wilder. Tough, dark-barked branches pushed against the buildings, choking the spaces between them. Most city trees, of course, thought Eric, died long ago. Boulder, like Denver, had once been covered by beautiful trees, all gone now without constant watering.

A thin, mechanical sound drifted to him from somewhere deeper in the campus. It was speech, but high and tinny and he couldn't make out the words. Someone on a bullhorn, he decided.

Eric peered over the top of the rubble. From here, the red brick of the C.U. campus stood out from the dusty green and gray brush.

He'd seen little evidence of fire damage in Boulder, which surprised him. Fires swept through the prairies around Littleton every five or six years, and none of the thousands of wood frame houses still stood. Only the most solid of the brick homes and the steel and glass businesses remained relatively unscathed. But here, the city's empty buildings rattled and clattered and creaked in the breeze, and downed power lines flapped against their lonesome poles. Boulder was a true ghost town. All the damage seemed to be caused by vandalism, wind, rain or the plain old weight of time. "You know what makes me feel better," Eric said, "is that I haven't seen anything motorized. They may have guns, but no trucks or tanks."

Teach grunted. "We're on foot too, you know." He scanned the buildings across the street sourly. "The problem is all this brush. It's so thick. I don't see but one or two ways through, and if Federal's got any sense at all, they're guarded. How are we going to get to your library? And for that matter, the campus is so big. How are we going to find the kids?"

Eric swallowed his fear. Since they'd reached the Boulder city limits, it had been all he could do to resist calling out for Dodge and Rabbit. They were out there somewhere, among the deserted houses, stupidly moving toward whatever goal he'd planted in their brains. "We ought to wait a bit . . ." said Eric, ". . . to see their routine. If we can get into any of those," He waved at the structures across Broadway. "We might be able to make the library. Besides, the best we can do to meet up with the kids is to go to the place they know we're going to. Either they're there already, or they will be soon."

"Okay," said Teach. "We wait. You watch." He propped the water skin beneath his head, shut his eyes, and within seconds, seemed to sleep.

Eric crawled a few feet away from Teach to a low spot in the foundation they hid behind. He could see both stretches of the street and the paths between the closest buildings. Rabbit, he thought, Dodge, where are you? He imagined them held captive or shot outright. How could he live knowing he'd brought them to this danger? He should have sent them home when they joined him days ago. Nothing was gained by bringing them. He stared at the backs of his liver-spotted hands, turned them over, made fists of them, and the bony knuckles stood out from the near translucent skin. I'm an old man, he thought. I needed them to be young for me, and, he admitted, closing his eyes, I wanted to be a better grandfather to Dodge than I was a father to Troy. If Dodge could see the books, he'd know. If he could see all the learning man has piled up, he'd know what man is capable of. We don't have to fall back to the beginning. We can rise again, but we have to do it with him and his generation. Another handful of years, and it will all be too late. The secret is in the books. We find out what is making Littleton sick, then we go on and rebuild. That's what we'll do.

He could see in his imagination an older Dodge leading them bravely into the new world. No mistakes this time. It'd be a smarter, happier people who learned from the missteps of the past.

But first we'll have to find them.

The tramp of feet caught his ear, and he slid back a foot, pushing his chin into the dirt. Two more soldiers passed by, turning onto the same path the first two had followed. Ten minutes apart, or so, he thought.

Eric jostled Teach. "Now's the time," he said.

Instantly alert, Teach rolled to his hands and knees, checked the street himself and nodded. "What's the plan?"

"We start there." Eric pointed to the damaged building.

*

In the basement, mostly by feel, Eric found it. The building's boiler room had been stripped of almost anything portable. All that remained was junk, and the boilers themselves, two bulbous iron shapes bristling with pipes and dangling wires. The trap door was behind the second boiler. Eric strained to raise it. The metal door moved up an inch, then stopped. Teach slipped his hands beneath the edge and yanked hard with no more luck.

"I'm right," said Eric. "It's locked from the other side. We'll need to pry it open."

Teach broke a four foot length of two-inch pipe from its junction to the boiler. "This'll give me enough leverage," he said, balancing the pipe in the middle. "Now I need a thin edge of the wedge."

Eric pulled a short-handled bolt cutter from his pack. "Will this do?"

Teach stuck the handle into one end of the pipe, jammed the bolt cutter under the trap door, used a brick as a fulcrum and leaned his weight on the free end of the pipe. The door groaned; something snapped, and Teach flopped to the floor.

Teach handed the bolt cutter to Eric. "Pretty convenient thing to be toting around. No wonder your pack's so heavy. Any other surprises in there?"

Eric pushed the cutter back in place. "Standard equipment for a scavenger."

Teach only raised his eyebrows when Eric produced a candle lantern from the pack, lit it and climbed down a short ladder into a passage. He paused before stepping to the bottom. The flickering light revealed parallel lines of thickly insulated pipes and conduit reaching into the dark. Water covered the floor, but there was no way to tell how deep it was. Eric looked up. The candle gave Teach's skin a yellow hue. "Coming?" asked Eric. He took the last step; the water barely lapped over the rubber soles of his hiking boots.

"Do we have to?" asked Teach weakly.

After splashing along for a couple of minutes, ducking their heads beneath low-slung I-beams every ten feet, Teach said, "Will this get us there?"

Eric kept his hand on a conduit next to him. The water wasn't deep, but the footing was slippery. "It's not a direct route. This passage ought to take us to the Heating Plant where all the heat and power originated."

"So, what were those boilers for?"

Eric thought about it. Their steps echoed in the passageway. The air smelled dank, but not dead. He guessed that there must be circulation. "Maybe they're for back up. I studied the maps and a schematic of C.U., but they didn't say anything about that."

They reached an intersection, and Eric stopped. Teach bumped him from behind.

"Where's this go?" asked Teach.

Eric held up the lantern, but the pale light showed only a few feet of passage. "It wasn't on the map." A sign bolted on the wall said, "B-82."

Eric had always had a good memory for things he'd read, and in his mind's eye he could see the map of C.U. on his dining room table, the late afternoon sun slanting across it as he placed his finger on each building and looked for its name in the key. He smiled to himself. "It's to the theater. We started from the basement of the Geology Center. Next to it was Economics. This passage wasn't on the map, but that's the theater's number from the schematic." Eric pointed to the sign. "If this goes where it ought to, we'll be underneath the Ekeley Chemical Laboratories Complex in a few hundred yards, which will put us close to the library."

"The place gives me the creeps. If it weren't for the kids, you couldn't have gotten me down a hole like this for a year's supply of firewood." Teach's deep voice rumbled in the dark, but he sounded unsure, a little panicky. Eric gritted his teeth. The reminder of the lost kids made him quiver, and Teach's nervousness set him on edge. Here, in the service tunnels beneath the campus, Teach looked out of place. Water soaked his soft leather soled moccasins, and goose bumps stood his leg hairs on end.

They started forward again, Eric holding the lantern ahead of them, feeling each step carefully, although the floor had not varied and the water had remained a uniform half-inch in depth so far. "It's a scavenger skill," said Eric patiently. "For years, we've explored the Gone Time places, hunting for supplies, looking for the treasures that had been left behind. I've spent thousands of hours in the dark."

They came to a ladder. Eric climbed a few rungs and shown the light on the trap-door above. A huge padlock was snapped shut around a pair of sloppily welded rings to hold the door closed. Here a sign said, "B-19."

"Right on path," said Eric. "That's Chemistry. Arts and Science should be directly ahead, and the library will be on our left."

Eric moved the light close to the ladder rungs. "See this," he said and showed Teach how a thin layer of flaky rust coated each step. "The middles are scraped clean, though. Whoever locked the doors did it pretty recently. Probably in the last year. Either somebody is living in the tunnels, or there is one door that's locked on the outside."

Teach rubbed his finger on the rung and held it up. "Damp. It would rust in a couple of days. Somebody uses this ladder a lot."

Eric smiled. "Give me a couple of months and I'll make a scavenger out of you."

Teach shuddered. "Jackal's life isn't for me. Too many poisons. If it's Gone Time I say leave it lie. Good for cooking fire talk, but don't play with their toys."

"You'd rather a bear ate you, or your children died from measles, huh? Are you happy knowing that your expected life span is twenty years shorter than mine?" Suddenly angry, Eric stomped down the corridor, splashing dark splotches against both walls. He felt the blood rising in his face. We're so close, he thought. The library's right around the corner, and this . . . this . . . caveman doesn't know why we're here.

Behind him, Teach said evenly, "I've heard a lot about the Gone Time. Mostly horror stories I've got to tell you. Stuff my parents told me. What Ripple's found out. Even the things you've said. I've heard about Gone Time magic, tales I can hardly believe, but you know what I never hear anyone say? That Gone Time people were happy. For all the cars and trains and subways, for all the medicine and telephones and computers, for all the manufacturing and invention and television, I haven't heard a single word about how happy the Gone Times were. So why don't you answer your question? Were you happy in the Gone Time? When was the first time you were really happy?"

They pushed on in the dark in the silence punctuated by the hollow slap of their feet on the wet floor, and Eric thought back, and he remembered the first time:

Between conscious and unconscious he drifted, and he was thinking, I'm warm again, and he floated. Slowly he felt himself moving upwards, out of the lethargy and dreaming of sleep, and briefly he thought of going back to the soft blankness, but he didn't, and slowly he became aware that he was lying on his side. He was wrapped in warmth. It pushed against his back and sides, even over his ears and the top of his head. He breathed in the moisture of his own breath. His head rested on soft, warm cloth.

Vaguely, he wondered where he was and how he got here. It was like he'd been sick when he was a child. He'd hide under the blankets with his fevers and chills, and listen to the gentle hiss from the vaporizer, smell the rich penetrating odor of Vick's Vapor Rub, and he'd stay covered up until the fever broke and he was wet with perspiration. For hours he'd stay wrapped, interrupted only by his mother checking on him. Being sick was no fun, but afterwards, wrapped and warm and tired, he felt content.

That's how he felt now, but he knew he wasn't a child, and after a while he started to think about what had happened in the last few days: the cave, the long bike ride, the destruction in Golden and the ghost cop, Meg and the basement, wind, the long run from the fire, hail, snow, cold, and Leda. None of these memories worried him. He was just sorting them out lazily, as if they'd slipped out of place, and he needed to file them again.

Where am I? he thought. What does it matter? he answered,

and he let his attention drift away again almost back to sleep. His right arm seemed to be trapped, but he didn't feel energetic enough to move it. His left arm was draped over something, and the weighty softness of cloth pressed around it all. Beneath his left hand, he felt a warm, damp, smooth surface, and he rubbed it gently.

Still not awake, sleep like a great, fuzzy presence in his mind, he massaged the surface beneath his hand and it stirred. An arm tightened around him, and he realized he was holding Leda. They were in bed, and he remembered the white bungalow with blue trim, the blue goose with "Welcome" painted on it on the front door. He felt a hand on his back move; fingernails scratched lightly by his shoulder blade, not purposefully, accidently; she was still sleeping. Her forehead rested on his chest, and he could feel her breathing. He pressed against her back, pulling her closer and continued rubbing. Skin rippled under his palm, her backbone a gentle line of bumps, her skin slick with sweat. The tiny hairs at the back of her neck felt like mouse fur. He left his hand there and moved his fingers in tiny motions, stroking lightly, holding her, and gradually, through his drowsiness, he realized they were naked, that she had saved his life with her body warmth. Her chest rested against his own. His left knee lay on top of her knee.

This wasn't what he'd imagined being in bed with a woman would be like. He thought of the scenes from movies he'd seen, the arching, violent couplings; the athletic, frantic gymnastics in film after film, but here he was in bed with Leda, holding the back of her neck, feeling her breath on his skin as she slept, and it felt comfortable and lazy and . . . and . . . right. Not even sexual as he'd always thought of it. Just good. He lay like that for a long time. A half-hour or more he guessed.

Then, her hand moved again, rubbing his shoulder blade, and he tightened up. She's awake, he thought, and this moment will be over. I'm warm and safe and we'll climb out of bed. She'll never talk about it. She just had to save my life. That's all.

But her hand kept moving, and he began to relax again. It was so warm. There was no light at all. He felt as if they'd transported themselves into a different universe, one no larger than the womb of blankets and each other. The only sounds were the sounds of their breath, the rustle of skin on skin. The only smells were the smells of each other, moist, rich human smells. She rubbed one shoulder blade and then the other, and Eric moved his hand down from her neck to rub her shoulder blades, mirroring what she did with her hand, massaging high on her back on one side and then the other; the thin sheen of sweat helped his hand glide effortlessly. For a long time she just rubbed his shoulder blades, working on one gently for minutes, sometimes stopping as if she'd dropped back off to sleep, then switching to the other for more time. Then her hand found larger circles, now high on his side, now reaching all the way around him. Her stomach touched his. Eric followed her lead, letting her hand tell his where to go. Against his chest, in his ear, he could tell her breathing was deeper now. She trailed her fingertips against his backbone, tracing them, bone to bone, from his neck, slowly down his back—his hand did the same; her skin flowed smoothly under his hand—lower and lower until she was in the small of his back rubbing the delicate areas over his kidneys, pulling his stomach against hers with each motion, pulling himself against her, and he was breathing deeply too, not sure if he should be scared or excited, but desperately, desperately sure he never wanted this to end.

Then Leda reached farther until her hand was rubbing his bottom, and he let his hand do the same; she gasped slightly as he passed the dip in the small of her back to mimic her, and she pulled her knee out from under his, pulling him even closer, shifting her legs. She wrapped her leg over the top of his, used her foot against the back of his legs to pull him against her. He panicked, and all his muscles locked up. "No," he choked out, his breathing as ragged as if he'd just finished a hundred yard dash.

She kept him close. "It's all right, Eric," she said between her own gasps. "It's all right." And after a moment, he relaxed and let her guide him.

It was the first time he could truly remember being happy.

And it was after the Gone Time was done.

Teach said, "Do you remember?"

Eric looked around. He had lost track of time and the tunnel surprised him. "Have we gone by any other passages?" he said.

Sounding puzzled, Teach said, "Of course not."

"Good. We have to find the library."

"I know. You said that." They splashed on. Teach said, "Are you all right?"

"Just keep your eyes open is all," Eric snapped. He bit the skin inside his mouth until he tasted a little blood. Getting lost in a memory like that, even a wonderful memory, disturbed him. Concentrate, he thought. Stay in the present.

A few paces later they came to another junction. The sign read, "B-61."

"Hah," said Eric. "This is the way."

The tunnel jogged left, then right. They made the second turn, and a line of lights in the ceiling flicked on, revealing the end of the tunnel and a ladder up.

"Someone knows we're here," said Teach.

Eric blew out the candle. "Maybe, maybe not. That's a motion detector I think." He pointed to a pair of boxes mounted on the sides of the tunnel. "I tripped it when I crossed between them."

"Motion detector?"

"It's an electronic thing. The lights may have gone on automatically. Of course, if the lights go on here, an alarm may have gone off somewhere else." Looking up the ladder, Eric continued, "You're right that one door wouldn't be locked on the inside." Taking a deep breath, he said, " This is it," and started up. Teach followed.

At the top, Eric pushed the trap-door open an inch and peered out. From what he could see, he was in a basement like the one they'd started in. Broken boiler equipment, moldy-looking boxes bursting at the seams, and a flight of stairs leading to a shut door. The difference was that this basement was lit by electric light. Eric wondered where the power came from as he opened the trap door the rest of the way.

Teach was just climbing out when the door at the top of the stairs opened revealing an older woman in a white smock, who was saying as she stepped through, "It's about time you got back . . . ." She looked at them a second, mouth open, screeched, and slammed the door in Teach's face as he bounded up the stairs.

Teach grabbed the handle and twisted it to no avail. He threw his shoulder into the panel, but it didn't even rattle. He sat on the top stair. "Now what?" he said.

"I guess we wait," said Eric. "It's their library."

He heard a voice on a bullhorn coming from outside the building, the voice he couldn't understand earlier. It chanted the same phrase over and over without intonation, almost without intelligence. "Give up your books for the good of the people. Give up your books for the good of the people. Give up your books for the good of the people . . . ."

Chapter Eighteen
GOING HOME

I t'll be good for you, Eric. You've got to eat." Leda sat cross-legged on the bed, her shirt untucked, the sun a hazy circle in the dark curtain behind her.

"We've got to hit the road," he answered. Then, embarrassed, he opened his mouth again and let her spoon in another helping of cold tomato soup. "It's gross," he mumbled. The unthinned soup felt like a clot in his mouth, like a wad of chicken fat.

"Hypothermia's no joke." With business like efficiency, she leaned forward with a spoonful, and he swallowed it without tasting. "If you don't fuel the engine, you won't have any get up and go."

Eric tried to read her expression, but her concentration on not spilling the soup revealed nothing. He hadn't awakened when she got out of bed. The first thing he remembered was her pulling the covers off his face, and she was already dressed.

Has she forgot last night? he thought. Trying to keep the irony out of his voice, he said, "I've got get up and go." It came out sounding whiny to him.

She grunted noncommittally and scraped the can for the last bit of soup. "Well then, get up," she said finally.

Keenly aware of his nakedness, he waited until she left the room, then he pushed the blankets off and searched the floor for his clothes. He thought, I don't feel any different. Today's like yesterday.

His jeans lay in a puddle behind the door and felt as if they weighed ten pounds. They splashed when he dropped them.

I don't know why everyone makes such a big deal about it, he thought, but he could still feel her cheek against his, the breath on his neck, her hands on his lower back pulling against him. He shook his head and opened a dresser drawer where he found a pale green long-sleeve shirt two sizes too small that smelled faintly of mint. An old man's clothes, he thought—a dead man. He couldn't bring himself to wear the boxer shorts folded neatly in another drawer. In the closet, next to a half-dozen flower print dresses, hung five identical pairs of pressed, gray rayon pants. The cuffs didn't reach his ankles, and the waist left a six-inch gap when he stretched it away from his stomach. He cinched them tight with a narrow black belt. Since water still soaked his sneakers, he decided against a pair of argyles and slipped his bare feet into the cold shoes instead. Pausing at the door, he took a deep breath, then walked out of the bedroom, through a short hall and into the kitchen.

Leda knelt on a counter top, reaching deep into a cupboard. "All canned soup. Nothing else. Stuff in the fridge is spoiled too. That's all there is to eat." Her muffled voice sounded cool, competent, as if she were addressing a stranger.

She didn't pull her head out of the cupboard as she spoke.

Tentatively, Eric said, "My dad's probably got plenty of good food. We're only ten or fifteen blocks from there now."

"Right." She slid off the counter. "Don't we make a pair?" she said, as if she were kidding, but she didn't laugh, didn't smile, didn't even meet his eyes. She wore a maroon man's shirt with the sleeves rolled above her elbows and a baggy pair of gray pants that matched Eric's, although the cuffs piled up on her shoes. "Let's go then."

"Okay. Fine," said Eric, and he decided to forget about last night. It was a freak thing, he thought. Maybe it didn't happen at all. Like a dream. But as he followed her out the door and into the bright sunlight of the morning, he felt heavy and bleak, and he wanted to hug her, to feel her reality in his arms—to be hugged back. She strode purposefully to the street, down the sidewalk, away from the blue-trimmed white bungalow with the blue goose and its warm, hand-painted "Welcome."

On the lawns, the reminders of yesterday's snow existed only in the shadows as thin sheets of slushy ice, retreating as the sun advanced. Steam tendrils wavered from wet spots on the asphalt, and already half the street was dry. Eric guessed it might be seventy degrees. For the first time in days, he couldn't smell smoke, just wet grass and spring air.

"We go that way," he said and pointed up the hill of Littleton Boulevard. Although they were only a quarter-mile from the river, trees and houses blocked his view and he couldn't see how extensive the fire had been. Littleton seemed almost untouched. Some trash on parking lots, some boarded up stores, but little of the destruction he'd seen in Golden or West Denver. His shoes squished with each step as they walked on the broad sidewalk toward the King Soopers shopping center and East Elementary, where Eric had once gone to school. Across the street, the Crestwood, a restaurant his family sometimes went to, looked sad and deserted. The fountains that sprayed into twin decorative ponds weren't running;. No newspapers filled the stands, and one of the heavy wooden doors canted away from the other, attached only by the bottom hinge.

He caught up to her so they'd walk side by side and he could cast quick glances at her from the corner of his eye.

"What are you going to do if you find your dad?" she said abruptly. Her voice sounded too loud.

"*When* I find him."

She sighed. "Sorry, when."

They reached the top of the hill, and a few blocks farther the intersection of Littleton Boulevard and Broadway awaited, normally the busiest intersection in Littleton, but the crossing lights were dark, and the streets empty.

He said, "You know, I haven't seen a car in two days."

Water gurgled down the gutter beside him, rushing toward sewer grates. The last of the snow melt echoed tinnily down drain spouts in the houses to his right. Drops pattered into the grass from sodden trees. Water sounds splashed and slithered softly all around them. Other than the bark of a distant dog, he heard nothing else. No planes. No cars. No children. As long as he had lived in Littleton, he remembered that if he stopped and listened carefully on a summer day, he had been able to hear children and horns, the roar of lawn mowers, the pounding of hammers in garages. On Friday nights in the fall, the music of the high school band playing at half time reached his yard. Littleton was a place of friendly noise. Even late at night when he stepped outside, he heard the rumble of cars on Broadway. But now, nothing. Just the water sneaking away.

Leda said, "It's too creepy here. Can we get off this road?"

"Sure. We have to cut right anyway." They turned up Lakeview Street into an old suburban neighborhood where small brick one-stories nestled side by side. For a second, Eric thought that it had been colder here, that ice shards were catching the sun and reflecting it off the lawns. Then he realized it was glass. In front of where the picture window of each house they passed used to be lay broken glass. They reached Shepherd Avenue and crossed, heading toward Ketring Park. Its trees waved above the roof tops. More broken glass. House after house. In some houses, torn drapery and broken curtain rods indicated the windows had been broken from the outside.

As they walked he grimaced. We're almost to Dad, he thought, and right after that, he thought, What's going on with Leda? His gut ached. Cold tomato soup sloshed nauseatingly with each step. A hot spot on both of his heels told him that his sockless feet in the wet shoes were blistering.

He glanced her way again. She kept her eyes resolutely forward. He thought of reasons why she changed. Yesterday we could talk. Yesterday was cool. He cast theories around. Maybe she's embarrassed. I mean, I'm a just a kid to her. Or maybe she's got a boyfriend. Maybe she's married! He checked her hands as they swung by her side. No rings. But none of the theories rang true, not emotionally true, and he concluded that she hated him. Nothing else made sense. He'd done a terrible thing, and now it was all she could do to tolerate him. He felt an urge to apologize. The words danced on the tip of his tongue, and he almost said them, but what came out was, "Why all the vandalism?"

A block ahead, in Ketring's parking lot, two backhoes glistened dully yellow in the sun. Beside them, a flatbed truck piled high with body bags attracted a cloud of flies, writhing and twisting above the black forms like a huge, angry ghost. Eric turned a block early to avoid the park.

Leda said, "Fear." She walked silently for a dozen strides. She shook her head, as if she'd come to a decision. "How far away are we?"

"Ten minutes, tops," said Eric. They turned onto West Aberdeen Avenue. When he was five, he had chased an ice cream truck down this street. He'd delivered papers here when he was twelve. He knew who lived in most of the houses. The white-bricked one with the lavender trim belonged to the Stewarts, whose two daughters were on the student senate at the school. The Isenbergs lived in the cedar house. Their son, Chaim, was the only Jew Eric knew. Beyond them were the Johnsons, the Cardwells and the Gizzys. All with busted in windows and no signs of life. Home, he thought, I'm nearly home.

Leda said, "A couple of week ago, gangs started going around setting cars on fire, breaking windows, beating anyone well enough to be on the street. Not just kids either. Old guys. Sick, angry. People shot anyone coming to their doors. Scary stuff. They were just afraid, I guess, and they couldn't do anything about it, so they lashed out." She brushed hair away from her face, then waved her hand at the houses. "Probably this happened late. One or two guys with baseball bats or something, fever just starting, little bit of itch in their throats. Nothing left to do. Everybody dying and all that glass unbroken. Must have seemed like some kind of metaphor."

Eric sighed gratefully; his shoulders relaxed, and he realized how tense he'd been. It was the most she had spoken since this morning.

A movement behind a mini-van parked in the Gizzy's driveway across the street caught his attention. A Doberman, its ears up and pointed, watched them intently. As they passed, Eric saw that its muzzle was torn, and part of the side of its head was ripped as if it had been in a fight or had collided with some barbed wire.

Leda continued, "Of course, the gangs only lasted a few days. The bug caught 'em, or the National Guard or the helicopter boys."

The Doberman stood. Another dog, a collie, emerged from the shadows by the house and joined him. A couple others lay in the shadow, their mouths open, panting.

"That's a big dog," said Leda. It stepped toward them. "Nice puppy," she said.

"Looks well fed." Eric scanned the ground for a rock or stick, but grass lapped against the sidewalk, and the dead roses in the flower bed sprawled over mud. He shuffled along sideways, keeping his face toward the dog. Sweat beaded under his arms although it was still cool. "What do you think he's been eating?"

"Gross thought," said Leda, walking backwards, watching the dog. "Kibbles and Bits?"

Growling and stiff-legged, the Doberman crossed the gutter onto the edge of the street. Leda raised her hand over her head and mimed a throw. It ducked and retreated a step, then started barking. The other dogs stood, heads low, growling deep.

Eric said, "They don't seem too friendly. Maybe we just need to get out of their territory." He remembered dogs from when he carried papers, and he thought he recognized the collie from the Kissle's house up the block. It had always greeted him at the door with slobbery licks on his hands when he collected once a month, but it didn't look playful now with its lips raised off its gums and its tail straight down and still.

Eric kept moving, thirty feet, fifty feet. Heads low, the dogs crossed the street, matching their pace. The Doberman led, still barking: loud, repetitive, explosive, insane-sounding.

"How big's their territory?" asked Leda. Her low, calm voice comforted Eric. He swallowed dryly. Step by step, the dogs advanced.

Eric said, "No sudden movements." Then the other three dogs started barking. "Run!" he yelled, and he sprinted up the lawn.

Arms pumping, breath tight, Leda beside him, he headed for the broken picture window above a knee-high growth of shrubbery. Barking stopped, but a frantic clatter of claws on asphalt spurred him on. He thought of his Achilles tendons, unsocked, glaring below the short pants, crying out "Meat, meat, meat." And he knew the thought should have been funny, but it wasn't.

He dove through the window, trying not to land on the broken glass, Leda right with him, and they slid across a hardwood floor into a gray and blue pin-striped sofa. A Tiffany lamp on an end table, teetered, fell, and shattered on the floor. "Up! Up!" he yelled, pulling on her arm. Barking boomed outside the window, and he saw them hesitating. He thought, maybe going into a strange house was too new for these dogs who'd learned to adapt so fast. The Doberman circled twice, howling, all black gums and shiny teeth, then charged the bushes, the others in tow.

"Shit!" Leda pushed him in the back, and they scrambled into a short hall with three closed doors.

Eric tugged at the first door knob, and it didn't turn, then things began to slow down for him, became almost dream like. Leda reached for the knob when Eric's hand slipped off. She'd cut her palm; a shallow flap of skin waved free and blood streaked her wrist. Her dark hair hung down, covering her face. Eric thought, we'll have to get that cut wrapped.

Still, while he stared at her wrist (a drop of blood broke free and floated lazily to the floor), since so many horrible things had happened to him in the last few days, since so many times he'd been running or scared, the oddness of his detachment occurred to him. He thought, four months ago I was going to school, watching MTV, and now I'm hoping a stranger, an older woman I slept with last night, can get a door open in sombody's house before a man-eater dog can attack me. He thought it almost laughable.

A scratching noise in the living room and then a series of thuds told him of the dogs' progress. Then a distinct metallic sound from beyond the locked door. Leda pulled, and he heard from the other side a semi-loud *chink-chink*, like someone shaking a bottle full of coins up once then down. I know that sound, thought Eric.

"Get away!" hissed a voice on the other side.

Leda looked toward him in surprise, her hair flying in her face in slow motion, her own teeth bared, her hand on the knob. The Doberman rounded the corner, tensed his thighs and sprang for Leda's throat.

A connection flashed in Eric's mind, a sound memory from a scene in *Terminator II*: Linda Hamilton stalking the second terminator, the one made of liquid metal. Mad as hell, she marched toward it, her one arm hurt or broken, and in the other hand she held a pump shotgun. In a real strength move, one that marveled Eric then, she chambered a shell home with one hand. She jerked the gun up and down once. *Chink-chink.*

Eric caught Leda's arm and threw himself backwards. Her head jerked. The dog sailed toward them.

They fell.

Suspended, the Doberman hung in the air, mouth agape, teeth luminous.

Then a section of the door blasted out, catching the Doberman, throwing it against the wall. It almost seemed to stick for a moment, and Eric thought he saw, in the second before it slid wetly to the floor, a look of profound disappointment in its furious face. Cordite and burnt wood smoke eddied to the ceiling.

Cowering, the other dogs stood at the entrance to the hallway. Eric thought, I didn't even hear the shotgun.

Chink-chink.

Grabbing Leda's collar, Eric scrambled backwards to the next door, which swung open easily under his pressure. Still on his backside, he pulled Leda after him. She kicked the door shut.

"You're choking me," she gasped, and he let go of her collar.

"Get out of my house!" screamed a voice, and the roar of the gun was deafening this time. In the hollow ringing that followed the explosion, the sound of alphabet blocks scattering across the floor seemed unnaturally loud.

"Get away from my baby!"

On the wall adjoining the other room stood a crib, a tightly sheeted bundle resting in the exact middle of a bare mattress. *Chink-chink.* Another shell in the chamber! thought Eric. A pie plate-sized hole appeared in the wall, knocking a corner off the crib, blowing sheetrock dust in on them.

Eric stood, picked up a kid's rocking chair and heaved it through the unbroken window. While Leda flopped a blanket over the ragged knives of glass and went through the opening first, the repetitive metallic cocking of the gun followed by a *click* beat out a manic rhythm, and a rising wail penetrated the wall. Filled with grief and death, and hardly human, the sound chased them out of the house.

Later, after they'd crossed two more lawns, passed through two more picture windows (careful to yell out before entering, "Anyone home?"), down two more bedroomed hallways, shutting doors behind them, and crawled out two more bedroom windows to throw off the dogs. They sat with their backs against a sun warm cinder block garden wall.

Eric said, "Looks like you cut your hand."

Sweat soaked Leda's maroon shirt in wide circles from her armpits to the her belt. Her head was back and her eyes closed. "Yeah." She breathed deeply and when she exhaled, she shuddered. "Guess not everybody's dead yet." Quietly she watched as he tore a sleeve off the shirt, then wrapped her hand.

Next to them, water dripped sporadically from drooping branches of a willow. Nearly touching the grass, the longest branches appeared to set the drops down as if they were washing the ground, or baptizing it.

Silence stretched between them—she sat, cradling her hand in her lap, staring blankly across the grass—but the silence calmed Eric. He didn't feel awful about her anymore, sad that she hated him, but not upset. They'd shared sex and near death, and of the two, death was more overwhelming. Nearly dying unites people, he thought. "How long do you think we were in that house?" he asked, making small talk. He guessed that the whole incident from the time they dove through the picture window until they hurdled the chain link fence in the back yard was less than a minute.

"An hour and a half . . . a lifetime," said Leda.

Far away, dogs barked. Eric listened intently; they didn't seem to be getting closer. "Let's go," he said. "We're nearly there."

Leda nodded and pushed herself upright.

When they rounded the corner onto Panorama St. a few minutes later, and his house finally came into view, he thought, how will I face him? They turned up the driveway. What will I say? Glass sprinkled the front yard here too. One of the curtains hung outside the window. He thought, I'm not the same as I was a week ago. I'm not the same kid.

He opened the front door.

Chapter Nineteen
SACRIFICIAL BOOKS

T hat's an elaborate story," the quaky voice on the other side of the door said after Eric finished explaining who they were and why they were in the library's basement. The voice, who had introduced himself as a Gone Time survivor, asked, "How do I know you're not just a clever liar?" Despite the quiver, the voice seemed learned, each word carefully pronounced.

Eric pressed his forehead against the wood. Outside, the bullhorned announcement boomed over and over, "Give up your books for the good of the people." His feet hurt. Water from the tunnel had soaked his boots, and now his feet felt hot and damp.

"Let us in," Eric said, exasperated. "I tell you, I'm seventy-five years old and have walked all the way from Littleton because I thought you might be able to help us. My friend here lives in the mountains. We don't have anything to do with those people threatening the library."

"So you say. If you *are* seventy-five, than you're lucky to have got this far." The voice sounded as old as Eric felt.

"Ask me something from the Gone Time. Not something I could have read in a book. If *you're* as old as *you* say you are, then *you'll* know what to ask."

Through the wood, Eric heard a whispered discussion, but he couldn't catch any of the words.

Sour-faced, Teach sat on the trap door at the bottom of the stairs behind Eric, scraping the last of the muck off his water-darkened moccasins.

Finally, the voice said, "Okay. Three questions. If you answer them correctly, then we will open the door. If not . . . we will use the Old Science against you, and you will die."

Eric smiled wryly at the phrase "old science" and the doomsday tone the voice used to say it. He guessed that the people in the building, whoever they were, had held off Federal's men with such a warning, but it sounded ridiculous to him, almost superstitious.

"Ask away," Eric said.

The three questions were, "What did the phrase, 'Plastic or paper?' mean? What exactly was the Pepsi Generation? and, What was call waiting?"

After he answered, several locks clicked, then the door swung open revealing the same white-smocked, elderly woman who'd surprised them as they exited the tunnel, and a truly ancient appearing man in a wheel chair.

Nearly bald except for a fringe of wispy white hair that reached to his collar, and dark liver spots that marred the smooth skin on his head, he scrutinized Eric through a milky-gray cataract haze, but he seemed to see fine as Eric crossed the threshold. The woman stepped protectively to the old man's side. Eric looked past them. His eyes widened. Rows of books stretched behind the man in the wheelchair, thousands and thousands of books, lit only by narrow shafts that slipped through the cracks between the boards on the windows. Grinning broadly through yellowed and broken teeth, the old man extended his hand toward Eric. "I'm Pope," he said, "the Librarian. I thought Federal had killed all of the Gone Timers but myself."

"Yes," said Eric, and shook his hand absently. As far as he could see, stretching into the darkness, from floor to ceiling, were books. He walked past the old man, down the nearest row, trailing his fingers across the bindings. "Yes," he repeated. Eric thought, I'm here at last, and the books survived.

A smile ached on his face. Fatigue dropped away from his legs and back. Leda, he thought, if you could only see this. You were right, about the learning, about the persistence of knowledge.

At thirty-nine, when she'd discovered she was pregnant, she'd said, "The child has to be taught, Eric. Promise me that we'll teach him to read." Even after fifteen years together he still shivered in amazement at her love. Her dark hair framed her face, and the only signs of age were tiny crow's-feet in her eyes' corners, but her gaze was so intense that he'd been taken aback. "Of course," he said. "Why wouldn't he?"

She hadn't smiled, didn't break the stare. She'd said, "If something happens to me, you will have to be his teacher."

Not enough light penetrated for him to see titles, but the backs of the books felt fine and solid. He passed his fingers across the embossed letters of a thick, leather-covered volume, then inhaled deeply and smelled the library smell, millions of pages pressed together, the weight of thought and information heavy in the air. "Oh, Leda," he whispered. "Oh, Troy."

Something lightly touched the back of Eric's leg. Pope sat in his chair beside him. Eric had not heard the chair rolling. "We share our time in books, don't we?" whispered Pope. "This has been my life work."

Eric grasped Pope's wrist and squeezed gently. "They are beautiful." Deeper back in the rows, more narrow streaks of sun penetrated through the boarded windows, casting thin, buttery light on other books standing neatly on dustless metal shelves.

From behind him, the woman said, "We ought to go upstairs. It's not safe down here."

Reluctantly, Eric turned away to follow Pope, the old woman and Teach to an elevator. "How do you power it?" asked Eric.

Raising himself slightly from the chair, Pope pushed the up button and the doors slid open. "Generators on the roof and solar panels spread throughout the campus." Eric, Teach and the woman stepped into the elevator. Pope blocked the doors with his chair. "Tell me again why you're here." He rested his chin on his chest as Eric told him of the troubles in Littleton, of the illnesses and stillbirths. Pope nodded his head slightly at each detail, as if in agreement.

Teach cleared his throat after a few minutes of this. "Seems like a closet's an uncomfortable place to get to know each other."

Pope let the door close and pressed a button. Teach's shock as the elevator rumbled into movement tickled Eric.

On the second story, a muslin curtain covered one tall, partially open casement window that overlooked the quad in front of the library. Pope said, "We can see out, but they can't see in."

Seven large army tents filled the back third of the grassless area, and five heavy machine gun nests built of sand bags faced the structure. Behind the tents, and on both sides between red stone buildings, the ubiquitous scrub and greasewood stood, a wall of tough vegetation that encircled the camp.

The loudspeaker, still blaring its message about giving up the books, hung from a pole beside the middle gun nest. A few yards from the broad marble steps that led to where Eric guessed were the front doors a rolled barb wire fence blocked the entrance. Behind that, a ditch paralleled the long front of the building. By leaning close to the muslin, Eric saw the ditch and wire made a neat ninety-degree turn at the far corner. No soldiers were visible.

Pope said, "Federal surrounded us two weeks ago. It is pathetic, really. His men lie in that ditch, watching twenty-four hours a day. Meanwhile, my people come and go as they please through the tunnels. They think the buildings are haunted, because of us, so they are even unaware of the tunnel entrances."

"People?" said Teach.

Pope squinted at the big man. "A library requires more manpower than you would suspect."

"What do they want?" asked Eric. He wondered if the men who had carried out the execution the day before were in the camp now. A soldier dressed in green, pushing a wheelbarrow, appeared between the tents and headed for the library. He dumped his load between the machine guns and the ditch. Eric strained to see what the small pile was. A second soldier followed the first with a similar wheelbarrow, and after him the line continued.

"Books," the woman whispered. "Oh, Pope. Do you think they've found the Chemistry library, or the Bio lab's?"

"So much for the ghosts," said Eric.

"The traps would not discourage them forever," said Pope grimly. "It doesn't matter if they did." Despite his words, he still sagged into his chair, as if someone had severed one of his strings. More books joined the pile, a barrow load every few seconds.

The message booming over the loudspeaker clicked off. Through the open window came the thud of books piling onto books and the metallic squeal of the barrow wheels as the low stack grew and spread out.

Teach said, "Why the library? What's he want?"

More books hit the ground. Eric looked back. The old woman gripped Pope's shoulder; he had closed his eyes. Behind them, rows of books spanned the distance from light to dark. Shadowy glass display cases stood beside dusty tables, and Eric imagined students working quietly, heads down, pens scratching notes.

"Many things, I suppose. Federal knows knowledge is power. He fears our existence here. The books frighten him. The building itself too maybe. The campus. We foiled him in Commerce City by luck. I did not even know of him," wheezed Pope. "I had sent an expedition to warn them about the water, and all but the stubborn moved north and into the mountains three days before Federal arrived. He conscripted the remaining young men, killed most of the others and tortured the oldest to find out where the rest had gone. An eleven-year-old girl saw it all from hiding and warned us of his approach. We had time to prepare." He coughed dryly into the flat of his hand and wiped it with a handkerchief the old woman gave him. "Federal thinks he is the new Gheghis Khan, riding with his warriors over the wastes of the world. He thinks we will oppose him, so he decided to eliminate us first. He thinks that our power comes from the books. Just the Old Science between him and a crown. The man who would be king of nothing."

Pope coughed again, then said to the woman, "Contact the staff. Events are moving faster than I planned." She nodded and disappeared between the rows.

"Why nothing?" Eric paid attention to the men piling books. At first he thought that they were innumerable, the uniformed men coming like an infinite line of men and wheelbarrows, but he'd seen the same soldiers several times now, and he realized there must be only fifty or so of them.

"We have preparations to make. But come, I will show you why Federal is a fool." Pope turned his chair and wheeled himself to the elevator. When he reached the doors, he looked back at Eric as if to say something, then frowned. "Where is your young companion?" Teach had gone.

Puzzled, Eric said, "My grandson and two of his friends may have followed us here. Perhaps Teach went to look for them."

Pope grimaced. "That complicates matters, but nothing can be done about it."

Another floor up, Pope led Eric into what looked like a fully equipped radio lab. Silver and black consoles packed a counter top that ran around the large room. Eric found the soft, electric lighting bouncing off the dust-free surfaces nostalgic, reminding him of his dentist's office, everything clean and fingerprintless.

"Federal's ambitions may be larger than the world. Do you know anything about SETI?" asked Pope as he flipped several switches. A low, subsonic hum that Eric felt in his teeth filled the room . Pope continued. "It was the Search of Extraterrestrial Intelligence. C.U. took part, as did numerous other universities, building huge radio dishes aimed at the stars specifically with the idea of picking up other civilization's signals." Two large speakers mounted next to the ceiling on shelves hissed into life when Pope rotated a dial on a console packed with needle gauges. Lightly, the smell of ozone and warming electrical components filled the room. "We never found any. Why not?" He twisted another dial, and the speakers crackled as Pope rotated through the radio bands. "The SETI project theorists struggled with several possibilities: one, we weren't searching the right bands. Maybe extraterrestrial communicated with gravity waves or ESP. Two, our equipment wasn't sensitive enough to pick up their signals, or three, we were alone."

He threw a switch and spoke into a microphone. "Staff members," he said, "take your positions. We are at . . ." He glanced at his watch. ". . . five minutes and holding. Wait for my signal please."

Then he continued, as if he hadn't interrupted himself. "Millions of star systems with planets are within radio distance of Earth." Pope hunched forward. The dial he reached for was an uncomfortable reach for a man in a wheel chair. "Millions of chances for intelligent life to develop, and it might have. But time is vast, and maybe intelligent life isn't stable. Perhaps it's an evolutionary dead end. Intelligence just flickers in time and we have missed it all around us in our own eighty-year radio flicker." He rotated the dial from one extreme to the other, and only light static came from the speakers.

Assembled on the shelf next to the radio array sat an obviously home-made panel. Over a hundred toggle switches pointed down, each neatly labeled with a number. On the wall, along with other charts, diagrams and pictures, hung a map of the campus with corresponding numbers marking buildings and the gaps between them. Pope flipped a switch to one side of the panel, and small lights glowed red above all but two of the switches. He tapped them both with his fingernail. One lit, but the other stayed dark. He spoke into the microphone again. "Davis or Courtney, check connections on fifty-seven." A speaker crackled on the radio panel, and a sexless, nervous sounding voice said, "Fifty-seven. Yes, sir."

"What's all this?" asked Eric. He bent down and looked past Pope's knees and under the shelf. A massive bundle of wires from the panel plunged through a sloppy hole in the sheet rock.

"Old science for Federal," said Pope. "As I said, we had warning he was coming. But I've always known about him. My real preparations started the summer I realized I wasn't going to die in the plague, sixty years ago."

Pope turned off the panel lights and sighed deeply, and in the sigh Eric heard a profound sadness. "It is difficult to accept, but all the evidence, all rational thought argues that humanity is the sole intelligence in the universe. There is no one out there."

Pope went back to the radio array and rotated the dial again. Other than a steady beeping that Pope identified as a satellite signal, he found nothing. He said, "But I'm not scanning the stars anymore. My equipment is now tuned to receive Earth's signals, and I have picked up no other stations for years. I am searching the right bands. My equipment is sensitive enough. Like the SETI project years ago, I am left with only theories to explain this. One, nobody else is signaling, or two, we are alone. Undamaged radio equipment must exist everywhere, in every corner of the Earth. The ability to power it, and the knowledge to use it must still survive if the percentage of surviving population is similar elsewhere as it was here. I now ask the same questions that deviled SETI. Why are the radio waves empty? Why has no one visited us?" Pope's milky eyes blazed at Eric; his knuckles whitened on the wheel chair arms.

The same voice broke in on the radio again. "Loose wire at fifty-seven. Should be good now, Sir."

Eric thought of the small parties of explorers who had left Littleton over the years, one trying for Colorado Springs, one for Kansas City, one for Salt Lake City, that had never come back.

"I have concluded that rational thought must argue all of the rest of human kind is dead. The planet is empty of intelligence except for this narrow strip in the Rocky Mountains," said Pope.

"That doesn't make sense. Why would we be the only ones left? Diseases don't strike geographically." Eric searched for an argument. Surely Pope must be wrong, he thought. Surely more than a few hundred people survived. But he thought again of Littleton's isolation. Why hadn't they been contacted? Where had all the young explorers gone? He said, "It didn't miss Colorado. So many died here too!"

Eric remembered sitting on his porch in Littleton the last few years. As the sun dropped below the peaks and cast their long shadows across the plains, he'd imagined little communities like his own, dotted across the country. Only space and the need to attend to the daily needs of survival kept them isolated. But the sense of those other people, the sure faith in their existence, had inspired him as he rocked in his chair watching the eastern horizon darken. A wall of pink-lined clouds had caught the last of the sun; an evening breeze ruffled the edge of the blanket he'd draped on his lap. He had been resting from a long day. We'll fill the highways again, he'd thought. We'll expand ourselves and be great again. Humanity has been set back, but this is only temporary. Knowledge will heal and bind us.

He was ashamed to remember he'd then thought that the plague might have been a *good* thing. He'd thought that before, too. We were close to killing ourselves at times. Overpopulation, territorial jealousies, friction over historical occupation of the land had caused war and suffering. As the last of the sun edged the mountains pink, he'd thought, no one's shooting at each other in the Golan Heights. They aren't lobbing molotov cocktails in Dublin anymore.

He said, "Why might they all die everywhere else?"

Pope cut the power to the radio. "The plague began it, but my guess is we did the rest ourselves. Various, persistent toxins, I believe, both nuclear and chemical. At least in the Rocky Mountain region, the water table has gotten worse. The farther from the Continental Divide, the worse it is. The community in Commerce City, for example, drank from a water supply that had become increasingly poison. Too much upstream: rotting, underground gasoline tanks, stored pesticides and chemical solvents that were leaking from their barrels. I don't know what all caused it. Maybe just buildings and cars and roads melting back into the land."

With one push on his wheels, he crossed the room, opened a cabinet and took down what looked like a walkie-talkie, but where Eric expected to see speakers, there were instead several switches. Pope shrugged wryly. "It's a poetic image, don't you think? All our cities and factories, houses and stores, dissolving in the rain like sugar cubes, and all their toxins stored within and beneath them letting go, one corroded storage container after another. In Commerce City, the people were getting sick. Babies miscarried or were born deformed. I sent them into the mountains."

"That's what's happening in Littleton too. Is it our water?" Eric thought of the South Platte that ran by the edge of town. Most water came from there, but the stream had been crystal clear for years, its water sweet and cool. "Should we move up into the mountains too?"

"Mountains may be the last to go, but they'll go if the pollution continues." Pope linked his fingers across his chest and closed his eyes, squeezing a tear in their corners. "It's getting worse, I told you. We started measuring here thirty years ago when we began losing contact with other survivors. The water table's going bad, and the lower in elevation you go, the higher the toxin level is. I can't tell from here—there is no way to know without sending an expedition—but the seas may be sick. Nothing is more downstream than the sea."

Ripple's words about upstream and downstream came back to Eric. She'd said of the Gone Timers, "They took upstream and disposed downstream like upstream was forever and no one lived below."

In the background, an amplified voice started shouting again, but the words were indistinct in the windowless room. Raising a hand, Pope pointed to a chart hung on a wall. "Somehow we poisoned the water, and if the sea dies, we will die too. Most of our breathing air comes from ocean-based photosynthesis, but I've been graphing other changes in the air."

A timeline marked the bottom of the chart, and a line starting at five years after the plague climbed like stair steps to today. In the last five years, the steps came closer together.

"What's being measured here?" asked Eric. His thinking centered on Pope's last words. Surely he is wrong, thought Eric. The water table may be polluted, but it has to vary! A local problem in some places maybe, but not a global one—not one that could take in the sea. In the books somewhere there must be a solution!

Outside, the voice shouted incessantly. Pope twitched a finger toward the main library area.

"Push me, would you? My arms aren't what they once were, and we need to keep an eye on him." Grabbing the handles, Eric maneuvered the chair through the door and toward another muslin-covered window. When they reached it, Pope plugged an AC adapter from the walkie-talkie into a wall socket. On the quad below, the pile of books had grown to several feet thick.

"Remember the nuclear accident at Chernobyl?" Pope waited for Eric to nod. "The graph shows the rise in air-borne radiation. The plague killed too quickly. Not all nuclear power plants around the world must have been shut down safely. What I think we are seeing here in each one of these jumps . . ." He drew in the air the stair steps on the graph. ". . . is a power plant losing containment. They are burning and pumping radiation into the atmosphere."

An image of a slowly rising tide of poisons came to Eric. Each year his community could move higher, but in the end there would be no place to retreat to, and the air could kill them before they reached the top. "Is this what you see?" asked Eric, thinking of his own vision. "That humanity is finished?" He thought, if all this is true, then why try to save the library? What's to be gained? The last barrow full of books hit the pile, and soldiers scurried around the pod, picking up guns, heading this way and that.

As if answering the thought, and not the question, Pope said, "As long as we live, we live. I have work to do here, and I am not ready to quit it quite yet." He cranked open the small ventilation window that rested at the bottom of the tall, narrow expanse of glass so they could hear the loudspeaker. "Besides, I still want to deal with Federal."

"But why?" Eric wanted to collapse. As quickly as the euphoria of seeing the books had come, the weight of his age had returned. "Why not walk away and give him the library if he's going to die anyway?"

Through the open window, the voice boomed, "Surrender the library or we burn the books." Beside the stack, two soldiers stood with torches. Two others flanked them, their M-16s held ready at waist level. The rest had taken positions in the ditches; some pointed their guns at the library doors, while others watched the roof and windows.

Pope said, "Fairly illogical request, don't you think? I know his intent is to burn these books too. He knows I know that. What makes him think the threat to burn part of the books would make me give him the rest?"

Eric gasped. "Not *burn* them. He wouldn't *destroy* them. Wouldn't he want to get their power, if that's what he believes they represent?"

Pope fingered the switches on his walkie-talkie. In this pose, with the gauzy muslin-filtered light falling on him, he looked almost like a statue, something hewn out of white marble. "I imagine the librarian at Alexandria must have thought the same thought in ancient Egypt as the hordes descended." His voice grew sarcastic. "'Surely they won't damage the papyrus scrolls! Surely they won't destroy all of mankind's learning.'" Pope barked out a short laugh. "They estimate a half-million documents were lost at Alexandria."

The soldiers extended their torches over the books.

"We will burn them," shouted the voice. "We will burn them all."

The amplifier crackled. Wherever the unseen speaker was, he had not released the "send" button; his breathing washed behind the static.

Eric's hand pressed against the wall. The pressure ached on his wrist as he leaned to get a better look down into the quad.

Twin plumes of torch smoke, thin and gray, trailed straight up.

Soldiers' eyes, white and wide, swept over the building.

Federal's breathing rasped in and out.

"Drop them," his voice said metallically.

Torches fell.

The thuds of their impact sounded dully on Eric's ears as he looked at the floor. It begins this way, he thought. Threats and fear hold the barbarians out for a while, but they always seem to conquer. How could I get so close, he thought. How could I get so close and not find an answer? All the lessons I tried to teach Troy. All the learning we've put away, all the proof of where man's been, about to go away. If man lives, this is the beginning of the new dark age.

Heavy as spring time mud, despair weighted him. He took one shaky breath, closed his eyes, and held it.

"No!" shouted a voice from outside.

Eric brought his eyes up. From the wall of greasewood thirty yards from the pile of books, sprinted a small figure, arm upraised. The soldiers' heads swiveled to spot it. Soldiers in the trenches whipped around and repointed their guns. Still running, half the distance covered, the arm snapped down and one of the soldiers by the fire dropped; his hat flew one direction and the rock flew another.

Clawing the muslin out of the way, Eric slapped his hand against the glass. A smothering sense of deja vu swept through him. "Rabbit! Stop! Stop!"

Even from the window, Rabbit's scar was visible, his face contorted with effort and rage. "Not the books!" he shouted, and another rock smacked one of the soldiers who had held a torch.

Rabbit reached the pile of books, snagged a torch, and flung it away. One of the soldiers in the ditch fired a long burst, missing

Rabbit but shredding the side of a tent. The loudspeaker erupted in a panic, "Don't shoot, you idiot."

Eric drummed the flat of his hand against the glass. "Run, Rabbit, Run!"

Rabbit bent over the pile and grabbed the other torch. Flame had barely touched the books. As if breaking a paralysis, the second soldier with a gun, reversed it, stepped forward, and delivered a business-like blow to the back of Rabbit's head, sending him sprawling into the books. The torch tumbled away across the bare dirt.

Hand on the window, Eric's breath froze.

For a moment, all was still.

"Kill him," said Federal, and the soldier who had hit Rabbit put his gun to his shoulder and fired four single shots into the still body.

In Eric's thoughts, nothing.

Nothing.

Nothing.

Something strangled sounding came from the loudspeaker.

Another scream. Inarticulate. From the same wall of greasewood, Dodge lunged into the quad, Ripple hanging on to the back of his shirt, pulling him back. Cloth ripped. Ripple fell back; Dodge tumbled forward, began crawling toward Rabbit and the books.

The soldier, still aiming his gun at Rabbit's back, looked at Dodge. As huge as a bear, a dark shape, bent low, emerged from one of the tents. Moving with dark fury, it crossed the distance, swept through the soldier who never saw it coming, and met Dodge who was still crawling, carrying him and Ripple into the brush.

"Get them away, Teach!" yelled Eric through the glass. He pounded the glass again. "Away, away," he wailed, dimly aware that Pope was pulling at his belt. Soldiers boiled out of the ditch, some running to the tents, some standing as if struck dumb, some pointing their guns at the library. Pops of light flashed from the ends of their muzzles.

"Get down! Get down!" bellowed Pope, as he, in a move surprisingly strong for a wheelchair-bound man of his age, yanked Eric from the tall window that seemed to crystalize, suddenly going opaque, cascading to the floor all at once.

"Damn," said Pope. "I didn't want it to go like this." Bullets whizzed over their heads, knocking holes into the high ceiling tiles. He crunched over the broken glass. "Get me to the radio room. I broke the remote."

Numbly, Eric pushed him across the library. Glass shattered elsewhere, then the shooting stopped. They made it to the radio room, and Eric rested his back against the door frame after propelling Pope in. Black dots swam across Eric's vision. Bands of pressure pulled in his chest. He wheezed painfully.

He pushed the palm of his hand against the pounding in his forehead. The last glimpse he'd had out the window rose before him: Teach and the children were gone; the soldiers were firing at the building; and in the middle of it, bright as a sun, the pile of books blazed around the silhouette of Rabbit, his arms thrust straight from his sides, his legs together, burning, burning, burning in the mid-day light.

"Eric," said Pope, and something in his tone brought Eric out of the pile of books. Leaning back, his head resting on the back of the chair, Pope almost looked as if he were relaxing, but his hand pressed hard against a growing patch of red on the white smock shook Eric out of his anguish.

"Can't let the barbarians sack the library," Pope gasped. "Can't have them spreading our books about, ripping pages they can't read." He sucked a breath in sharply and shuddered. "Quick," he said. "Turn on the radio and say, 'five minutes and counting.' Then you have to flip all the switches on that panel. Get to the tunnels." He pointed to the array he had tested earlier, to the far right switch on the bottom row. "Last one is the front doors. No delay."

Trying to help the librarian sit up so he could breathe easier, Eric reached around the chair and braced his hand against its back while moving Pope. Eric's hand came away red, and he wiped it on his pants. Pope looked at the stain.

"Hardly slowed, did it." He coughed a fine spray of blood.

"What will happen?" asked Eric, hugging the man close, as if by holding him he could keep him alive. Through the blood-soaked smock, Eric felt the rapid flutter of Pope's heart.

Pope bubbled, coughed again, and Eric thought he might die right then, but Pope took another breath and said, "Diesel bombs on timers in all the buildings and in the brush." He moaned. "Campus . . . surrounded. They won't get out."

"How does that help?" said Eric. "We can't burn the library ourselves."

Breathing in short, quick puffs, Pope twisted in his chair. "Got . . . to. For sixty years . . ." He grabbed at Eric's arm and gripped. " . . . I've planned on Alexandria."

He panted twice more, then seemed to relax, breaths coming slower and slower until after five or six, he quit.

Eric faced the array. All the switches pointed down. He thought, the last switch is the library. If Pope is right, then this might be the last library. There aren't others in other cities. This is it. The world is empty. Just a few hundred people, maybe a thousand, and no one else. All the learning is here. All the books.

Outside, shots were fired. More glass broke. Shouting.

He turned on the microphone and said, "Five minutes and counting." He thought of Rabbit dying for a pile of books. Rabbit, who had rubbed his legs when they were sore, who smiled only secretly when he thought no one was looking, the orphan boy with scars on his face who believed everything that an old man had told him about the value of knowledge.

Using both hands, he flipped all the switches but the far right one. Their lights glowed at him. His finger rested on the last switch. Its sharp plastic edge felt sharp against his skin. He pulled up until it jumped into the upright position, and its light lit. A dull thud of a vibration against his feet and a slight pressure against his ears told him the diesel burned in the library below.

Chapter Twenty
LOST AND FOUND

A stranger's house would feel less threatening than this, Eric thought. He stepped cautiously across the threshold. Glass littered the living room carpet. A needlepoint, a gift from one of his mother's friends, hung crookedly on the wall. It doesn't feel like home, he thought. Nothing's right. We're in the wrong house.

Eric recognized titles in the hanging bookshelf above the couch, *Time Life Home Repair Series: Plumbing, Finding the Lost Railroads, Birds of the Rocky Mountain West.* A yellowed and water-stained newspaper lay on the carpet beside his father's chair, its headline still readable: "Military Enforces Quarantines."

It didn't smell like home. Even with the picture window broken, a rotten, wet stench permeated the room. None of the familiar smells came through: Chapstick, Old Spice, toast, fingernail polish, Mr. Clean. The light was wrong. Unimpeded sunlight cut sharp shadows on the walls instead of the soft lights and darks he recalled.

None of the right sounds. No washer groaning in the utility room. No big band tune from the stereo, no vacuum cleaner. Glass crunched beneath his foot. Like an empty church or a mortuary, the noiseless air seemed expectant and patient, even brooding. The entrance into the hallway that led to the bedrooms and his dad's office loomed like an abyss. He heard a whimper, a tiny, beat puppy thing that sounded pathetic in the empty living room. He realized he'd made the noise himself.

He stepped back and bumped Leda, who caught the backs of his arms. "Steady," she said. "What's the smell?"

Eric tried to speak, swallowed hard, took a deep breath and said, "In the kitchen." He walked slowly, attempting to make no sound, and he stared, fascinated, as each step revealed more of the room: first, the pantry, next the can-opener beside the bulletin board, then the cabinets and stove, and finally the refrigerator and freezer, its doors part way open. Spoiled meat oozed gray slime from the white package's seams, and mold choked the vegetable drawers.

"Somebody's been in the house. Front door was unlocked," he said. "Dad always double checked before we left. He'd unplug appliances, turn the main water off, close the curtains." Eric shut the refrigerator. Putridness wafted past him. "He was a careful man."

Leda's shoe squeaked on the linoleum; Eric jumped. It sounded, for an instant, like his father's shoe. Every line in the kitchen spoke of his father. Eric could see his dad's hand in the smudges on the cupboard handles, in the way the three plates, three cups and three sets of silverware—remnants of the last breakfast they had eaten before leaving to the mountains—rested in the sink, in the color of the walls, each barely visible brush stroke a picture of Dad painting. Dad had said, "From the top down, son. You'll leave dribbles that way," when they had worked together on it two summers ago. Dad's presence smothered the room.

Leda exhaled, and Eric jumped again. "This his?" she said as she lifted a blue and black flannel shirt from a basket around the corner in the utility room.

"Sure." He backed away until his rump hit a counter. Was Dad wearing that shirt when he left the cave? he thought. Was he? Eric tried to picture the last moment when he'd seen Dad at the exit to the cave holding his bicycle. He saw the graffiti on the wall, the feel of the wool blanket under his hand, the shapeless hump of his dead mother under the blanket, even his dad's last words, "I'll be back before sunset," but Eric couldn't remember what Dad had worn.

"Yes," he said, but did it mean Dad had been here? The thought brayed in his brain. Clearly he wasn't in the house now. The broken window would be fixed; the door would be locked; the dishes put away. But had he been here? Where was he? Balanced perfectly, the feelings that this was no longer his home, and the . . . the . . . he couldn't come up with the word to describe the emotion . . . the anticipation? the hope? the dread? that his father had left some sign teetered precariously within him.

"Let's do the rest of the house," he said, and walked out of the kitchen, not waiting to see if she followed.

He looked into the rooms in order. Diffuse light filtered through glazed glass in the empty bathroom. A purple throw rug, centered exactly in front of the sink, still sported a speck of dried toothpaste from Eric's haste to leave the house almost six weeks earlier. He tried the faucet—his throat seemed petrified with dryness—but the fixture creaked when he spun it, and nothing came out.

His closed bedroom door swung open easily. Model airplanes hung from the ceiling; rock group posters covered the walls; books and knick-knacks lined the tops of the dresser, the desk and nightstand. A wadded up sheet and some dirty clothes blocked the path to the bed. Only the gaps in the bookcase that represented the comics he'd packed when they'd left the house for the cave, the dozen empty hangers in the closet and a fine layer of dust made the room any different than it had been earlier in the year. But, like the rest of the house, it felt weird, as if aliens had come and stolen everything, replacing it with this well done but not quite right duplicate. Eric couldn't imagine himself on that bed anymore. He could barely recollect what it was like to live in this room. And still every element screamed, Dad! Dad had given him that book; Dad had hated that album; Dad had helped him with that homework; Dad criticized that pair of pants; Dad had sat on the edge of this bed late at night asking about Eric's grades. When the door was shut, it was to keep Dad out. When the door was open, it was to invite Dad in. No part of it lived or died or moved that it wasn't measured in some way by Dad's inescapable scale.

Eric remembered with amazement that when he'd left the cave a few days ago, it was with the thought that maybe he could *rescue* Dad, that Dad needed his help, but now that Eric was home again and could feel again the atmosphere of his Dad's house, the idea seemed ludicrous. How could a son rescue a dad? Dad lived removed and remote from the world of the son, his only connection through a thread of rules and expectations. Dad passed laws. Dad rendered judgement, then Dad moved on.

Something touched his arm, and he whirled.

"Sorry," Leda said. "I didn't mean to rush you."

Concern colored her features, but all Eric could think was that for the instant he'd feared it was Dad's hand on him, that when he turned, Dad would be there. And what would he say? Would his abandonment of the cave be a mistake? Would Dad glower over him and say, "You left mother alone?" or would he, magnificently, like a god, forgive him, take him in his embrace and make it all right again?

"This is your room?" she said. "Nice models."

"I used to do them when I was a kid." He touched the wing tip of a bright red tri-plane above him. It turned slowly clockwise on its thread.

In the hallway, in front of his parents' room and its closed door, Eric paused with his hand extended, not quite touching the door-knob. Leda stood beside him. A swish of drapes from the living room told him that a breeze had picked up outside. He clenched his jaw and put his fingers on the cool metal, but didn't turn it. How many houses, he thought, have neatly closed their doors on tucked-in corpses? All the possibilities frightened him: the door opens on a covered form on the bed. Eric pulls back the blanket and finds Dad, or the door opens and Dad is sitting on the edge of the bed, or the door opens and the room is empty—Dad has left no sign. A scream circled in the back of his throat. If there was a chance that devils packed the room, he could hardly be less fearful. Trepidation filled him, like a cold, heavy metal.

Finally, he turned his hand into a fist and rapped lightly on the door. "Dad?" he said. The breeze outside calmed. Nothing made a sound. Only Leda's breathing prevented the hallway from being dead silent. He gripped the knob, twisted it, and pushed the door.

The door swung open on an empty room. Blankets were folded tidily away from the pillows. Family pictures sat on the dresser. On Dad's nightstand, the television remote waited for someone to pick it up. Eric walked to the side of the bed feeling like a time traveler—the closed drapes belied the world outside. No evidence of change existed here: a TV Guide, slippers, a robe hanging in the open closet, an open paperback face down on his mother's nightstand, some clean towels resting on a chair. All seemed like relics now, like a carefully designed set or a museum display. And the fear didn't vary. His chest strained against it. His throat ached with it. Goosebumps flashed down his arms.

"No one's here," Eric said. It was all he could do to speak.

"Try the next room?"

"Okay."

In the office, Eric used his finger to draw a line in the dust on the bare desk top. Then, disturbed by the messiness, he wiped the whole desk clean with a tissue that he dropped into the otherwise empty waste basket. Photographs lined the room, mostly pictures of his dad receiving various awards and commendations from work:

Journalist of the Year (three of them), Colorado Editor's Choice
Award (seven of these), Denver Jaycees Community Service Award
(just one), and other photographs of Dad shaking hands with or
standing next to politicians or celebrities. Twenty-five or so pictures
of Dad, surrounding him in the office.

But Dad wasn't here. He knew it before, but it wasn't until
he'd opened the door that he accepted it. Dad wasn't here, and he
felt like throwing up. Blood flushed his face. He gritted his teeth,
and suddenly he knew what the emotion was that had boiled up
inside him, that had been building for days. It wasn't fear; it was
abandonment. Dad left. He hadn't come back, and not only that,
but he'd started leaving years ago, not just when he'd left the cave,
but years earlier he'd started separating himself from Eric. He
thought, how long ago did I lose him?

Eric felt small again, as if the boy within had risen and taken a
place in his heart, and the boy wanted to weep, wanted to lie on the
floor and wait for Mommy and Daddy to make things better.

One of the pictures on the wall showed his dad, smiling, shaking a hand across his chest with some important person, and for the
first time Eric really looked at the black and white photo. Clouds
muted the light. Grays dominated. Dad gazed into the camera, his
tie loose and off-center. In the background, unfocused and barely
discernable, stood Mom. By her side, clinging to one leg, was a little
boy, no more than a white smudge of a face topped with a dark
smear of hair, himself, not looking at Mom, not looking at the camera, but looking at Dad, leaning a little bit toward him, frozen in the
photograph in a state of yearning.

Leda said, "Wow. Did you meet any of these people? That's
the Governor, isn't it?"

"My dad is dead," murmured Eric. As low as he spoke, the
words still filled the room. Eric dropped his head. The lone tissue in
the waste basket uncrinkled while he watched.

Leda turned away for a second. Eric could tell from the lines in
the side of her face that she'd squeezed her eyes shut. Then she
faced him, eyes dry and open, stepped toward him, and rested a
hand on his shoulder. "I know," she said. "So is mine."

Seconds passed. Then her fingers pulled gently on him, and he
moved into her arms. She held him long. He pressed his face against
the top of her head, smelling her hair. Gradually, the fear . . . the
abandonment . . . went away. It drained, like water. It flowed out of

him until he almost felt whole. The office metamorphosed into just a room—not a monument to a harsh and distant deity. Leda's cheek rested against his chest. She'd locked her hands behind his back. He told himself, it doesn't matter if Dad made it home or not. Maybe I'll never know what happened to him. He died like the millions of others, moving from one destination to another or hiding away in some unsafe place, leaving behind a lot of unfinished business. Eric tightened his grip. Leda raised her chin and met his eyes. He kissed her forehead.

"Thanks," he said.

She gasped, like she'd been holding her breath, and then let it go. "I was afraid you hated me." He started to release her, but she held on tighter. "After last night. I knew it was your first time." The words rushed out. "I like you, Eric." Her breath hitched up in her throat. "I'm alone, and I just don't want you to hate me."

He straightened a bit, in shock, and his first impulse was to say, "I thought you hated *me*," but he bit back the sentence. Her words, "I'm alone," triggered a completely different way of looking at the last few days—it was a revelation—her way. What must it have been like for *Leda*? What griefs had she endured? What fears? She wasn't hidden in some cave. People must have fallen sick all around her: her friends, her family, her neighbors. What must that have been like? When she climbed in her car that last time and started her drive across the city, where was she going? Was she seeking or fleeing? And what, he thought, have I been doing? He held her tightly, her shoulder blades pressing firmly against his forearms. Have I been seeking or fleeing?

Eyes closed, he leaned against her, and she against him, until finally he relaxed. The crisis passed. Breathing felt fine and normal and smooth. Goosebumps faded away. The sense of emergency that had harried him for days dropped off. Something else had changed too; he felt bigger, somehow—not older really, just bigger, as if the room had shrunk a little bit, as if he had grown within himself. He gave her one last hug and said, "Help me move this desk, will you?" Dad had said the key fit a drawer behind it. She let go, rubbed the back of her wrist under her eyes and took a position on one corner.

"Sure."

Crushed between the back of the desk and the wall, a bundle of papers fell over as they pushed the heavy piece of furniture. Eric gave his side one last heave, moving it another foot, then picked up the bound sheets. Setting it on the desk, he undid the ribbon that held them together and looked at each wrinkled document: the house mortgage, a list of bank accounts and their balances, a handful of stocks, a legal looking paper with a key taped to it giving Eric the right to open the safety deposit box, and all the warranties to the major appliances in the house. Forty-two twenty dollar bills filled a new, white envelope, and at the bottom, he found a will and power of attorney naming him as the sole executor of the family's assets.

"He must have thought that you might outlive him," said Leda. Her hand rested on his back as they leaned over the papers. "Looks like they were dropped, then the desk was pushed up against them. Why were they on the floor?"

"Don't know. They seem kind of useless now," said Eric. "Let's see what he left me in the drawer."

Eric dropped to his hands and knees behind the desk. At the bottom in one corner, he found a small knot-hole big enough for his key to fit it, and when he looked very closely, he saw the outline of the drawer in the wood, about the right size to hold the papers on the desk. The grain and finish hid it well. Only someone who suspected that the hiding place might be there would have a chance of finding it.

He inserted the key and unlocked the drawer.

Inside, Eric found a single sheet of note paper. He read it, sat for a moment, reread it, then handed it to Leda.

Eric relaxed against the wall, his feet braced against the desk. Leda put the paper down. "It's complete now," said Eric. "No unanswered questions."

Dad made it, thought Eric. They blew up the tunnel so he couldn't come back to me. There were no ambulances in Golden. He saw how bad things were. There was no place to go but home, and that's what he did.

Eric thought about the trip to see the eclipse when he was ten. Dad assumed I knew what an eclipse was. A thousand mile drive and he never once asked his ten-year-old son if he knew what an eclipse was! Dad must have *continuously* assumed I knew things. Mom said Dad never shared what he thought, but there, at the end, he tried. He made it home to leave me a message, not knowing whether I'd find it or not. He died not knowing.

That knowledge hurt.

Dad left it anyway, Eric thought. At the end, he must have realized what Mom knew, that he assumed too much from me. At the end, he wanted to leave one thing, and this is what he left. It must have been the most important thing.

Eric reached up. Leda handed him the note. He read it for the third time. In shaky script—recognizable but not firm: not well—it said, "I have always loved you. Dad."

*

"There's advantages to the downfall of civilization," said Leda as they walked out of the Littleton Target with new clothes, backpacks and supplies. She had chosen a man's blue work shirt and had tucked them into her jeans. Eric thought the look complemented her. "I don't need to go to work in the morning."

Eric struggled to fit the stiff, surgical tubing over the aluminum rods of the new sling-shot while at the same time carefully picking his way between the tumbled and smashed shopping carts that littered the parking lot. "No driver's license test for me," he said.

"No April 15th." She led them toward the river. "We ought to find a place close to the water. Bottled stuff we can drink, but bathing could be a problem."

"Sounds good," said Eric. "You can forget Superbowl Sunday hype."

"Yeah, and Christmas decorations up before Halloween."

"Or elevator music."

"Rock and Roll rules," she said.

The late afternoon sun turned the river a mellow gold, and they walked south along its bank until they found an empty house with unbroken windows. After knocking loudly several times, Eric pried open the front door with a crowbar. "Useful tool," he said. "We don't need keys anymore."

Leda checked the bedrooms, and Eric looked into the basement. Her voice floated down the stairs. "I don't need to remember my social security number."

They met in the living room. "All clear," she said. "This will do for now, but we're going to have to do some planning. Find other survivors. Set up for the long haul."

"The government should send help eventually." Eric shrugged his shoulders out of his backpack, letting it drop to the carpet.

Leda seemed to contemplate that comment for a bit before saying, "Could be a while." She crouched next to her pack and began removing canned goods, big cans in back, little ones in front, like kids for a school picture, which Eric thought amusing. He realized there was much to learn about her.

He opened the drapes and windows. Having dropped below the mountains, the sun turned the clouds violet and pink. Light painted the foothills a soft blue and the plains a dusky yellow. "You know," he said without turning from the window, "I don't know your last name."

She stepped beside him. An empty road between them and the river followed its contours in both directions until it was lost to sight. No traffic. Not a single, mechanical or human sound. Farther up stream, the water rushed over and around the broken cement of what once was a bridge.

"We don't need last names anymore," she said.

That sank in for a while. Then, he nodded in agreement.

Later that night, long after he'd drifted to sleep in a four-poster single bed decorated with beige lace, with the windows open and the river mumbling its secrets in the dark, his bed moved, jarring him awake. Leda snuggled against him, and they made love. In the midst of it all, in the heated, passionate ecstasy of it all, Eric imagined their sounds echoing among the empty buildings, the silent town, with no one to hear.

Chapter Twenty-one
ALEXANDRIA

Lost in shock, Eric was shrouding Pope's face** with a clean smock that had been draped over the back of a chair, when a young man rushed into the radio room. Eric ignored him. The motion of hiding the face felt studied and graceful. He released the smock's shoulders and the cloth settled on Pope's features. Only the hands resting on the armrests remained uncovered. "He asked me," said Eric, and he waved at the switches, each with its ominously glowing light above it. He added, "You know, they killed a boy."

The man stared at the dead librarian, his mouth open. Finally, he stuttered, "We only have a minute or two. Hurry." He hustled Eric out of the room and down the stairs. Apathetically, Eric allowed himself to be led.

At the basement entrance, the young man blurted to the elderly woman what he'd seen and heard, then joined a line of people heading through the basement door. She turned to Eric. "You helped him?" Eric nodded. "Thank you," she said. Her lined eyes scrunched closed for a second. "He was a visionary. The staff will miss his guidance." She gripped his hand tightly, then returned to directing the line of people.

"I'm sorry," Eric said to her back. He thought, I should find this fascinating. Where did these people come from? What were they doing in the library? But he felt numb. He could see Rabbit running across the quad to save the burning books. The unyielding surface of the glass still rested on his palms. He thought of a term from the Gone Time, the slow motion replay, and that's what was happening in his head, over and over, Rabbit dashed toward his death. Everything else seemed to be happening too rapidly—events rushed— and he didn't feel he could keep up.

"Quickly, quickly," she said and coughed. An acid bite flavored the air. She patted each person on the shoulder. All wore white smocks. Most were young, under thirty, and several children took their place in line. A few carried boxes, a few, one or two books, but most were empty-handed, their faces nervous but controlled. The evacuation seemed rehearsed. Noxious smoke billowed across the ceiling. Within a minute, the last one passed through. Eric bent low to avoid the fumes.

"You need to hurry too," she said.

Age and brittleness overwhelmed him. Joints ached—elbows, knees and fingers—skin and muscles dangled from his bones. He felt like an empty vessel. Eric sat on the floor. Flame crackled but he couldn't see it through the murk. This seems fitting, he thought. He didn't have a plan, just an urge to quit, to let the library burn all around him. Rabbit died, he thought, because of me. I brought him here, and he died for nothing. I destroyed the library. The long journey's a failure. We can't be helped.

The effort to keep his head up seemed too much. "I'll stay," he said. Metal groaned from deep in the smoke, and then something crashed heavily.

"Come on," she said urgently, and pulled at his arm. "The building's doomed. You're not." She dragged him backward a few feet, and mostly through her effort, not his own, he clambered through the trap door and into the tunnels.

"Move," she said. Low wattage bulbs lit the tunnel until it curved out of sight. The last of the other people disappeared around the turn as he watched. "We have to be beyond the campus before the perimeter goes up."

"Perimeter?" said Eric dully.

"Yes." She pushed him in the back, almost knocking him over. He staggered forward through the shallow water, splattering gray splotches onto the curved walls. She said, "We've extended the tunnels."

"The perimeter!" Eric could see again the scene in the quad, but instead of Rabbit, he watched Teach carrying Dodge and Ripple into the greasewood, the thickly wooded, dry brush that choked nearly all the open space in Boulder. Eric picked up his pace, out-distancing the elderly woman. "Teach is with my grandson out there. I've got to warn them!"

Eric turned into the first cross-tunnel, even though no lights illuminated its length. Blind, he ran forward, brushing his hand against the wall, feeling for a ladder. He pictured Pope's map on the wall, each number representing a bomb in the outlying buildings and the spaces between them. Even on a still day, the ring of fire would close in and burn out the center. The fire would create its own draft. Federal and his men would be trapped—that would be Pope's Pyrrhic victory—but so would anyone else.

Behind him, the elderly woman shouted, "It's too late. If they're within the perimeter, it's too late."

Sound and touch guided him as the rough cement ripped at his palm and each step shot splashes of water up his pants legs. She shouted something undecipherable behind him. Still, he ran, sucking great gulps of moist tunnel air. Finally, his hand slammed into a ladder, and he swarmed up the rusty rungs. But even as he climbed, comprehension came to him, and the futility of his effort slowed him down. With no surprise, he found the padlock holding the trap door closed at the top of the steps. Back down the tunnel, he heard the cautious footsteps of the old woman.

"We're on a countdown," she called. "We have to get out." Her disembodied voice came up to him. "You can't help him by dying down here."

Eric said, "Why burn the whole university? Why burn the books?"

"I'll show you, but you have to come right now. We may already be too late. Besides," she said as Eric descended, "with all the shooting, your friend would have been smart to leave. He's probably far away."

Bile rose in Eric's throat. Teach's strategy isn't running, he thought, it's to get off the main path and then not move. Teach's strategy is to hide. He could be crouched behind some bush *on campus* right now, still as a deer.

"Hurry," she said. "Time is running out." She beckoned, her form outlined by the light behind.

"We're at least ten feet deep," Eric said, defeated, realizing that what she'd argued was true: he could do nothing. "Burn it to the ground and we wouldn't know." Everything's gone, he thought. Dodge outside, unaware of the danger to come, and in the library, flaming fingers reaching everywhere, flowing across the rows and rows of books. Perfect tinder, a book: dry, thin, crisp. Irreparable.

"It's not that," she said, panic rising in her voice. "The tunnel's wired too. We have to be beyond it or we'll be trapped. You weren't supposed to stop."

Again, he found himself running, more like shuffling now, following her through the lit tunnel, passing one cave-black side passage after another. Whatever youthful energy that had spurred him up the ladder was gone. He sucked thin lungfuls of air that came and went too quickly to help; water weight dragged at his pants' legs. He thought, How long since I threw the switches? They went past another side passage.

She talked as she kept up behind him, panting out words. "Big explosive . . . seals the tunnel . . . little ones . . . along the way . . . finish it. . . . All entrances . . . blocked. Tunnels . . . collapse."

He thought he heard Dodge's voice in his mind. "Grandfather," it called. Fear and guilt spurred him on. Maybe, he thought, Teach will get him off campus. We'll meet up. Then I can take him home.

Eric pushed the possibility that Dodge might die down as hard as he could, determined not to think about it. He picked up his pace. Lights flicked by faster. We have to get home, he thought. Pope's message was not all negative. I'll get Dodge—oh God! let them escape!—and we'll warn Troy and Littleton. We can get upstream into the mountains, drink only rain water. Pollution may be rampant, but it might be slowing. Radiation might be higher, but maybe not deadly; Pope didn't say.

"There," she gasped, pointing ahead to a large green box mounted on the side of the passage that became more visible as they rounded the slight curve. It blocked two-thirds of the tunnel, leaving just enough room for a person to fit through. "The bomb . . . We have to be . . . beyond it."

"How much time?" The box loomed before them, and as Eric approached, he sidled to the opposite side, away from the explosive.

She slowed, as if a sudden movement might set it off. Her white hair had pulled free of the ribbon that held it back, and strands of it stuck to the sides of her face. "Chemical fuse. Five minutes minimum. Eight or nine minutes tops."

Dodge's voice came to him again, a remote echo, "Grandfather?" Eric stopped and cocked his head, listening, the bomb within arm's reach, and the old woman collided with him, her eyes wide and wild. "Go," she hissed, and pushed by, careful not to touch the box.

"Did you hear that?" He remembered the vivid memories that had come more and more often lately, the inability to separate what was happening with what he recalled. But the voice sounded real.

"What?" She kept moving farther down the corridor, putting distance between her and the bomb.

Indecisive, he took two steps the way they'd come.

"Don't be a fool," she said, backpeddling.

"I thought I heard something."

She kept retreating. "I have to go," she said, almost apologetically. "I've got a responsibility. Pope's dead." She started running again and shouted back to him over her shoulder, "I'm the Librarian now." Her footfalls banged away.

Eric ran to the first cross tunnel. "Dodge?" The sound bounced back from an unseen, far wall. He listened intently. Water seeped out of a crack over his head and dripped steadily onto the floor. Around each small bulb suspended from the ceiling, a subtle nimbus glowed, casting edgeless shadows of pipes and conduits on the walls. "Dodge?" he cried again.

Clanging echoes of his own voice bounded around him. He looked back. The woman was gone, and he staggered forward, alone, in the tunnel whose bare walls offered no hope in either direction. Chest hurting, hand scraped, wet and loggy with fatigue, he felt profound isolation, like a marble in a long tube rolling nowhere. Forward or back, he could barely tell the difference.

Further down, from the next branch, a voice called, "Eric?" It was Teach.

Slime underfoot nearly cost Eric his footing as he rushed to the opening and turned into it, running several paces away from the lit tunnel. "Dodge!"

Out of the darkness emerged Teach and the children. Teach said, "When the library caught fire, I guessed you'd go underground. I broke another lock."

Dropping to his knees in the shallow water, Eric pulled the slender young boy to him. Dodge's wet face trembled against Eric's own.

"Rabbit," sobbed Dodge.

"I know." Eric stood. Tears marked the dust on Ripple's cheeks. "We have to run. There's a bomb." Catching Teach's eye, Eric said, "What about Federal?"

Looking grim and determined, Teach fingered his knife. "He's dead."

They started toward the lit corridor.

The lights went out.

Dodge tightened his grip on Eric's hand. Ripple inhaled sharply. Pure blackness.

"Was this supposed to happen?" said Teach.

Eric extended an arm and walked forward until a damp wall blocked his path. He lost his orientation. Which way? he thought. Did I come from the left or the right? Sickly, he recalled reversing directions several times before he'd got here. And, he thought, how much time has passed?

He'd thrown the switch—that started the bomb's timer—covered the body, ran down two flights of stairs, climbed into the tunnels, ran some distance in them, went back for Dodge, Teach and Ripple. How much time?

"Left or right?" asked Ripple, parroting Eric's thought.

"I don't know. Right," said Eric, pulling on Dodge's hand, keeping his arm in front. Teach crowded behind him. Underfoot, the cement vibrated, then Eric's ears popped.

"Was that it?" asked Ripple. "Are we too late?"

Her voice seemed to come from nowhere, as if she were drifting in space. The blackness was absolute, as solid as obsidian. "No. Too small. Too far away." He thought, I turned *right* to get them. "Back, back, back!" He about-faced, put his hand out again and straight armed Teach. "We're going the wrong way."

Within a few strides, Teach's silhouette took form, and a few steps more around the gradually curving tunnel showed the bomb. Ceiling lights in a line beckoned beyond. Must be a different circuit, he thought. Breath came to him in quick sips. "Quickly, now," he said. "That's it."

In Eric's head, a large stopwatch ticked off seconds. He giggled, a high pitched giggle that echoed metallically around him. He'd drug up a weird Gone Time association. It's *Sixty Minutes*, he thought. Now for a few words from Andy Rooney. Only they won't be words, and there will only be one.

Looking larger and more ominous than before, the box raced toward them. How long, Eric thought, is five to nine minutes? Surely twice that time has passed.

Ripple reached it, ran by. Teach turned his shoulder, ran by, letting go of Eric's hand, Dodge faced it, then ran by. Finally Eric slid his back along the cement, the box's smooth surface catching a glint from the ceiling lights. His own breathing thundered in his ears; heartbeats throbbed, a death-clock.

From within the box, a sharp snap, like a mouse trap.

Eric froze.

It's a dud, he thought, and then he was beyond, following Teach, Ripple and Dodge who waved frantically at him to hurry from thirty feet farther along. He tried to laugh in relief, but he had no wind for it. All urgency fled. Dodge's alive. We're safe now. Besides, he thought, I'm an old man. What can they expect from me?

Running toward them as best he could, he attempted to get out the words about the bomb, to let them know the danger had passed. Then their faces lit up as if the sun peeped through a gap in the clouds, and a mammoth hand picked him up from behind. His last thought was, I'm flying.

*

Something on his forehead cooled his brow and felt fine. For the longest time, Eric let the pressure of it hold him down, and he drifted. How old am I? he thought. Where am I now? Sounds swam around him, water whispers like voices murmuring, and for a while he believed he was in the house in Littleton where he and Leda had first stayed after he'd discovered the note from his father. He'd woken once in the middle of that night, her arm under his head, the bedroom window shimmering with moonlight, and the river gurgling and chuckling outside. She'd shifted in her sleep, snuggled closer but hadn't wakened. I just need, he thought, to roll over and open my eyes, and there she'll be, black eyelashes pressed together, her face an inch from mine. I'd kiss her on the corner of the mouth. Press my lips lightly against her, a clandestine declaration of love. She'd never know I'd seen her sleeping by the silvery sheen of the summer moon.

The damp weight lifted off his forehead—he wrinkled his brows—the compress returned.

"You're awake," someone said. Eric struggled to hold onto his unconsciousness, the pleasing lassitude, the painless ease of the past, back to the four-poster bed done in beige lace, but it was too late.

Dodge leaned over him. "Grandfather?" he said. Eric tried to sit, and a grating pain in his left shoulder jerked him into full wakefulness.

"It's broke," said Dodge. "You're not supposed to move." The dark-haired boy adjusted the blanket under Eric's chin. "You slept all night," he said.

Lifting his head hurt too, but he did enough to see the dark-rock walled room lit by a single frosted bulb hanging from a wire. "Help me." Bracing with his right arm, he pushed himself up from a thin mattress. A wave of dizziness swept through him, and he nearly fell back. Dodge supported him. Shifting the weight of his arm ignited new pains in his shoulder.

"They said you should stay still," said Dodge. "I *told* them you wouldn't go for it." The young boy sounded triumphant.

"Where?"

Dodge helped Eric stand. Steady now, the shoulder only ached. A sling held it tight to his chest. Keeping hold of Dodge's thin shoulder, Eric limped to the door.

"You'll see," said Dodge.

Outside the door, hundreds of lights circled a large, high-ceilinged room that at first Eric thought was a mausoleum. Black, square recesses, wide and tall enough to accommodate coffins, checker-boarded the stone walls. Fifteen feet away, in the center, around a cement table sat Teach, Ripple and the old woman.

"Welcome to the *real* library," the old woman said, smiling. Eric joined them. The old woman looked at him keenly. "With Pope gone, you are now the last of the Gone Timers. This can be a place for you to stay. You can help us preserve the past. From here, the Gone Time will be restored."

Confused, Eric glanced again at the deep gray stone walls, and the clearly man-made space. The impression of a tomb struck him even more: the walls of stone, the carved niches side by side and stacked to the ceiling. Despite the electric bulbs, shadows dominated the room, and no light penetrated the squares cut into the stone.

She stood stiffly. "Cool air catches me in the joints." Then she shuffled to a wall. "Did Pope say anything to you about the ancient libraries?" She faced them, her form bent and haggard in the room's harsh light. "It was his greatest fear that we'd suffer the same ignominy here." Her voice cracked. Despite her age, she sounded like a lecturer, a college professor. "Three years after the plague, he drafted his plans." She waved her hand inclusively. "It was a two-part strategy. Part one was the excavation of the chambers, and part two was this." The old woman put her hand into one of the niches and removed a mirrored plate about the size of a tea saucer.

"It's a . . ." Eric moved closer, searched for the word, "a computer disk."

"Compact disk, with enough space for hundreds of megabytes of information. If it's pure text, this disk will hold more than a full set of encyclopedias." She carefully placed it back in its spot. "Within this chamber are over eighteen-thousand disks: the entire library, including pictures and diagrams, speeches and video. For the last fifty-seven years, Pope and the library staff have devoted themselves to preserving all the learning we have on these disks. They wore out and replaced computers and scanners and laser disk recorders, but they didn't quit. He wouldn't let them. Oh, his perseverance." Her tone became reverential. "He knew the technology. He nurtured it, and he had the drive to make this all real."

Eric looked into one of the niches. Several score of disks stood side by side on edge in a marble tray. From where he stood, each disk caught a little of his reflection, an eye and a portion of his forehead. Behind that tray, a line of trays extended to the end of the four foot deep cavity. He plucked one disk out of its slot. It was nearly weightless, blunt-edged. The mirrored surface caught the chamber's light and broke it into spokes of color radiating from the hole in the middle.

The old woman cackled. "The plan's beauty is that the library itself will motivate man to rebuild. All knowledge is here, but when our last computer breaks down, it will be unavailable until technology can duplicate the readers. Pope thought of everything. He carved instructions on gold plate just inside the surface doors to the repository. Mankind must rise to learn." The old woman sounded like an apostle now, filled with zeal and passion. "Of course, he hid the entrance. We can't have the hordes in here before they are ready. No, that would be no good at all. The doors are hidden, but man will find it again. That was Pope's dream: man will discover the treasure under the mountain. None of it disappears."

She scanned the room, her survey deliberate as her gaze wandered from section to section, as if she couldn't believe the achievement herself. "Archival quality polymers in the disks. Highly stable," said the old woman. "Under ideal conditions acid free paper might last a couple of hundred years, but it would be susceptible to fire, moisture, insects and wear and tear. Compact disks resist heat, cold, pests and mildew. They may last . . . well . . . forever. Until man is ready again."

In wonder, Eric replaced the disk. All was not lost. The building was gone and the books burned. The library, however, still stood. He rested his palm on the top of the disks. From little finger to thumb, how many millions of words? he thought. How big a pile would the tomes beneath his hand make? Then, suddenly, in swelling horror, he thought of something else. "All the library's books?" he said. "The Chem and Biology libraries too?"

"Yes."

He fell against the stone wall, pressing the back of his wrist to his mouth. An image flashed before him again of the pile of books starting to burn, of Rabbit tossing away the first fire-brand, of the rifle coming down. The futility of it. The stupid, misguided futility of his gesture. That was all it could be. Rabbit had to have known when he'd dashed into the quad that he couldn't stop all those men. He must have known.

In each niche, hundreds of disks stood upright in their marble slots, each tray sporting a number carved into its base. They glinted sharp light back to him as Eric passed. I wanted this, he thought, for the library to be here and all the learning saved for my son and grandson. I wanted to build cars again, planes, schools, hospitals . . . .

In Littleton, Dodge and Rabbit had brought him books. They dug deep, bringing him poetry and texts, and manuals and novels. Rabbit always brought the most. Quietly he'd lay the book down, waiting for Eric to pick it up, to nod approval or pat him on the hand. "Books, boys, it's books that will save us," he'd told them. "Books will make man great again."

The labor to carve this crypt and to preserve the library staggered him. But a vision of the stack of burning books that Rabbit tried to save rose up within. Looking at all the disks in the niche before him, stepping back so he could survey the other niches circling the room and reaching to the ceiling, Eric couldn't justify Pope's effort. The room and what it represented lost its magic. It was just a stone cold tomb. A museum not of the old, but of the alien, of a world that no longer existed and could never exist again. The chamber was a sepulcher of the Gone Time. "Come on," he said to Dodge, Teach and Ripple, "We need to go home."

"Eric," said the woman, "stay. You're the last of the Gone Timers. This is your place."

They headed toward the exit where stairs led to the surface. The old woman looked beseechingly at him, then bent into a niche, reaching in as if to make some minute adjustment to a disk. "Maybe the Turks at Alexandria," Eric added, "knew what they were doing."

*

Late in the afternoon, a few miles west of Boulder where the first of the foothills cupped the two-lane highway out of town, Eric slogged determinedly forward. Not only did the broken shoulder throb with every stride, but his whole left side felt bruised. The first hour or so of hiking had loosened it some, but now the pain intensified the farther they walked. He'd leaned gratefully on Dodge several times. Soon, though, they outpaced him. They were a hundred yards ahead and out of sight. "Go on," he'd said. "Need some time to think, that's all."

From Boulder, a thick column of black smoke rose straight up, marking the ruins of the smoldering campus. Before they'd left, Teach had reconnoitered, but found no sign of Federal's men. "Lots of melted guns," he had said. "The tents were full of them."

The road wound steadily uphill, and Eric watched his step. Years of thawing and freezing had buckled the asphalt and made walking difficult. Waist-high, scraggly limbed, loose-barked bushes poked up here and there, so the hike was more a matter of weaving than a straight path.

For the first time, instead of thinking about clearing the brush and estimating how much work it would take to recondition the road, he thought of the inexorable progress of change. In another hundred years, he thought, no one will know that this was ever a highway. Why, a person hiking the other direction in two-hundred years might well think that no other human being had ever been there, and if he continued on, only right-angled mounds of brick will mark the foundations of the buildings in Boulder. A hunk of cement sitting in the middle of a field, vines growing all over it, might be all that's left of an overpass. He might dig himself a fire-pit and find some other remnants, a key-chain maybe, or a beer bottle.

Eric imagined the hiker turning the dirt-crusted bottle over in his hands, watching how the firelight cut through the muddy-colored glass. He would have come from a mountain community, High Water perhaps, one of the first explorers, pushing the boundaries of his world, hoping that the poisons had receded and the world was safe for people again. He would put the bottle aside, finally, and make his bed next to the fire, and then, before he went to sleep, he'd look up at the stars and make up stories about them, never knowing that mankind had once aspired to visit them, had once seen themselves as the inhabitants of a tiny planet, circling a star as beautiful and remote as the ones that wheeled over his head right now. He'd sleep, his next frontier the hill he hadn't hiked over yet. To him, the world would be new again, filled with wonder and danger, a place to learn from.

The image of the future hiker didn't seem either good or bad, just interesting. The sun now nearly touched the hills ahead, and the shadows lay long behind him. In the still air, the steady chirping of mountain wrens and the crackle of the occasional twig or dry leaf underfoot were the only sounds. He hadn't seen Teach and the children for some time, and the stiffness in his legs as he climbed toward High Water slowed him considerably.

To loosen his calves, he walked backwards a few feet. Boulder's plume of smoke hazed the air. It's like Golden, he thought, years ago when I first came out of the mountains looking for Dad. The feeling of experiencing it again swept over him powerfully. Goosebumps raised on his back and legs. Smoke in the sky, he thought. A city is burning, and I'm searching.

The sense of then and now filled Eric so thoroughly, the sense of connection with himself at fifteen and himself at seventy-five felt so solid, that he almost wasn't surprised when he turned around and saw striding toward him down the road, the figure of a man who could easily be his father. Dodge held the black-haired man's hand. Behind him, came Teach and Ripple.

"Troy," said Eric.

They stopped, a few feet apart. Dodge looked from his grandfather to his father and back expectantly.

"I searched for you," said Troy. "I was worried . . . you know . . . the boy. I didn't think you were serious."

In wonder, Eric saw that Troy's eyes were glistening, that he was shaking.

Troy said, "I thought you were gone forever, Dad. You never said goodbye."

Silence stretched between them. The feeling of connection held on. Eric felt fifteen; he felt seventy-five. He was a son searching for his father; he was the father the son found. Everything circled around, he thought. Everything circled around.

He said, because he knew it was the only thing to say, the words that had been written but never spoken, the words he had carried with him for sixty years, "I have always loved you, son."

*

Late that night, in their campsite beneath two old pines, Eric suddenly awoke. Only moonlight cast any illumination. The hillside glowed with its light. He canted his head from one side to another. Was that a bird? he thought, or did I only dream it? It was a bird, a meadowlark. I know that call; my father taught me.

$$\frac{45}{1966}$$
$$\frac{45}{2018}$$

About the Author

James Van Pelt grew up in Littleton, Colorado, where his dad worked for Martin-Marietta designing rockets, and *Sky and Telescope* magazines were neatly stacked on the coffee table for light reading. His mom, a voracious reader, encouraged James by buying books whenever he wanted them and giving him the freedom to read (as long as she didn't check on him too often long after he was supposed to be asleep).

Since then, he has taken his dad's interest in science and mathematics, and his mother's love of books, and turned them into his own life as a teacher and author of science fiction and fantasy. James teaches English at Fruita-Monument High School and Mesa State College in western Colorado. His short fiction has appeared in numerous magazines and anthologies, including *Asimov's, Analog, Talebones, Realms of Fantasy* and many others. He was a finalist for the John W. Campbell Award for Best New Writer, and his works have been finalists for the Nebula, the Theodore Sturgeon Award for Best Short Fiction of the Year, and others.

His first collection, *Strangers and Beggars*, was named as a Best Book for Young Adults by the American Library Association, and his second collection, *The Last of the O-Forms and Other Stories*, is a finalist for the Colorado Blue Spruce Young Adult Book Award.

His website can be found at http://www.sff.people/james.van.pelt. He can be contacted at Vvanp@aol.com.

Printed in the United States
79626LV00002B/292

9 780974 657387